ENDANGERED SPECIES

Mariner's Library Fiction Classics

STERLING HAYDEN
Voyage: A Novel of 1896

BJORN LARSSON
The Celtic Ring

SAM LLEWELLYN
The Shadow in the Sands

RICHARD WOODMAN
The Darkening Sea
Endangered Species
Wager
The Nathaniel Drinkwater Novels:
The Bomb Vessel
The Corvette
1805
Baltic Mission
In Distant Waters
A Private Revenge
Under False Colours
The Flying Squadron
Beneath the Aurora
The Shadow of the Eagle
Ebb Tide

ENDANGERED SPECIES

Richard Woodman

SHERIDAN HOUSE

First U.S. edition published 2000
by Sheridan House Inc.
145 Palisade Street
Dobbs Ferry, New York 10522

Copyright © 1992 by Richard Woodman

First published in Great Britain 1992
by Little, Brown and Company

Library of Congress Cataloging-in-Publication Data

Woodman, Richard, 1944-
  Endangered species / Richard Woodman.—1st U.S. ed.
    p. cm.
  ISBN 1-57409-076-3 (alk. paper)
    1. Great Britain—History, Naval—20th century—
  Fiction. I. Title.

PR6073.O618 E54 2000
823'.914—dc21

3138 3283 12/04   00-021000

Printed in the United States of America

ISBN 1-57409-076-3

For Ned

'It seems now that the sea has almost retreated from our lives, and that ships are leading a twilight, marginal existence, like senior officials who resist being pensioned off.'

The Bay of Noon
Shirley Hazzard

'There is no home left for universal souls except perhaps Antarctica or on the high seas.'

The Life and Times of Michael K
J.M. Coetzee

'All our virtues are forms of fear.'

The Harbour Master
William McFee

Acknowledgement is given to William Orford for his permission to use the poem on pages 283–284.

Contents

CHAPTER ONE

The Middle Watch

'One bell, Sec!'

Stevenson rolled over and grunted.

'One bell!' The persistent Liverpudlian accent wrenched him from sleep and he sat up with the tired discipline of long practice.

'Okay, Pritch.' Stevenson swung his legs over the edge of the bunk. As the door curtain fluttered behind the exit of Able Seaman Pritchard, Stevenson eased his feet to the deck, feeling for his flip-flops.

At the sink he groped for his toothbrush and dashed water into his face. He jerked the *sarong* off, drew on underpants, shirt and shorts, combed his hair and left the cabin.

The wind of the ship's passage ruffled his shirt as he climbed the bridge ladder. Above him soared the mute majesty of the tropical night sky, a black, velvet arch pierced with a myriad stars. He marked them with a seaman's instinct: Canopus blazing low in the southern sky, coruscating with iridescent shots of blue and red as its burning gases were fracted by the earth's dirt-laden atmosphere; higher up the limbs of Orion dominated the sky, Rigel cold with the blue fire of a super giant, Bellatrix white as ice and Betelgeuse red with blood on the hunter's spear arm.

'Morning, Chas,' Stevenson said curtly as he crossed the bridge-wing to the dimly lit chart-room.

1

'Morning, Alex.' Charles Taylor turned and acknowledged the arrival of his relief, then resumed his review of the horizon ahead of the ship. In the chart-room Stevenson made himself a cup of tea, glanced at the log and read the Master's night orders written in Captain Mackinnon's elegantly archaic hand. He scribbled his initials against them, then picked up his mug of tea and re-emerged to lean on the rail alongside the Third Officer.

'Sleep well?' Taylor asked as he always asked, as though courtesy demanded it, at the same time drooping languidly over the teak caprail. Such dubious mannerisms tended to set him apart from his shipmates, as though he was unwilling ever to let them forget the social differences that separated them.

Even Captain Mackinnon, Stevenson thought with a mild pucker of irritation, stood slightly in awe of Chas Taylor.

'Not bad, thanks,' he replied. 'All quiet?'

Taylor straightened up, stretched and yawned, as if palpably slipping off the responsibilities of officer of the watch and emphasising his four-hour stint was now over. The product of private education, Taylor had come to sea in a misdirected quest for a genteel way of life. He was some fifty years too late and the result was a rather disdainful young man who nevertheless possessed a certain impervious superiority that neither Captain Mackinnon nor Chief Officer Rawlings could deflate. Indeed, such was the man's charisma that he was regarded by them with a caution bordering on respect, despite the fact that Taylor was thirty years younger than the Captain and eighteen younger than the Chief Officer.

Stevenson found this conviction of class paradoxical. He in no wise considered himself a man of lesser competence than Taylor, but the Third Officer's natural assumption of superiority was so easily borne that it was hard to confound. Taylor came from stock which possessed the confidence that money brings, something Stevenson had never experienced. Every fact Stevenson knew about Taylor was quietly notched

2

a little higher than in his own case. The photograph in Taylor's cabin showed his wife a cool, blonde young woman, with the high cheekbones and square jaw of lasting beauty, and whenever Stevenson saw the picture he felt a slight resentment; the fact Taylor was married seemed somehow to claim a pre-eminence. Inevitably it made Stevenson consider his own love affair with Cathy. Cathy was enviably lovely, but she was not as beautiful as Caroline Taylor. It was as if the Third Mate had some sort of right to these things.

Taylor's junior status was irrelevant, for Taylor radiated the experience of countless generations in a way that Stevenson found confusing. And, because Stevenson was a straight, almost humourless devotee to his profession, Taylor's sardonically charming attitude abraded Stevenson's own self-esteem at times, while at others it attracted him. This vacillation troubled Stevenson's relationship with his younger colleague, leaving him always the clumsy loser.

'Only seen two ships,' Taylor remarked laconically, reporting the significant events of his watch. 'And the Old Man turned in about an hour ago.'

'Beautiful night,' remarked Stevenson between sips of tea. He looked forward. The old-fashioned crutched derricks reflected faint highlights from the stars and the foremast rose like an advancing cross as the ship hissed through the calm, windless sea. Beside him Taylor yawned again.

'You're a romantic bastard, Alex.'

'Thanks.' Stevenson felt the familiar irritation, then Taylor confounded him by one of those disarming remarks of which he was occasionally capable and which Stevenson felt resentfully flattered to receive.

'I often stand up here and wonder,' Taylor said slowly, almost experimentally, 'whether it is possible to define infinity on a night like this.' He paused. Beside him Stevenson stirred into full consciousness and looked sharply at the Third Officer, to see if he was being mocked.

'I keep thinking it should be possible to work it out; after all we're looking at it, not just contemplating it mathematically, but actually staring at the reality. The trouble is trying to find the words to accompany the thoughts. D'you know, several times this evening I thought I had it, was convinced I was within an ace of the thing, then' – he snapped his fingers – 'gone!' Taylor laughed at himself; a bitter laugh, Stevenson thought suddenly, forgetting his earlier irritation. 'And then here I am,' Taylor went on, 'back on the bridge of the old *Matthew Flinders* ploughing a furrow across the Indian Ocean.'

He looked at Stevenson and abruptly asked 'D'you think I'm mad, Alex?'

Taylor had never previously asked him anything, and he thought the question ironic. When put on the spot, Stevenson's seriousness became his foremost characteristic. Besides, the night was worthy of a few secrets.

'No, you're right,' he said, adding with an awkward diffidence, 'these nights are bloody romantic. I usually become convinced there is a God. Don't have the slightest shred of doubt. I just worry for four hours about His exact composition.'

Stevenson was gratified by Taylor's low chuckle of appreciation. 'It's all very poetic,' Taylor said. 'The trouble is it's so bloody beautiful it almost hurts . . .'

The candour of this frank remark disarmed Stevenson for a moment and he lit a cigarette, recoiling from its taste. Then, recalling he was the older of the two, he asked, 'Have you got something on your mind, Chas?'

Taylor's silence was that of assent. After a brief pause he inquired, 'You're not married, are you, Alex?'

'No.'

'Thinking of it, are you? The photos in your cabin, I mean . . .'

'I finished with Cathy the day I got orders to join this ship,' Stevenson said with a sudden harsh edge to his voice. 'I just like to have a bird's picture to ogle,' he added tritely,

4

ineptly trying not to break the mood of intimacy that existed between them.

'Bad for the image, eh?' Taylor mocked. 'Don't want the crew to think you're fruit?'

Stevenson grunted and drew on the cigarette. A pale orange glow suffused his even features. 'What's the problem then? Your marriage?'

'Caroline,' Taylor said slowly, as though measuring out the confidence, 'is a natural blonde with beautiful legs and that indefinable quality of being a prize bitch.'

From forward the single clear note of the ship's forecastle bell indicated the lookout had spotted a ship to starboard. The two officers raised their eyes, both aware that they should have seen it long before the seaman forward.

'I've got her, two points to starboard.'

'Right then, she's all yours. Steering o-eight-nine. Should pick up Pulo Weh sometime during my forenoon watch. Good night.'

'Good night.'

Stevenson lifted his binoculars and studied the distant, twinkling masthead lights of the approaching ship as Taylor shuffled away, the mood broken by the intrusion of duty. Stevenson thought he had gone when his voice called from the ladder: 'Ever read Conrad?'

'A bit,' Stevenson replied.

'He knew what it was like to stand a middle watch. D'you know what he said about humanity?'

'Haven't a clue,' admitted Stevenson.

'He said mankind on this earth was an unforeseen accident which did not bear close examination.'

'Oh.' Stevenson tried to find some relevance in the remark.

'Something for you to chew over, old son; see you in the morning.'

It was only after Taylor had finally departed and left Second Officer Stevenson to the magnificent loneliness of the night that the latter wondered if Taylor had been less than

5

ironic earlier, in doubting his own sanity.

The approaching ship passed two miles to starboard, heading westwards, its phosphorescent wake splashing into the bow wave of the *Matthew Flinders*.

Stevenson began to pace the bridge, from wing to wing, passing regularly through the wheelhouse where the dull hum of gyro-compass and radar, and the orange flicker of the automatic pilot rendered a helmsman redundant. Only the isolated lookout two hundred feet forward on the old-fashioned forecastle head maintained the vigil above decks. A few other lonely souls stood their watch in the engine-room below.

The London-born child of Scots parents, Alex Stevenson had nursed an ambition to go to sea since childhood. Characteristically he had never wavered from his intention. Up to the beginning of this present voyage he had been quite content, his master mariner's certificate secured at last, the passport to eventual command.

But the *Matthew Flinders* was on no ordinary voyage; this was to be her last, for she was already consigned to breakers in the Far East, one of a last pair of cargo-liners which had once formed part of a substantial, privately owned British merchant shipping company. Relegated first to the Isle of Man registry her disinterested owners had recently flagged her out under the ensign of Panama to avoid complying with British government legislation and the supposedly 'high' wages demanded by British seafarers. Mercifully, for this final trip, the owners, anxious to rid themselves of their last ships, had not bothered to import a crew from Taiwan or the Philippines, but merely scooped up whatever was available on the international pool. By a perverse coincidence the complement of the *Matthew Flinders* was largely as it had always been, with British seamen on deck and Chinese greasers below. Her deck officers and engineers were a handful of the company's

6

remaining long-term employees, hanging on in the forlorn hope of redundancy payments.

This uncertain future had contributed to Stevenson's rupture with Cathy. Casting about for possible alternative employment he had been forced to face the fact that his country had turned its back on its maritime past; no one gave a tuppenny damn about the so-called Merchant Navy. There were, quite simply, no more ships.

Walking up and down, his bitterness grew. Others were cushioned against the inevitable. Captain Mackinnon was retiring, as was the Chief Engineer. Mr Rawlings, the Chief Officer, had some contingency plan, while Taylor's family had money. Besides, the lovely Caroline was rumoured to be something smart in her own right in the City of London. But Stevenson, with the indigent respectability of the lower-middle class, needed his job, the only job he had ever wanted to do, the only job he had trained for. In fact it was his very way of life that was to be torn from him by the harsh facts of economic change.

Resolutely, he turned his thoughts away from such embittered contemplation. If this was to be his last voyage, or at least the last voyage before he had to hawk his skills round manning agencies, sell himself to any bidder and sail for his subsistence in ill-founded rust buckets, he wanted to enjoy it.

But he no longer had the consolation of Cathy; he had ended their affair, as he had said, when he received instructions to join the *Matthew Flinders*. He leaned disconsolately on the rail and reflected on the wisdom of his act, painful though it was. Taylor had spliced his life to that of the beautiful Caroline and it was clear that he was unhappy. Even so, they had been a month at sea and the sensuous warmth of the night was compelling . . .

He gave in to the insistent vision of Cathy in the shower, her dark hair piled on her head and her face held up to the splashing rose. He could see again her straight nose and the

7

ever-so-slightly receding chin which threw her lower lip into pouting prominence. Hers was not the patrician beauty of Taylor's Caroline, yet it was the flaw in her looks that gave them their special charm.

'What are you staring at?' he could hear her ask from beneath the hissing water, turning those level grey eyes on him lying in bed. 'Eloquent eyes' he had privately and poetically named her, for she seemed to say more through them than through her lips, as if the latter were maintained for purely carnal purposes.

'You,' he answered, suddenly embarrassed that he had spoken out loud. But it was insufficient to drive Cathy's image from his mind. She emerged from the shower, pink and brown and deliciously shameless, bending to towel her thighs so that her breasts swung with a detached and lascivious oscillation . . .

Stevenson lit another cigarette and resumed his furious pacing of the bridge, silently cursing the girl.

Cathy had been the first woman with whom he had had more than the briefest of relationships and he had ditched her. She would, he guessed, probably marry a farmer and have dozens of healthy children, farmers being the very antithesis of seafarers. The thought of farming brought him back to Chas. With Cathy and people like her, the presence of mankind on the earth was scarcely 'an unforseen accident', but rather a preordained fruition of some cosmic purpose provided with its own internal dynamic.

'And here I am back to God again,' he muttered irritably to himself. Dismissing the whole train of thought he made for the compass repeater and occupied himself by taking an azimuth of Jupiter.

In his cabin below the bridge Captain Mackinnon tossed restlessly, unable to sleep. He too wished to savour this last voyage, for though he looked forward to its end, he knew that retirement, no matter how well-deserved, diminished him as a man. At that moment, and for all the succeeding moments until he handed the *Matthew Flinders* over to her Chinese breakers, he and he alone was responsible for the ship and her company, some thirty-six souls, as tradition had it. And he was master under God, elevated to a most culpable position, not merely responsible but answerable for many of the misdemeanours of his crew. Sometimes the burden of it weighed upon him intolerably, but he was shrewd enough to know that he would miss it.

Besides, he had a most unsailorlike affection for the ship herself, having been her very first Third Officer, sent to Belfast to join her at the builders because Mrs Dent had specifically ordered it.

'You've impressed the Old Woman,' the Marine Superintendent, Captain Shaw, had said to him, referring familiarly to the widow of the company's founding chairman, a woman whose influence in the Eastern Steam Navigation Company remained pre-eminent. 'She insists on you occupying the Third Mate's berth.'

Shaw had regarded him through his rheumy eyes, his yellow face already betraying the cancer that, with the overwork of six years of war, would lay him in his grave before the maiden voyage of the new *Matthew Flinders* was over.

'Don't let the Old Woman down, laddie,' Shaw added, repeating the nickname by which Mrs Dent was known throughout Eastern Steam.

'I'll do my best, sir.'

'Aye, see that you do or I'll have your hide.'

He had stepped happily out into Water Street, disregarding the sleeting rain driving up from the Pier Head and the restless chop of the grey Mersey beyond. He and Shelagh had high hopes now the war was over, and the approbation of the Old Woman and a berth on a brand new ship meant that they would be able to marry soon, their future secure. Britain, he had thought with the experience of war behind him, would always need her Merchant Navy.

9

It was odd, Mackinnon thought, how easy it was to remember these things: the elation, the rain, and Shelagh's pleasure when he had phoned and told her he would be crossing to Belfast that night. And all because the 'Old Woman' approved of him.

Mackinnon's memory flashed back to the events that had earned him the Old Woman's good opinion.

It had been raining that black night, a stinging rain coming up astern of the convoy with a following sea that made the old *Matthew Flinders* roll and scend in a twisting that racked the creaking hull. The first of her name, she grossed eight thousand tons, a coal-fired steamer capable of no more than nine knots, built for profit out of the reparations greedily scooped up by Dent and his partners after the First World War. She had been obsolete when she had slid down the ways and into the grubby Tees and was over twenty years old that foul and bloody night the U-boats found her off Rockall.

'Almost home and dry,' Taffy Davies had said as Apprentice Mackinnon relieved him on the starboard Lewis gun at midnight and about five seconds before the first explosion. Mackinnon had still been shaking the sleep out of his weary young frame after what seemed like weeks of endless, mind-numbing watch-and-watch, four hours on and four off, with sleep in short snatches of three hours if undisturbed by the ship's motion or the enemy. When the night split apart and the gouts of orange and yellow flame shot skywards to die to a flickering before the concussion rolled over the water towards them, he was conscious of shock, and then the relief of knowing it was not them.

'Jesus!' blasphemed Taffy as he made way for Mackinnon in the sand-bagged gun pit, 'that's the *Patagonia*.'

Mackinnon needed no further enlightenment. After days of weary plodding across the Atlantic, they knew the relative position of every ship in those four, strung-out and irregular columns; knew the dawn reshuffling that took place after the

10

destruction of the nights as the Commodore of Convoy HX 987 rearranged his battered charges. They knew the *Patagonia* well, having laid ahead of her in Newport News and become friendly with her apprentices, penniless like themselves.

'The poor bastards,' whispered Davies as the flames were extinguished by the sea and the night was lit by the cold glare of the starshells thrown up by the questing escorts. The SS *Patagonia* had ceased to exist, for she had been laden with high-explosive ammunition.

'Can you see anything?' a voice asked, as behind the two boys the Second and Third Mates stared through their binoculars.

The adjacent ships were thrown into monochrome relief by the flares. Only a gap in the extreme starboard column attested to the missing *Patagonia*, a gap into which, her Aldis light flickering, the corvette *Aubretia* was moving. Of the U-boat which launched the attack there was no sign.

'They won't have known anything,' observed the Third Mate with an exhaused sigh, and then the night blew apart again, blew up around them with a fiery savagery that seared them as a torpedo struck the *Matthew Flinders*. Momentarily blinded by the flash of the impacting warhead, Mackinnon felt the deck beneath him rear up, throwing him against the gunshield. Its steel angle caught his shoulder with a sickening pain which brought the taste of bile into his throat as he fell to the deck.

Shakily he got to his feet. He was suddenly, inexplicably, alone.

He felt sick from the effect of the blast, but conscious that he was less frightened and more aware of his surroundings. Above the increasing roar of escaping steam he could hear the klaxon alarm, and someone shouting an unintelligible order. The angle of the deck increased sharply, then seemed to stop, and this sudden change enabled him to recover his wits. He scrambled out of the gun pit and up the tilting deck, like an

11

animal in a flood, instinctively seeking high ground. Oddly, there was no one in the wheelhouse and he continued upwards until he came to the opposite side of the bridge where his watch mate, Apprentice Dave Kingsley, should have been.

'Dave?' he shouted, casting about with a sudden panic as the starshells were extinguished by the sea. The utter darkness filled him with a rank, sweating fear. Then above the venting steam he could hear orchestrated shouting.

'The boats!' he cried in sudden comprehension, and half-slid, half-skidded back down the sloping bridge through the deserted wheelhouse, making a grab for the ladder rail that wrenched his shoulder again. Then he stumbled down on to the boat-deck where, in the gloom, he could see the white flash of men in singlets, the dull gleam of oilskins and the grey outline of the starboard lifeboat.

'Is that you, Mackinnon?' Captain Robson's harsh voice cut through the wet night air above him. Mackinnon turned. At the head of the ladder the Master stood, the pale stripes of his pyjamas showing beneath his bridge coat. A pale square of paper fluttered from his right fist.

'Sparks is waiting for this in the radio shack . . .'

Reassured that some discipline prevailed and aware that the Captain must have been in the chart-room while he scuttered foolishly about the bridge, Mackinnon ran back up the ladder and took the message form. The radio shack was abaft the tall funnel and inside, under the battery-powered emergency light, the Radio Officer was dragging on a cigarette, his headphones clamped round his balding skull and a nervous hand poised over the morse key. Without a word he tore the chit out of Mackinnon's hand and began transmitting the fate of the SS *Matthew Flinders* to the outside world. Mackinnon stood for an uncertain moment, then the sparks flung off his headphones, pulled a duffle coat from a hook on the bulkhead and shoved past the apprentice.

'Come on, she's going!'

The ship gave another lurch. More starshell burst

overhead and the crump of exploding depth charges could be heard in the distance above the shouts and the roar of the steam.

'Come on.'

Mackinnon followed the Radio Officer. Back on the boat-deck the struggling figures were thrown into stark relief by the flares. Above their heads a white plume vented from the funnel and then a series of tremors rumbled beneath their feet and the ship suddenly fell back on an even keel.

The surface of the sea, tossing up towards them with the curl and hiss of breaking crests, was much nearer as the *Matthew Flinders* began to settle in the water.

The Bosun had the after end of the boat swung out and was exhorting the men to heave on the forward guy of the old-fashioned radial davits to carry the bow out over the ship's side. The boat swung clear, hanging over the black Atlantic twenty feet below, and they began to clamber into it.

There was a terrific noise, so unfamiliar they stopped and looked at one another for a petrified instant. Then more depth charges exploded on the far side of the convoy and the black hull of a following ship steamed silently past them, her wash spreading out from her bow and striking the sides of the *Matthew Flinders*. Plumes of water shot vertically and were torn across the boat-deck, dousing the already rain-soaked men who swore with true, seamanlike ferocity and began again to scramble into the lifeboat.

At the same instant a starshell went out and the unexplained noise grew louder, shaking the ship.

'Lower away there!' yelled Captain Robson, motioning Mackinnon into the boat. A moment later the lifeboat began her jerky descent. A rising sea struck her and she was lifted bodily and swung outwards, away from the ship's side which rose now like a black wall beside them. Then the sea fell away with a suddenness that brought Mackinnon's stomach into his throat, the falls snapped tight and the boat whipped

13

the length of her keel and swung inboard, striking the rusty steel topsides, her frames cracking as she bounced off with a flexing of her gunwale.

'Lower, lower!' Captain Robson was shouting and the boat resumed its progress until another wave caught her and, ready for it, Captain Robson roared, 'Come up!', and the men on the falls threw the turns off the staghorns.

The boat wallowed into the sea and the falls were unhooked. The side of the *Matthew Flinders* seemed immensely high, looming up into the night sky like a great cliff.

'Christ, she's breaking up . . .'

'She's rolling over!'

Split in two as her exploding boilers tore her apart, some quirk of the destruction wrought to her ancient fabric caused her to roll away from the boat. The men who had lowered it and should have followed down the rope ladder went with her. It was over in a matter of less than a minute.

The lifeboat was alone on the empty, heaving ocean, the centre of a small circle of black sea circumscribed by a pall of rain and spray. The crumps of the depth charges of the counter-attacking escorts seemed much farther away and the starshells finally went out.

All that remained of the ship's company of the SS *Matthew Flinders* were two able seaman, the Chief Steward, three greasers, a fireman and Apprentice Mackinnon. He was sixteen years old.

He remembered few details after that nightmare evacuation of the old ship. Memory told him his exemplary conduct during those next few days had recommended him to the 'Old Woman' and she, after the war, had insisted he became the Third Officer of the brand new *Matthew Flinders*.

Now, as his thoughts came full circle and he drifted off to sleep, he felt the prickle of disappointment that his ship no longer carried apprentices. The lack of them had been the

14

surest indication that the owners no longer considered there was a future for their ships, or cared very much. This was now proved by their voyage to the scrapyard. This, Mackinnon considered as he rolled over, was a tragic shame; true, the system had been abused to provide cheap labour and not even a war had prevented sixteen-year-old boys being exposed to its merciless rigours, but it had provided thousands of young men a chance in life . . .

It was history now and he was an old man approaching retirement. Slowly his brain relinquished its hold on consciousness and he drifted to sleep.

Dawn had found them quite alone on the heaving sea. The Chief Steward took nominal charge and the older of the able seamen sat aft at the helm. The rest of them huddled disconsolately on the thwarts shivering in the damp chill, for it still rained, a cold drizzle that obscured everything.

Once, and then so briefly that afterwards they could not be certain, they thought they heard the hiss of a bow wave and the grey loom of a ship, perhaps the *Aubretia*, sent back to quarter the wake of the convoy in search of survivors; but although they raised a shout, it ended in a senseless stream of blasphemy as the insubstantial apparition vanished.

'It might have been a U-boat,' said Mackinnon, asserting himself for the first time and voicing a fear which, for him, was greater than that of impending death. He was too young to imagine death might be about to claim him; the fear of imprisonment in German hands was far stronger.

But as the day wore on he learned how very easy it is to die. The fireman, shuddering uncontrollably in his singlet, was dead by noon; a greaser passed silently from them an hour later. The very ordinariness of it filled Mackinnon with dread.

It began to dawn on him that the others in the boat did not expect to survive and were incapable of exerting themselves to no purpose. After three years of war they had seen others die and there was a strange kind of comfort in numbers. The Chief Steward dished out water and biscuit, though for the most part they slumped helpless and hopeless in the wallowing boat, silently awaiting their fate.

Mackinnon had no idea how long they remained like this, for the rain swept over them for hour after dismal hour, until, as dusk overtook them, the sky began to clear. A blood-red sun sank towards the horizon.

The sunset reminded him sharply of yesterday, of the *Matthew Flinders* and his chums in the half-deck, of Taffy Davies and Dave Kingsley . . .

'Almost home and dry,' Taffy had said.

'We've got a compass, haven't we?' he asked Able-Seaman Bird whose crouched figure huddled over the kicking tiller gave a specious appearance of order in the boat.

Bird looked up at the first-trip apprentice and nodded.

'Why don't we sail the boat then?'

Bird stirred, frowning, and shook his head.

'We could get the mast stepped by dark.' Mackinnon saw intelligence kindled in the eyes of the men around him. It dawned on him how far inside their instinctive selves they had retreated. They had become feral creatures, each facing the inevitable end with a silent resignation.

'Which direction do we steer then, son?' asked the Chief Steward quietly, his tone that of exhaustion. 'D'you know?'

Mackinnon did not know; not exactly. His duties had been confined to cleaning his quarters and the bridge, doing odd jobs and mounting lookout duty in the bridge gun pits, to be ammunition server if needed. It had seemed a glamorous enough task, sitting by the Lewis gun as the old *Matthew Flinders* struggled along, belching black smoke in an attempt to keep up the speed ordered by the Commodore. Now it struck him that it might have been of more value to have known roughly where they were. He supposed he had actually possessed the information on the chit Captain

16

Robson had sent him to Sparks with, but the Master had been a man of old-fashioned prejudices. Apprentices were the lowest form of animal life and the chart-room was a hallowed sanctum . . .

Nevertheless, Taffy Davies was an apprentice of two years' experience and Taffy seemed, at least to young Mackinnon, to know everything. Taffy had said with his usual confidence, 'Almost home and dry . . .'

'If we steered east . . .'

'We usually get sent up towards Iceland, son,' said the Chief Steward. You did not need a master's certificate to know that east of Iceland lay a lot of ocean before one hit German-occupied Norway. Mackinnon felt the older man's patronising rejection as a spur to anger. He was incapable of comprehending the Chief Steward's quiet courage in waiting for the end. He was an elderly, unfit man. War had called many back to the colours, and the red ensign of the Merchant Navy was the least glamorous, least regarded of them. The Chief Steward felt overwhelmed with pity for Mackinnon; the boy's youthful spirit would not allow him to die quietly.

'Steer south-east, then,' Mackinnon persisted, a complex feeling of anger and adolescent petulance seizing him. He struggled forward and began unlashing the mast and the lugsail rolled round its yard.

'South-east . . .' Bird looked up from the compass. 'Maybe the kid's right.'

By nightfall the starboard lifeboat of the SS *Matthew Flinders* scudded south-east, the tiny glim of her binnacle light radiating hope on the face of Apprentice Mackinnon at the helm.

CHAPTER TWO

Distant Storm Clouds

Taylor sighted Pulo Weh at 1030 ship's time the following morning and the lush green hummock lay on the starboard beam of the *Matthew Flinders* by noon. This proximity of the land released Stevenson from the necessity of attending the bridge for the ritual of taking noon sights. Instead he enjoyed a quick beer in the bar before having lunch and relieving Taylor in the endless round of the ship's routine.

There were several other officers already sipping their pre-lunch drinks. The Radio Officer was picking up a gin and tonic when he caught sight of the Second Mate.

'Hullo, stranger.' He turned to the Chinese steward behind the bar. 'Here, Woo, give Second Office' a nice cool beer.' The Radio Officer signed the chit and Stevenson gratefully accepted the dripping glass, grinning like a boy let out of school early.

'Cheers, Sparks.'

'Cheers.'

'Any news from the big outside world?'

Sparks shrugged. 'Rioting in Ulster, fuel shortages in Eastern Europe which are imposing great hardships on British tourists, and another load of Vietnamese boat people picked up in the South China Sea. SNAFU . . . situation normal all—'

'All fucked up,' Stevenson completed the acronym. 'I

18

know the graveyard watch go out of circulation but I'm not a complete zombie.'

'Oh, scoff not, it's the best thing to be,' grinned Sparks, eyeing Stevenson over his glass. 'I've ceased to react to news from Ulster and being stuck here scarcely gives me cause for concern for British tourists in Yugoslavia or wherever. Strikes me the bastards have too much money and too much time off.'

'Who? The Yugoslavs?' asked Stevenson.

'You are bombed out, old lad. No, the bloody British tourists.'

'What about the Vietnamese, then?'

'Oh, come on, Alex, do me a favour; you're bombed out on night air. The world's full of poor suffering bastards, isn't it? At the moment I feel one myself.' Sparks swallowed the gin and tonic and held his glass between thumb and forefinger, making it oscillate conspicuously. Stevenson took it and passed it across the bar.

'Another gin, Woo, please.' As he signed the chit, Stevenson said, 'Only think, Sparks, you'll have to find something else to gripe about after this trip.'

'Oh, I reckon the wife will provide me with ample fodder for thought.'

'Hullo, Alex.' Mr Rawlings, the Chief Officer, joined them. He was a man of raddled good looks, his once fair hair fading, the flesh of his face slackening its hold on the skull, his blue eyes beginning a slow retreat into watery sockets.

'Beer?' asked Stevenson, not waiting for an answer as Woo automatically responded to the arrival of the Mate. He signed the chit and passed the glass to Rawlings. 'I was just saying . . .'

'He was just saying depressing things,' interrupted Sparks, 'and I refuse to be depressed. This may be the last voyage, but I will not allow that to disrupt my lifestyle.'

'It must do,' said Stevenson with a hint of bitterness.

'Now look, Alex, these little lunch-time sessions of ours

have, for years, been an oasis of civilisation in a turbulent world. We don't want you swinging down from the awning spars spoiling things, do we, Roger?'

'No, we bloody well don't,' said the Chief Officer. 'Chap's got to have a *chota peg*. Keeps the flag flying, old boy.'

Stevenson was aware they were ragging him, but he refused to be drawn. 'Well, I find it depressing,' he said seriously. 'I mean in a few weeks we'll actually be doing this for the last time.' He looked from one to the other, expecting reaction. 'I think it's a bloody shame.'

Sparks sighed and put his glass down. 'So do I, Alex, so do I. I've left Mary and the kids in a bungalow on the Wirral three times a year for the last God knows how many years and I've complained every time we've parted. I've even tried working ashore, but it was a disaster.' He shook his head. 'This has been my life and I've stuck it out and so has she, in expectation of better things at the end of it. Clearly we asked for too much. *I* didn't think it would end like this either.' Sparks buried his bitterness in his drink.

'No, none of us did,' put in Rawlings guardedly. 'That's what makes it difficult, it defies reason; it's completely incomprehensible. Great Britain needs a merchant fleet.'

'Not that it ever gave a tuppenny fuck for its sailors, mind,' added Sparks. 'Remember Nancy Astor.' He wagged an admonitory finger and they laughed. Whatever Mrs Astor's virtues as the first female Member of Parliament, she was held in permanent obloquy by the men of the Merchant Navy for suggesting they wore yellow armbands when landing from foreign voyages as potential carriers of venereal disease. Hers was an attitude felt to be typical of the regard the British had for its seafarers.

'They,' Sparks went on, referring to the fateful, unnamed but blameworthy force that might have been the shipowners, the government, the British public at large or an amalgam of all three, 'are hardly aware of our existence, let alone our becoming extinct. Anyway,' he made an attempt at brightening with obvious effort, 'now I know what it felt like to be a dinosaur.'

'I knew there was something bloody odd about you,' joked Rawlings, signing for another round as the dinner gong sounded from the saloon alleyway.

'Not for me,' said Stevenson, swallowing the dregs of his beer and hurrying below.

'That young man's too bloody serious,' said Sparks, accepting the recharged glass. 'Cheers, Roger.'

'He wants to hang loose,' said Rawlings, imitating an American accent.

'Well, I can see his point. He endured four years of apprenticeship, struggled to get all his tickets and then not merely the company, but the ethos of the whole fucking country tells him he's too expensive a luxury to keep on,' said Sparks. 'He's a young man, he's allowed to be angry. Bitterness, on the other hand, will blight his life.'

'Christ, you are philosophic,' grinned Rawlings fatuously, stiffening as they were joined by the Master.

'What'll it be, sir?'

'Thanks, Sparks,' said Mackinnon rubbing his hands, his powerful forearms dark beneath the immaculate white of his open-necked shirt with the stiff board epaulettes bearing their four gold bars. 'The usual, please.'

'Gin and tonic for the Captain, Woo, please.'

'We were just saying that young Stevenson's future isn't looking too good, sir,' said Rawlings.

'There's no future for him or the other youngsters,' snapped Mackinnon with a hint of exasperation at the Mate's smooth, hypocritical tone. 'It makes my blood boil to think what we're throwing away. God help us if we ever get ourselves into another mess like the Falklands. We don't have the resources to do that again.'

They were silent for a moment, considering the implications of the Captain's comments, then Sparks remarked, 'I suppose it all started with the oil crisis in the seventies.'

21

'Yes, but you can't blame the Tory government for that,' said Rawlings defensively, resuscitating an old ideological war between the two of them.

'It's much more complex than that,' said Mackinnon. 'It's partly to do with our loss of an imperial role; partly to do with the ineptitude of British shipowners in trying to carry on in the same old way, like building expensive ships and refusing to change quickly enough.'

'And perhaps our own refusal to relinquish some of our privileges and change our work practices,' put in Rawlings. Mackinnon and Sparks exchanged glances. Rawlings, who had swallowed the dogma of monetarist economics to his occasional embarrassment, was the most reactionary person on board the *Matthew Flinders*, increasingly jealous of his status as his chances of command evaporated.

'Indeed,' agreed Sparks, raising an eyebrow. 'But we have been undercut by the subsidised merchant fleets of the Warsaw Pact and displaced by the rise of the national fleets of the Third World.'

'Oh, they've been a bit of a mixed blessing,' chuckled Rawlings dismissively. 'Half of them have run into trouble due to graft and corruption.'

'That may be the case,' said Mackinnon, 'but they had the effect of releasing on to the maritime market sources of cheap labour willing to put up with unsafe working practices and dubious ships. The shipowner hasn't been so spoiled for choice since the Depression.'

'No wonder the bastards have been rubbing their hands with glee,' added Sparks, his socialist instincts fully roused. 'They've a limitless source of cheap labour at a time when international legislation is freeing up things so that the registered nationality of a ship is meaningless.'

'I thought you were all for the international brotherhood of man, Sparky,' jibed Rawlings.

'In an ideal world, that would be fine,' said Mackinnon, backing the Radio Officer and ignoring Rawlings's facetiousness, 'but you ditch a national asset, which not only provides you with the fourth arm of defence, but actually earns you invisibles to set against a balance of payments deficit, at your peril. I know we, as seafarers, have to compete more than any other section of the workforce in a truly international market place, but unless you subsidise a merchant fleet, an advanced country like Britain, irrespective of its geographical identity as an island, isn't going to have one. Not for defence, not for earning invisibles, not for anything.'

'I agree, sir,' said Rawlings with a mixed air of ingratiation and faint exasperation, aware that Mackinnon was ignoring him, 'but you can't really blame the shipowner, you know.' He turned on the Radio Officer. 'He has to make his profits where he can. If it's cheaper to register a ship in the Bahamas, or Panama, or Liberia and hire Filipinos because they cost less than a bunch of Scousers—' He looked at Woo, polishing the glasses as the other officers drifted off to their lunch. 'I mean Eastern Steam have employed Chinese in the engine-room and as stewards for damn near a century.'

'But they retained a genuine, philosophic interest in the ships and their employees,' said Sparks, finishing his drink and siding with the Captain in an unusual display of loyalty to his employers, 'including their Chinese.'

'That's the first time in all the years I've known you that I've heard you say something complimentary about the shipowner,' Rawlings scoffed.

'But it's true,' snapped Mackinnon. 'They were tough and uncompromising, and wanted only a profit. Some of them were absolute bastards and fed us shit – you both know the old story about the condemned food: "fit for cattle feed or ship's stores" – and that's quite true, quite true. But companies like Eastern Steam *did* care up to a point. You joined Eastern Steam, not some nebulous organisation called the Merchant Navy. As a navy the thing never

23

existed, no matter how many ignorant journalists write about the *QE2* being the "flagship of the British Merchant Navy". No, companies like Eåstern Steam did value loyalty and, though not really paternalistic, they looked after their employees in a generally responsible way.' Mackinnon paused to finish his drink. 'None of this sort of thing would have happened in Old Mother Dent's day, I can tell you.' Mackinnon put his glass on the bar and nodded at Woo before moving towards the door.

'Times change, sir. Even the Old Woman would have been unable to resist today's pressures.' Rawlings handed his glass to the steward then turned to find Mackinnon blocking his exit.

'She'd have found another way, mister,' the Captain said with sudden vehemence, 'not cast us off like rubbish!'

Mackinnon felt irritated at the small breach with Rawlings. He did not like the man, but he was a tolerable Chief Officer, efficient in a lacklustre way. In common with many of his background, Mackinnon was entrenched behind the conservatism of the 1950s; he respected order, stability, and a pecking order in society, and viewed the arrest in their erosion as a necessary brake on an otherwise undisciplined descent into chaos. The industrial anarchy of the 1960s, and in particular the seamen's strike of 1966, had marked a low-water point in John Mackinnon's professional life. Nevertheless, he sympathised in general terms with Sparks's robust and committed socialism, increasingly so as he watched the demise of companies like Eastern Steam; but he had worked too hard for what he had achieved to donate it, uncompensated and unguaranteed, on the altar of socialist fraternity. The change would come by evolution, and, as far as Mackinnon was concerned, socialist government in Britain had proved the worker was as capable of being corrupted by power as king, count or counsellor. By such associations as he had enjoyed with old Mrs Dent, with

Captain Shaw and through the experience of his own advancement in a capitalist trading company, he acknowledged the old order and largely approved of it.

To Captain Mackinnon, precisely because he was a seaman as well as a ship-master, the pragmatic necessity of checks and balances, of authority and underlying freedom of will, were essential foundations of civilisation.

'Without order and discipline,' he was fond of saying, quoting an eighteenth-century admiral, 'nothing is achieved.'

And precisely because of this received wisdom he did not believe that society did not exist, nor (as was becoming political dogma at the time) that it was a haphazard collection of individuals. If economic reason was to prevail, it required an underlying structure upon which to work. As far as Captain John Mackinnon was concerned, the collection of ships that went under the one-proud misnomer of the Merchant Navy were as fundamental as Parliament or the Bank of England. At the point of its being declared redundant, Captain Mackinnon's views swerved violently off what had now, distressingly, become the tracks of orthodoxy. Therein lay the roots of his dislike of Mr Rawlings.

Rawlings, though adequate enough in his glib way, was not what Mackinnon wanted in his Chief Officer. The man was facile and dutiful only to the point of routine. He was the product of the post-war age, touched by the euphoria of victory, when the Merchant Navy offered not only a way of life but an alternative to conscription. Rawlings had stayed due to idleness and a liking for a loose, mildly alcoholic life. But he had a formidable asset in his marital connections, for he had married into the hierarchy of Eastern Steam and, though he had missed a command, he remained employed until the end, unassailable and easy-going, cushioned from harsh reality.

Such a background made his politics comprehensible

without making them admirable, for they were the refuge of an expedient, not a convinced, man. Nor did they make Rawlings any the more likable, thought Mackinnon irritably, as he returned to his cabin after lunch.

Mackinnon woke from his post-prandial nap at precisely 1430, as he had done every day when at sea on passage since he had had command. Excepting, of course, when fog, tempest, Act of God or any other circumstances demanded his presence on the bridge.

He began undressing, intending to go aft for a swim before having his midafternoon cup of tea, his invariable practice when in the tropics. He was a short, fit, powerfully built man whose weatherbeaten countenance ended at his neck and began again at his elbows. Around his knees he appeared to wear athletic bandages of similarly weathered skin. The rest of his body was pale and covered in dark hair. His crew called him 'Gorilla' Mackinnon, a soubriquet which sounded as well as it suited the Captain.

Grabbing a towel, he padded out into the blinding sunshine on the boat-deck and turned aft. To starboard the fading coast of Sumatra lay like a blue mark along the horizon, crowned by boiling white thunderheads. The ship slipped smoothly through the rippled sea as she made her way into the northern entrance of the long Strait of Malacca. Fanning outwards from her rushing bow and its white bow wave, flying fish lifted and beat their long tail fins against the surface of the water to extend their flight.

The Captain splashed into the pool with a gusto that would have done credit to a younger man. The old exhilaration flooded through him; he lay on his back and wallowed contentedly. Above him the blue of the sky was contrasted by the random passage of fluffy white fair-weather cumulus. Staring up at the infinite sky he wondered how badly he would miss this life, this pleasant solace of the ship's routine. It suited a man of his years

26

better than the young men, with the preoccupations of desire and ambition never out of their minds. Then he thought of the patient waiting of his wife, who had longed for this, his last voyage, for thirty-four years.

She had such plans for them both; now they had the money to do those things they had always longed to do, and the time in which to indulge themselves. They would visit Florence and Rome, spend night after night after night together in gentle intimacy unshadowed by any approaching departure to what Shelagh Mackinnon jealously called 'the other woman'. Mackinnon smiled to himself. Eastern Steam had named their ships after masculine explorers, but they were plain bitches to their crews and seductive harpies to their wives!

Now the other woman was about to relinquish her hold upon him. *This* was the last voyage . . .

A testy little hope borne of anxiety that nothing should go wrong crossed Mackinnon's mind, but he dismissed it, allowing his memory to traverse the years, reflecting on his luck, on Shelagh . . .

He had no idea how many days they spent in the lifeboat, though afterwards they reckoned it to be nine. With so few of them there was adequate water and biscuit, though the ceaseless motion of the boat induced seasickness in men who thought themselves immune. The wind remained west or south-west and when it grew strong they learned to stream a rope astern to hold the boat's stern to the tumbling wave crests.

Moreover, Apprentice John Mackinnon was learning lessons of a more lasting nature. The sudden arousal of his young anger had provided the motivation for the stepping of the mast and hoisting of the sails. It had also usurped the leadership of Able Seaman Bird who, without obvious rancour, relapsed into a grumbling contemplation of their fate. He constantly drew their attention to the fact that their pay ceased the day the ship had sunk, excepting Mackinnon, of course, whose father's premium paid for his training, and must be gradually reimbursed to the son in lieu of proper pay. Bird made no particular play of this difference, but beat ceaselessly upon the drum of the injustice he exposed. It was almost, the young Mackinnon thought, as though Bird regretted his survival, for it put him in the position of subjecting himself to this awful inequity and he would rather have died than suffer this final humiliation at the hands of capitalism.

At the time, this revelation of the perversity of human nature seemed incomprehensible; afterwards it seemed that the ordeal in the boat was marked not by days, nor the issue of victuals by the Chief Steward, but by the thump-thump of Bird's relentless, irrefutable polemic.

With the wind on their starboard quarter they sailed south-east amid the rain and mist of autumn low pressure. The coast, when they sighted it, loomed suddenly, terrifyingly close. Unfamiliar, its appearance was hostile, grey cliffs set about with the white pounding of breaking seas. They stood inshore and drew closer, seeing a rolling countryside and re-entrant bays, the white oblong of a farmhouse, the huddle of a village and the sharp yellow strand at the head of an inviting bay.

They drove recklessly inshore as the sun set unseen behind the grey veil of the persisting overcast. The lifeboat's keel struck the sand with a grating, the boat broached and lurched amid a welter of breaking seas that rolled up to the high-water mark and spent their energy in a sibilant roar.

Staggering over the gunwale while the waves thumped on the bottom of the heeling boat and broke over it in deluges of bitterly cold spray, they found their legs incapable of bearing their weight and fell full-length in the shallows. After a while Mackinnon floundered ingloriously up the beach and lay gasping beyond the reach of the waves. Eventually he heaved himself shakily to his feet and found a path. Calling his intention of getting help he followed it inland.

He seemed to walk miles before, in the last of the twilight, he stumbled into a muddy farmyard and found a solitary figure scattering kitchen scraps to a bevy of hens. The girl looked up and gave a little shriek. She retreated, calling her alarm at Mackinnon's approach. A door flew open and a lozenge of orange lamplight spilled out across the yard. It was instantly disfigured by the shadow of a large man with a shotgun.

'And who the divil are you?' the man challenged, the click of the gun lock sounding clear in the evening air.

'Seamen,' Mackinnon gasped, 'British seamen . . . we've been torpedoed.'

He remembered clearly standing there while the big Irishman came up to him and, finger on the trigger of the shotgun, cautiously scrutinised him. The man walked round him before asking, 'How many of you?'

Mackinnon told him and led him back to the beach while the man sent his daughter to inform the police.

'Where are we?' Mackinnon asked as he stumbled down on to the sand where his shipmates had huddled and the lifeboat looked like a beached whale in the darkness.

'County Antrim,' the man said gruffly and they returned to the house until the police arrived. The girl came back with the police, peering at the survivors with shy curiosity, a girl of his own age with large dark eyes and hair that looked brown until the lamplight caught it and it flared into a rich, dark gold.

Mackinnon heard the man called her 'Shelagh'. He did not then know that she was destined to become his wife.

Ah, well, Mackinnon concluded chuckling to himself, Shelagh deserved a reward for her constancy; if, he thought looking down at his pot-belly floating like an island between his chin and his toes, she considered the reward worth having . . .

A splash woke the Captain from his self-contemplation.

'Afternoon, sir,' said a head bobbing up beside him. It was Taylor.

'Afternoon, Three-O,' replied Mackinnon and began a slow dismissive crawl to and fro, irritated because his solitude had been broken.

The thunderheaded cumulonimbus clouds Captain Mackinnon had observed over the distant mountains of Sumatra produced an electric storm during the first watch, the eight to twelve in the evening. For hours the flickering of vast electrical discharges illuminated the huge nimbi from within, deluging the forests of northern Sumatra with torrential rain. It was an awe-inspiring sight which reached its crescendo around midnight as the Second Officer once again relieved the Third.

'The odd thing about it is the lack of noise. It must be over a hundred miles away,' drawled Taylor.

Stevenson agreed. 'All the same, it's pretty impressive.'

'I wonder,' Taylor went on musingly, 'what the Spanish and Portuguese thought of it when they first came out here. I imagine they'd have regarded it as an omen.'

'I expect they consulted their priests and clutched their crucifixes.'

'Do I detect a touch of ancestral Scots Calvinism? Tut, tut, prejudice and all that – not allowed today.' Taylor stared south again as the lightning flashed on the two figures, throwing sudden, momentary shadows and lighting the disembodied face of Stevenson fighting his annoyance over so thrown-away a remark. 'Still,' Taylor went on archly, 'it was an improvement on examining the entrails of goats.'

Irritated and unthinking, still half-doped from his brief, two-hour sleep, Stevenson said, 'The Portuguese didn't do *that*. It was the Greeks and Romans . . .'

But he need not have bothered. The next lightning flash illuminated Taylor's face in such stark relief that the contempt of his expression seemed to hang between the two of them long after darkness had returned. A pent-up fury burst from Stevenson.

'You really can be an arrogant sod, Charles,' he snapped.

Taylor turned and Stevenson knew from his voice that he was smiling. 'I know, Alex. And it *does* annoy you, doesn't it?'

Then he was gone, his tall, thin figure dropping down the bridge ladder so that Stevenson had the very distinct, though quite ludicrous, impression that Taylor had dropped down to some hellishly subterranean level, and not the boat-deck of the motor vessel *Matthew Flinders*.

Charles Taylor stepped out of the shower and wrapped a towel round himself. Padding back to his cabin he opened a can of beer. Between vigorous rubs of his limbs he knocked the beer back. When he and the can were dry he picked up a book and threw himself on his bunk.

He was tired and the print danced before his eyes; he was unable to read a word. He snapped the bunk light off and lay staring upwards into the darkness, but he found it impossible to compose himself for sleep. He was angry with himself for annoying Stevenson, angry at his self-revelations of the night before and vaguely hurt by Captain Mackinnon's obvious unfriendliness of the afternoon. It seemed, in keeping with his strained marriage, he, Charles Taylor, was incapable of maintaining a single human relationship.

He felt the big Burmeister and Wain diesel engine thumping relentlessly far down below. It missed a beat as the governor cut in. Every turn of the screw took them thirteen feet away from home.

Home . . . what the hell did that mean, anyway?

With the inevitability of a clock hand ticking away the moments to the hour of execution, Taylor's mind crept inexorably round to thoughts of Caroline. It was incredibly true that as his mind's eye fastened itself upon her image his

31

heartbeat increased, so that his reaction was as real as if she had walked into the room and was, even then, sliding out of her silk robe, her white body a pale flame in the gloom.

He turned over restlessly, but she did not leave. He rolled over on to his back again and she bestrode him like a succubus, her wide smile tormenting him until, as always, he forgave her and succumbed to the blandishments of her remembered flesh.

CHAPTER THREE

Singapore

'Hujan! Hujan!'

Stevenson looked up from the cargo plan. The air was suddenly much cooler now, and clouds had overrun the brazen dome of the sky. The first heavy raindrops fell as the Chinese stevedore came running up.

'Rain come, Second Mate. We put hatches on now.'

'Sure.' Stevenson nodded assent, folded the cargo plan and, stuffing it hurriedly into the breast pocket of his khaki shirt, began walking swiftly aft to the seamen's accommodation. Already the labourers were emerging from the hatches, chattering happily at the respite from their work, grinning at the hurrying officer.

'Rain coming,' one remarked, proudly demonstrating his knowledge of English. 'Plenty rain.'

The alleyway was dark after the glare of sunlight and he blinked as he stopped in the doorway of the crew's mess-room.

' 'Ullo, Sec. What can we do for youse then, la?' The unmistakably Liverpudlian accent of Able Seaman Pritchard greeted him from a haze of cigarette smoke. From within this uncomfortable fug came the familiar pop and hiss of opening beer cans.

'Rain's coming,' he said. 'Get the hatches closed.'

Pritchard rose, but his watch-mate, Able Seaman

Macgregor, continued to swig the freshly opened can. 'Don't be all bloody day,' Stevenson added, staring at the reluctant sailor whose eyes shifted from the Second Mate to Pritchard as the latter flicked him on the shoulder.

'Come on, la. Get your arse into gear.'

Macgregor slammed his beer can down hard on to the Formica-topped table so that a fleck of froth flew from its opening.

Stevenson strode out on deck again, irritated by the silly incident. The glare of the sun had gone and the sky was darkly overcast. The billowing cumulus that had drifted up from the Rhio Islands of Indonesia twenty miles to the south were no longer picturesque adornments on the horizon but vaporous sacks sagging overhead from which dark curtains already swept the tank farm on Pulo Bukum.

The raindrops, huge, heavy and icy after the heat, struck Stevenson and made dark patches the size of old pennies on the *Matthew Flinders*'s deck. He clambered on to the nearest hatch-coaming, seized the end of the hatch-wire and pulled it. A snag in a steel strand bit painfully into his palm and he swore, tugged the greasy wire free and unscrewed the shackle pin, all the while hauling the heavy wire across the gaping pit of Number Five hatch.

'Hold on there, Sec.'

Pritchard, his hands encased in leather gloves, took the shackle and made it fast to the lug on the Macgregor hatch cover. Looking up at the cargo winch, Stevenson watched with mounting annoyance as Able Seaman Macgregor, with an air of proprietorial leisure, put the thing into gear, disengaged the derrick cargo runners and set the wire tight.

'Okay, Rob Roy,' Pritchard called, jumping clear. With a grinding banging which reverberated from bulkhead to bulkhead and from the ship to the godown walls on the wharf, the huge steel slabs were jerked by their tie chains one after the other from their neat vertical stowage under the overhanging deck of the contactor house and slammed horizontally over the opening of Number Five hatch. Even as Macgregor lazily swung himself from the forward winch control to the after one, Stevenson and Pritchard had run round to repeat the operation at Number Six hatch.

'In de good ole days,' grunted Pritchard as the two men attached the wire to the cover sections of Number Six hatch, 'the bloody 'prenticle boys would've given us a hand.'

'Yes,' said Stevenson, 'and I'd have stood and bawled at you from under my solar topee.'

Pritchard grinned at the Second Mate as he waved at Macgregor and both men backed off. So much for the lifestyle of bourgeois privilege enjoyed by officers of the latter-day Merchant Navy, thought Stevenson, with a twinge of resentment. The numbing clatter and bashing that followed silenced his repartee.

'Come on, Rob Roy,' Pritchard yelled at Macgregor, 'there's more work forrard,' adding, as he followed Stevenson along the starboard outboard alleyway where the labourers were settling down on coconut mats amid cigarette smoke and a universal hawking, 'I know de bloody things have the same name as him, but you'd think he invented dem. If youse hurry, Sec, you can drive the winches and let that little sod earn 'is keep.'

Stevenson was pleased that Pritchard disliked Macgregor Perhaps the Liverpudlian was just ingratiating himself, Stevenson thought as he heaved himself up the steel ladder on to the top of the contactor house between Number Four and Five hatches, but he considered himself a fair judge of character. Pritchard was a grafter and Macgregor a waster. The resentful glare that Macgregor threw him when he eventually caught up with the Second Mate and Pritchard confirmed his judgement.

'Where de fuck 'ave youse been?' Pritchard greeted him as the rain began to pour with a seething hiss that drummed on the steel deck. A foot above the well-deck a heavy mist seemed to hang as the raindrops bounced back before finally falling and forming a shallow lake that gurgled its way into the scuppers and poured over the side.

By the time they closed the last hatch they were all three soaked to the skin. Stevenson climbed down from the forecastle winch controls and they stood for a moment under the overhang, catching their breath before running aft to the shelter of the accommodation.

'Thanks Pritch, Macgregor . . .'

The Glaswegian looked up slyly. 'That should be worth a wee beer, eh, Sec?'

Stevenson stared at the man, the effrontery of the suggestion silencing him for a moment. Pritchard snorted, contemptuous of his watch-mate, and began to walk aft, as though braving the rain was preferable to being a party to Macgregor's ploy.

'Ah'm bluidy soaked, mon,' Magregor whined, looking down at himself, his voice wheedlingly pathetic, as though he alone had taken the full force of the rain.

'You cheeky bastard . . .' Stevenson knew the instant he spoke he had been trapped. Macgregor's mood changed instantly to a posture of truculence; his eyes blazed with hatred. He was the affronted one now and Stevenson bit his indiscreet lip with annoyance.

'You canna talk tae me like that, mon. Ah'll take the matter up wi' the Union. Nae struck-up prick of an officer's going tae call me a bastard.'

Stevenson turned angrily away, strongly tempted to hit Macgregor and stop his silly blather but determined not to put himself further in the wrong. He made to follow the disappearing figure of Pritchard.

'Hey, you stuck-up English snob, ah'm talking tae you . . .' There was no mistaking the provocative aggression in Macgregor's voice and Stevenson swung round, holding his clenched fists by his side with an effort at self-control.

Macgregor stood with his jaw thrust belligerently forwards. Stevenson could have sworn he wanted the

36

Second Mate to hit him, to fulfil some ancient, imagined or inherited grievance.

'Listen, Macgregor, you know very well I didn't use the word seriously, so button your lip! As to my being English, just remember I'm as Scots as yourself!'

Stevenson saw the fox cunning of quick-witted malice appear as a gleam in Macgregor's eyes.

'Bullshit,' he said contemptuously, 'and just *you* remember that ma name's *Mister* Macgregor tae you.'

Stevenson choked off a reply and began to walk furiously aft. It came to him, in a bitter moment of recollection, that somewhere, long ago, he had read or heard his profession traduced, the British mercantile marine described with contempt as the pickings of the prisons officered by the sweepings of the public schools. It was, like most generalisations, inaccurate in the particular, but possessed the tackiness of wit to stick, to lodge among those disposed to that most English vice, snobbery. The reflection grated on his nerves, reminding him he had abandoned Cathy for this life, this life that gave him Macgregor for a colleague.

'Shit!' swore Stevenson.

The rain, falling from the overloaded clouds in a solid mass, chilled him and he dripped water on the labourers now dozing on their mats along the outer alleyways. They shouted their protest. Gone were the days of the white *tuan*; now even an involuntary dripping of rainwater brought down the complaints of coolies upon him.

He was in the shower when he heard the knock on his cabin door.

'It's only me,' sang out Taylor's voice. 'I've a beer for you.'

Stevenson rubbed his hair vigorously, wrapped the towel round his waist and stepped out into the cabin. Taylor was lounging on the daybed; he handed Stevenson a beer.

'Thanks, Chas.' He threw his head back and sucked greedily at the can.

'What's up?' asked Taylor, seeing the preoccupied look on

37

Stevenson's open face.

'I'm bloody furious and this is just what I need. Thanks.'

'What's happened?' Taylor persisted.

'Oh, nothing much. That bloody man Macgregor gave me some lip . . .' Stevenson outlined the incident. 'My own fault, really. I shouldn't have called him a bastard.' He finished with an unhappy shrug.

'Oh, forget it, Alex. We're all guilty when it comes to bad language. It doesn't signify except when a troublemaker like Macgregor wants to make something of it. Here, have another beer and drown your sorrows.'

With a sense of diminishing unease Stevenson slowly dismissed the incident from his mind. Beyond the jalousies the rain lashed down and a peal of thunder rumbled across Keppel Harbour. Stevenson looked at his watch.

'There won't be any more cargo work this shift,' he remarked, accepting the second can of beer from Taylor.

'That's what I came to see you about. The Mate says he'll stand this evening's harbour watch so you and I can take a run ashore together. How about it?'

'That's unusual for old Randy Rawlings, isn't it?' asked Stevenson, pulling on a clean white uniform shirt and musing on the Mate's philanthropy. Second and Third Officers were customarily on watch and watch in harbour with no time to socialise beyond the brief few moments when they handed over the deck.

'I suspect he has ulterior motives. I heard him asking Woo for a Chinese special chow tonight; I expect he's invited someone aboard. Hasn't he got relatives here?'

'Oh, yes,' Stevenson recalled casually. 'I think you're right.'

'Anyway, I thought it would be a good opportunity for you and I to enjoy a modest little piss-up and, er—' Taylor rolled his eyes with exaggerated significance at the picture of Cathy on Stevenson's desk. Stevenson turned from drawing on his shorts and for a moment both men stared at the photographed face that smiled back at them.

'She's very attractive, Alex. She seems to me more like the kind you marry than the kind you screw.' He sighed. 'But I suppose you were screwing her just the same.' Taylor caught Stevenson's eye. The latter was oddly discomfited by the remark and swung round to gaze in the mirror and comb his hair assiduously.

'Sorry, old man,' said Taylor. 'Didn't mean to tread on any toes.'

Stevenson heard the supercilious pomposity enter Taylor's voice with the outmoded words. He was assailed from both flanks. First Macgregor's sly attack on the imagined privilege of his being Alexander Stevenson, Second Mate of the ageing motor vessel *Matthew Flinders*; now, from somewhere above him in the social pecking order, came the mild contempt of the blond aristocrat. He felt bowed under the martyrdom of being middle class and in a flash had lost his temper.

'Oh, for Christ's sake, Chas, don't be so bloody condescending!' He rounded on Taylor and whipped him verbally, transferring the anger he felt for Macgregor to the lolling figure of the Third Mate on the daybed. 'From what you told me the other night, you're no great Lothario yourself . . .'

And for the second time that afternoon he regretted what he had said the instant the words had left his mouth.

Taylor looked like a man physically struck.

'Oh, fuck it! Chas, I'm sorry, I really am . . .' Stevenson was abruptly aware of the difference in their ages. Taylor was suddenly a silent, crushed boy and Stevenson realised that his superciliousness was a facade, bred in him, or cultivated, it did not really matter.

'I am sorry, I shouldn't have said that. I didn't mean it. Macgregor got under my skin.'

Very slowly Taylor uncoiled himself and stood up, facing the contrite and apologetic Stevenson.

39

'Forget it, Alex. I'm going down to dinner.' He made to push past Stevenson as the notes of the steward's gong sounded.

It was the Radio Officer who saved the situation. His appearance in the cabin doorway was without the time-honoured formality of a knock and the obvious excitement on his face was sufficiently unusual to distract them both.

'Hey, you guys, come and have a butchers at this lot.' He paused, sensing reluctance and insisted, *'Come on!'* Stevenson and Taylor followed him on to the boat-deck, dodging the streams of water that cascaded down from the lower edges of the sagging awnings. By the rail and beneath the awning's shelter they joined Captain Mackinnon and Chief Officer Rawlings who were staring through the persistent rain.

The long line of merchant ships of many flags and nationalities lying alongside the shallow curve of the wharves of Keppel Harbour stretched as far as they could see on either hand. From the adjacent fairway, the muted grumble of slow-running, high-performance diesel engines announced the approach of a curious sight. The five Britons stood silently, staring at the rain-splashed strip of grey water and the burden it bore.

A sleek, evil-looking patrol launch of the Singapore Defence Force was coming up Keppel Harbour. A filthy brown haze of exhaust smoke trailed astern, throwing into sharp focus the light grey paintwork and the red and white of her ensign, but partially hiding what she was towing. As the big launch came abeam of the *Matthew Flinders* they saw clearly what it was.

Trailing astern of the immaculate patrol boat came a mastless junk, half the size of its tug. It was crammed with people, so crammed that no one individual could be discerned from the mass, like ants round the entrance to an ant hill, but with one important difference: the ants would

40

have heaved with a common energy, a mass of moving legs and bodies.

The people aboard the junk were immobile.

They sat, or lay, or stood like statues and it seemed to the watching British officers their stillness was not that of exhaustion, or hunger; not even of an oriental fatalism or hopelessness, but the awful dignity of silent reproach and this had, in some extrasensory way, preceded them, alerting the watchers to their coming.

They were towed the length of Keppel Harbour, past the idle ships of two dozen nations; past the manifestly opportunist convenience of, perhaps, no more than half that number of so-called national flags. It seemed, too, they dragged more than a cloud of the patrol boat's foul exhaust gases behind them, for as they passed the *Matthew Flinders*'s officers, surprise had changed to a sort of half-comprehended embarrassment. The five men looked sheepishly at one another, and then avoided each other's eyes as though they were in some way guilty of something they were unable to put words to.

Then, in a hiss of intensification, heavier rain swept down the harbour, driving in under the awning and the watchers turned away for the shelter of the accommodation and the five-course dinner awaiting them in the saloon.

Stevenson was the last in the queue as they stumbled over the sea step in their haste. Perhaps because of the upsets of the last hour he felt most acutely that dumb accusation. He looked back.

The heavier rain had overtaken the boatload of refugees. They were blurred against the brown diesel fumes of the still-audible patrol boat, and then blotted out, as though nature itself was affronted.

But Stevenson was left with the indelible memory of several scores of people remaining perfectly motionless.

Captain Mackinnon was depressed and aware that if he did

41

not put a stop to this solitary drinking he was going to go to bed drunk and wake up tomorrow with a thumping hangover. In defiance of common sense he poured himself another gin and slopped the remains of a tonic bottle into the glass after it. Not wanting to drink the gin so undiluted he rose unsteadily to his feet, barked his shin on the corner of the coffee table and bent to reach in his drinks locker. He withdrew the last bottle of tonic, opened it and filled his glass.

A faint sensation of nausea uncoiled itself in his belly and perspiration broke out on his broad forehead. He swore horribly and trenchantly under his breath. He had been here before.

Alcohol, the inescapable lubricant which oiled the working of human imperfection, was too easily obtained, too freely part of the everyday, aboard ship. It accrued to itself a host of little rituals, small steps and bobs and curtsies of a sinister measure, the dance of a slow death.

There was no denying the sight of those unfortunate refugees had disturbed the self-confident equilibrium of Captain Mackinnon's life. He did not know quite why, for he was largely an unimaginative man, except that their plight had raised doubts in his mind. Firstly he doubted his own right to happiness, and his imagination in contemplating retirement saw his future solely in such terms, though the practical difficulties and trials of his life had conditioned him also to doubt its actual existence. Moreover, such an occidental assumption that he had earned his retirement was palpably unjust in the face of the misery he had just witnessed. And finally he doubted the value of human endeavour that seemed, eternally, to fail to achieve what must be achieved to improve the reality of existence.

He had found the imposition of these depressing considerations too gloomy, too insuperable to shrug them off ashore, and had settled to his longely binge, putting off the agent's invitation until the following evening.

Bleary-eyed he stared about him round the cabin and swore again. Yes, yes, a thousand times yes, he would abandon this, this obverse of the panoply of command, to be sitting with Shelagh who had long ago pulled him back from the abyss upon whose edge he now teetered, remembering . . .

And, remembering, he knew the answers to his doubts: his love for Shelagh, their love for each other, marked him as lucky. He was a lucky man and Shelagh proved it. Not as lucky as some, he thought reasonably, but luckier than most; luckier than many men he had sailed with, *was* sailing with at the moment, and a damned sight luckier than those poor devils of boat people that had been towed pathetically past them three or four hours earlier.

Lucky he might be, but happy he was not.

It was foolish to imagine the world would ever be free from strife and injustice, poverty and hunger. There were so many people, more than the earth could support, even if the hugely rich and, perhaps, the not so hugely rich, relinquished some of their excess wealth.

Was he, a self-acknowledged lucky man, too greedy? The thought troubled him. He did not acknowledge what some had embarrassingly called heroism when he had brought the lifeboat ashore, but he reckoned he had paid the tariff by fighting in a war and skirting the edges of other conflicts. His uneasy feeling of not having paid enough, or not having kept his payments up, worried him. He felt touched by disappointment and uncertainty.

He experienced a surge of self-justification, falling back on a fierce, defensive pride in that to which he belonged. The Merchant Navy had fought the longest, most vital battle of the Second World War, the Battle of the Atlantic. He had read somewhere that proportionally more of its men had died than in any of the so-called 'fighting-services', but they were mere sailors, scarcely men of the pipe-and-slippers/missus-and-the-nippers variety, and few wept over their

43

copious drownings. Now, Mackinnon bitterly reflected, they were going down the tube, redundant, too expensive (though God knew they cost little enough, now as then). Only merchant seamen could be treated with the cavalier dismissal which stopped their pay the moment their ships were sunk. He remembered Bird railing about the outrage in the YMCA in Belfast . . .

But it was in the past now. The world had turned; their fates were governed by the accountants and even the old oligarchs, like Mrs Dent, were *outré*. It was bad luck on Sparks and Stevenson, of course, and even on that square peg Taylor who, Mackinnon considered, would never have survived in an open boat and had never been asked to, but it was not as bad as being aboard that rotting junk with the detention camp looming.

For himself, Mackinnon concluded, compromising an old man's selfishness with a due appreciation of good fortune, he could acknowledge his luck, deserved or not. There was no doubt about that. He had only to keep his nose clean for a week or two more, then Shelagh, and Rome and Florence, and the thing would come full circle . . .

His eyes fell on the big art book Shelagh had insisted he bring with him. He had trouble focussing on the gilt title, printed in Times Roman on its dark spine, but he had no need to read it. He knew it and its new, unopened state reproached him: *The Uffizi*.

He wondered why he had not opened it, aware that he had been moved to do so several times but had drawn back and postponed the moment. For pleasure? No, for wholly superstitious reasons, as if the physical act of opening the book and feasting his eyes upon the illustrations would be a direct challenge to providence, inviting its malice in thwarting his desire. So he had left the book, promising to look at it the moment he came down from the bridge for the last time, an act of finality which marked his passing from active employment to retirement, an act marking his transition from operating as John Mackinnon, Master under God of the motor vessel *Matthew Flinders*, to pensioned status under the direction of his wife. He laughed at himself, then thought again of Shelagh, of her handing him the book and he asking, laughingly, 'What the hell's the Uffizi?' And she had given him one of her silent go-on-with-you looks so he was still not quite certain.

He had not much noticed the girl in the Antrim farmhouse. It was only after they had reached Belfast and were kicking their heels waiting for a passage back to Liverpool that he found himself thinking of her. Then he almost forgot her; but not entirely, so when John Mackinnon caught sight of the girl at the bus stop outside the David Lewis hospital in Liverpool he recognised her at once.

'Hullo,' he had said, filled with cocksure manhood, coming up to her in the twilight while the gaunt outline of Bibby's bombed warehouse reared up against the pallid wash of the sunset. 'You're Shelagh, aren't you?' He paused as she stared at him not denying her identity, confused. 'From County Antrim,' he added helpfully. 'D'you remember me? The apprentice that was washed up in the ship's lifeboat? We arrived at your farm one evening and I frightened you.' He thought he might be frightening her now, but he ploughed on. 'I'm John Mackinnon and I remember you very well.' He had held out his hand while a curious mis-thumping of his heart told him, though he did not know it at the time and only recalled it now, that they had been brushed by the passing wings of fate. And then, after she had recognised him, he walked her into town and paid for two seats at the cinema, learning of her arrival in Liverpool and her desire to become a nurse. He was uncertificated Third Mate of the *George Vancouver* then, just paid off from a fourteen-month voyage and already signed on the *James Cook* preparing to sail to join the Fleet Train in the Pacific in the final struggle with Japan.

45

Before the ship sailed for Manaus he and Shelagh had, as the saying went, been walking out together for long enough to know.

Yes, Captain Mackinnon mused with the persistent profundity of the mildly drunk, he was a lucky man, and leaving the glass two-thirds full, he stumbled through to his night cabin and fell across his bunk.

Stevenson passed a glass of beer to Taylor and both men crossed the tiny dance floor and sat down.

'Chas, I – er – I'm really sorry for what I said earlier.'

Taylor shook his head. 'Forget it, Alex. I asked for it anyway.' He made an obvious effort to change the subject. 'The Mate certainly wanted to get rid of us this evening, didn't he? Practically kicked us down the gangway.'

Stevenson agreed, relieved after the tense taxi ride that Taylor bore him no ill-will. 'We don't want to talk shop, let's make the most of tonight.'

They both stared round the bar. It was still early, but already a couple of Norwegians were necking furiously in the shadows. The girls were Chinese and writhed with sinuous enthusiasm round their captors. The sight made the two Britons uncomfortable. As yet only one other 'hostess' was in the place, a beautiful Malay girl who sat alone at the bar, apparently content with her own company. It was obvious to Stevenson that she was having a disconcerting effect on Taylor.

'Odd about that boatload of refugees this evening,' Stevenson tried.

'Sorry?' Taylor turned from the girl, abstracted.

'Odd about those refugees. I mean, I couldn't help feeling, well . . .' Stevenson's voice trailed off uncertainly.

'Ashamed?' suggested Taylor.

'Yes, something like that.' Stevenson struggled with words adequate to fit the deep impression the sight had made on him, aware too that the mood of confidence between them had been damaged by his earlier insult, yet eager to re-establish it even if he did run the risk of a rebuff from the younger man. 'It left me feeling guilty that we could do nothing, but certain that we ought to do something . . .'

Taylor smiled engagingly over the rim of his glass. 'Ah, that's the guilt engendered by your pampered overfed western lifestyle. You see, you haven't been bred to accept it as your birthright; you are full of the Protestant work ethic that automatically conditions you to suspect the good things of life whether they are in your lap or someone else's, while at the same time it drives you to accumulate more and more material wealth and to justify your existence by hard work.'

Stevenson digested Taylor's words, aware of the underlying irony but uncertain whether or not it was aimed at Stevenson or turned upon himself. Taylor did not give him time to arrive at a conclusion.

'I don't suppose those poor bastards in that junk would actually feel real envy for you. Their predominant feeling is probably one of relief at getting to Singapore with an underlying fear about what happens next.'

'That sounds a bit callous,' Stevenson said, warming to the conversation and driving to the heart of the matter. 'I get the impression that your well-to-do forebears bore the burden of their wealth with – what shall I say? – commendable fortitude.'

Taylor laughed. 'Ah, the old Whig philosophy was pretty good. Had distinct advantages, you know. A lack of conscience was one of its first attributes. Very useful, did away with all awkward moral dilemmas.'

'I hope you're not intending to employ it tonight with her.' Stevenson nodded at the solitary hostess.

'Why not?' Taylor grinned again, then his mouth twisted and his expression hardened. 'Oh, don't say "because you're married", for Christ's sake, because as far as I'm aware the instant I'm at sea Caroline forgets I exist. If she occasionally recalled me I might get the odd letter. No, Alex, if you want to make me the conscience of the western world, forget it.' He stood up and added, 'I'm not in the mood.'

Taylor walked across the bar and Stevenson watched him strike up conversation with the girl. She seemed reluctant at first, but Taylor was gently persistent. Stevenson felt a prickling of lust followed by a wave of jealousy. He took a long pull at his beer. When he looked again Taylor was sitting alongside the girl and the barman was pouring them both drinks. He sat in the gloom of his secludedly desolate table and printed aimless patterns on its top with the condensation formed round the base of his glass.

It occurred to him that this was Taylor's retribution. This abandonment in the face of Taylor's success at picking up the girl was a refutation of his own accusation that Taylor was no great Lothario. Stevenson watched the pair, their heads close together. No, there was no triumph in picking up a bored professional, and so cheap a revenge was too shabbily obvious to be Taylor's style. If, Stevenson concluded as he motioned the barman for another drink, it *was* revenge Taylor was meditating, then it was a more profound one than a levelling of a petty score with himself. Taylor had mentioned Caroline's failure to write; perhaps it was she whom he wished to humiliate.

'Don't you want to be introduced?' Stevenson looked up. Taylor loomed over him, the girl at his side. She was undeniably lovely, with a skin-tight black dress cinched at the waist. It had a high neck, though her shoulders were bare, and a short hemline. From his observations when she had been at the bar, he knew its back was non-existent. He struggled, gentlemanly, to his feet.

'Sharimah,' Taylor said, 'meet Alex.'

'Hi.'

Stevenson felt again the prickle of intense desire. Her breasts swelled the soft, slightly elastic material of the dress, but it was her face that transfixed him.

48

He was no first-trip apprentice to be cunt-struck by the first painted trollop who squeezed his knee, but he would have had to have been insensible not to have been moved by her genuine beauty.

'Hullo . . . what are you drinking?'

'It's all right,' put in Taylor, 'my shout' – meaning hands off, I picked her up.

Stevenson sat again, opposite the girl. Raven hair fell to her shoulders and the light brown of her skin was taut over high cheekbones. Her face escaped full oriental flatness by a well-made nose suggesting the miscegenation of a Portuguese seaman somewhere in her ancestry. From eyes as dark, Stevenson thought, as the tropic night, she confronted his scrutiny, carried out with the thunderstruck wonder of half-drunk admiration. She pouted crimson lips around a cigarette and seemed to blow a mocking kiss as she withdrew it from her lips.

'You like girl too?' she asked him as he inhaled the smoke from her lungs. Taylor was on his way back from the bar, his eyes daring Stevenson to poach.

He shook his head and she shrugged. 'Pity,' she said with honest, whorish candour. 'You very good-looking man.'

Someone put some music on and one of the Norwegians was dragged on to the tiny dance floor by a giggling Chinese girl. Taylor had just eased himself alongside Sharimah.

Stevenson stood. 'Would you like to dance?' he asked and then stared at Taylor. The girl looked from one to another and Taylor shrugged. 'Okay,' he said, his tolerance edged with a touch of sarcasm, 'I buy the drinks, you dance.'

'Just one,' said Stevenson placatingly, holding out his hand to Sharimah.

'Just one.'

They swung into the faintly ridiculous gyrations of the dance, Stevenson awkwardly, his eyes on the body of the girl, while she, automatic in her movements at first, abandoned herself to the music and the inflaming of

49

Stevenson's passion. Beyond her bare shoulder, he could see Taylor's smouldering eyes devouring Sharimah's figure.

They danced until the last guitar chord slashed the air, leaving them breathless and suddenly self-conscious in the silence.

Stevenson caught Sharimah's elbow and turned her back to the table, but Taylor had gone to relieve himself, and another song, slow and smoochy, crooned lugubriously from the tape recorder somewhere behind the bar. Both the Norwegians, huge blond men, swivelled slowly, the tiny Chinese women engulfed in hugs.

Stevenson slipped his arms round Sharimah's waist and drew her to him. The scent and touch of her overwhelmed his senses. He thought, distantly, of Cathy. Sharimah's face was averted so he pressed closer as they began to sway to the slow beat. Her pelvis thrust forward to meet his, and she turned her face up to him. His tumescence intruded between their contiguous bellies.

'You want me, tonight?'

He swung her round and found himself facing Taylor. Sharimah sensed some conflict within him and drew back her head. Not thinking he would spurn her, given his obvious urgency, she sought elsewhere for explanation.

'You married man?'

Stevenson looked down at her, his agony clear on his face.

'Yes,' he lied, feeling her fall away and himself shrink feebly.

She sighed, and, as if to compound an image of star-crossed lovers, he embraced her tighter. Lust unaccountably gave way to a sudden, overwhelming feeling of tenderness.

They drew apart, holding hands.

'I'm sorry,' he said.

She shrugged. 'Okay. Your friend he wants me tonight.' Stevenson nodded. 'I like you best but I am business girl. Your friend good business, okay?' She squeezed his hand then let it go and walked towards Taylor who was watching them from the table.

'Sure,' murmured Stevenson following her, as her buttocks wiggled away from him.

Stevenson stumbled at the top of the gangway. He was not drunk, just a little unsteady, his coordination a touch awry. As he came level with the deck two figures could be seen in the pools of light from the bulkhead lamps. The Tamil security guard greeted him with a respectfully indulgent grin.

'Good evening, sir.'

Stevenson paused on the gangway table, hauling himself upright before stepping on to the deck. The second man straightened from leaning on the rail and the deck lights high-lit the tight-lipped, malicious smile.

'Well, well; if it isna our Second Mate, an' pissed out o' his skull an' all!'

Stevenson paused for a moment, glaring at Macgregor, but possessed of sufficient sobriety to hold his tongue; then he plunged through the door into the athwartships alleyway and dragged himself unhappily up to the boat-deck accommodation.

A giggle came out of Rawlings's cabin and the door curtain was suddenly rent aside. A naked girl, her face flushed and laughing, backed out, her arms extended as though restrained. She twisted free with a toss of straw-blonde hair, still giggling, and made to run. She found herself confronting the astonished Stevenson. Both of them stood stock-still, the lights playing across the girl's breasts as they heaved with excitement and exertion. Then she turned and fled in the opposite direction, just as Rawlings, a towel draped discreetly round his paunch, looked out into the alleyway.

'Dawn? Dawn? Are you all right? Good God, Alex . . .!'

'She went that way.' Stevenson nodded towards the Captain's end of the alleyway.

'Oh, shit.'

51

Rawlings padded barefoot in pursuit. For a moment Stevenson stood, wondering if he had really seen the naked girl, then the intense whispering from the turn in the alleyway and Rawlings's reconnoitring head made him turn away. He let himself into his own cabin. As he shut the door he heard the flap of their feet and the suppressed giggles of the girl.

'Was that one of your friends?' she asked with the voice of a fallen angel.

CHAPTER FOUR

Cargo Work

During the lonely night watches of the outward passage, Taylor had seen no very good reason for Caroline's fidelity. In his unhappiness her acceptance of his proposal in the first place and their subsequent splicing among the liturgical trappings of the Church of England seemed equally incomprehensible. Perhaps she had changed afterwards; perhaps, after all, she had made a mistake, in which case it was a common enough one.

Had she written even the dullest of letters to meet the ship's arrival at Singapore he might have felt some amelioration of the self-doubt and low self-esteem he so competently buried in his cultivated air of superiority. But Caroline had failed him and his disappointment was so acute he came ashore intent on desperate and immediate solace.

Thus, he rode with his wounded pride silent in the taxi alongside Stevenson whose very words had precipitated the crisis, knowing what he contemplated had its own compensations the instant he caught sight of Sharimah alone at the bar. The girl's beauty made her price unimportant and it pleased Taylor to excite his tormentor, then to cheat Stevenson of her.

He woke at dawn. Above him a large fan gyrated slowly against the cracked plaster of the ceiling. He rubbed his eyes and the movement disturbed a gecko high up on the far wall. The little house lizard was hunting dozing flies. Outside, beyond the open jalousies, the air was heavy with the land smells and the persistent stridulation of cicadas.

Alongside him Sharimah stirred. Even after his passion was spent and remorse crept upon him with the awareness of the events of the previous evening, he could lie and admire her beauty. The grey light made her seem insubstantial, ethereal. One breast was uncovered and she had caught a stray lock of her black hair in her right hand as she had turned in her sleep.

Memories of the yielding softness of her lips came to him, and he stared in fascination at the high cheekbones and the delicate darkening of the skin of her almond eyelids.

He was suddenly disgusted by the sweat-stained grossness of his own body, already stirring again with its automatic and primaeval reaction.

She opened her eyes, gauging his mood, suddenly cautious and insecure, he realised, as she must always be on waking next to a client. He watched her as she turned anxiously to the bedside table and the crinkled heap of dollars. He followed her gaze and then their eyes met again. It was all they had in common, he thought, with a sudden pain, knowing she liked him no more than any of the others, that pile of paper money, left incautiously for him to retake if he had the mind to. He had wanted and paid; she had wanted and sold.

He lay back on the pillow and stared at the ceiling. The gecko had gone.

Beside him Sharimah rose. In an oddly private gesture she turned away from him and drew on a wrap. It was the signal that he had had from her what he had paid for: his time was up. She walked to the window and sat down upon a rickety chair, indicating he should dress and leave. She lit a cigarette from a packet lying on the window sill. A faint cloud of smoke blew back into the room.

He got up and began dressing.

'Can I see you again when I come back to Singapore?' he asked. Was he coming back to Singapore? Did he want to buy this girl who did not like him again? Why not? The illusion of love was better than the wasted passion he had known with Caroline.

The rapidly growing light caught her face in haunting profile. The cigarette smoke trailed from her mouth like ectoplasm.

'Maybe you not want to scc me when you come back.' Her face was expressionless. 'Maybe you have 'nother girl in Hong Kong.'

'Maybe.' He made to leave, then paused with his hand on the door handle. 'Sharimah?'

She only half-turned her head, so he could see the angle of her cheek but not her eyes.

'Did . . . did you like me?' It was a stupid, gauche question and she turned full face and stared at him, her eyes wide, disbelieving. He thought, for a moment, she was going to shrug indifferently and play the bored whore, but, miraculously, her expression softened and she looked as she had in the first, innocent, uncomprehending moment of waking. 'You okay,' she said, then swung to the window. Taylor did not see she was crying as he backed out of the room.

Mackinnon woke parched and priapic, disturbed by vague feelings of remorse. The empty gin bottle and half-finished drink stood evidence of his indulgence as he collected his thoughts. Such lapses of rectitude were rare, but they brought the taste of guilt to his lips.

There had been a time . . . but it was best not to think of

it, to close the cupboard door and lock it on the skeleton within. It was a long time ago and the man who never made a mistake, Mackinnon consoled himself, never made anything . . .

He slaked his burning thirst, relieved his abused bladder and, having showered, wound a towel round his waist and padded about the dayroom clearing away the bottle and glass, then walked out on deck. The first light of dawn flushed the eastern sky and the morning smell of the tropics, even on the edge of this teeming city, was refreshing. He thought, with a pang of nostalgic regret, that he would not smell it many more times, and he drew long draughts of the cool, scented air into his lungs. The faint suggestion of a headache lurked and he leaned on the rail and stared down on the empty wharf.

Ahead and astern lay the crescent of moored ships, the brilliant glare of their deck lights gradually fading, superseded by the rapidly growing daylight of the equatorial latitude. The wharf was dusted with detritus alongside each of the *Matthew Flinders*'s hatches. Stacks of pallets stood by the locked doors of the godowns while wisps of straw and chips of polystyrene packing bore witness to the cargo discharged the day before. Mackinnon looked at his watch. In an hour the scene would be transformed with the arrival of the 'wharfies', the tally clerks, the foremen and stevedores. The security man coming on duty would bring him a copy of the *Straits Times* and the agent's runner would be aboard with the day's paperwork. Mackinnon hoped that he would not have to deal out summary justice this morning and there were no drunks to log. If there were his reading of the newspaper would go hang.

He became aware that he felt an anticipatory sensation of resentment against anything that threatened to upset the tranquil passing of this voyage. It was a rather selfish indulgence, his conscience chid him; perhaps it was nature's way of telling him it was time he retired.

He grunted his objection to the uncomfortable thought and put it down to a touch of alcoholic remorse. A second later he had remembered the cause of his private binge and the vague, premonitory feeling that had disturbed his equanimity the previous evening: the boat people.

He sighed and gazed out over the Lion City. How different it appeared, with its tower blocks rising in white columns above the old, colonial-period architecture, dwarfing the once massive structures of the *tuans*, visible evidence of the triumph of largely Chinese capitalism.

How different to its appearance when, in those first weeks of peace, the *James Cook* had berthed in the Empire Dock and the pomp and circumstance of British reoccupation had taken place. For Uncertificated Third Mate John Mackinnon, eighteen years of age, the bugle-blowing had a hollow ring. He remembered the pictures of General Perceval's surrender when the unthinkable occurred and now he was here to witness its aftermath. The lorries arrived at noon, a convoy of them, and the crew of the *James Cook* watched as their pitiful cargo was unloaded. It was a cargo that was to occupy the vacant 'tween decks of the *James Cook*, fortuitously fitted out at the ship's building by an opportunist Sir James Dent with a view to transporting Indonesian and Malay Muslins on their annual pilgrimage to Mecca. The ship had never been employed on this hadji run, but today the 'tween decks were filled with a human cargo of another kind.

After several months' service with the Fleet Train based at Manaus, the crew of the *James Cook* had heard of the Burma Railway and of Changi jail. They had heard, too, rumours of Japanese atrocities matching the revelations of Belsen, Auschwitz, Ravensbruck and the rest, but they had seen nothing. For them the war had been between their inadequately armed ships with their over-stretched escorts and the unseen U-boat. Then, in the Pacific, they had conveyed stores, fuel and ammunition to the British Pacific

Fleet, raising to an art form the replenishment and subsequent efficiency of the great aircraft carriers with their screen of long, lean destroyers.

But they had seen little of the enemy apart from the desperate, doomed and incomprehensible heroics of the pilots of the Emperor Hirohito's divine wind, the *Kamikaze*. Those old hands among the *James Cook*'s company who remembered Japan before the war talked not of politics, of the invasion of China or the rape of Nanking. Instead they remembered nights ashore in Shimonoseki or Kobe, Nagasaki and Yokohama, of the gentle giggles of the knocking-shop girls, whom they gallantly termed *geisha* but who were nothing of the kind. They complained, seeing in it perhaps a manifestation of that arrogance that was but a flatteringly sincere imitation of the white man, of the indignity of the 'short-arm inspection', when the port doctor publicly examined the penises of the crew for signs of primary syphilitic lesions. Even this formality had its admirers, who contrasted it with the head-in-the-sand hypocrisy of 'homeside'.

In liberated Singapore, however, they saw something else as those trucks set down the released prisoners of war.

Mackinnon remembered it so well. The staring eyes, the shrunken limbs and cadaverous bodies, the uncertainty and fear in their faces.

'They don't realise they're safe,' he remembered one hard-bitten able seaman observe in a wondering tone. 'Yer okay now, mates,' he yelled, as if the gruff reassurance set all to rights. And as the bellowed and intended kindness fell upon uncomprehending ears, the seaman turned aside and let fly a muttered torrent of obscenities that expressed his disgust and impotence.

Had Mackinnon felt something of the same futile exasperation the previous evening? Had it been the same stunned disbelief, compounded by a bleak despair that nothing ever changed, that man's inhumanity to man stalked his vaunted progress like a shadow?

As the daylight finally triumphed and along the wharf the deck lights were put out by tired nightwatchmen, he found himself swearing under his breath like that old AB. The recollection had been vivid and he could almost smell the foul stench those poor men gave off. It permeated the *James Cook* and lingered for weeks as they engaged in the melancholy duty of repatriation.

Mackinnon was distracted from these morbid recollections by the arrival of a taxi at the foot of the gangway. He stared curiously down to see its occupant get out. It was Taylor.

So the Third Mate had spent the night with a prostitute. Mackinnon was disappointed. He did not expect his officers to be angels, even those who were married, though the folly of risking HIV infection appalled him. There had once been a lapse in Mackinnon's own marital probity, though Akiko had not been a whore. The intimations reaching Mackinnon that Taylor's private life was unhappy did not, in the Captain's opinion, entitle him to vengeful immorality. The Captain would have more readily forgiven Taylor a brief descent into a bottle. To do otherwise would have been sheer hypocrisy

'Morning, sir.'

Startled, Mackinnon turned to find the Radio Officer behind him, already immaculate in his white shirt and shorts.

'Morning, Sparks. You're up early.'

'I wish I could say I was an early bird catching worms, but I didn't sleep too well.' He peered over the rail as the taxi pulled away and Taylor's feet clattered on the gangway. 'Night on the tiles, I see.'

'Yes. Pity. What kept you awake?'

'Oh,' Sparks shrugged, 'I don't know . . .'

'Was it those boat people?'

Sparks met the Captain's eyes. 'Bothered you too, sir?'

59

'Yes, and if I'm honest, more because I don't want any similar complications on this of all voyages than from any great notions of compassion.'

Sparks nodded. 'Know what you mean. Upsetting, just the same. If they've got this far south, the China Sea must be full of them.'

'Yes, that's what's worrying me . . . Morning, Mr Taylor.'

Both men watched the Third Mate climb sheepishly to the boat-deck.

'A bit knackered, eh, Chas?' grinned Sparks, trying to head off any censoriousness on Mackinnon's part.

'Morning,' said Taylor, recovering himself. 'No. I had an excellent sleep, thank you.' He made for the accommodation.

'Mr Taylor!' Mackinnon called, and Taylor swung round expecting some interference with his private life.

'Sir?'

'What,' asked Mackinnon, 'was *your* reaction to those boat people?'

The question had sprung almost unbidden into Mackinnon's mind, as though it had risen spontaneously from the depths of his subconscious. It was not what he had seen yesterday that had upset him so much as how it had made him react. He had experienced the feeling of impotent shame at being who and what he was all those years ago when, in the first flush of victory, he had walked the streets of Singapore – a youthful liberator.

He had read accusation in every pair of eyes he had encountered: the white man had failed, the mantle of imperial protection had proved an illusion. To an eighteen-year-old raised on Churchillian oratory and imperial mythology the effect had been profound. This morning he realised how permanent was the scar.

That failure had properly belonged to his father's generation, he had thought, feeling the weight of history upon his young shoulders. Had his generation similarly

60

failed? Yesterday he had read the answer in the countless pairs of eyes staring at the moored ships, and even, he fancied (for it was powerfully nostalgic), smelt again that smell . . .

Captain Mackinnon wanted to know how his youngsters had felt, and how would they react if, as seemed highly possible to the Captain's haunted imagination, they too encountered a similar boatload of human wreckage.

'What did *I* think?' Taylor turned back and Mackinnon saw his eyes were opaque, inward-looking. 'It was pitiful,' said Taylor in an agonised tone of voice, raising his hands palms outwards then dropping them by his side in a gesture of helplessness. 'Pitiful . . .' He turned away.

Mackinnon found Sparks watching him. 'He's not a bad lad, sir.'

'Did I say he was?'

'No,' agreed Sparks, with a wry smile.

'And I'm surprised to find you leaping to his defence.'

'Because he's a sprig of the landed gentry?'

'Yes.'

'He's unhappy, and therefore redeemable.'

'The whole bloody world's unhappy, but it doesn't appear to be redeemable.'

'No. It was a bloody depressing sight.' Sparks paused, then said, 'There's nowhere to go now, is there?'

'What d'you mean?' asked Mackinnon abstractedly.

'Well, a century ago there were the colonies, and, earlier, we shipped our social misfits to Botany Bay. The Irish went to the States, along with the Poles, the Eyeties and the Russians, those that weren't sent the otherway to Siberia courtesy of the Ochrana. Even the Yanks themselves went west and grew up with the country . . .'

'What you mean is you could once relocate deprivation and dissent, today it goes to sea.'

'Got it in one, sir. The world's too crowded and distances have shrunk; so, like rats in a cage, we'll end up fighting for space to live.'

'I seem to remember someone else pleading the necessity of *lebensraum*.'

'Who?' Sparks frowned. 'Oh, yes, Hitler.' He shook his head and added, 'Well, the more of us there are, the less our individual lives matter. That's something the Chinese have known for generations. Now it seems we must digest the lesson.'

'But it leaves us exposed to exploitation, to the assumption of power by the unscrupulous,' protested Mackinnon.

'Only if we remain governable, sir,' Sparks said grinning wickedly.

In his microcosmic world it was not merely the fact that he was a ship-master that made Mackinnon believe in order and discipline, but a deep inner conviction that iconoclasm and anarchy produced chaos, and chaos was inimical to a full belly.

There was an atmosphere of anarchy prevailing in the saloon at breakfast, Mackinnon thought irritably when he took his place at table and exchanged greetings with Mr York, the Chief Engineer. It was a consequence of their being in port, of course; what old Captain Shaw had called 'the trammels of the shore'. Had the *Matthew Flinders* been at sea the airy space would have been redolent of all the freshness of a tropic morning when, it seemed to Mackinnon, God's act of creation could have been a comparatively recent event. Officers, deck and engineer, would have come in, muttered polite good mornings, taken their breakfast under the bobbing attentions of the Chinese stewards and then gone about their business. Their lives would have been subordinate to the overwhelming demands of the great steel soul of the ship. This morning, however, their private lives obtruded and their demeanour was a consequence of the night before.

First at table were the stone-cold-sober, those who had

62

been on duty: Sparks, the Second and Fifth engineers. Then other engineers drifted in, sniggering over the events of a run ashore, and Sparks was joined by Stevenson who pulled a face at Sparks's interrogatively raised eyebrow.

'Tut-tut,' ticked Sparks, mocking Stevenson with a smirk of exaggerated self-righteousness. It was not yet time for Sparks to go native, besides he had a mountain of correspondence to deal with from his wife who was somehow managing to move house and keep two unruly boys in the vicinity of their proper place of education. These were, he mused over his bacon and eggs, the small, irregular wars in life that people fought. It was not indifference they felt to the plight of those like the boat people, merely a more immediate preoccupation with the minutiae of their lives. He decided not to write and tell his wife about the refugees. Such problems were for politicians to sort out, otherwise there was no point in electing them.

Taylor joined them, his hair still wet from the shower he had taken as soon as he arrived on board. He sat down and ordered, avoiding the others' eyes.

'Good night?' enquired Stevenson quietly.

'Wonderful,' grunted Taylor. Stevenson exhanged glances with Sparks who pulled another face.

Then the girl walked in. She was pretty and blonde, with an irresponsibly wide mouth and breasts prominent enough to stir both the monastic and the jaded in the gathering. The impression her entrance caused amused and pleased her; she was quite unaware of any improprieties it might engender, improprieties which choked Captain Mackinnon with their effrontery, and astonished Stevenson who recognised her. She paused, uncertain where to sit, yet unashamedly enjoying being the cynosure for all eyes. Behind her came Chief Officer Rawlings who ushered her to the seat next to Mackinnon.

'Dirty old bastard,' murmured an incredulous Sparks, scooping marmalade from the dish.

'Bloody exhibitionist,' agreed Stevenson.

'I wondered who the extra place was for,' growled Mackinnon, half-rising while the girl sat.

'My niece Dawn, sir . . . Dawn, Captain Mackinnon,' Rawlings drawled. An inquisitive silence hung in the saloon like a smell. 'She was unable to get home last night,' Rawlings explained. 'Had to kip on my settee, didn't you, my dear?'

The girl nodded, looking round her. She began to see that her behaviour was not passing as uncensured as her uncle had assured her it would.

'I trust you had a good night,' Mackinnon remarked, his voice heavy with sarcasm. Next to him the Chief Engineer made a scoffing noise and renewed sniggers ran among his junior staff. Sparks whispered, 'Good old Gorilla.'

A flush began to suffuse the cheeks of the girl.

'Pissed as a newt, Pritch,' confided Macgregor, opening a can of beer as he shoved the grease-rimed plate away from him and belched.

Able Seaman Pritchard ignored him, scraped up the last of the egg yolk with the remains of a slice of bread and reached for the mug. It was decorated with the badge of Liverpool Football Club and contained an acidulous brew of orange tea. Holding it to his mouth with both hands he stared at Macgregor over its rim. 'So will you be if you drink dat stuff at dis time of day.'

'Fuck it,' snarled Macgregor. 'Nae shit-faced officer'll be telling me what tae do this morning. Ah had the night watch, so ah did, an' ah can tell you Stevenson was pissed, Rawlings was screwing a young piece of stuff, the dirty, lucky bastard, and Taylor was having his hole ashore. He didna' get back till an hour ago.' He belched again. 'Sae fuck you. Ah'm for my pit.'

He tossed the beer can into the tin-plate rosy standing in the corner of the mess-room. It missed, clattered on the deck and rolled away. Macgregor ignored it and stood as the other men in the mess turned and regarded him with distaste.

'Pick that up,' said an older seaman at the next table.

Macgregor made a kiss with his lips. 'Fuck you, Braddock,' he said and walked out of the mess-room.

'Good riddance,' said Pritchard as Braddock dropped the can noisily into the rosy.

'There's always one fly in the ointment,' he said as the Bosun came in with a handful of mail to turn the dayworkers to.

'Three letters here for you lot,' he said. 'Two for Braddock and one for Pritch.' He tossed the letters expertly, so they skidded across the Formica table top and were equally expertly caught by their addressees.

'Ta, Bose.'

'I'll give you two five minutes to read 'em, then get cracking on those derrick runners for Number 6. They'll be opening that hatch after dinner and the Mate wants them ready. The rest of you on the foredeck and let's get the jumbo organised.'

Captain Mackinnon was drinking a final cup of coffee as the crew noisily went forward to rig the 'jumbo', a special derrick mounted on a trunnion abaft the ship's foremast for handling extra heavy lifts out of the capacious hold below it. There were two enormous electric transformers to be discharged and the agent's young Chinese runner, who had joined the Captain's table for coffee and cast quizzical looks at the Mate's niece, brought confirmation that the low loaders would be alongside the ship at ten o'clock.

'That'll be the lads going forrard now to get the jumbo ready, sir,' said Rawlings urbanely. He turned to the agent's man, 'Would you mind seeing Miss Dent ashore, Mr Chang?' He rose and turned to the girl, who now looked awkward and embarrassed. 'Well, Dawn, I think it's time to go.' The girl got to her feet and muttered her thanks to

Mackinnon. Rawlings held her chair and escorted her to the door as the agent's runner followed. 'Tell your mother I'll try to catch up with the family news tonight if I can get ashore. Nice to see you, my dear.' He kissed her cheek and went back into the saloon. Resuming his seat he winked at the Chief. 'Don't be an old stick-in-the-mud, Chief,' he said, stirring his coffee. 'I remember you in Sourabaya . . .'

'She wasn't my niece, for God's sake,' spluttered Mr York.

'She was somebody's niece,' remarked Rawlings facetiously.

'I'll see you in my cabin, Mr Rawlings,' Mackinnon said, getting to his feet, 'just as soon as you're satisfied with the heavy-lift gear.'

'Aye, aye, sir,' said Rawlings, unruffled and again addressing the Chief. 'It's the last voyage, Chief,' he said, and left the air full of implications.

Mackinnon was well aware that Rawlings's smart-arsed remarks to Ernie York were, in fact, addressed to him, a heading off of any reprimand Captain Mackinnon felt he might be entitled to give his Chief Officer. He opened the *Straits Times* but was unable to concentrate on its contents and sat discontentedly until Rawlings arrived, tapping punctiliously on the mosquito door that Mackinnon had left open to catch the growing sea breeze.

'The jumbo's ready for the low-loaders,' Rawlings said smoothly, adding as a casual afterthought, 'You wanted to see me, sir?'

'You know what about, Mister,' said Mackinnon, wishing he was not sitting down. 'What the hell d'you think you're playing at? That girl . . .'

'Is my niece, sir. Her parents went out to dinner last night and she felt like paying me a visit.'

'I remember her when she was a kid, for God's sake! How old is she now?'

'Eighteen. She'll soon be starting a university course.'

'Did she have to stay all night?' asked Mckinnon. He knew he was going to lose this fencing match with words unless he made a direct accusation, but his old-fashioned sense of propriety prevented him from airing so horrible a suspicion, even of Rawlings.

'You're not, er, alleging that anything improper occurred, are you, sir?' Rawlings enquired archly.

Out-manoeuvred, Mackinnon felt anger rise in him like bile. He suppressed it with difficulty. 'What you and your eighteen-year-old niece do or do not do is of no interest to me, mister. What concerns me is that you flagrantly brought her into the saloon this morning.'

'If I had sneaked her down the gangway this morning the whole ship would have said I'd knocked her off, wouldn't it? You know how well a secret is kept aboard ship. She's part of the family,' he said, shrugging, 'part of Eastern Steam. She's known these ships since she was a kid.'

'Aye, and this is the last voyage.'

'Exactly, sir.'

'Get on with your duties, Mr Rawlings.'

In the wake of the Mate's departure what disturbed Mackinnon most was not Rawlings's amoral conduct, but the girl's immorality.

Any assertion that it was no business of his was a lie, for it disturbed him just as the plight of the boat people disturbed him. If he felt a measure of responsibility for the one, it followed he accepted a measure of responsibility for the other. As he paced back and forth across the forward end of the boat-deck, in front of his cabin windows and immediately beneath the now-deserted bridge (ostensibly keeping an eye on the preparations for the discharge of the transformers), he found the conundrum perplexing.

Why did he not feel quite the same about Taylor's transgression? Below him cases of Guinness were following Ford Escorts out of Number Three 'tween deck and

Stevenson, wearing the khaki drab of cargo duty, walked slowly forward discussing something with the Chinese stevedore. There, thought Captain Mackinnon indulgently, was a good officer, and he vaguely wished he had a son like Alex Stevenson.

He and Shelagh had no children. There had been a daughter once, who died mysteriously, a babe in arms. The doctors had called it 'a wasting disease', but this unsatisfactory diagnosis only masked their ignorance and insulted the intelligence of the grieving and separated parents. Mackinnon supposed himself lucky again, in that he had had a ship's business to immerse himself in, and even had the child survived he would have had little part in her upbringing. No, the burden of loss had fallen, as always, upon Shelagh, and she had stood it better than he. It had been a bad enough voyage, that eleven-month jag on the *William Dampier*, without the sense of loss and the worry about his wife; it was not surprising (though it remained unforgivable in Mackinnon's personal canon) that he had almost succumbed to the temptations of alcohol . . .

It was, of course, Miss Dent's youth that made her conduct with Rawlings so inexplicable to Mackinnon. He had never debauched a woman in his life and the realisation reminded him that, for all his years, for all his imminent retirement, in some ways he was an innocent. The idea made him chuckle ruefully. At least privately he could laugh at himself. He felt the deck under his feet incline gently. The shock of fear never left him when the deck moved, for this was not the easy roll of a ship in a seaway but an induced heel, like the death throes of the old *Matthew Flinders* during the war. He immediately suppressed the instinctive reaction; this was no more than a gentle angle of heel as the jumbo, its threefold topping-lift purchase of heavy steel wire-rope taut with the sixty-tonne weight, swung ponderously over the side and lowered the huge transformer on to the low-loader on the quayside.

Well, he thought as the ship recovered and swung back, the purchase wires suddenly running slack and the low-loader creaking under its burden, thank God he *could* still laugh at himself! Those damned refugees had unsettled him rather more than he cared to admit.

But suppose he picked some up? The anxiety tormented him. He could ignore them – there were stories of such things happening, of patrol boats of various embarrassed governments towing the cranky craft outside territorial waters and leaving them adrift to their fate – but such a consideration was unthinkable to John Mackinnon, himself a survivor from a drifting boat. The notion appalled him. Had he sunk so low in his comfortable life that he could even contemplate such an action? He shied away from the selfishness of it.

Nevertheless it was early August. Navigational conditions in the South China Sea took a turn for the worse about now. The typhoon season was upon them and, judging from the news and the evidence they had seen, there were at that moment several hundred, perhaps thousands, of people afloat on the bosom of the ocean. Captain Mackinnon had a feeling of inevitability lurking in the pit of his stomach. A premonition. He swore again, recognising the existence of the law of imbuggerance: that if something could go wrong it would.

Captain Mackinnon was a seaman to his fingertips and what he lacked in knowledge of the seduction of eager young women he more than made up for in his knowledge of sea lore. Instinct played a significant part in the practicality of his mind; it was instinct that made him plan for eventualities, and it was instinct which combined with the discipline of his mind to make him the kind of shipmaster that he was. 'Gorilla' might be his soubriquet, but it was one containing its own kind of grudging admiration, expressing the impression of gentle strength Captain Mackinnon generated.

The *Matthew Flinders* was fortunate in having such a commander, though at that moment John Mackinnon privately thought he had run out of luck.

CHAPTER FIVE

The South China Sea

Stevenson straightened up from the gyro-compass repeater on the port bridge-wing, rubbing eyes tired from the last hours of cargo-working in Singapore. He let the Horsburgh Lighthouse flash a couple of times before bending again, aligning the needle of the azimuth mirror with the winking light as it came on to the alter-course bearing.

'On, sir!' he called to Captain Mackinnon standing expectantly in the wheelhouse door, and hurried into the chart-room to plot the ship's position.

Mackinnon spoke softly to the helmsman and the *Matthew Flinders* swung slowly to port, her deck heeling slightly under the influence of the rudder.

'Steady on o-two-six, Cap'n,' reported the shadowy figure of Braddock at the wheel as he took off the counter-helm and fingered the Turk's head on the amidships spoke. Above him the illuminated tell-tale showed the rudder come to rest on the division between the red and green sectors. The ship eased out of her heel and Stevenson emerged from the chart-room.

'Right on track, sir, making sixteen and a half.'

'Very good, Mr Stevenson. You can put her on auto pilot now . . .'

Clear of the Singapore Strait the ship headed north-north-east into the South China Sea between the mainland of the

Malay peninsula and the off-lying archipelago of the Anambas Islands. Stevenson set up the Arkas and dismissed the helmsman.

'Okay, Brad. You carry on.'

'Fancy a cuppa char, Sec?'

'Good idea. Better ask the Old Man if he wants one.'

Stevenson waited by the Arkas a moment, checking the automatic responses of the machine's sensors. Then, satisfied with its performance, he reported to Mackinnon. 'She's on auto, sir, steady on o-two-six.'

'Very good.' Mackinnon straightened up from the bridge rail on which he was leaning. 'She's all yours, then.'

'Aye, aye, sir.'

But Mackinnon lingered, turning forward again, both elbows on the teak rail. 'It's a beautiful night,' he remarked, 'if you've an eye for these things.'

'Yes, it is,' Stevenson agreed, taking the remark as an invitation to join the Master. Both men stared ahead. The ocean lay dark, like rippled silk below the stars which twinkled in their millions, displaced in brilliance only where the moon shone among them. High and full, it lit the ship with a pale fire in which details stood out with almost unnatural clarity.

'Tea, Cap'n . . .'

Mackinnon accepted one of the mugs Braddock held out to him and Stevenson took the other. 'Thank you.'

'I'll be in the mess-room, Sec.'

'Sure.'

Both white-shirted figures turned forward again, studying the bow wave curling out from the cutwater and the moonlit highlights along the lengths of the crutched derricks.

'You'll be staring out over a load of boxes next trip,' said Mackinnon.

'If there is a next trip, sir.'

'You're not packing it in, are you?'

Stevenson shrugged. 'I think it'll be a case of having to,

don't you? That or sailing on some rust bucket under a foreign flag with a crew that don't know a reef knot from a refrigerator.'

'We're under a foreign flag now,' said Mackinnon sadly. 'Besides, you don't need that acquired wisdom really, do you? The fruit of experience is just so much excess baggage. In fact you're better off without it. It reminds you of what you're not any more.'

'You mean all the sailors died with Nelson?' asked Stevenson.

'A bit after his time, son, if you don't mind.' Mackinnon chuckled ruefully. 'There was a time when you had to be bred to it, right enough. You had to serve your time and learn the job from the bottom up. It was tough, but we had to go through it one way or the other. Now technology has . . . well, you know . . .'

'Depersonalised it.'

'Yes.' Mackinnon sipped his tea, then asked, 'What'll you do?'

'I don't know, sir. See what turns up, I suppose. When this ship goes it's the end of Eastern Steam. Suddenly the phrase "on the beach" has a nasty ring to it.'

'Aye. I read somewhere that to live a full life a man has to experience poverty, love and war. The first and last have little to recommend them.'

'And the middle one has its complications, *that* I do know, sir.'

'So does the Third Mate,' Mackinnon threw in shrewdly.

'Er, yes, so I believe, sir,' Stevenson said guardedly.

Mackinnon drained his mug. 'It's downhill now,' he said, staring out over the vast emptiness ahead of the ship. Somewhere away on their port bow beneath the rippled surface lay the wrecks of the *Prince of Wales* and the *Repulse*, the British battleship and battle cruiser lost to overwhelming Japanese air superiority in the dark days of the Second World War. The bodies of their companies had

73

long ago dissolved into the ooze of the seabed. No, not all the sailors died with Nelson . . .

He sighed and cast the Second Mate a sidelong glance: if only he and Shelagh . . .

'I had a wee daughter, mister,' he found himself saying. 'If she'd lived she'd have been about your age.' For a moment he regretted the confidence; he could not recall ever having mentioned the lost child before and wondered what had made him reveal the intimacy at that moment.

'I'm sorry,' Stevenson said. 'I didn't know.'

'No reason why you should.' Mackinnon lapsed into silence, then said, 'I'm not complaining. But sometimes you wonder.' He straightened from the rail, suddenly formal. 'Well, good night to you, Mr Stevenson. Keep a sharp lookout and call me if you need to.'

The time-honoured formula uttered by every shipmaster leaving his bridge to a subordinate expressed the utmost discharge of Mackinnon's duty before he could turn in. Stevenson responded in the time-honoured way:

'Aye, aye, sir.'

It was as punctilious an exchange as the preceding remarks had been personal. Both men, the older with his hands on the ladder rails as he paused for a moment, staring astern at the orange glow in the sky above the city state of Singapore, and the younger as he began to pace the wide bridge of the *Matthew Flinders*, knew that its historical utterance would soon be a thing of the past.

'Old bugger,' Stevenson muttered affectionately to himself, smiling in the moonlight as Mackinnon's bulk faded into the shadows of the boat-deck below.

In his cabin Mackinnon found he was unable to sleep. Perhaps he had brought something of the disturbing magic of the night with him from the bridge, magic which had prompted him to expose himself to Stevenson, for it was uncharacteristic of the Captain to be so candid. Oddly he felt

74

no guilty regret over a momentary lapse of reticence, but an odd anxiety that the frankness did not disturb him. The paradox made him restless and he sat on the settee in the darkened cabin. It was lit only by the shaded desk lamp which illuminated the scattered remains of the bureaucracy of Singapore littering its top. He sighed. The windows which looked forward were uncurtained, the neat chintz fabric looped tidily up to hooks on either side of them. In the old, munificent days, the Master of the *Matthew Flinders* would have had his personal steward, his 'Tiger', a Chinaman whose sole task was to minister to his wants and one of whose duties would have been to draw the curtains at sunset. Now Mackinnon had to remember to attend to the matter himself, and since he had been on the bridge for the past three hours the task remained undone.

He declined to move; as long as the cabin remained lit only by the small, shaded bulb in the desk lamp it would not affect visibility from the bridge above.

How odd it was, the paperwork, the curtains, the trivial stuff of which his life had been made with its rituals and rather pompous little formalities. Some marked the point at which the machinery of a state touched him as Master of a foreign-going merchant ship, some irked him with their burden of responsibility, some reminded him of his diminishing status.

Woo still liked to call himself Mackinnon's 'Tiger', because once he had occupied the office and could not now lose face; but he no longer attended to the Captain's curtains at sunset and both men knew their respective positions had shifted upon the uncertain sand of social change.

Such changes, Mackinnon thought, made the leaving palatable just as they made confidences easier, though why he had felt the need to make them to Stevenson he was not sure. Was he expressing some quiet satisfaction that his own life had been full? He had known war and love, and if not abject poverty then something like it in the indigence of the

75

merchant seaman. But the recollection of those lost warships, which he had never traversed this point on the surface of the earth without recalling, had tonight touched him with an almost potent poignancy. He well remembered news of their loss, remembered his boyhood sentiments as first they, and then Singapore, had fallen to the Japanese. His arrival at Singapore on the *James Cook* had seemed to his young and fanciful imagination to have been a renewal, a picking up of the torch of British maritime endeavour, a carrying on after the reverses of adversity.

How was it put in the words of the prayer alleged to have been written by Drake to support his near-mutinous crews in his circumnavigation?

It is not the doing of a thing that yields the true glory, but the continuing until it be ended.

Would it be ended when the *Matthew Flinders* was passed to the scrapyard? Or was he just morbid because it was the end of him personally?

No, it was Stevenson who had touched him tonight; Stevenson who had prompted the confidences; Stevenson who was a natural seaman and for whom there was no future. He liked and respected the Second Mate and would have wished to hand on the torch to the younger man, but he knew the thing was impossible, a sentimental chimera. Stevenson would wait in vain for something to turn up . . .

Sadly Mackinnon heaved himself to his feet and stood for a moment looking down at his desk. Something tugged at his memory which, he realised regretfully, was not what it had once been. His eyes fell upon the gilt title of the book about the Uffizi and he thrust aside any thought of Shelagh. Then he remembered, riffled among the litter of papers on the desk and picked up the telex the agent's runner had left with him at the very moment of departure.

'It's not urgent, Captain,' the runner had said, handing over the envelope, 'you can open it when you have sailed.'

Mackinnon tore it open now.

To the Master, MV MATTHEW FLINDERS
From DENTCO, LONDON
Anticipate ship may be resold for further trading. Shanghai
interests indicate this now likely. Do not prejudice vessel's
condition.
    Dentco.

Mackinnon grunted and let the flimsy telex fall upon the papers on his desk.

'Do not prejudice vessel's condition,' he murmured disgustedly. 'What do they think I'm going to do? Sell the brass clocks?'

As Captain Mackinnon shuffled irritably to bed, Alex Stevenson lit a cigarette and settled to his watch. He was glad to be at sea again, clear of the taint of the land with its disquieting distractions. His envy of Taylor lost its immediacy and if he was still unable to think of Cathy without a deep yearning, at least here, beneath the majesty of the tropic sky, it was poetry that seeped into his mind, blunting the keen edge of lust.

He ground out the cigarette, took one last fix on the coast of Malaysia and marked up the departure position on the chart. Recording it in the log, he worked up a dead-reckoning position for 0400, after which he resumed pacing up and down. The ship cut through the smooth level of the calm sea with an occasional flash of bioluminescence. The dull rumble of her engines rose to a muted grumble; a faint cloud of exhaust gases and the occasional spark spewed from her tall funnel as she laid her wake straight astern to where the loom of the Horsburgh Light dipped below the rim of the world. Low on the eastern horizon a bank of cloud was building, the roiling heads of the rising cumulus catching the moonlight. Above them the impassive stars rolled their sidereal paths round the earth and it was as though the *Matthew Flinders* and her officer of the watch were at the very hub of the universe.

Alexander Stevenson was as near absolute and profound happiness as anyone has a right to be.

Far ahead a point of light caught his eye, vanished, then reappeared, to grow in intensity. Soon it resolved itself into the navigation lights of an approaching ship. The red and green of the sidelights indicated the two ships were on reciprocal collision courses. Stevenson studied the Singapore-bound stranger through his binoculars, then walked into the wheelhouse and gave the *Matthew Flinders* a five-degree alteration of course.

Out on the port bridge-wing again, he raised his glasses. The other ship's lights were clearly opening their bearing on the port bow and an occlusion of her green starboard light indicated she too had responded. It was odd that the lookout had not yet indicated the presence of the oncoming vessel. Stevenson shifted his glasses to the forecastle head and adjusted the focussing. The powerful 10 x 50s that he favoured showed the moonlit forecastle clearly. He could see no solitary figure in the eyes of the ship and at once his mood of contentment vanished.

'Shit!'

Striding into the wheelhouse he picked up the internal phone.

'Yeah?'

'That you, Brad?' he asked.

'Yeah, Sec, d'you want some more tea?'

'No thanks. Macgregor's on lookout, isn't he?' Stevenson asked, cautiously, double-checking his facts.

'Yeah . . .' replied Braddock, an edge of doubt creeping into his voice.

'I can't see him on the fo'c's'le, Brad, and he failed to ring for a ship.'

'Okay, Sec, I'll take a look.'

Stevenson put the phone down and stared at the forecastle again in case Macgregor had nipped off for a leak, but the place remained deserted and now the passing ship was no more than four miles away, a fast container ship, Stevenson could see clearly, the flat surface of her cargo of boxes reflecting the moon in a smooth plane.

While he waited for Braddock to report back he wondered what story the able seaman would concoct. He fervently wished the *Matthew Flinders* had carried apprentices. This was just the mission for a lively apprentice. Braddock, though no lover of Macgregor, would probably cover for him, clinging to the mistaken solidarity of the peer group. Stevenson could see Braddock's figure going forward and he was suddenly angry. He hit the forecastle telephone bell, expecting Macgregor to jerk into sight like a puppet, but nothing happened and already Braddock was ascending the forecastle ladder. A few moments later he rang the bridge.

'I'll take over the lookout, Sec. Macgregor's in the shithouse; says he's not feeling well.'

'Is he pissed, Brad?'

'He's not feeling well, sir,' said Braddock with flat and false formality.

'Okay.'

Braddock would not be so indulgent towards his watch-mate after standing both his own and Macgregor's stint as lookout, Stevenson thought with petulant satisfaction.

The passing ship was drawing abaft the beam and Stevenson pulled the *Matthew Flinders* back on her course, fuming at the turn events had taken. Somewhere below him, as immune from apprehension as if he was on the moon, Macgregor was sleeping off his binge. Shackled by duty to the bridge, Stevenson contemplated calling Captain Mackinnon, but old Gorilla had not turned in until very late and he had no wish to burden him unnecessarily. Besides, Stevenson had enough against Macgregor for leaving his post to drag him up before Mackinnon in the morning. Worst of all, and the most unforgivable element of the incident, was that Macgregor's irresponsibility had ruined Stevenson's equanimity.

*

'Come in!'

Captain Mackinnon looked up sharply at Stevenson as the Second Mate, dressed in clean whites, complete with cap tucked formally under his arm, pulled the door curtain to behind him.

'May I have a word, sir?'

Mackinnon could smell trouble and the cap confirmed it; he nodded and listened while Stevenson explained what had happened during the middle watch.

'I see,' he said when Stevenson had finished. 'And you're quite sure?'

'I'm positive the man was not at his post when he should have been, sir. That's the bottom line.'

Mackinnon grunted and picked up the telephone on his desk. 'Ah, Mr Rawlings: pop in a moment, will you please? Alex Stevenson wants me to log that Glaswegian beauty of yours.'

A few moments later the Chief Officer came in. Mackinnon outlined what had transpired.

'Right, I'll get him up, sir.' Rawlings turned away.

'Hang on a minute, don't be too hasty. We've got to be sure of our facts these days. What was Macgregor doing yesterday before we left Singapore?'

Rawlings scratched his head. 'Well, I think he was out lowering the derricks like the rest of them just prior to sailing . . .' Rawlings was clearly not too sure of the precise deployment of his hands.

'Was he on derrick gang last night?'

'Er, I'm not sure, sir. I'll go and ask the Bosun.'

Mackinnon's skin went a shade darker than usual. 'You'll do no such thing, mister. Perhaps you could contrive not to have so much to distract you from the ship's business in future, Mr Rawlings.'

It was Rawlings's turn to flush.

80

'Macgregor was off duty last evening, sir, up until sailing,' offered Stevenson, embarrassed for Rawlings but equally pleased Mackinnon had had a go at the Mate.

'How d'you know?' snapped Mackinnon.

'Third Mate and I passed the mess-room several times when the gangs were closing up. I saw him in there myself.'

'Drinking?'

'Well, yes, sir, but I'm not specifically alleging . . .'

'No of course not, Mr Stevenson, but a few beers, and so on,' Mackinnon said, staring at Rawlings, 'tend to make a man sleepy.'

'Sir,' Stevenson said, averting his eyes from the Mate's face.

'Right, Mr Rawlings, now let's interview Macgregor; bring him up with the Bosun. Mr Stevenson, perhaps you'd pass word for the Purser to join us.'

Macgregor was deprived of a day's pay on the charge of failing to keep a proper lookout. He took the punishment without demur, casting his eyes down with suitable acquiescence and murmuring an apology to the Master which reiterated the substance of his defence that he had been 'caught short' and had felt unwell. He denied drinking and Mackinnon did not adduce Stevenson's evidence. Macgregor assured the Captain it would never happen again. Indeed, he said it had never happened before. No one in the Captain's cabin was deceived. It was a well-worn pantomime and after the verbatim entry in the Official Log was read out, Macgregor was asked if there was anything further he wished to add. His humble 'no, sorr' was contrite enough to melt the hardest heart. But the malice in the glance he cast Stevenson as he left the cabin told the Second Mate there was to be a curtain call as old as the pantomime itself.

Almost exactly twenty-four hours after Stevenson had discovered Macgregor missing from his post as lookout, when the two of them were alone on the bridge, the seaman uttered his threat. By then the *Matthew Flinders* was north of the Anambas Islands with the Natuna Archipelago some eighty miles on her starboard beam; Braddock was pacing the forecastle and Macgregor's pretext for attending the bridge was a routine visit prior to going forward to relieve his watch-mate.

Tonight the moon was veiled, and the northerly breeze had an edge to it that did not belong to the tropics. Macgregor sidled up to the Second Mate to report, with punctilious correctness, his rounds of the ship had been completed.

'Thank you,' Stevenson responded, never once taking his eyes off the horizon ahead.

'Aye, mister, ah'm no surprised you canna look me in the face. You're a right bastard, that's for sure, a right fucking bastard of a bluidy shit-face . . .'

'All right!' snapped Stevenson, swinging on Macgregor, his clenched fists held tightly by his sides before they gave way to the impulse to pummel this stupid troublemaker. 'You've had your say. Now leave the bridge, Macgregor.'

'*Mister* Macgregor, to you!' the seaman said vehemently, his jaw jutting forward and his right index finger arrowing upwards to within an inch below Stevenson's nose.

For a second the two men confronted one another, then a voice as chilling as the wind cut between them, imperious and compelling: 'Get off the bridge, Macgregor!'

At the top of the ladder, his torso naked, a sarong flapping about his legs, stood Taylor.

'Och, ah see. There's two of you bluidy bastards, is there?' Macgregor drew back from Stevenson, and Taylor stood aside. 'Ah'll see you when . . .'

But neither of the two officers heard Macgregor's threat as he descended the ladder. Stevenson stood beside Taylor as they watched Macgregor go aft. At the after end of the boat-deck he turned and they saw his hand jerk obscenely.

Stevenson let out his breath. 'Thanks; you arrived just like the cavalry.'

'You looked as though you were going to kill him.'

'That little sod was about to tell me he would get even with me Hong Kong-side.'

'They always say that.'

'Yes.' Stevenson recovered himself and turned from the contemplation of the now-empty boat-deck. 'Anyway, what's the matter with you? Can't you sleep? You were yawning when I relieved you at midnight.'

'I'm all right. Got a bloody headache, that's all.' Taylor shivered.

'You'll have pneumonia if you hang around like that,' Stevenson said. 'There are some paracetamol tablets in my toilet cabinet; help yourself.'

'Thanks . . . thanks, I will.' Taylor turned back to the ladder.

'Thank *you*, Chas.'

'Good night then.'

'Good night.'

In the radio-room at the after end of the boat-deck Sparks finished scribbling on a jotter, took off his headphones and began to copy out the message on a proper form in a fair hand. When he had finished he rang the telephone to the bridge.

'Hullo, Alex. I'm getting a preliminary typhoon warning . . . What? Yes, from Hong Kong, though I don't think . . . No it's a good way off, er' – he consulted the chit in his hand – 'a hundred and thirty-three degrees twenty minutes east and six degrees fifteen minutes north. That's the other side of the Philippines, isn't it? Yes, thought so . . . No, that's the lot for tonight. See you *mañana, buenas noches.*'

Stevenson pulled out a general chart of the Northwest Pacific Ocean, turning over in his mind the doggerel he had been made to learn as a young brass-bound apprentice: *July, standby; August, almost; September, remember; October, soon over.*

Just our bloody luck, he thought to himself.

Captain Mackinnon saw the message when he went on the bridge before descending to the saloon for his breakfast. It elicited no comment from him. The typhoon was only beginning to develop. Time, in the tangible form of further reports, would indicate whether it posed any threat to the *Matthew Flinders*. They were three days away from Hong Kong, and though they might not be the last three days the ship had left to her, they were most certainly the last three days during which Mackinnon bore the sole responsibility for her safety.

He filed the brief facts away in the recesses of his mind and went below to enjoy his breakfast. Three more days, three more breakfasts at sea . . .

He remembered the ship's stay of execution. Perhaps he would remain for a few days, run her up to Shanghai . . .

But he might be expected to spend time handing over to her new master . . . a Maoist zealot half his age. He did not think he could bear that . . .

Perhaps after breakfast he would open that book about the Uffizi.

At smoke-oh time in the seamen's mess Pritchard listened once again to Macgregor's diatribe against the Second Mate. As he rolled his second cigarette and threw his feet off the corner of the table he looked at Macgregor, his patience exhausted.

'Ah've had just about enough of your bleedin' whimperin'. Why don't you sod off?'

Macgregor's mouth flapped open, then shut as he saw Braddock grinning his agreement with Pritchard. The Liverpudlian Welshman stood up.

'The Sec's okay,' he said, flipping the cover back over his Zippo lighter with a metallic click. Then he stalked out of the mess. Braddock rose and followed him and one by one the remainder of the seamen did the same, sharing, like most folk, a desire to be left alone.

'Aye,' said Macgregor indignantly to the empty mess-room, 'you're a fine bunch of arse-licking bastards, for sure.'

On the bridge during the afternoon watch Stevenson recovered his good spirits. Taylor's intervention had, he considered, effectively trumped Macgregor. It was true that in less than a week he would be facing the most crucial crisis of his career but the intervening days of routine suddenly seemed imbued with a desperate significance and he felt compelled to enjoy them with an unadulterated enthusiasm.

Ahead of the ship the navigation was straightforward, the standard hybrid mixture of dead reckoning and astro-navigation that had served the mariner since Harrison invented the chronometer and Cook proved its accuracy. They would pass between the Paracel Reefs and the Macclesfield Bank and finally raise Wang Lan lighthouse, Hong Kong's southern outpost and the *Matthew Flinders*'s last landfall.

If happiness is that state of contentment which in retrospect seems ideal, then Stevenson was happy again that afternoon. Even the photograph of Cathy failed to disturb him as he took his pre-dinner shower. It was in the bar that he encountered the first shadow over his continued contentment.

'Headache gone?' he asked Taylor conversationally, sucking a moustache of froth off his upper lip.

'No, I feel bloody awful, Alex,' Taylor muttered, and Stevenson noticed the Third Mate's pallor. It was obvious he had been sleeping badly, if at all, but there was something else about him that pricked the conceit of Stevenson's happiness with the sharp needle of reproach.

For Charles Taylor wore the unmistakable look of a haunted man and Stevenson read in his eyes terror and premonition.

CHAPTER SIX

Encounter

They received a second typhoon warning from Hong Kong Radio during the first watch of the night, the evening eight-to-twelve. Taylor was on duty at the time and he made a mistake in copying down the position Sparks dictated from the radio-room. Preoccupied and introverted, obsessed by what was happening within him, Taylor carried out the task carelessly, his mind elsewhere. He plotted a position ten degrees east of the reported location of the typhoon's centre. Upon the general chart of the North-West Pacific on which such disturbances were routinely monitored, Taylor, having transcribed the erroneous position, then drew a line from Stevenson's first plot through it. Finally he extended this line northwards to the predicted recurvature latitude of twenty degrees. Thus projected, the eye of the typhoon seemed destined to pass up the eastern side of the Philippine Islands before swinging away into the vast wastes of the Pacific somewhere in the Luzon Strait. It would not threaten them in the South China Sea, lying west of the Philippines.

But at the moment Third Officer Taylor dismissively folded the chart away, ninety-knot winds were already roaring through the forested heights of the island of Mindanao; outriders of the typhoon tore the leaves of the *atap* palm from hut roofs on the shores of Palawan, while the land-locked Sulu Sea was heaving ridges of spume-crested waves to leeward like the grey North Atlantic in winter.

Nor, when Stevenson relieved the Third Officer at midnight, was there any evidence of Taylor's misdemeanour. Only in the radio-room, darkened now that Sparks had hung his headphones up for the night, was the correct position displayed on the uppermost chit in a bundle bulldog clipped and hooked on the bulkhead.

They were approaching a bend in the river beyond which an outward-bound steamer could be seen. She was in ballast, on her way downstream towards the open sea from Shanghai. The brown waters of the Whang-Pu were littered with small craft and the steamer, like themselves in the *James Cook*, frequently blew its whistle. Short, impatient whoops were betrayed by the puffs of white steam escaping from the trumpet on her tall, stovepipe funnel long before the sound reached the *James Cook* two miles away.

Third Officer Mackinnon stood in the wheelhouse, beside the elderly Chinese Quartermaster at the wheel, at his station by the engine-room telegraph, monitoring the tachometer; on the starboard bridge-wing Captain Hooper and the Pilot jointly conned the ship and indulged in desultory conversation. The Pilot had boarded at Woosung and brought with him an air of uncertainty and excitement. The Communist Chinese were said to have crossed the Yangtse-Kiang in force and the Nationalist opposition was crumbling. It would not be long before the Red Army was at the gates of Shanghai. The city's fall was only a matter of time. Looking out over the flat landscape that spread either side of the levéed banks of the Whang-Pu, little evidence of a violent civil war could be seen. Only a dull and distant rumble, like thunder, told of artillery far to the north-west. The dusty brown plain, reeking with the stink of human sewage used as fertiliser, faded with distance into a brown haze. Figures could be seen tending the fields, their sensibilities inured to the smell, their slow, patient actions with hoe and mattock indifferent to the far-away bombardment.

There was greater activity on the river. Apart from the stinking night-soil boats, sampans and rag-sailed junks worked up and downstream in an endless procession, impervious to civil war and even to the intrusion of the two large ships closing the bend at the lower end of Pootung Reach.

The approaching steamer blew a long whistle-blast announcing her arrival at the bend. Moving expectantly to the *James Cook*'s own whistle lanyard, Mackinnon waited for the Pilot's nod, then tugged the wire. Above their heads the boom of the compressed-air-driven siren blared magisterially. The steamer swung into the bend, straight-stemmed and counter-sterned, her tall, woodbine funnel venting a heat shimmer and a column of black smoke into the warm, spring air. She was flying light, topsides and exposed boot-topping red with rust, half her screw thrashing impotently in the air under her counter.

'Starboard easy,' ordered the Pilot, moving the *James Cook* out of the centre of the channel. 'We'll have to watch that fellow,' he remarked to Captain Hooper, indicating at a junk just about to tack under their starboard bow.

''Midships . . . steady . . . steady as you go.' The *James Cook*'s bow pointed at the outside of the curve and the junk's bearing drew slowly but steadily aft. 'Slow ahead, mister.'

'Slow ahead, sir.' Mackinnon obediently swung the telegraphs, waited for the repeaters to jangle their acknowledgement from below, and recorded the instruction in the engine-movement book. Then he watched the tachometer needle drop back to thirty r.p.m.

'Engine turning slow ahead, sir,' he reported, and Hooper nodded, still in command and, in law, only taking the Pilot's 'advice'.

Master and Pilot straightened up from the rail and walked

across the bridge through the wheelhouse. Hooper paused behind the Quartermaster. His eyes moved from the junk, whose hull was now disappearing under the flare of the *James Cook*'s bow, to the rapidly nearing steamer and then to his own ship's head.

'Nothing to starboard,' he growled intimidatingly into the Chinese Quartermaster's ear.

'Not'ing starboard, sir,' the old Chinaman confirmed. Hooper joined the Pilot on the port wing as the steamer swept past with a sudden apparent acceleration as the two ships came abeam. A pre-war relic, no noisy diesel engine thundered within her. Only the gentle hiss of escaping steam, the thrash, thrash of her screw and a shouted exchange between the pilots marked her passing. She had huge Union Jacks of stretched canvas on her topsides and her crew were spreading more, painted on tarpaulins, over her hatches. The *James Cook*'s crowd had just peeled their own back, prior to their discharging cargo on arrival at Shanghai. They were an indispensable safeguard in those troubled waters.

'Hard a-port!' The Pilot's imperative command followed the exposure of the next reach beyond the passing counter of the steamer.

'Hard a-port,' echoed the Quartermaster, already spinning the teak wheel. The *James Cook* heeled slightly under the sharply applied helm.

'Half-ahead!'

Mackinnon swung the telegraphs again and repeated the formal ritual of recording it. He was interrupted by Hooper's sudden shout, 'Mr Mackinnon – watch that junk!'

Mackinnon ran out on to the starboard wing. He could see the angled peak of the sail battens of the junk under the starboard bow moving down the ship's side. The junk was close below him, its sails shivering, the rents in them fluttering distressingly as the huge bulk of the cargo-liner stole the wind. Already the junk pitched violently as the

89

James Cook's bow waves passed under her. On her deck an old man in a huge straw hat was wrestling with her heavy tiller, while a younger man forward clutched a shroud and shouted. He was joined by a young woman in black *samfoo* pyjamas. On her back a baby's head bobbed, so that it seemed to Mackinnon, from above, that it was the child who screamed at them. On the high poop, squatting by the cooking fire, a toothless and balding old woman joined the venomous tirade. A cat clung to the top of the chicken coop in which two startled hens cackled, and a mongrel barked furiously.

'Is she clear?' bellowed Hooper, now standing in the wheelhouse door as though he could not bear to look. The ship's stern swung outwards as the increase of speed took effect.

'Nearly, sir,' replied Mackinnon, craning over the rail as the junk seemed about to be overwhelmed by the *James Cook*'s quarter. He could see their own Chinese, off-duty greasers and a cook, grinning and trading insults, aware of their superiority and the prospect of imminent disaster overtaking the unfortunate occupants of the junk. Mackinnon's heart thumped with acute anxiety. The junk disappeared under the stern and he ran across the bridge.

'Port quarter, sir,' he called to Hooper by way of explanation as the Master drew aside for him. The Pilot was already looking aft on the port side as Mackinnon leaned over next to him.

The junk bobbed clear, unscathed. Only the equanimity of her crew had been shaken, though her clearance had been a mere inch or two, but the piping invective followed them and the Pilot faced smartly forward.

'Our red barbarian grandmothers apparently had intercourse with goats, Third Mate,' he said, adding in a louder voice, ''Midships . . . steady . . . steady as you go . . .' closing the incident with laconic imperturbability.

With his heart still thumping and adrenalin pumping in his

arteries, Mackinnon lingered a moment, staring astern. A small black dot appeared above the junk's sail. For a moment guilt made him associate its manifestation with the junk, for he was not unaware of the cavalier nature of the encounter, no matter how commonplace its occurrence in the crowded waters of the Whang-Pu. But the black shape seemed inexplicable, though it grew larger and was no longer a dot and then spread into a recognisable shape.

Mackinnon's war-trained reflex was to yell in alarm, but he caught himself in time from making a fool of himself.

'You're not on daddy's yacht, mister,' Hooper's voice chid him from the wheelhouse, recalling him to his duty beside the engine-room telegraph. 'A miss is as good as a mile, they say.'

Rebuked, Mackinnon walked back to his station, aware that Hooper seemed to be manipulating something in his pocket. Mackinnon idly wondered if it was true the Captain always carried a rabbit's foot for luck. He forgot about the aircraft as the Pilot ordered full ahead.

A moment later it strafed them. The shells tore up the immaculately scrubbed teak planking of the bridge-deck so that it splintered, standing like petrified grass. A series of holes were torn through the bridge bulwark and the gunfire smashed into the forward contactor house. The plane roared overhead, then banked sharply, the stink and smoke of its exhaust assailing them. On the bridge-wing Hooper and the Pilot stood up, miraculously unhurt despite the furrow of damage that marked the deck beside them. The Pilot was ashen-faced, but Hooper was bellicose with indignation.

'That was a bloody Yank aeroplane,' he ranted, 'one of the Nationalist air force, the bastard!' The Captain raised his glasses and attempted to identify the American-built fighter-bomber. The aircraft cruised round in a leisurely circle and then steadied on a second approach.

'Fucking hell!' roared Hooper, diving for the cover of the

wheelhouse where Mackinnon was nervously standing over the shaken Quartermaster and striving to keep the ship on course.

'Come to starboard more,' Mackinnon hissed, and the Quartermaster spun the wheel. Ahead of her, the junks and sampans drew aside, under the shelter of the raised riverbanks, leaving the fairway of the river to the foreign devils and the rogue aeroplane. Unable to take any avoiding action, the *James Cook* waited passively. Again came the stutter of cannon fire and the crash of the shells; again came the roar of the fighter overhead and the swift, malignant passing of its cruciform shadow. But this time it was different. The bomb dropped alongside them, missing the *James Cook* and plunging into the mud of the riverbed where, perhaps striking some wreckage, it detonated. The explosion, shook the ship, causing her to whip from end to end like a schoolboy's boxwood ruler. A column of brown water rose fifty feet to port, then fell upon the boat-deck like something solid. It seemed to the four helpless men on the bridge that, for a moment, they had difficulty catching their breath. As the roar of the aircraft's engine diminished, they stared after it. It banked as it had before, then, to their relief, straightened its course to the eastward. Visibly shaken, Hooper and the Pilot emerged cautiously on to the bridge-wing. Trembling uncontrollably, Mackinnon answered the jangling bell of the engine-room telephone.

'Chief's asking what's going on, sir,' he said, a sheepish grin of reaction on his face.

'Tell him a slant-eyed bastard has just peppered his bloody funnel and dropped a—'

But he got no further, for the Pilot shouted, 'Hard-a-starboard,' and the Quartermaster spun the wheel ineffectually.

'She no steer, *Tze-foo*, he said, and with a barely perceptible movement in the deck under their feet, the *James Cook* ran aground.

'Jesus Christ!' blasphemed Captain Hooper, slapping his forehead and advancing on the wheelhouse with a malignant stare at the Quartermaster. 'I fucking knew it.'

'She no steer proper fashion, *Tze-Foo*,' the Chinaman hissed desperately at Mackinnon. 'I speak before.'

'Telemotor pipes damaged by the bomb blast, sir,' Mackinnon said.

Hooper stopped in the doorway. 'Bad luck, Mr Mackinnon, bad luck, damn it,' he said, intoning a favourite formula for misadventure. He turned away, shaking his head and raising his binoculars after their late assailant 'Bloody bad luck . . .'

The retiring aircraft droned away, its shape gradually merging with its trail of exhaust smoke until that, too, became a smudge in the haze above the distant horizon.

Smoke began to uncoil from the forward contactor house. For half an hour the screw thrashed astern in a welter of churning mud and water while forward hose parties mustered and extinguished the blaze. The junk they had so nearly run down passed them, the four generations composing her crew grinning at the *James Cook* from her deck.

It was six hours before the tugs, two from Shanghai and one from Holt's Wharf at Pootung, succeeded in plucking the *James Cook* off the mud and into deep water, allowing her to resume her passage to Shanghai under tow.

As she slid free Mackinnon heard Hooper, a man who made an affectation of superstition, grumbling irrelevantly to the Pilot: 'It's bad enough *ju-ju* for a company to name their ships after men, but most of Eastern Steam's heroes came to a sticky end.'

'You'll have a job using such a justification for a grounding, Captain,' replied the Pilot, laughing now that the Garden Reach and the tall buildings of the International Settlement came into view. 'You'll be all right if you note protest on arrival at Shanghai. That bastard,' he added with a jerk of his head at the sky, 'was probably supposed to be beating up the Reds beyond Woosung.'

'Well he's cost me an *ex-gratia* payment plus towage to the buoys, damn him.'

'Oh, a little *cumshaw* will eradicate the worry over repercussions locally, Captain. The tug skippers are flexible men.'

Nothing was ever made of the incident outside the board minutes of the Eastern Steam Navigation Company. Relatives at home learned only through the letters of the ship's company how a British merchant ship had been bombed and strafed by a lone fighter-bomber of Chiang Kai-shek's demoralised air force. The British papers were full of a more newsworthy story of the China coast, a story about the escape of a Royal Naval sloop, HMS *Amethyst*, from under the guns of the Communist Chinese and down the Yangtse Kiang. Beyond the Yangtse bar Admiral Brind waited for the *Amethyst* to rejoin the fleet while less than a hundred miles away the *James Cook* lay at her buoy off the Bund and her Master cursed his luck . . .

Mackinnon woke from his dream in a sweat. It had all come vividly back to him so that he could still hear Hooper's ridiculous, superstitious claim, a claim he continued to press as the real reason for the calamity with a persistence persuasive enough to make his officers doubt he was in full control of his mental faculties. For them the official indifference and public ignorance of what had occurred merely fuelled a bitterness engendered during the war and increasingly endemic among them.

Staring into the darkness Mackinnon knew his own resentment, born in those days and simmering in his brain while he slept, had cooked up the dream from his memory. He sighed and rolled over. It would be over soon and there was consolation of a kind for him, at least. It was a pity for Stevenson and the others, of course, but times had never been easy for fools who went to sea for a living.

94

To compound Taylor's dereliction and further lull Mackinnon and his officers into a false sense of security, the presence of the Philippine archipelago to windward acted like a great breakwater to the South China Sea, preventing that natural harbinger of bad weather, a heavy swell, from alerting them to approaching danger until only hours before the first onslaught of the wind.

Mackinnon noticed it first, fourteen hours after they had received the second storm warning, a low ground swell which rolled the *Matthew Flinders* in a lazy motion. It was already late morning, and he was pacing the forward boat-deck, glancing up at the overcast sky and entertaining doubts as to their sighting the sun at noon.

He went on to the bridge, acknowledged Taylor's report about the overcast and remarked on the swell.

'Yes, sir,' was Taylor's non-committal response. Mackinnon thought he looked strained and tense.

'You all right, Mr Taylor?' he asked gruffly. 'You look a trifle under the weather.'

'I'm fine, sir,' Taylor said hastily, almost visibly pulling himself together. 'I don't think we're even going to get an ex-meridian,' he added, changing the subject.

'No,' Mackinnon agreed, turning his attention back to the navigation of his ship. The ex-meridian, an observation of the sun close to its midday culmination, could be corrected to obtain a latitude. It was not an absolutely accurate method, but, if based on good dead reckoning, was of substantial value. 'Nevertheless,' he went on, hefting his sextant, 'we'll hang on for a while.'

The radio-room telephone rang and Taylor answered it.

'Link call coming in from Hong Kong,' Sparks told Taylor. 'Tell the Old Man, will you, Chas? We're turn four, so it may be a while yet.'

'Okay.' Taylor hung up and returned to the Captain on

the starboard bridge-wing. Stevenson and Rawlings had made their dutiful appearance, both with their sextants.

'More in hope than anger, I think, sir,' said Rawlings pulling a face at the cloud cover. Mackinnon grunted.

'There's a link call coming in, sir,' announced Taylor, joining the knot of waiting officers. 'Sparks says we're turn four and it may be some time.'

Mackinnon stared through his sextant in a vain attempt to sight the pale, obscured disc of the sun as it promised to make a fleeting appearance. He thought of the telex from Dent's; it was not surprising the company should supplement it with further instructions now the ship was approaching Hong Kong.

'Dentco, I suppose,' ruminated Rawlings, echoing Mackinnon's thoughts.

'On a Sunday?' queried Stevenson. 'Modern management will be out to play.'

Mackinnon had forgotten what day of the week it was. Stevenson's perceptive remark, in tune with the bitter aftertaste of his dream, lodged in his mind a disquieting conviction the incoming call was both personal and significant. He remembered another such, long ago, when he received the first intimation his baby daughter was ill. He wondered how long the three other ships included in the radio station's traffic list would take with their own calls.

'Eight bells, sir,' Taylor reported as the mystic hour of noon came and went, and the sun stayed behind the thickening veil of stratocumulus.

'Nothing today, gentlemen,' said Mackinnon. 'It'll have to be dead reckoning.' They trooped into the chart-room to mark up the ship's position and then dispersed. At the time, no one realised just how prophetic Captain Mackinnon's remark had been.

The Captain was leaving the bridge bound for the saloon and lunch when Sparks phoned from the radio-room.

'Our turn next,' he said and Mackinnon hurried aft,

96

grabbing at an awning spar stanchion on his way as the *Matthew Flinders* leaned to a particularly heavy roll.

'I think it's a personal call, sir,' said Sparks, holding out the handset as Mackinnon entered the radio-room. The Captain's heart thumped with irrational foreboding. He took the handset.

'Hong Kong Radio, this is *Matthew Flinders* – Golf, Oscar, Kilo, Echo. All attention. Over.'

The deadpan tone of the operator sounded in his ear. 'Golf, Oscar, Kilo, Echo, I have a call for you from the UK. Stand by . . .'

Mackinnon waited and then Shelagh's voice had replaced the operator's.

'Hullo . . .?'

'Shelagh!' he broke in, not wanting to put her to the embarrassment of the formalities of radio-speak. Sparks retreated discreetly. 'Darling, it's wonderful to hear your voice. How are you?'

'I'm fine, John, fine. Where are you?'

'I'll be in Hong Kong about midnight the day after tomorrow.' The ship rolled heavily again and he found he had to brace himself against the radio-room desk. 'Maybe a bit later. I think we've a blow coming on. I'm not too sure when I'll get away, though. They're selling the old hooker to the Chinese. Over.'

'I've got a surprise for you, John. I'm coming out; flying Cathay Pacific tomorrow night . . . Over.'

'What? Darling . . .' Captain Mackinnon's eye fell on the neatly clipped wad of pink message forms hung on the hook under the stencilled label: WEATHER. Something very primitive stirred in his stomach.

'Johnnie? Did you hear? I'm flying out to meet you in Hong Kong. Over.'

'Yes, yes, I hear you, Shelagh, that's wonderful news. Over.'

'You don't sound very pleased . . .'

There was something wrong, something appallingly, dreadfully wrong, though he could not be certain . . . And then he realized it was the proximity of the position written on the storm warning in Sparks's neat hand with the noon position he had just had entered in the deck log. The figures were still fresh in his mind. Instantly he knew a mistake had been made in plotting the typhoon's centre; knew, too, why the swell was building with such rapidity and why an instinctive uncertainty had been clamouring for his full attention. Christ Almighty, he even knew the dream had been a premonition!

Mackinnon experienced a wave of nausea and in mute rebuke the *Matthew Flinders* rolled with a ponderous reminder of what was to come. In a few hours the *taifun*, the great wind, the hurricane of the China Sea, would be upon them. While he had been worrying about boat people and the disquieting inconvenience of their meeting, fate had been storing up the oldest of challenges to meet man on the sea, a great storm . . . He concluded the telephone conversation with an almost heartless brusqueness.

Somebody – he looked at the received time of the warning and realised it had been Taylor – had made a mistake, but Mackinnon sought true guilt nowhere other than in himself. He felt old and beaten. He eased himself into Sparks's chair and caught his breath. It was the last quarter of the twentieth century; he had information technology at his fingertips even on an ancient ship like the *Matthew Flinders*. There was no possible excuse for being caught out . . .

Had he been a younger man he would have welcomed the challenge, perhaps even gone in search of it, but now, within days of the end of his last voyage, it was simply not *fair*.

The unworthy petulance of the thought stirred him. Sparks was coughing pointedly at the radio-room door.

'Everything all right, sir?' Mackinnon remembered the content of the link call. A few minutes ago he had been talking to Shelagh in distant England. She was coming out to meet him and the marvel of the thing struck him at the same instant as Sparks recalled him to the present. He stood up and faced the radio officer.

'Well, yes and no, Sparks,' he said. 'The missus is flying to Hong Kong to keep an eye on me, but first I think this typhoon is going to give us a bit of a dusting.'

The banality of the exchange steadied him. Perhaps it was Sparks's quite unconscious deference, perhaps merely his own automatic assumption of responsibility, but he felt the sensation of fear recede.

'Typhoon David,' Sparks said casually 'Yes, it looks as if it might be getting a bit close.' Both men braced themselves against another heavy lurch of the ship. 'And feels it.'

'Why the hell,' said Mackinnon as he made to leave, 'do they give the bloody things male names nowadays?'

'It's called progress, sir. In the name of sexual equality.'

But for Mackinnon it held a hint of superstition. He thought of Captain Hooper and his rabbit's foot as he made his way back to the bridge. Out on the boat-deck he was aware the wind was increasing in force. White horses already dotted the sea and, although no more than a strong breeze at the moment, the wind had an edge to it. He looked up; the cloud base was lower than when he had searched for the sun at noon.

In the chart-room he pulled out the chart on which first Stevenson and then Taylor had plotted the positions of the tropical revolving storm, for so it had been denoted at the first report. By the time Taylor had bent over this chart the previous evening, it had already been upgraded to the sinister dignity of a typhoon and given the code name 'David'.

Mackinnon studied the two positions. Whilst he realised the early movement of such disturbances is both unpredictable and irregular, the data about them can confuse. Premature judgements based on scanty information mislead, but the distance between them was suspiciously short and the predicted recurvature unusually abrupt. The mistake he should have spotted earlier was now so obvious that he found it difficult to understand why he had not questioned it before.

He knew, too, that the almost (at least in meteoreological terms) sudden generation of the storm meant that it was probably relatively small. That would account for both the size of the swell and the present moderate wind force they were experiencing. It would, however, be foolish in the extreme to think of its lack of size as grounds for dismissing it. The warning spoke of winds of force twelve, sixty-five knots. His only consolation seemed to be that it would probably not last long. But, equally, its arrival could not be far away.

Fourteen, fifteen hours ago the centre of the typhoon had passed over the *west* coast of Mindanao and must by now have traversed the Sulu Sea and be assaulting Palawan. Unlike Mindanao, Palawan was only about twenty-five miles wide. No wonder there was a swell . . .

Mackinnon strode out on to the starboard bridge-wing. He had not misjudged the steady rising of the wind. The inevitability of their passage through the typhoon and his estimation of its likely duration made the whole matter bearable. There was nothing he could do about it beyond nursing his ship through it. Shelagh would be waiting for him in Hong Kong. It was something to look forward to; a carrot to dangle in front of the donkey, allowing him to thrust to the back of his mind the stick of his own guilt which threatened to beat him. He must turn out the crowd and send them round the decks to make all secure, double-check the derrick lashings and tighten the wires on the drums of deck cargo on the after well-deck.

Young Stevenson was on watch and Mackinnon found him staring to windward through his glasses. There was no purpose in pointing out the error in the plotting of the typhoon warning. Stevenson would be better employed supervising the securing of the upper decks.

'Mr Stevenson, I want a word . . .'

Stevenson turned. 'Ah, sir, I was just about to call you. I think you'd better have a look at what's four points to starboard.' He held out the binoculars to Mackinnon. 'Four points to starboard, sir,' he repeated.

Mackinnon took the glasses, levelled them at the horizon and, focussing them, swung them forty-five degrees on the bow.

He did not want to acknowledge what he could see. For upwards of a minute he stood staring at the image in the glasses. Suddenly his confidence waned. The memory of his dream and Captain Hooper's words came back to him. Eastern Steam's eponymous heroes had mostly come to a sticky end. Cook hacked to pieces on the beach at Hawaii; Hudson and his son frozen in a small boat after the mutiny of their crew; Dampier dying of neglect; Fitzroy by his own razor, and Flinders, poor Flinders, whose luck changed after his encounter with Entrecasteaux . . .

Slowly Mackinnon lowered the binoculars.

'Put the engines on stand-by, Mr Stevenson,' he said expressionlessly. 'Get a man on the wheel and then ring down and ask the Mate to come up.'

'We are about to make our own encounter,' he murmured to himself and then chid himself for his foolishness. He remembered the law of imbuggerance and the premonition he had sensed in Singapore. He had run out of luck, sure, but it was nothing he should not be able to handle.

Captain Mackinnon raised the glasses again and, on the rim of the typhoon, he considered how best to recover the sodden refugees in the waterlogged boat to windward.

CHAPTER SEVEN

Refugees

The jangle of the engine-room telegraph alerted almost everybody on board the *Matthew Flinders* to the fact that something unusual was happening. On some merchant ships it had once been the practice to ring it at noon by way of a test, allowing bridge and engine-room clocks to be synchronised. Telegraphs are rung when a vessel moves into fog, heavy rain or snow, but the crew are usually alerted to this by other symptoms such as their own senses, a call for lookouts, or the peremptory blare of the siren. Normally the telegraph remains silent from manoeuvring at one port to manoeuvring at the next. When, therefore, Stevenson rang it that afternoon, even those dozing in their watch below stirred uneasily in their bunks.

Only for Taylor, alone in his cabin after lunch, did the noise come as a welcome distraction. Unable to relax despite the fitful and unsatisfactory drowsiness of the past nights, he was exhausted to the point of nervous insomnia. He had come to dread his watches below and the awful isolation of being unable to live with himself.

The headaches he had complained of were secondary symptoms of his malaise, products of his intense anxiety and lack of sleep. For several days now he had suffered the agony of the damned without respite, too ashamed to confess it to Mackinnon, too obsessed with the conviction it

102

masked a more terrible disease. The periods of acute pain were interspersed with long intervals of worry, of putting off the next onslaught, yet all the time imagining the desire to urinate was pressing. The foul truth of the gleet would not let him forget, while the greater fear of either syphilis or AIDS burdened every thought he had. And though Taylor had made a reprehensible mistake in the matter of the misinterpreted typhoon warning, he clung to his sanity and hid his shame with an almost heroic determination. When the telegraph rang, Taylor reacted immediately, beating Chief Officer Rawlings to the bridge.

The seamen, just turning to on deck after their dinner, crowded to the rail. Off-duty engineers and greasers appeared and the T-shirts of stewards and the cook sprinkled the gathering as that other, esoteric shipboard telegraphy sent the fact of their encounter through the vessel with the speed of rumour.

Mackinnon shouted down to a seaman on the foredeck, summoning him to the bridge. Macgregor came up and took the wheel as Stevenson switched from automatic to manual steering. With her engines slowed and her helm hard over, the *Matthew Flinders* worked round the wallowing boat.

'Midships . . . full astern . . . stop her.' Macgregor and Stevenson obeyed Mackinnon's commands as he stood on the starboard wing and brought his ship to windward of the castaways. When she finally lost way, the ship lay motionless some hundred yards from the object Stevenson had sighted eighteen minutes earlier.

The *Matthew Flinders*, beam on to wind, sea and swell, rolled heavily and drifted slowly to leeward. Her greater windage thrust her inexorably downwind towards the junk. From the bridge Mackinnon, Rawlings, Stevenson and Taylor watched the gap between the two disparate craft narrow.

'East meets West,' murmured Rawlings.

The wooden vessel was some seventy or eighty feet long

with an ugly midships superstructure. The remains of what had once been a tall mast was capped with a single navigation light, proclaiming her conversion to diesel propulsion, but a ragged sail lay collapsed and unused upon the cabin top.

Stevenson took in these details automatically. What impressed his consciousness was the junk's human deck cargo. It was only later he learned one hundred and forty-six persons were crammed together in that tiny hull. For the moment all he saw were the upturned faces, pale with privation and despair, apparently unmoved by the appearance of the great ship above them.

'Poor bastards,' said Mackinnon. Along the ship's rail similar opinions were being expressed in similar vein. East and West indeed met and in that moment of suspended animation, each adjusted to the other's presence.

Stevenson watched the gap between them diminish, the heavy leeward listing roll of the old cargo-liner drawing closer to the wallowing, waterlogged lolling of the overloaded junk.

Taylor stood appalled. He felt cold, chilled by so much misery, so many people in a desperate situation like himself, for he was incapable of entertaining any consideration which did not, in some way, reflect his own plight. As he stared down, a very curious thought occurred to him. Since the outbreak of gonorrhea he had wiped any thoughts of Sharimah from his mind, neutralising his memory of her, for fear he should find that attraction he had felt for her turn into hatred. He knew from some primitive instinct that if he let this happen such hatred, cheated of outlet, would introvert. Suicide would disgrace his name. Instead, seeing the upturned faces, he felt a keen and overwhelming compassion for Sharimah in which a measure of self-pity was to be found.

'Cargo nets,' said Mackinnon, galvanising his officers. 'Get some cargo nets over the side, and the pilot ladder for those who can climb.'

Rawlings duplicated the Captain's orders, shouting down

on deck. Turning to Taylor, he said, 'Come on, Three-O,' and slid down the bridge ladder to take charge. The staring groups of seamen burst apart, running about the decks in search of the bundled nets and the rolled and lashed ladder by Number Three hatch.

'Work up a DR position, mister,' Mackinnon ordered and Stevenson obeyed, glad of something to do.

'Christ,' he muttered to himself, surprised at the strength of his own emotional response. There were women and children down there . . . Unaccountably he thought of Cathy, then he dismissed the thought and picked up the chart pencil.

Mackinnon remained staring down at the junk as it crashed alongside the *Matthew Flinders*'s shell plating. Hull struck hull with a loud grinding, splinters flew and the human cargo aboard the junk shifted away from the point of contact causing it to lurch dangerously, rolling her outboard rail under. Anxiety passed across the faces of the occupants as, from the great ship rolling high above them, they transferred their attention to the dark slick of water suddenly running over their feet. A moment later, squealing with fear, they stared up again.

Mackinnon shook off the appearance of those faces. They haunted him, disturbing old ghosts, reminding him of the faces he had seen in Singapore in 1945. He closed his eyes momentarily and became aware of someone beside him. It was Taylor, standing white-knuckled as he clasped the scrubbed teak caprail. The Third Mate was glaring down into the junk, rooted to the spot, oblivious to Rawling's order. His face was sallow and oiled with sweat, like a seasick man. Shaken himself, Mackinnon put it down to emotional response, forgetting Taylor's fault and, in a rare, paternal gesture, he patted Taylor's shoulder.

'Best to do as the Mate says, Mr Taylor. You'll get over it. Nip down and lend a hand.'

Taylor gazed blankly at the Captain. 'Aye, aye, sir,' he

said mechanically. As he went below the Captain's words echoed in his head. Would he get over it? Would this anxiety and guilt ever leave him? For Taylor had not been seeing the seven score faces as he stared down. For him they had fused into the half-closed eyes of Sharimah, Sharimah bucking in sexual ecstasy beneath the urgent thrusting of his own body with an enthusiasm that had both surprised and pleasured him. It had rarely been like that with Caroline, especially lately . . .

But the pleasure was short-lived, and cold comfort to him now, for the Malay girl had chilled as soon as she ignited, had used him as he had used her, and left a legacy of their mutual self-abuse. He felt no personal animosity to her; but the thought that she herself might have sought her own revenge on him, that the source of her disease was someone like himself, made him feel ill. His palms sweated afresh as he stumbled down the ladder to the main-deck, and he fastened his mind on the Captain's advice to assist the Mate with a desperation no longer rational.

The cargo nets had not been over the side more than a minute before Mackinnon realised they were useless. To Rawlings and his men it was quickly obvious that the occupants of the junk were too weak to attempt the fifteen-feet climb to the *Matthew Flinders*'s deck. Braddock and Taylor scrambled over the side to help and clung like monkeys by one hand, the other extended to assist at the point at which the junk ceased her upward surge, before she fell back into the trough of the swells. None of the Vietnamese moved; they stared impassively at the well-muscled and bronzed white men. Braddock began shouting encouragement and the exasperated words floated up to Mackinnon fifty feet above.

'Come on, you daft buggers . . . come one! 'Ere you, missus, for Christ's sake give us the kid . . .' Braddock's free hand beckoned frantically.

106

The woman moved forward slowly. Others helped her, passing her forward until she was on the edge of the crowd. A foot or two separated her from Braddock's outstretched hand. Swaying uncertainly she held out her baby.

Mackinnon could already see what was going to happen.

The junk rolled inwards. The woman was propelled two steps forward, losing her balance. She cannoned into the steel wall of the ship's side. Braddock had anticipated it too; with surprising agility he moved sideways and leaned down. He caught the child as the woman found her footing falling away from under her. He wrenched the tiny bundle from her arms before she was even aware what was happening and was too busy recovering himself and his prize to see her dragged down the ship's side. Her hands scrabbled and caught in the netting. Taylor moved across to help her. Her feet had left the junk's deck before it reached the bottom of the swell. Taylor, stretching across the net, could not get her to let go one hand and seize her wrist as he descended as far as he dared. He reached out to grasp her arm, but she reacted violently, twisting and screaming before the rising junk caught her legs. The wild cry of fear turned to a piercing screech of agony as her feet were crushed. Mackinnon shouted a futile warning while the crowd on the junk, watching helplessly, seemed to draw a corporate breath. It was all they could do, for the thing happened so quickly.

The woman lost her grip and fell back on to the junk's deck. Alongside the Captain, Stevenson, alerted by Mackinnon's shout, could see her lower legs were a bloody wreck.'

'This is no fucking good,' muttered the Captain, then he raised his voice: 'Mr Rawlings! This is useless! I'm going to stand off. We'll have to use a boat. Get the motorboat away as quickly as you can!'

Rawlings had to shout at Taylor to get him back inboard. The Third Mate seemed transfixed, staring down at the

107

injured woman alone on the bare patch of deck while splinters struck from the junk's gunwale fell about her and the other refugees remained motionless. Eventually Rawlings got him on deck and they followed Braddock and his bundle aft.

On the bridge Mackinnon turned to Stevenson. 'You take the boat, mister. Don't overload it, for God's sake. We'll hoist you up with each load.' Mackinnon glanced up at the sky. 'I don't think we've much time.' He strode over to the telegraph and rang full astern, then rubbed his forehead, an expression of extreme perplexity playing over his face. 'Wait here a moment and keep an eye on that junk.'

Stevenson looked over the side again. With a shudder the ship gathered sternway. Seeing the two white men disappear with the baby, and left with the unconscious body of the unfortunate mother bleeding on the deck, the hitherto motionless refugees suddenly began to surge towards the nets. One or two leaped upwards, but most faltered, the violent motion of the junk dissuading them. Then the *Matthew Flinders* began to back away, her greater windage forcing her down upon the junk, while her stern swung into the wind. The frail junk disappeared under the flare of the bow, the terrified occupants wailing piteously at their apparent abandonment.

Stevenson, expecting the junk to reappear on the other bow in a capsized state, was relieved to see her still upright but the anguished cries of the refugees left him in no doubt as to the dangers of swamping once he got alongside in the motorboat. He rang stop engines as Mackinnon puffed back on to the bridge.

'Here.'

The Captain nudged him furtively, masking something from the helmsman with the bulk of his stocky body. 'Keep it out of sight. It's loaded. That's the safety catch. Tuck it inside your life jacket and don't use it unless you have to. We don't want to antagonise those people.'

Stevenson failed to grasp the significance of Mackinnon's last remark. He was staring at the cold object pressed into his hand.

'The Mate's nearly ready,' Mackinnon said. On the boat-deck below the bridge a crowd of officers and men were mustered to swing out the motorboat. 'If they look like swamping you a shot in the air should do the trick, but if it doesn't work,' Mackinnon sighed, 'I leave it up to you . . .'

'You mean . . .?'

'Yes, of course I bloody mean it,' Mackinnon snapped. 'I can't *tell* you to use it, but I want boat and boat's crew back in one piece, mister.'

The Welin-Machlachlan davits rumbled down their trackways and threw the swaying motorboat outboard until, tamed by the tricing pennants, it swung with a bump alongside the edge of the boat-deck.

'Go on, son. Get on with it.'

He watched Stevenson leave the bridge, saw him vanish for a moment, then reappear with an orange life jacket.

'Second Mate's taking the boat, Mr Rawlings,' he roared.

Three or four men jumped in. The Fourth Engineer's greasy boiler suit bent over the engine. A moment later Stevenson hung over the boat's stern, forty feet above the sea, and shipped the rudder.

They had done well to man the boat so quickly, Mackinnon thought. Their compassion had lent speed to their actions. The Captain waited anxiously, wondering if the engine would let them down. The humped backs over the crank jerked in unison and a cloud of thick black smoke belched from the exhaust, then died. Three times the cloud appeared before a shattering roar sounded from the boat. Rawlings held a thumb up towards the bridge.

'Lower away!'

The tricing pennants were slipped as the *Matthew Flinders* rolled to starboard, the boat swung outwards and began to descend, crashing inboard as the rolling ship heeled to port.

109

The motor lifeboat struck the ship twice more before she slammed into the water, shaking her volunteer crew.

A swell picked the boat up and the falls hung slack.

'Unhook! Into gear . . . give her full ahead . . .'

The boat sheered out from the ship's side, her crew dodging the swinging hooks and a moment later was clear of the protecting mass of the *Matthew Flinders*. The immensity of the sea was born in upon Stevenson as a physical reality rather than an intellectual consideration. The flat familiarity of the distant horizon was gone, replaced by the rearing crests of the waves and the physical onslaught of the rising wind. It was no longer a benign cooling agent, but the implacable, unseen force generating the huge irregularities of the sea's surface.

A wave burst on their bow and their thin cotton clothes were instantly saturated. Stevenson felt suddenly, shockingly cold. Astern of the motor lifeboat, the *Matthew Flinders*, which only a few moments ago had loomed over them, was lost behind the swells, vanishing as both lifeboat and ship fell into the hollow troughs. She diminished in size with startling rapidity as they drew away from her. From the bridge fifteen minutes earlier, it had seemed to Stevenson no more than a short distance to the junk; now it appeared much greater.

Mackinnon's sense of urgency and this feeling of isolation twisted a worm of apprehension in Stevenson's belly. He leaned on the tiller, cleared his throat with an assumption of authority, and bellowed instructions at his crew.

'Whatever happens,' he concluded more confidently, 'we mustn't let them swamp us. We'll have to make several trips.'

They climbed over the crest of a wave, the bluff bow of the boat throwing spray out on either side. The white foam broke around them with a seething hiss and a fulmar petrel swept out of the wave trough, turned neatly on rigid wings and quartered their wake, otherwise unperturbed by their presence.

Then, on the next wave crest, hard-edged against the sky, Stevenson saw the overcrowded hull of the helpless junk. He

110

put his free hand inside his life jacket. The steel butt of the .38 calibre Smith and Wesson dug uncomfortably into his stomach muscles.

Taylor had delivered the message given him by Rawlings and stood beside Mackinnon, watching the progress of the boat.

'The saloon's fine,' the Captain said, absently approving the Mate's dispositions and intentions. Recollecting Taylor's earlier nervousness he added, 'You and Braddock did well down there.'

Taylor was exhilarated. He envied Stevenson's command of the boat, but there was no denying he had enjoyed the sensation as he had swung outboard with Braddock in a futile but gallant attempt to assist the refugees aboard. Somehow their failure added to his heightened sense of achievement, for he had been *there*, at the point of action, his disease quite forgotten in the thrill of it. He felt for the unfortunate woman, of course, but some primitive instinct had been undeniably assuaged by her injury, for the sudden red of blood conferred upon the incident a savage reality.

As the motor lifeboat closed with the junk, a profoundly shocking realisation hit Taylor: he had forgotten his own chronic dilemma in the acute agony of the woman's pain. It was a quite irrational, inexplicable thought, the kind a man can never publicly admit to, *schadenfreude* of a most private type. It was not himself that was hurt; someone else was in pain. Suddenly the indifference of the woman's companions was comprehensible.

While he waited alongside Mackinnon, Taylor realised he had discovered something important. His illness, debilitating and reprehensible though it was, was a result of *life*; he could not deny an intensity of feeling as this realisation occurred to him. He quite suddenly understood that he had, in his expectations, calculated his entire future in terms of safety, and his disease threatened this stability. His ruined

111

marriage was seen thus when set against the expectation of perfection he had thought it should produce. It was, he now realised, extremely foolish, based entirely upon the arrogant assumptions made by civilised and sophisticated western man.

This, he realised, staring about him from the Olympian height of the bridge at the white dot of the motor lifeboat as it ploughed through the deteriorating conditions, this was adventure, an enterprise of hazard, an exciting and stimulating experience. He felt a surge of new-found confidence, aware he had caught an echo of the past, in tune with the intrepidity of his ancestors, excited by his proximity to risk and death. Such sentiments, he was convinced, came to him as of birthright. He was piqued Stevenson had command of the boat, but a typhoon was in the offing, and the sea state and sky promised far worse was to come. Like a hound he sniffed at the wind, seeking opportunity.

As to his present predicament, it was no more than bad luck.

Standing on the windswept bridge-wing he resolved with quixotic intensity to see Sharimah again. He could, no, he *would* travel home via Singapore, use his leave up if necessary, for there could be no denying the warm passion of the girl, her own affliction notwithstanding. It almost made him laugh to consider the disease might draw them together. It was shaming but curable

The resolution, once formed, was irrevocable. He braced himself, drew the rising wind into his lungs and felt full of vigour. The venereal infection was a temporary embarrassment. Great men had suffered thus and it had not affected their achievements. Caroline was forgotten, dismissed as she had long ago dismissed him in the moment of his departure.

Raising his glasses he observed Stevenson with a critical eye as the motor lifeboat bumped alongside the junk.

Stevenson wished he had had the foresight to bring one of the

112

Chinese with him to act as interpreter, but they had melted away when the boat was being prepared. It occurred to him that he did not know whether or not Cantonese and Vietnamese were mutually comprehensible, then concentrated on bringing the lifeboat alongside.

The refugees surged across the junk, their faces alight with expectation; the waterlogged craft wallowed dangerously.

'Ease her, Tony,' he called to the Fourth Engineer and the engine note dropped. A crescendo of excited jabber rose above the hiss of the sea and the noise of the wind. They were to leeward of the junk as it rolled, drifting towards them. He ought to get the injured woman off first, Stevenson decided, his heart thumping as he measured the rapidly closing distance by eye.

'Stop her!'

They were a boat's length from the junk as they lost way, the sea tossing the two craft wildly about.

'Anyone speak English?' Stevenson called and was surprised by a stir in the crowd. A girl in shapeless slacks and a cheap cotton blouse emerged from the press of humanity. She looked utterly exhausted.

'Yes. I speak English.'

Stevenson's relief was overwhelming. 'Good. Listen carefully. I want the woman who is hurt first, then the children. Not more than twenty-five people at a time.' He held up the extended fingers of his right hand five times. 'You savvy?'

She hooked a strand of black hair back behind an ear. 'I understand.' She turned away, explaining. The refugees listened for a moment, then wailed and remonstrated in protest. The sudden movement on the junk made it wallow sluggishly, so that Stevenson knew it was not far from foundering.

The two boats bumped alongside each other. The castaways surged towards their rescuers and the junk again listed dangerously. Only the example of the injured woman, the relative motion of the two craft and the exhaustion of the refugees prevented disaster. This hesitation saved them from catastrophe. A moment later and the alerted boat's crew were staving off a too-hasty evacuation of the junk.

'I promise we come back,' Stevenson shouted at the diminutive figure of the girl as the first group of Vietnamese settled in the tossing motorboat. 'I want you,' he said, pointing at her with deliberate emphasis, 'to wait until the last time. Okay? You wait. Tell the people I will come back.'

It took forty minutes to make the first trip, ten of which were spent in hooking the lifeboat on to the long wire falls with their heavy steel blocks. Lifeboats were designed for evacuating a ship; they were not working craft to be hoisted back on board with any ease. Braddock, the bowman, nursed a gashed forefinger uncomplainingly for the remainder of that long, arduous afternoon. Lifted to promenade deck level, willing hands helped the refugees aboard, especially the now-senseless woman whose legs had been roughly bound and upon which crude tourniquets had been improvised. Then they descended again on the second of what would prove to be seven trips, taking over four hours to complete.

As the boat headed back to the junk for the last time, the wallowing craft was visibly lower in the water. Stevenson was seriously concerned about the wind. Captain Mackinnon had patiently worked the unwieldy bulk of the *Matthew Flinders* upwind of the junk, cutting down the transit time, but the disparate sizes and windage of the two vessels caused the ship to drive to leeward faster than the waterlogged junk. To avoid overwhelming it he had been compelled to move away as the penultimate load of refugees was disembarked.

Having made several of his trips almost entirely in the shelter of the ship, Stevenson now found himself exposed. There was a savage note to the wind and the sea was building rapidly. The wave crests broke about them with a malevolent roar, striking the sides of the boat with a jar.

Mackinnon had passed a message down to the Second Mate

114

that he was to personally check the junk before finally leaving it. As the last of the wretched boat people scrambled or were pulled aboard the motor lifeboat, Stevenson jumped nimbly across on to the bare timbers of the pathetic craft.

The girl interpreter had remained until last. Although Stevenson had asked her to, he had not expected to be obeyed so punctiliously. For a moment he caught his balance, swaying with the motion of the junk. She was dead in the water, lolling dangerously at the end of each roll and only her internal subdivision, a feature introduced to boat-building by the Chinese in the middle ages of European history, prevented the free-surface effect capsizing her.

He caught the painter Braddock threw him and took a turn round the junk's mast.

The girl observed him. Her small moon-face was framed by her tangled, shoulder-length hair. She had more prominent cheekbones than he had first observed, and her tiredness shadowed her beauty.

He tried to smile reassuringly. 'You go now,' he said, waving at the boat bumping alongside and noticing, for the first time, how they had sprung the gunwale capping in two places.

'What you do?'

'I search,' he said vaguely, not certain what was expected of him.

'All go,' the girl said. 'I wait, like you say.'

'Okay,' Stevenson said, a hint of impatience in his voice as his men grew restive.

'Dat fucking t'ing'll sink in a minute if youse don't get a shift on, Sec,' said Pritchard, voicing the opinion of all the boat's crew.

'We're making water ourselves, Alex,' added the Fourth Engineer.

'You go,' Stevenson almost shouted at the girl. There were tears in her eyes and she swayed with exhaustion. Instinctively he put out a hand and grabbed her arm.

Steadying her he was aware of the thinness of her, of her dry, exposed skin, her lacklustre hair.

'She's at the end of her tether,' he said, passing her over to the boat's crew who lifted her aboard with a rough tenderness and set her gently on a thwart.

Stevenson slipped below. The junk's hull consisted of three compartments. Forward, a small space had once provided accommodation for the junk's crew, abaft which was a cargo hold containing pieces of wood with which, Stevenson supposed, the boat people had built makeshift sleeping quarters. Both of these were half-full of dangerously slopping water on which assorted filth slowly revolved, evidence of the ingress of water. The air was thick with the sickly sweet smell of urine.

He made his way aft, and dodged through the hut-like wheelhouse which also contained an old propane stove. Muck and debris were littered everywhere. He ducked inside, past a leaking bilge pump which showed signs of recent use, and lowered himself into the space below, a dark and foul engine compartment awash with oil bilge water. The junk was filling fast, though void of humanity. Stevenson turned to leave when something bright caught his eye. It was partly concealed under a wooden box. He bent and picked it up. Without knowing precisely how it worked, he guessed its function.

It was an empty ammunition clip for an automatic weapon. The neatly dovetailed box it had been shoved under was an ammunition box. Someone he had just put aboard the *Matthew Flinders* was armed.

116

CHAPTER EIGHT

The Stuff of Heroes

Captain Mackinnon waited, anxious and impatient, a churning sensation of extreme discomfort in the pit of his stomach. He felt a repugnance for the responsibility he had assumed. As Stevenson leaped into the motor lifeboat and it cast off from the junk, he knew his problems were only just beginning.

'Sorry to bother you just now, sir . . .'

'What is it?'

Almost apologetically Sparks handed him a message neatly written on Eastern Steam's own signal paper.

'Another typhoon warning, sir.'

Mackinnon grunted irritably, going into the chart-room and reaching for the general chart of the North West Pacific. He remembered the purpose for which he had come on the bridge six hours earlier. It was too late to reprimand Taylor; the man was showing signs of stress and it would do no good now, when more pressing matters demanded his own attention. Besides, the Third Mate had done pretty well in trying to assist the boat people aboard, even though their first attempt, for which he held himself responsible, had ended in failure. Mackinnon sighed and bent over the chart, reaching for his reading glasses.

Christ, he felt tired.

*

Plotting the reported position of the storm's centre, Captain Mackinnon did not see Stevenson bring that last boat load of castaways back to the ship.

With her engines stopped, the *Matthew Flinders* lay beam on to the wind and sea, rolling so heavily that it proved beyond the capabilities of the boat's tired crew to grab the wildly swinging falls with their heavy blocks and catch them under the steel hooks in the bow and stern.

Braddock succeeded in hooking on the bow, but the boat fell into the trough of a sea and the boat's bow was jerked high in the air, jolting the occupants violently. The next moment the ship rolled over on top of them, the falls hung slack and the un-moused block dropped from the hook and swung dangerously past the already injured Braddock's skull.

Alongside them the *Matthew Flinders*'s shell plating went up and down with the relative motion and rapidity of a lift shaft viewed from an erratic and runaway lift. It was clear to Stevenson that they had pushed their luck beyond the point of safe return.

'Chuck the boarding ladder over!' he roared at Rawlings, whose slackly handsome face wore an unfamiliar expression of real concern as he leaned over the boat-deck fishplates high above him.

The Mate acquiesced immediately. The coiled rope ladder, intended for evacuation, was flung out from the boat-deck looking like a weapon of repulse, but it uncoiled harmlessly as it descended and, with a snaking rattle against the ship's topsides, hung invitingly besides them.

'Astern a touch, Tony,' Stevenson ordered, trying to keep the boat somewhere laterally close to the bottom of the rope ladder, the lower rungs of which alternately dipped into the water then shot several yards above their heads, catching with a momentary explosion of splinters between the shell plating and the boat's damaged gunwale.

'Jesus Christ . . .' someone muttered, wondering who was to be the first.

'I think one of us had better lead,' Stevenson began when the girl, waiting for the boat to rise and the ship to lean over them, made a sudden grab for the ladder.

Stevenson watched with anxiety as she scrambled upwards, out of reach of the rearing boat. Already figures appeared at the main-deck rail to help her inboard and, as soon as she was clear, others quickly followed her example. Somehow the information that this was their final chance transmitted itself to the last of the refugees. It seemed, too, this final boatload consisted of the fittest and most able. Stevenson wondered if any of them had concealed arms about their persons. It was a stupid, suspicious thought, for they wore only the thin, sun-bleached cotton rags they stood up in. He hoped the weapons had been dropped overboard from the junk.

The Fourth Engineer deftly threw the boat's engine in and out of gear, ahead and astern, to keep the bottom of the rope ladder as near steady as he could. One by one the refugees clawed their way up the ship's side, until only the boat's crew remained.

'Up you go, Brad.'

Stevenson saw the Able Seaman's bloody finger for the first time, saw him wince as he clung to the ladder and began his hurried ascent. Pritchard followed.

'You too, Tony.'

Stevenson waited for the Fourth's feet to clear, then he too left the boat. Its engine chugged in neutral as it bumped against the ship's side. Almost at the rail, Stevenson looked down. From this height it seemed a relatively simple matter to hook on those blocks and save it. He hesitated, half-minded to go back and do the job by himself.

'Get inboard, Alex!' he heard Rawlings bellow from the deck above. 'Leave the bloody boat!'

He clambered over the rail, accepting a helping hand from the Bosun.

119

'The wind's piping,' the Bosun said by way of a compliment. 'She'll not be needing a motorboat in the scrapyard.'

Taylor, who had been watching, reported the boat's loss to Mackinnon and the Captain returned to the starboard bridge-wing in time to see the motor lifeboat drop slowly down the ship's side and disappear under the curve of the quarter.

The loss of the boat increased his isolation and anxiety. In all his years as Mate and Master he had husbanded the owner's property as though it had been his own, a prudent, careful and responsible man in a position of trust. Considerations of scrapyard redundancy never entered his head. As the boat drifted out of his sight he felt carried back to an earlier time, a time when the loss of a boat was inconsequential, when the ocean was dotted with abandoned boats and the wreckage of broken hulls. The sensation of *déjà vu* was almost overwhelming and with it came the inevitability of cyclical crisis, of a second testing being upon him when he was bereft of the resilience and assumed immortality of youth . . .

'They couldn't hook on, sir,' Taylor was saying.

Mackinnon raised his eyes to the horizon. The weather continued to deteriorate and the ship could no longer be left to roll at the mercy of the increasingly heavy sea. As if synchronising with his thoughts a wave broke against the weather side of the *Matthew Flinders*. The whole ship shook from the gigantic blow. Mackinnon and Taylor spun round as a huge column of white water, the dissipated mass of the thwarted wave, rose high above them. It was instantly demolished, torn downwind to scour their faces like shot-blasting. Both men lowered their heads, then Mackinnon, spluttering with the cold shock of the spray, revived.

'Ring on half-speed, mister!' he ordered and Taylor

responded, glad to be active again. 'Hard a-port!' Mackinnon made for the wheelhouse door to stand behind Macgregor as the Able Seaman brought the ship head to wind. 'Midships and steady,' he ordered, adding to Taylor with an uncharacteristic clue as to his mental state, 'Keep her so, mister, while we sort ourselves out.'

Mackinnon desperately needed time to give his full consideration to the problem of the typhoon, a problem that the sighting of the boat people had compelled him to shelve for a fateful five hours. Yet even now he could not entirely dispel the image of the boat drifting astern under the quarter. He recalled the junk they had nearly run down on the *James Cook*, and how he had craned to see it clear of the stern's overhang.

Satisfied he had settled the *Matthew Flinders* on a comfortable course that effectively hove the ship to, he strode out on to the port bridge-wing and raised his glasses to stare astern. The boat bobbed white in their wake. To starboard the junk had vanished.

'She's gone, sir,' a voice said and he lowered his glasses to find Stevenson beside him, wet and shivering, his teeth chattering. 'We were just in time. She was filling fast. They must have been pumping all the time.'

'You did very well, Mr Stevenson.'

'I'm afraid there's something else, sir.'

Afterwards, several of the *Matthew Flinders*'s crew remarked that Rawlings had surprised them. The Mate's talent for organisation had possibly been spurred by Mackinnon's recent admonition, or perhaps, like many a man promoted slowly and gradually losing drive and ambition in an uninspiring world, he simply rose to the occasion, revealing talents they had never known he possessed.

Between them Rawlings and Freddie Thorpe, the Chief Steward, had marshalled the women and children into the

121

officers' smoke-room, the men into the saloon. The injured woman, her legs still bound in the rag tourniquets applied in the junk, had been given a shot of morphine sulphate from the drugs chest.

Rawlings, who periodically eased the restriction of the cinctures to allow blood flow to inhibit mortification of her ragged flesh, considered some form of operation would have to be performed if she was to live. Armed with a rough list of the rescued, he climbed to the bridge to make his report.

Captain Mackinnon was not there. Having hauled the ship head to sea and hove-to, he had left the bridge to Taylor and Macgregor and gone down to his cabin with Stevenson. Rawlings retraced his steps to the boat-deck and knocked on the open cabin door.

'Come in, mister,' Mackinnon said and Rawlings stepped inside. 'The Second Mate has something to tell us. We're going to have to search every one of them.'

'Why, for Chrissake?' asked Rawlings. The Second Mate told of the ammunition clip he had discovered.

'That's wonderful,' Rawlings muttered with dismal emphasis.

'I'm putting the pistol back in the safe,' said Mackinnon. 'It's all we've got if things get rough, but I don't want it flashed around and rousing anyone's suspicions. Everything will probably pass off all right. They're exhausted and should be relieved we've rescued them, but' – he paused to let his words sink in – 'in case there are problems about landing them and so on, this is the combination number.' He bent to his desk and scribbled a few digits down on two scraps of paper handing one to each of the officers. 'We don't know what's going to happen, so you two learn it and if you think circumstances demand a shooter and I'm not available . . . well, you know how to get hold of it. Okay?'

The two officers nodded solemnly.

'This seems a bit serious,' Rawlings said as Mackinnon put the Smith and Wesson back into the safe.

'Yes, it is,' said Mackinnon, shutting the heavy door with a clunk. Straightening up he turned and faced them. 'I've got her hove-to at the moment. I'm going down to see the Chief. I want you to secure the deck; we're in for a bit of a blow.'

'What about the woman, sir?' asked Rawlings. 'We're going to have to do something about her and I'm no quack.'

The weight of all that was happening bore down on Mackinnon again and the problem of the typhoon waited like a guilty secret, demanding attention that he could not give.

'The ship's pretty comfortable at the moment,' Rawlings prompted.

'I'll see the Chief,' Mackinnon repeated, an edge on his voice, 'and then we'll have a look at her.'

'The officers' duty mess?'

'Yes. Go and tell Freddie Thorpe to get things ready, then take a turn round the deck. When you're happy with the deck,' he said to the Mate, 'you take the bridge. Send Taylor down to help.' He turned to Stevenson; the Second Mate had already done his whack in the boat and in any case, with the middle watch to keep, the man never had more than a few hours' sleep. It was already long past his relief time and Rawlings should be on watch. Mackinnon wanted a stellar fix before it got dark if cloud cover permitted. 'See if you can get some stars.'

Rawlings agreed.

'I'll see to the deck, sir,' volunteered Stevenson helpfully.

'Very well,' Mackinnon said. 'Then you get your head down. Freddie and the Third Mate are enough to help with the woman.'

As he spoke the *Matthew Flinders* rode high on an approaching sea, broke through the crest and dived into the following trough. Even at her reduced speed she hit the advancing face of the next wave with a jarring crash and made them rock on their feet. The flare of the bow threw the water out on either side where the wind caught it and flung it

123

back at the front of the superstructure. The windows of Mackinnon's cabin were opaque with white spray striking with a violent whoosh.

He hurriedly issued some further orders concerning water, food and a watch on the boat people. 'Any questions?' he finally asked. 'Right, let's get on with it.

The officers' duty mess was a small, bare chamber off the galley alleyway used by deck and engineer officers in port when working flat out. Its central item of furniture was a fixed, Formica-topped table over which a clean sheet had been spread. In one corner stood a locker bearing a sink, draining board and hot-water urn. When the Captain arrived after his consultation with the Chief Engineer, Freddie Thorpe, the Chief Steward, and Taylor were already there, the urn bubbled encouragingly and beneath it, on the draining board, lay the case of surgeon's instruments thoughtfully provided by Eastern Steam. In the matter of expertise, the company were laxer. It was, in the directors' combined opinion, a matter of historic precedent. As with most things on board the ultimate responsibility lay with the Master. While common usage condoned the delegation of most routine activities, the extraordinary nature of their present task demanded Mackinnon's personal attention. If the woman was to die through ineptitude, only Mackinnon's ineptitude, backed by the consoling motive of his best endeavours, would satisfy the coroner at Hong Kong. Moreover, as far as Mackinnon was personally concerned, notwithstanding the ensign waving above the *Matthew Flinders*'s wildly pitching stern, anything else would be a dereliction of duty on the Captain's part.

The Chief Steward finished swabbing the table as Mackinnon arrived.

'Very well, Freddie,' Mackinnon said, placing a large roll of towels on a steel-framed chair shoved in one corner, 'bring her in.' The Carpenter and one of the seamen brought

124

the stretcher in and they clustered round, transferring the groaning woman on to the extemporised operating table.

'Shut the door, Chippy,' he said as the Carpenter withdrew. Mackinnon addressed Taylor. 'D'you think you can help us, Mr Taylor? We'll all need strong stomachs.' Unrolling the towels he produced a bottle of whisky and set it on the table alongside the inert body of the woman. 'You'd both better have a damned good swig.' He indicated the bottle, aware of his own nervous apprehension. 'Wash the outside, Mr Taylor. I've a feeling we're going to need more of that before we're finished,' he added, rinsing his hands in the bowl of disinfectant Thorpe produced. The fat, elderly little Chief Steward was sweating profusely, his face unnaturally pallid, his silence a testimony to his self-control.

Mackinnon remembered Freddie was due to retire and had seen this sort of thing before, during the last war.

Last war? The words shamed him. What lay between them was human wreckage from what was, essentially, only a long, if intermittent continuation of the same cataclysmic event. A great, apparently endless uprooting of humanity. He stood and waited for the bottle while the woman groaned.

Mackinnon watched Taylor shudder as the raw whisky hit his stomach. 'I've had Sparks call Hong Kong for some advice, but with nothing there but a handful of patrol craft we can't expect the Navy to help at this distance. The Yankee helicopters at Subic Bay will be grounded in this weather, so it's up to us . . .'

The reluctance of the three men to do anything was nearly tangible. Almost unconsciously the whisky bottle went round again, the occupation of drinking from it more important than the shallow panting of the drugged woman. Taylor felt a prickling desire to urinate and shrunk from the thought. The recurring fear made him shift uneasily on his feet and this shambling recalled Mackinnon to his task. He examined the assembled kit and cleared his throat.

'From what I can remember my wife once telling me about amputations . . .'

The gruesome collection of stainless-steel carpentry tools that lay in the bottom of a large, drained, still-hot saucepan made Mackinnon pause. He nodded appreciatively and, he hoped, encouragingly at Thorpe as the man mumbled inaudibly, indicating the pre-threaded sutures that lay on a piece of lint.

'Is there some surgical thread?'

Thorpe rummaged in a box brought down from the ship's dispensary and produced what the Captain sought.

'This is very well organised, Freddie . . . have another slug,' he said casually. 'Now . . .' He turned his attention to the woman, drawing their eyes to their hapless patient. 'Let's have those drawers off, Mr Taylor.'

Taylor picked up a pair of scissors. They were warm. He tried not to think of anything beyond the job in hand. He began to snip at one leg of the black cotton *samfoo* pyjamas. The desire to pass water was forgotten. There was an oddly virtuous feeling in what he was doing. He worked his way back to the lower end of the woman's left leg. The cotton had become entangled in the torn flesh and thickly congealed blood. He cut the bulk of the trousers away and dropped them on the deck, leaving the ribbons of their tattered hems buried in the darkening mess that had been her feet.

Moving to the other leg he repeated the process, finally ending the job by snipping the elastic waistband and pulling the remnants of the garment from under the woman's buttocks. She wore a thin pair of nylon knickers. He glanced enquiringly at Mackinnon.

'No, we can spare her blushes.'

Mackinnon felt the need to joke, to inject a reassuringly familiar obscenity into the situation, full, as it was, of paradoxes.

'Just ease her over, Freddie, on to one side, and I'll give her a shot.'

Mackinnon was aware that Thorpe, like Taylor, like himself, needed something to do. To the man's credit he turned her gently, pillowing her abdomen against his own beer-bred rotundity, though his breath came in gasps.

Mackinnon squeezed the fifteen-milligram tube of morphine sulphate until he saw a tiny worm of the drug wriggle from the attached needle.

'Pull 'em down a touch, Mr Taylor.'

The Third Mate eased the waistband of the knickers and Mackinnon pinched a large lump of pale and flaccid buttock, driving the needle in and squeezing the tube until it was flat.

'Looks as harmless as doll's toothpaste, doesn't it? Make a note of the time, Freddie.'

It was five past six.

Mackinnon moved down to the feet. They were quite crushed, a mess of blue-white bone and bloody muscle which terminated in odd and half-detached toes. He bent and sniffed, making himself think of raw steak and what Shelagh had long ago told him when he had confided his horror at being unable to help an injured man.

It was curious how things repeated themselves, he thought picking up the scalpel. Or perhaps it was not. Perhaps there were only so many things that could happen to a man during his life, given that he had spent it in, so to speak, the same place. The infinite variety of events that supposedly accompanied a career at sea were largely a figment of the imagination of novelists. It may have been true once, but even the proximity of death, he had learned, was not a concomitant of adventure but a dreary, inevitable and depressing business.

The man he had been unable to help was neither pirate captain nor cannibal chieftain. He had been a tall Dyak, crushed under an eight-tonne Ramin log being loaded from the rain forests of Borneo to be split into mouldings and sold

127

in high-street do-it-yourself shops back in Britain.

Oh, he had done his best. He had got his seamen to replace the parted bull-wire and re-reeve it through the snatch block and, as the unfortunate Dyak screamed, they had pulled the log with brutal efficiency from his crushed thigh. And then Mackinnon, grabbing the ampoule of Omnopon from the apprentice sent to fetch it, eased the man's pain until, for God Almighty's sake, the poor fellow smiled, asked for a cigarette and coughed at the unfamiliar taste of the apprentice's Capstan Full Strength.

'Ease the tourniquet a moment.' He waited for the gush of blood. Should take her pulse, he thought, but what was the use? These were desperate measures and the pumping action of the heart could be clearly seen. If it was weak there was nothing he could do about it. He ought to ease the tourniquet on the other leg, but the mess discouraged him. One thing at a time. *Festina lente.* The Latin phrase drifted out of his boyhood memory. How many hours had he dozed over such meaningless drivel? *Lucullus apud Lucullus, lux in tenebris.* He could do with some of that now: light in darkness. Why had they tried to ram such crap into his head? Why had they not taught him how to cut the crushed feet off another human being?

He felt angry. His hands had begun to shake again. The woman's blood was pumping out over the sheet.

'Okay, tighten up again.'

He recognised Rawlings's Parker ball-point pen wound in the strip of towel that Taylor gently twisted back and tucked in upon itself. He tried to remember how quickly gangrene set in.

'Let's hope we're not too late,' he said. Taylor grunted in agreement. The woman's breathing seemed easier, though her eyelids fluttered.

'Watch her tongue doesn't drop back and close her windpipe, Freddie.' The Chief Steward nodded, swallowing bravely as though extricating his own tongue from a dry

128

throat, and held the lolling head.

Mackinnon began to strip away the torn and broken flesh from the bones of the lower leg. Keep thinking it is just a bit of steak. Keep thinking of Shelagh boning a joint. Keep thinking of Shelagh and what she said. Just keep thinking of Shelagh as you scrape and cut. Shelagh . . . the bloody Uffizi . . .

'D'you know what the Uffizi is, Mr Taylor?'

'Yes, sir.' Taylor did not take his eyes from the woman's legs. 'It's the principal art gallery in Florence. Houses one of the finest art collections in Europe.'

'Very good. Titian and Raphael and all that lot.'

'Yes, I suppose so.'

'You haven't been there, then?'

'No, sir.' Mackinnon felt gratitude that Taylor had not visited the Uffizi. The utter inconsequentiality of the conversation struck neither man and Thorpe was too introspective to be listening. As Mackinnon debrided the leg, Taylor unthinkingly flicked the severed flesh clear of the table.

'Conrad called the sea life a useful calling,' muttered Mackinnon cutting away the final piece of wreckage from the woman's left leg.

'I'd say this was pretty useful,' said Taylor, 'though I don't know what she's going to do with no feet.'

The *Matthew Flinders* lurched into a wave, rolled in the growing cross swell and lifted her bow. The deck angled sharply as the bow drove out of the supporting wave.

'Hold tight,' hissed Mackinnon. The three men waited. The ship pitched downwards, pounding into the next wave, kicking her stern high into the air so that her screw raced and she stopped dead in the water, her bow buried. Its inherent buoyancy sought to lift it from tonne upon tonne of seawater. The whole fabric of the ship groaned with the strain imposed upon the hull. The crest of the wave under which she laboured rolled aft, exploded against the bridge front, further shaking the ship, then poured in cataracts down the main-deck alleyways. The *Matthew Flinders*'s stout teak doors withstood the onslaught, but nothing could stop gallons of water squirting in round their edges and flooding the interior. From outside they could hear the protesting squeals of the boat people, followed by a murmur of fear and accompanied by the roaring obscenities of the ship's company. They found themselves standing in a bare half-inch of water as it washed around the table legs and the gory remains of the woman's foot.

Both Taylor and Thorpe clasped the woman, their heads together above her near-naked loins, refusing to let the inert body submit to the peremptory demands of gravity. Mackinnon had hold of her left leg, his great fist tightly restraining it like a second tourniquet.

The ship settled.

'I read somewhere that surgery is rather like a mixture of carpentry and plumbing . . .' Mackinnon transferred his attention to the flesh above the crushed area, cutting back the muscles to expose the main blood vessels. He found the first and picked up a piece of surgical thread. 'And seamanship, I suppose.'

He fumbled the reef knot, but he managed it at last. As he exposed the second blood vessel Taylor had the thread ready and tied the ligature himself.

Good, thought Mackinnon, working on. The boy is proving himself. Perhaps this experience would be the making of him. There was no trace of his customary superciliousness.

Between them they secured all the identifiable veins and arteries. Carefully Mackinnon folded back the skin and the heavy pad of calf muscle he had saved, exposing the splintered bones of the shin. Then he reached for the saw. It was a perfect, miniature tenon saw made entirely of stainless steel. As he drew it across the tibia and fibula the Chief Steward passed out and slumped to the deck in a dead faint.

130

His fat bulk made a slopping sound in the water that washed back and forth.

'Never could hold his drink, you know.'

Taylor laughed with unnatural loudness. He liked the Old Man's jokes, but the off-beat sense of humour was something of a revelation. The axis of their relationship had shifted as they had been thrown together by the happenings of the afternoon.

Mackinnon folded the pad of calf muscle with its resilient covering of skin over the sawn ends of the bones emerging from the red ooze of the amputated leg. He reached for the sutures and began passing the stitches so the threads of the ligatures dangled clear. Supplementing the crudely stitched seam with butterfly closures, he poured Cetrimide solution liberally over the stump.

'I think you can ease that tourniquet now.'

Slowly, blood suffused the flesh of the stump through the lesser blood vessels and capillaries. There was no pumping flood; the ligatures were holding and it merely oozed along the jagged line of the stitched joint.

'So far so good.' Oddly he felt no more confident than when he had started. If anything the second leg daunted him. He wiped the sweat from his eyes and watched Taylor as, unbidden, the Third Mate wrapped lint around the ghastly wound and finally bound it with a length of bandage.

'Now the other one . . .' Mackinnon lifted the right leg. 'Pity Freddie fainted, he could have done this.'

'So could I.'

Mackinnon stared unhappily at the bloody mess. 'This isn't the Royal College of fucking Surgeons.' He sensed defeat. His hands began to shake again as he reached for the scalpel.

'Goddamnit . . .'

He raised his head, blowing the sweat off the end of his nose and avoiding Taylor's eyes.

'All right, sir. Here, give it to me.'

131

Mackinnon felt the scalpel taken from his quaking hand. He did not resist. A wave of nauseous exhaustion passed over him and he clutched at the edge of the table, willing himself not to topple on to the Chief Steward. For one awful, self-recriminatory moment he thought he might be drunk, but he knew he was still horribly sober. He watched, fascinated, as Taylor took over.

The Third Mate worked methodically, debriding the damaged tissue with a strange intensity. He doused the area with Cetrimide solution and exposed a length of the calf. He asked Mackinnon to plunge his hands into the warm mess twice to assist in the tying of the ligatures, and Mackinnon heard him muttering to himself in the ferocity of his concentration.

'Make her clean,' he seemed to be saying, 'kill all the germs . . . hate . . . fucking . . . germs . . . bacteria . . . streptococci . . . spirochaetes . . . microbes . . . the microbe is so very small . . . how does it go?'

With clinical brutality Taylor sawed through the bones and folded the preserved pad of flesh to form the stump, duplicating the captain's method.

'Nearly there.'

The curved needles of the sutures caught the light and then he straightened up.

'Dressing, sir . . .' Mackinnon passed lint and bandage. 'Now the tourniquet.' Both men watched anxiously for haemorrhage. A dark line of blood formed round the seam.

'No leaks.' Taylor was triumphant. They exchanged smiles across the body, shaking bloody hands in a spontaneous, ridiculous British gesture. At their feet the Chief Steward stirred.

'Well done, Mr Taylor.'

'Congratulations, sir.'

'I think we'd better give her some more morphine.'

Beside them the Chief Steward got unsteadily to his feet, staggering as the ship lurched heavily again.

'What's the time, Freddie?'

132

The Chief Steward looked at his watch. 'Er, half seven . . . I'm sorry, sir.' He gazed down disbelievingly at his soaked and stained clothes.

'Forget it, Freddie. Here, you missed the last round.' Mackinnon handed the bottle to the Chief Steward. There was barely a teaspoonful of Scotch in the bottom.

Being on the wheel Macgregor had seen little of the rescue. From Gorilla Mackinnon's and the mates' comments he had built up a picture of the scene alongside and in between frantic concentration on the steering he had glimpsed the motor lifeboat as it made its journeys to and from the derelict junk. Once, when the ship was stopped and he stood idly at the telemotor, he had left his station to peer curiously over the Old Man's shoulder, peevish that he was missing the action. Gorilla turned on him and sent him back to his post with such a blistering admonition that he spent the rest of his time sulking bitterly.

After Mackinnon had hove the ship to and Rawlings had relieved Taylor, he himself was relieved and went below. He was already irritatingly late for his tea. The accommodation seemed stuffed with squatting Chinks or Gooks, or whatever. The thin, wasted orientals slumped exhausted in odd corners, spread out from the saloon and the smoke-room in a kind of diaspora as they searched for and found their family groups. By this time most had eaten the fried rice prepared by the Chinese galley staff. The high-pitched and jarringly unfamiliar crying of small children and the smell of the strangers thickened the air.

He entered the mess-room to find Braddock nursing a tiny bundle and endeavouring to spoon thinned condensed milk into the baby's mouth. Opposite Braddock, Pritchard sat with a mug of tea, mouthing at the baby and diverting its attention from Braddock's best endeavours. The two men had discovered the child had no relative apart from the woman stretched out on the duty mess table.

133

'What's all this then?' Macgregor stared round the mess-room, his expression one of truculently false incredulity. 'Bairns an' wimmin in the fuckin' officers' saloon . . . What are youse, then? Stupid bastard you look!'

Pritchard watched the line of muscle ripple along Braddock's jaw. 'For Chrissakes drop it,' he said, before Braddock replied. But Macgregor was in no mood to take advice. Mackinnon's rebuke had angered him and he was in search of a victim. Braddock and Pritchard with a snot-nosed kid would give him no trouble.

'Och, piss off. Youse all runnin' round like daft kids. Youse wanna see the officers. Jeesus, bluidy faggots!'

Pritchard shook a cautionary head at Braddock who moved as though to pass the child over. Magregor turned away, opened a can of beer from his locker and then produced a bottle of malt whisky.

'Where the hell did you get that?' Pritchard asked, for Gorilla Mackinnon let no one below the rank of petty officer have a bottle. A tot or two, by all means, but not a bottle.

Macgregor leered, gratified to have excited envy. 'Ah'm no so stupid as youse think.' He found a mug and poured a chaser.

'Number Three upper 'tween deck,' Braddock said. 'He's got a whole bloody case of the stuff.'

Pritchard stared at Macgregor. The Glaswegian winked at him, a leering superior wink that bespoke, not the complicity of conspiracy, of jacks together, but the hard, selfish, city-bred snide of 'I'm all right'.

'You don't give a toss for anything do you?' Pritchard said, his eyes narrowing.

Macgregor grinned and shook his head. This sudden regard pleased him; the strength of excess, of being recognised as possessing no moral scruples, of actually shocking Pritchard, the tamed officers' arse-licker, gratified Macgregor immensely.

It was beyond Macgregor's capabilities to articulate this

134

sensation, but it flooded him with a fierce, primitive joy. He had never felt like this before and now knew where and how to seek pleasure. He did not realise this fact immediately, but it gradually dawned on him in the following hours with fateful consequences.

What shocked Pritchard about Magregor was the lack of any redeeming feature. He had known hard cases in abundance, tough, guiltless and unscrupulous men; but never had he known one who, during the course of a voyage, had not revealed some scrap of sentimentality, whether towards the *Mum* tattooed upon their arm, or a girl somewhere, even a dockside whore upon whom a rough affection was bestowed. But Magregor was past his comprehension.

Perhaps a woman could have discovered some good in Macgregor, but Macgregor had never had a proper relationship with a woman. The product of a broken home, whose childhood memories of a council flat were of a ceaseless arguing punctuated by parental violence, drunkenness and absence, Macgregor had escaped to sea. For the turbulence of what he knew of family life, of damp and neglect, of cold baked beans, bed-wetting and incessant noise, of the eternal televised images glowing amid the chaos of squalor, he had exchanged the harsh, lonely environment of a merchant ship. He had had a girlfriend once, more out of desperation than affection, an attempt to conform or be laughed at by other children, a slow, pathetic creature who had discovered an easy way of ingratiating herself with boys. The liaison had lasted until her mother caught them at the base of the stairwell. He had been thrashed senseless by his father and had run away for the first of many times.

The sea life had taken him up and offered him a purpose, but the easy access to drink, the loneliness and the temptations of open stows of cargo had proved too much for him. He had become a lost soul and Pritchard knew it.

'You're a rotten little bastard,' Pritchard said.

135

Stevenson's inspection of the upper deck was, of necessity, a cursory, torchlit one, for it was already dark. With the ship pitching into the heavy sea and the wind tearing at his clothing, reducing him again to a chilly state and reminding him his clothes were still damp, he made no attempt to venture too far forward of the main superstructure. To have ventured further would have invited certain death by being swept overboard, for the forward deck was already awash with every alternate wave that the *Matthew Flinders* met head on, white surges that foamed and hissed out of the gloom. Satisfied that there was nothing loose (and with Macgregor hatches he had at least the reassurance that the holds were secure), he made his way back through the occupied public rooms.

In the smoke-room he found the girl interpreter drying her hair on a towel given her by one of the stewards. A tired smile crossed her face as she caught sight of him and he experienced a surge of pleasure at her recognition.

He asked how she was. 'Okay,' she replied, the word set on two distinct notes. He was struck again by her good looks, her elfin face. The points of her small breasts showed beneath her ragged cotton shirt, raised by her uplifted arms. Desire, sharp and urgent, galled him.

'You are from Vietnam?' he asked, squatting on his haunches beside her.

'Yeah.'

'What is your name?'

'Phan Thi Tam.' He struggled to repeat the correct intonation. 'Okay,' she said, 'you say Tam.'

'Tam,' Stevenson repeated and she nodded with apparent satisfaction. He put his hand on his chest. 'My name, Alex.'

It was her turn to repeat the name. She attenuated the *l*, giving the sound a sing-song quality he found enchanting.

'Very good,' he said. 'Have you had something to eat?'

He held one cupped hand up to his mouth and made a scooping motion with the other, as though taking rice from a bowl. She laughed, an infectious sound redolent of relief and relaxation.

'Yeah, sure. Everybody eat.'

They were silent for a moment, weighing each other up, and then she said, with a positiveness which reminded him of how she had decisively seized and ascended the ladder from the motor lifeboat, 'I okay, Alex. Thank you.'

He stood and gazed down at her. The exhausted boat people were settling to sleep. The smoke-room was lit by only a single bulb and it side-lit her face, throwing the lines of her cheekbones, the ridge of her nose, the convolutions of her lips and the curve of her eyes into delicate relief. She would look like that on a pillow, he thought, then reality displaced romance and he asked, 'Does anyone else speak English?'

She flashed a quick glance about her. It was at obvious variance with the rapport he assumed they had just established, and he remembered the ammunition clip he had forgotten in her presence. She was no longer looking at him.

'No. Some speak French.'

'That's not good,' he said, 'no one speaks French aboard here.' He was troubled, annoyed that he had found the ammunition and that it somehow spoiled things with this girl. For a moment he was moved by her plight and his power, then he chid himself for an arrogant fool. What was he thinking of? 'You get some sleep now,' he said. 'Okay?'

'Okay,' she replied, smiling again.

But Stevenson was aware it was no longer a smile of spontaneity. He was wounded by the realisation.

'For God's sake . . .' he muttered at his own stupidity as he made for the bridge.

CHAPTER NINE

Master Under God

Captain Mackinnon regretted the whisky the moment he stepped on to the bridge. Indispensable as it had been to his recent performance as a surgeon, it was a disastrous accompaniment to what was now required of him. Out on the bridge-wing as the *Matthew Flinders* staggered under the onslaught of yet another heavy sea, Mackinnon could see he was in for a long and lonely night. In the darkness he studied the height and period of the waves as the breaking crests, exploding with a malevolent luminosity of their own, roared down upon them. The near-gale he had left the ship hove-to in had become a storm, the wind above fifty knots, he estimated, Force Ten on the Beaufort scale.

Waves of fatigue had swept over him as he had cleaned himself in his cabin, washing the blood from his hands, staring at the lined and bronzed yet pallid features in the mirror.

In a moment of weakness he had leaned his face against the cool glass and groaned. Shelagh was flying out to Hong Kong: the recollection stiffened him. In a day or two she would expect him to bring his ship into the 'fragrant harbour' of the Crown Colony. And the *Matthew Flinders* was *his* ship, despite the owners, despite the foreign flag their prostituting minds had seen to gaud her with, for he bore the responsibility. He had dried his hands and climbed to the bridge.

But on the bridge his resolution faltered. It was pot-valour, he realised, and with the self-knowledge came the cautionary thought that he had better be careful. The drinking of the whisky had reminded him of a time when consolation for all things lurked in alcohol.

He stood, bracing himself against the wild motion of the deck, and drew air into his lungs. He had come up here where he belonged, where duty bound him in an almost mystical bondage, to nurse his ship through the typhoon. He turned and made his way into the chart-room.

He found Rawlings bent over the chart-table, his legs widespread as he flicked the pages of his nautical tables.

'You got something then?'

'Not very good, I'm afraid, sir,' Rawlings said, scribbling a final line of figures and reaching for the parallel rules. 'The overcast was just about total and the horizon poor, but I managed three intercepts through gaps in the cloud, two of which were of Vega and similar enough to give me reasonable confidence in the fix.'

In view of the observational errors inherent in a poor horizon and quick glimpses of stars through rents in fast-moving scud, they could reckon the position to be accurate to within ten miles at the best. Nevertheless Mackinnon was pleased. It was better than nothing. Under the circumstances Rawlings had done very well, and he said so.

'Thank you, sir,' said Rawlings, 'there we are.' The Chief Officer stepped back and let Mackinnon peruse the chart and the neatly stencilled stellar fix. It showed the ship over one hundred and fifty miles south-east of Point Lagan on the coast of Vietnam.

'Those poor bastards made nearly two hundred miles in that wreck,' he said, laying down the brass dividers.

Rawlings grunted. 'Two hundred miles to *where*?' he asked.

139

'God knows. Beyond the fact that they were free.'

'This typhoon, sir,' Rawlings said anxiously, as if recalling Mackinnon to something he had forgotten, 'I've been looking at the nav. warnings.' The Chief Officer reached out for the signal clip.

'There's a mistake in the plotting,' said Mackinnon.

'Oh, I didn't think . . .'

'I spotted it earlier,' Mackinnon cut in, pleased not to have had Rawlings draw it to his attention and feeling it partially made up for his irresponsibility with the whisky bottle. 'Then we sighted that junk and' – he shrugged – 'the priorities shifted, you might say. Have we had any more warnings?'

Rawlings picked up a pink signal form lying under the lead weight holding one corner of the chart down. 'This came in five minutes ago. I was going to plot it the minute I finished the star fix and let you know.'

Mackinnon read the pink chit out loud:

De Hongkong Radio to CQ (all ships)
Severe Tropical Revolving Storm now Typhoon David centred on position 10° 30' north 115° east stop Winds within 200 miles of centre estimated cyclonic force 8 within 75 miles of centre force 10 to 11 gusting to force 12 stop Centre estimated moving NE at 12 knots stop Ships with information please report stop Ends

'This is already two hours old.'

Mackinnon looked to the barograph on its small shelf on the after bulkhead. The aneroid-driven pen had drawn its violet line in a steep downward curve. Setting time against atmospheric pressure on the instrument's printed graticule, Mackinnon drew cold comfort from the fact that in the last three hours the air pressure had dropped seven millibars. He swore softly, feeling a physical sensation of his belly knotting up with apprehension. He turned back to the chart-table.

140

Rawlings was again plying parallel rules and dividers, measuring the distance between the estimated position of the typhoon's centre and his own stellar fix. The legs of the dividers spanned over four degrees on the vertical scale of latitude, each of which represented sixty nautical miles.

'Two hundred and seventy-three miles away over the Tizard shoals, and the wind nor' nor' west, at force nine or ten.' Rawlings gave voice to Mackinnon's thoughts.

'It's a ten already,' he said flatly. 'It's either much closer than indicated, or much more severe.' He stopped and looked up as Stevenson joined them. The Second Mate stared down at the pool of lamplight illuminating the chart of the South China Sea with its two fateful positions neatly inscribed in Rawlings's pedantic hand.

'If we continue to lie hove-to with the wind on our starboard bow,' Mackinnon continued, 'we will probably find ourselves on the perimeter of the dangerous semicircle and in danger from the centre.'

His two officers were both nodding agreement, their faces grim.

'And if it doesn't recurve a touch, sir, as seems probable at this latitude, we'll be in a very dodgy position.'

'Dodgy would be an understatement, Mr Stevenson. Very well,' Mackinnon came to his decision, 'we put the wind on the starboard quarter and run out of the path of the storm, then.'

'We're as snugged down on deck as we can be, sir,' Stevenson reported. 'The Chief Steward's got one of his staff on duty with the refugees.'

'Good. Mr Rawlings, let the engine-room know. I've already warned the Chief we're in for a blow. Better tell the duty engineer to make sure the greasers use the shaft tunnel to get to and from their accommodation. The after deck will be far too dangerous.'

'Aye, aye, sir.'

'And ask Sparks to come up; we'll get a signal off to Hong

Kong. Carry on, then. I'll take the bridge for a while. I've sent the Third Mate to get his head down for an hour. You can put a man on the wheel, too. I don't care a damn what the makers of the bloody auto-pilot claim, I want flesh and blood on that wheel . . .' At the expression a vision of the Vietnamese woman's smashed legs swum into his mind's eye. He addressed Stevenson. 'You turn in, son. Oh, by the way, you did well in the boat this afternoon.'

'Thank you, sir.'

'You've all done well,' Mackinnon said to Rawlings, as Stevenson disappeared. 'Taylor surprised me. He did one of the amputations.'

'Good God!' exclaimed Rawlings, bracing himself as the ship crashed into another monstrous sea and lurched into the succeeding trough. He followed Mackinnon into the greater darkness of the wheelhouse. Ahead of them the night was pallid with spray and it struck the windows with a lethal rattle.

'How is the woman?' Rawlings asked.

He could just make out the shrug of Mackinnon's epauletted shoulders in the gloom.

'I don't know really. We aren't bloody surgeons.' An edge of defensive desperation could be detected in the Captain's voice, but it had steadied again when he added, 'If gangrene sets in she's had it, I'm afraid. How's her baby?'

'Last seen being given the feed of its life in the seamen's mess.'

'I'm glad of that,' said Mackinnon.

'Are you all right, sir?'

'We had a tot or two to get through the bloody business, mister,' Mackinnon replied harshly, realising his breath betrayed him, 'but I'm fine, fine. Now, let's have a man on the wheel, get Sparks up here and let the engine-room know what we intend doing.'

And as Rawlings picked up the telephone, Captain Mackinnon jammed himself in the forward corner of the wheelhouse and waited for his orders to be passed to the engine- and radio-rooms.

This was not the first typhoon Captain Mackinnon had experienced, though he felt in his bones it was to be the worst.

'Only two things really frighten me at sea,' he was fond of saying to his officers by way of a cautionary tale, 'fog and fire.'

Heavy weather was rarely a real problem to ships as stoutly built as the *Matthew Flinders*, ships which had been designed specifically for these unpredictable waters; for old as she was, she had scantlings more massive than the welded boxes passing for today's new tonnage. But there was in this wind, Mackinnon thought, something malevolent. The spooky conviction that he had been a lucky man for too long hovered again on the margins of his sensible mind, dragged from the dark recesses of his self-centred subconscious by the overdose of Scotch.

Not that Captain Mackinnon believed in a vengeful God. He merely knew the sea and the wind to be indifferent, and his career to be a piece of monstrous arrogance, a puny, quite insignificant attempt to attain some sort of superiority over these mighty elemental forces in the name of John Mackinnon, human soul. When someone coughed behind him he realised he had been leaning, his forehead on the glass of the wheelhouse windows for some time. He grunted interrogatively and stirred.

'Sparks, sir. You sent for me.'

'Oh, yes.' He led the Radio Officer into the chart-room and dictated the signal to Hong Kong Radio, giving the ship's position, the barometric pressure and the speed and direction of the wind.

Sparks raised his head, Biro poised: 'Anything else, sir?' he prompted.

'No . . . oh, yes, better let them know we intercepted a junk of refugees. Have we had a head count?'

'Freddie made it one hundred and forty-six.'

'Good grief!' Mackinnon's surprise was genuine. He had not imagined there were so many, despite the crowded appearance of the junk's deck.

One hundred and forty-six additional human souls were laid as extra responsibility upon him. He looked at the bridge log recording the navigational movements of the ship. In Rawlings's script he read out an abstract of the dead-reckoning position, the time and the bald entry: *Embarked 146 Vietnamese refugees from derelict junk. No. 1 m/boat abandoned due deteriorating weather. Proceeded, C º 015°T.*

'Tag that information on the end of the signal then, Sparks.'

'Aye, aye, sir.'

Mackinnon lingered a moment in the chart-room, bending to stare again at the barograph. It still plummeted: it was time to turn round. But a hundred and forty-six souls! A hundred and forty-six lives which fate had already decreed should not dwell in their native land and had then abandoned upon the indifferent surface of the South China Sea . . .

Did his intervention constitute some mild relenting on the part of fate? Or was it a fragment of the arrogance that gave John Mackinnon his identity as a ship-master? And if it was the latter, had fate regarded it as a challenge and hence sent the typhoon as chastisement . . .?

He dismissed the preposterous thought with a mental shrug. What purblind bloody foolishness! He had no time for such introverted nonsense. True, the operation on the woman had unnerved him; true, he had taken too much whisky for prudence, and, true, he was tired; but he had been scared before and he had been drunk before, really drunk, so drunk that he had damn near lost everything. And, come to that, he had been so dog-tired before that he had not cared whether or not death crept upon him, and yet he had survived.

He drew in a deep breath and braced himself. For Shelagh's sake, he thought, Shelagh who was even then preparing to fly out to meet him, he could not weaken now. He was Captain John Mackinnon, Master under God of the motor vessel *Matthew Flinders*.

'Come to take the wheel, Cap'n,' Able Seaman Williams said as both men met at the wheelhouse door. 'Sorry I'm late. Took a bit of time getting along the boat-deck.'

'That's all right, Williams,' Mackinnon said, glad to be dragged from his morbid introspection, bending to the auto-pilot controls and resetting them to manual.

'She's doing a dido and the wind—'

'Yes, it's bad,' Mackinnon cut in, in no mood for idle chatter. 'We're going to turn round in a minute, so get the feel of her. Steer three-three-five.'

'Three-three-five it is, sir.'

They were going to turn round, he had said so matter-of-factly, as if the manoeuvre he was about to carry out was nothing more than a simple alteration of course. In fact, to remove the ship from her situation of potential trouble, he would have to risk everything on a most dangerous evolution, for to turn meant swinging her broadside on to the seas, if only for a few moments . . .

It called for the finest judgement and to make it Mackinnon would have to call upon more than mere experience. To gamble on such a single throw would need instinct, and without instinct he knew he was unfit to occupy his lonely post. Struggling against the wind, which in theory was diverted from the exposed bridge-wings by the upward curve of steel dodgers, he went out to get the feel of the run of the seas and the weatherliness of his ship as she rode them.

Immediately he realised he should have put about hours earlier. Prudence dictated he left the ship as she was, hove-to and riding the waves in reasonable comfort. She could take the punishment to which she was currently subject for as long as necessary. But more cogent reasons nagged at the Captain's brain, reasons concerned with meteorology. The proximity of the typhoon's core demanded action with a more peremptory insistence than mere cavilling safety. Once turned away with the wind astern, the ship would be heading south as the typhoon moved west and north. It was impossible for a tropical revolving storm to turn towards the equator, for it was generated by forces inimical to existence at very low latitudes. Formed some three to six hundred miles north or south of the earth's midriff as a mass of warm air that rose, slowly at first, drawing in cooler air to replace it, it became a self-generating vortex of increasing violence, spun off towards the nearer pole by the rotation of the earth.

The whole system moved on two axes. Spinning about the funnel of rising air, a vacuous column of low pressure formed, the dead centre wherein extraordinary conditions existed, conditions of wholly vertical air movement that left the surface of the water a confusion of tossing seas and swells that rushed spiralling inwards to collide with dangerous and destructive force. No ship-master deliberately exposed his ship to this windless but chaotic area within which the very surface of the sea could be lifted by the lack of atmospheric pressure. But on its rim the wind circled with predatory force, roaring in horizontally before rising into the upper atmosphere, generating the furious waves it then relinquished to send against those tearing in from the opposite direction.

This indraught of air resulted in acute changes of the angle the wind made with the seawaves so that a vessel head to the heaviest swell might be struck by cross seas differing in direction by as much as forty degrees.

Not content with spiralling, the vast disturbance moved bodily westwards as the earth rotated towards the east, casting it off with a twist of geostrophic force which, in addition to initiating the spin, inclined its track towards the

146

elevated pole. As this polar component increased as a function of time and latitude, the typhoon accelerated, perhaps doubling its speed of advance. As time passed and latitude increased, somewhere near the appropriate tropic, the storm reached its vertex and began to recurve. Sometimes it headed north and west to enter temperate latitudes as a depression. Alternatively it struck the coast of Indo-China and lost its driving force overland, starved of the warm, moist air necessary to its existence, so that continental landsmen never knew its awesome violence, only its pale and localised relation, the tornado.

This, then, was the text-book theory, known by every navigating officer worth his salt. A local mass of humid air, generally produced by a tropical island, which coincided with a northerly, or southerly, movement of the dead air of the doldrums which in turn conferred the revolving spin of a latitude greater than five degrees. It was this slower, earlier stage that the mariner feared, for within it unimaginable winds, winds in excess of a hundred and fifty knots might be encountered. On these facts he based his decisions, knew not to get caught in the so-called 'dangerous semicircle', that area to the right of the storm's line of advance in the northern hemisphere, and vice-versa in the southern. More hazardous still was the dangerous quadrant, that quarter in which the winds tended to drive a vessel in towards the centre and where the fiercest winds would be encountered, for their velocity was reinforced by the forward motion of the typhoon itself.

As a black overcast covered the *Matthew Flinders*, it appeared to Captain Mackinnon that his ship lay in the path of this dangerous sector. His intention to turn, to take his ship south clear of the storm's eye, would have the opposite effect, where the wind speed was diminished by the forward component of the typhoon as it moved away.

There was a rule of thumb by which he could gauge the peril in which his ship lay. Named for the Dutchman who had first made the simple discovery, it was called Buys Ballot's law and it decreed that if an observer in the northern hemisphere faced the wind, the centre of the nearest low pressure was ninety degrees to the right.

So much for the theoretical considerations. There were now the variables to consider. With the *Matthew Flinders* hove-to and making no headway, her present position was extremely vulnerable in terms of the approach of the storm. As the disturbance approached, the wind would gradually increase and back round anti-clockwise, throwing up an ever-worsening sea. Though he had no doubt as to her ability to stand up to such punishment he had to think of the ship's burden: not merely her professional crew, nor the added one hundred and forty-six boat people, but her lashed and tommed break-bulk general cargo, of the three bulldozers and Ford cars in the 'tween decks, of the twelve cement mixers any one of which, breaking adrift in the vacant spaces left by the cargo discharged in Singapore, might alter her trim, leave her with a list and affect her stability.

Then there was one last twist in the tail of this train of thought: occasionally typhoons behaved quite otherwise than predictably. Occasionally they looped in their paths; occasionally they turned back on themselves, increased in violence as though they knew the land killed them.

The legacy of Captain Mackinnon's almost superstitious apprehensions was an unshakable conviction that this was one such monster. So he stood on his bridge and studied the beast with which he was about to do battle.

Above Mackinnon's head the scud raced downwind, oppressing the surface of the sea. This sensation was augmented by the warmth of the great wind. Here was no forbidding chill, but the almost luxurious enervation of tropical destruction. A typhoon had the seductive breath of a whore, warm, overwhelming, and potentially lethal.

Mackinnon turned his attention to the sea. The wind

speed was well over fifty knots now, force ten to eleven. Grey-white spume streaked the surface of the sea, almost entirely covering it. The waves were huge, well-defined ridges, the spume angled slightly across their direction of advance, their crests curled over, roaring in gigantic avalanches that flung themselves upon the ship with a roar that added to the shriek of the wind. This now produced a hostile diapason in the derrick topping lifts, the halliards and stays about the upper deck and a deeper and more significant booming heard intermittently from the heavy funnel guys. To communicate, all conversation had now to be shouted above the pervasive and deafening noise of the wind.

The *Matthew Flinders* staggered into each ridge of water, her bow rising before plunging downwards, the flare of her bows driving the sea clear until the wave stopped her dead, tossed her propeller into aerated water where it raced ineffectually. Forward, water cascaded aboard and sluiced aft as she fought back, crashing against the winches and the hatch-coamings, running this way and that, grey torrents that picked out her deck fittings as dark spots of resistance.

Then, by some magnificent combination of design, trim, buoyancy and the speed and course set earlier by her Master, the ship rose again. The water poured off the foredeck as the bow climbed towards the unseen sky and the cycle repeated itself, over and over, seemingly interminably.

Mackinnon found his hand caressing the teak rail, watching the ship gallantly defy the wind and sea. It made him feel better and threw off the sense of gloom that had clouded his mind. He had an odd sense of kinship with the *Matthew Flinders* and found himself grinning into the howling blackness.

Supposing he lost in the coming hours? Supposing in the next fifteen minutes he misjudged things and the *Mattheew Flinders* broached and rolled on her beam ends. No cargo lashings would restrain those bulldozers . . .

He thought of Shelagh with a brief regret, but everyone had to die and it was better to go confronting a challenge than to fade, incontinent and helplessly broken down. He thought of the western luxury of contemplating tomorrow, of working towards those pensioned years as though some guarantee, some convenant existed between a soul and its fate.

Good God, what folly! Life was a series of linked moments, that was all. The poor devils they had picked up that afternoon understood this: luck had given them another moment or two and perhaps, if Captain Mackinnon misjudged his moment, this would be their last too. Either way they had extended their existence by a few hours, for the junk would have sunk in this sea long since.

'We build such temples to the permanence of our lives,' he muttered, 'yet what are they? What do they amount to?' And he laughed to himself in the surrounding wildness, a laugh of mild wonder. 'We are no more than dogs pissing upon lamp posts to mark our passing . . .'

He did not hear the ring of the telephone above the roar of the wind, but Rawlings, still in the wheelhouse, answered it and bawled its news at the immobile figure on the bridge-wing.

'Engine-room are ready, sir. Ship's ready to put about when you like.'

Mackinnon found the Mate's use of the ancient sailing ship term appropriate, suiting his sudden access of energy.

'Aye, aye,' he replied, exhilarated, 'let's see what we can do.'

CHAPTER TEN

A Breaking of Lances

Taylor had not rested. The effort of the operation coming, as it did, after days of strain and worry, had simply served to string his nerves to a greater pitch. Finally, the achievement of the operation under the stimulus of the alcohol, had left him high as a kite. He sat in his cabin swaying automatically with the motion of the ship, staring unseeing in front of him. He felt like a spider at the centre of its web; as though the essence of his life was concentrated at some central point within him and the threads of his being, tired and only half-acknowledged, extended from this core outwards to the extremities of eyes and hands and feet. Periodically he moved to sip from the tooth glass, for he had persuaded Freddie Thorpe to part with another bottle of whisky, 'on Company Service', after the operation. He drank it without apparent effect.

He was unaware of being tired, even of being strained, tuned to the very pitch of nervous collapse. Indeed, if he was aware of anything beyond this centrical intensity it was a small, deep-seated glow of contentment. He had never known the sensation before, but it did not bewilder him, for he had known it must exist somewhere. His contentment compounded itself from the knowledge he had discovered it at last.

His life was circumscribed now, he knew that, knew it

151

with the terrible conviction his body harboured its own destruction. Somehow the fact fired him with a spirit transcending both fear and fatigue. He had slipped on to a plane of self-knowledge beyond reason and remorse, so he sat still, while the ship gyrated round him, quietly drinking the whisky, waiting.

Stevenson did not turn in immediately. Knowing the *Matthew Flinders* was soon to go about and she would roll abominably in doing so, he was concerned for the passengers, fearing the motion might excite them to a panic. He went below to the officers' smoke-room where the movement of the ship was much less pronounced than on the bridge above. Under the single bulb the women and children slept in conditions far better than the overcrowded junk they had existed on for the previous week.

Only an old woman was awake, a balding crone who bobbed and grinned and showed a row of gold-capped teeth. Stevenson smiled in response, wondering what exactly had driven these unfortunate people from their homes.

He stepped gently over the bodies on their makeshift beds of spare mattresses and blankets. The sleeping faces of the women were calm, passive with the patience of Asia; the children slept with the innocent charm of babies and tiny people the world over, unmarked as yet by the experience of flight. For a moment Stevenson remembered Cathy and her part in all this, her fertile enthusiasm, her delight in things maternal.

He found Tam before he realised he had been looking for her. She lay on her side, her legs drawn up, one cheek resting on a hand. Her face too, had the calm of exhausted sleep upon it. The closed, long-lashed eyelids were almond-shaped, and if her full lips robbed her of the rose-bud beauty her race idealised, she was infinitely desirable to Stevenson. He bent over her for a moment and heard the old woman wheeze and gurgle. She rocked back and forth, smiling and nodding even more vigorously, sucking approval through her expensively ugly teeth.

Stevenson was embarrassed the crone had discovered his interest in the girl. He retreated towards the door. Outside he sensed the ship heel as they began the vital alteration of course.

Mackinnon had been watching the pattern of the waves as they came at his ship, judging their height and power, counting the sequence as they worked their way to a culmination of large waves, after which they could be predicted to subside slightly before building to the next sequence. At such an interval he sought to turn the *Matthew Flinders*.

'Ready, mister?' He checked the Mate was at the wheelhouse door ready to relay the order. He could see the pale shape of the officer and behind him the helmsman in the dull glow of the binnacle lights.

'All ready, sir.'

Rain began to fall, driving downwind in torrents, abrupt and drenching so that Mackinnon was instantly deluged and soaked through. The sudden onslaught of the rain would moderate the breaking power of the wave crests. Not much, but a little, perhaps enough to offer him a chance . . .

He watched and waited.

The *Matthew Flinders* lifted her streaming bow and the rivets, stringers, panting beams and shell plating creaked as the whole length of her forepeak and Number One hold rose unsupported from the sea. Then she crashed downwards, her flared bow shooting the water clear yet again in a white flash, snorting two grey columns up her hawse pipes. The rising water was torn in a great curve. A billion droplets of spray struck Mackinnon's face like needles. This was the moment.

'Full ahead!' roared Mackinnon. 'Hard a-port!'

'Full ahead and hard a-port!' repeated Rawlings leaping

153

for the telegraph and wrenching the handle back before slamming it down against the stop. The jangling answer from the engine-room was gratifyingly instantaneous.

'Hard a-port!' grunted Able Seaman Williams as he strained with the effort of responding rapidly to the Master's orders. The telemotor pressure gauges registered his effort in the two narrow-bore pipes operating the four-ram steering gear two hundred and ninety feet abaft the bridge, under the greasers' poop accommodation. The rudder, a hydro-dynamically streamlined plate as high as three men standing upon each other's shoulders, turned through its regulation thirty-five degrees. Slowly at first, but then with mounting speed as the propeller responded and thrust its wash against the rudder, the *Matthew Flinders* fell off the wind and into the trough of the sea. She rolled heavily to port and from below came the crash and tinkle of lose gear going over to leeward, a chair, crockery, personal effects left inadequately secured, but trivial noises to Mackinnon for whom came the satisfaction of knowing he had judged the matter to a nicety.

On the main-deck seawater poured aboard, building up against the weather hatch-coamings before lipping over the Macgregor hatches and cascading to leeward. She rolled back to starboard but the wind held her from even reaching the vertical as she was lifted high on the crest of a sea and exposed to its full force. Then she dropped, still rolling with a violent twisting as the lesser crest passed obliquely under her, and fell forty feet into its following trough.

She rolled to port again, beam on to the next sea as it loomed up alongside them, a menacing cliff of white filigree concealing the dark, invisible mass of hundreds of tonnes of water. Mackinnon watched, aware that in its rearing lee they were suddenly sheltered from the wind. Somewhere above him must be the crest and if it chose this moment to break . . .

The ship suddenly lifted bodily with such speed

154

Mackinnon felt his stomach sink. The wave hurled them skywards as though they were a thing of no mass at all and the wind found them, tore at them for their insolence in cheating a wave that had just broken a quarter of a mile to windward and was yet gathering itself into that steep angle beyond which it was unstable and must break again.

The *Matthew Flinders* again fell into the succeeding trough, but now she was bringing her stern towards the wind, turning fast under the impetus of rudder and propeller. She fairly threw her starboard quarters into the next wave, just as it broke. The whole ship trembled with the shock and the propeller raced, whipping its shaft and adding a mechanical tremble to the steel fabric of the hull. It stopped the turn and though the wave was a pigmy in comparison with what had gone before, its frustrated mass crashed aboard, breaking a port glass and partially flooding the greasers' mess-room.

The ship slid off into the trough, rolling to starboard and flicking her bow high into the blackness of the sky so that her masthead lights looked like two brief meteors in their trajectory.

Mackinnon knew the moment of greatest anxiety was upon him. The turn had taken too long; the lull in the power of the waves was over. A new sequence of cumulative seas was building inexorably to windward and his ship must simply endure or be overwhelmed. What he had set in train he could now neither accelerate nor stop. He gripped the teak rail and prayed.

Then he saw it coming, an indescribable thing no simile could do justice to. It possessed something of the immensity and solidity of an escarpment, the grey streaks lending a striated credence to this, but it was a living thing, moving not merely towards them with the impetus of the wind, but hunching itself up with a demonic purpose. As it approached its leading surface angled increasingly towards the unstable vertical.

155

Rawlings had sensed it too, alerted to its mighty presence by the comparative absence of wind in its lee. Curiosity had drawn him out on to the bridge-wing to watch as the ineluctable *thing* rose above them.

'Lord Jesus Christ,' Rawlings said, quite without blasphemous intent.

But the ship was turning again, impelled by her own mechanical logic. The propeller and rudder reasserted their power as the stern sank into the denser water under the overhang of the great sea helped by the momentary shelter from the wind.

And then it broke. A spectacular avalanche, it fell upon them, burying the whole after part of the ship so that Mackinnon calmly acknowledged the fact that he had lost and it did him no dishonour. Facts were always far easier to bear than fears, even the final one.

He was quite unprepared for the noise, for he had never witnessed so terrible a pooping. There was a diabolical booming roar that was part water, part trapped air exploding under the compression of the curling crest, past wind noise striking them again and part the protests of the ship's assaulted hull.

Abaft the funnel, as high as the level of the boat-deck and almost up to the sea step of the radio-room in which Sparks was even then tapping out the last sentence of Mackinnon's signal to Hong Kong Radio, the wave inundated them. Mackinnon could feel the deck sink under the incalculable weight. It convinced him his ship was about to founder.

It seemed a miracle to the two watching officers that the ship survived. Nor could they ever afterwards quite throw off the incredible feeling; it remained the kernel of the experience which burnt into their memories. Intellectually, of course, they knew the matter to be simply the resolution of fairly simple opposing forces in accordance with the immutable laws of physics.

The *Matthew Flinders* did not founder, nor did her stern

sink much, for as well as inundating her after part, the huge breaker thrust her forwards so that her bow dipped as the oppressed stern with its fat and buoyant after body fought back. Perhaps much of the mass of the sea was not as heavy as it appeared, formed as it was of aerated water; however, it could be argued to the contrary for the smashed port through which an earlier sea had passed to partially flood the greasers' flat now funnelled a jet of pressurised water into the space. Those unfortunate men who were 'enjoying' their watch below found themselves flung like rag dolls into corners where only the compressed air trapped within the confined space enabled them to survive.

And while the greasers tumbled about in the shocking water in mortal fear of their lives, uncomprehending the nature of the disaster of the pooping, Mackinnon realised his ship would survive. He felt her very fabric groan under the effort of floating, felt this strain run like a tremor through her plates so that his shoe soles resonated ever so slightly and his instinct made him swing round and roar with unnecessary loudness at Rawlings:

'Midships!'

And then, a second later:

'Steady!'

Fortunately, the archaic standing orders that still prevailed upon even flagged-out remnants of the Eastern Steam Navigation Company's fleet were still obeyed. Mr York, the die-hard Chief Engineer, steadfastly refused to compromise and had dogged and locked the steering flat at 1800 hours. The latter was a precaution taken against piracy and dated from the early days of trading on the China coast when native crews, bribed by criminal elements ashore, disabled a steamer's steering gear and rendered her ungovernable for a crucial hour off some prearranged rendezvous where the junks of pirates appeared. Such lootings were commonplace and the precaution was still worthwhile with the modern prevalence of drugs, for the

157

steering gear was a lonely, vital place with a multitude of nooks and crannies for a would-be smuggler. It was also a vulnerable machine easy of disablement by a member of the crew nursing a grievance. All these things had happened to ships of the Eastern Steam Navigation Company.

But it was the dogging of the entrance door which saved the *Matthew Flinders* that night, the tight securing of the heavy water-tight door with its wedge-shaped closures that were levered into position by the heavy handles called 'dogs'. Though countless feet below the surface of the pooping sea, the steering gear was unharmed and continued to function as Williams first took off the full-ported helm, and then applied counter-rudder. The huge, four-ram gear punched at the quadrant and applied torque to the rudder stock. Set so deep, the rudder bit into solid water and the ship was steadied, sliding forward, accelerated by its thrust, and the *Matthew Flinders* raced down the face of the gigantic wave. All about her the breaking crest subsided, an almost luminous circle of white as it relinquished its terrible grip.

Aft in the greasers' flat the water levelled chest deep; desperate men found a perilous footing, filling the air with gasps and the blasphemous obscenities which are their sincerest prayers.

Below, in the engine-room, they had no idea of the hazard to which their lives had been exposed, for beyond a drop in the engine's revolutions caused by the extreme submergence of the propeller after its recent racing – and even that was common in such weather – nothing was untoward.

Nor, after the violent rolling, did the refugees in either saloon or smoke-room know what had occurred, though more water squirted in round the doors and added to the residue left from the earlier flooding. Not that the rolling had unduly disturbed them, for they had endured days of it aboard the junk and were now so tired it impinged upon their consciousness only as an event in a dream. They were safe in this ship.

Even Sparks in his radio-room at the after end of the boat-deck, hunched over his morse key, headphones clapped to his skull, had no idea the wave had washed to his very threshold.

Only on the bridge did Rawlings and Mackinnon appreciate their survival. The witnessing of so awesome an event was at once to diminish and to enhance them, to humiliate and to make wondrous their comprehension of the true nature of things.

As the ship steadied, the great sea passed beneath them and ran on, leaving behind no trailing crests of comparable size, for it had itself been a coincident climax where the multitudinous wave forms jockeying across the pliable surface of the sea had met in a crescendo of form.

Other seas surged up astern and Mackinnon adjusted the course to bring the wind exactly on the ship's starboard quarter. In the wheelhouse the helmsman struggled to keep the ship's head within ten degrees of the course as the ship corkscrewed, surfing downhill on the face of each advancing sea. Each passed under her and dragged her stern into the following trough, a succession of accelerations and brakings that wearied the body in its efforts to remain upright.

'I want the wheel relieved every hour,' Mackinnon ordered, adding, by way of justification, if such was needed, 'This'll take maximum concentration.'

'Aye, aye, sir.' Rawlings nodded concurrence.

'And take a look around. No risks, but check the poop and you'd better ask the Chief to put a bilge pump on the after hold suctions.'

'I was just going to suggest that. I'll get Taylor up here now.'

'Right.'

Neither man made reference to what they had just witnessed, but, even allowing for the noise of the typhoon, each spoke preternaturally loudly. Mackinnon resumed his post in the forward starboard corner of the wheelhouse and again leaned his head against the window. His eyeballs felt hot and gritty, burning in their sockets. For a moment he closed them. He was thirsty, very thirsty, the alcohol having leached the moisture from his body. Ironically he was sodden; the rainwater and spray drained from him. He did not care. It was a thing of no consequence and he had greater problems to concern him than wetness without and drought within.

The motion of a ship always felt better when you ran; the power of the wind was diminished by your forward speed and it lulled you into a false sense of temporary security. Mackinnon was aware he must guard against this, for running carried with it the omnipresent danger of being pooped.

What had occurred once could happen again. He must give the possibility – no, the probability – some thought.

'Come on, you bastard, wake up!'

Pritchard shook the recumbent form. Macgregor turned over lethargically, stretched and exhaled. Pritchard recoiled from the whisky stench of his stale breath. It offended him to a more extreme measure; he whipped the pillow from under Macgregor's head then pulled the man's feet off the bunk. As the ship rolled and pitched, Magregor tumbled on to the deck and woke, protesting volubly.

'You're on watch, you drunken bastard! Now get up!'

Understanding dawned in the befuddled recesses of Macgregor's brain, and with it outrage. 'It's nae my turn . . .'

'You wouldn't know whose turn it was. You've ten minutes to relieve the wheel. We're all on an hour about.'

Macgregor clawed himself to his feet, stumbling from the motion of the ship and his own unsteadiness. He groaned, gouging at his eyes with his fists. 'The fuck it is. It's nae ma turn, ah'm saying.'

'It fucking is, Rob Roy. Gorilla's orders. You an' me and the rest of 'em: one hour about on the wheel.'

'What for?'

Pritchard laughed wildly at Magregor's ignorance. 'You'll

see on your way up top.'

Fear had again laid its cold siege to the heart of Third Officer
Taylor. It had broken ground days earlier but the combined
effects of extreme anxiety, fatigue and alcohol swung his
mood unpredictably. After his wild elation and the plan of a
return to Singapore to rescue Sharimah, he felt again the saps
and mines beneath his very soul.

He no longer had the confidence of the spider; suddenly he
had become the fly transfixed in the web, the eternal loser, a
sensation made worse by the knowledge that his downfall was
largely self-inflicted. Taylor had reached the moment when
he had to decide whether God existed or not, for without
what he conceived God to represent, he was utterly without
resource. And although Taylor had glimpsed the infinite in a
tropical night, his search was no longer outside in the
wilderness of wind and water now battering the *Matthew
Flinders*. It had nothing to do with the typhoon; it was within
himself. He was bound to his body, unable to leap into the
infinite in search of the inconceivable concept, that which
cannot be grasped, that which 'God' was used to evoke.

But the numinous moment of hope had gone. Writhing
down into himself to discover a spark of fire divine enough to
light his weary soul to hell, he found – nothing.

And his isolation was the more terrible because, like
Prometheus chained to his rock, he was bound to this
battered ship while vultures ate his liver before his very eyes.

There was a knock at his cabin door.

'Ol' Man wants you on the bridge now, Turd.' The cheeky
Scouse pun on his rank made him look up. Pritchard stood in
the doorway.

'Aye, aye,' he answered mechanically.

'Ol' Man's up top an' its blowing like fuck,' Pritchard added
by way of encouragement, for Taylor's cabin stank of whisky
and his eyes were glassy in the harsh glare of the cabin lights.

'Thanks.' Taylor was conscious of Pritchard's stare and

161

rubbed his eyes.

'Oim jus' making a cup of tea. It'll be in de chart-room, okay?'

'Sure. Thanks. I'll be right up.'

Taylor lowered his hands. Pritchard had gone. He could wash the tears from his face now.

Mackinnon stood in the wheelhouse and found himself functioning in a somnambulist state, awake enough to be ready to react to the slightest demand on him, but in a kind of half-doze which conserved his energy. He could keep going for hours now. Inches from his nose the clear view screen whirred noisily, except that the noise was but one note in the howling cacophony battering his dulled senses. He stared down at the familiar foredeck of the *Matthew Flinders* burying itself to the rail as the stern lifted and the bow hurried forward in a scending motion, driving onwards in pursuit of the preceding sea. Spray filled the air, so he looked through a dense mist and came to rely upon the endless pull and flex of muscle and tendon, and the tremors of the twisted hull, to tell him of the stresses to which each thrust of the sea subjected the ship.

On the starboard quarter the white, shaggy heads of sea after successive sea reared and roared until they formed a backdrop to the other part of him, the spirit recharging itself from resources deep within him, leaking energy into his brain and muscles like intravenous glucose. In this trance-like state Captain Mackinnon preserved himself for a long time, deriving his strength from his communion with God. The God he knew existed beyond the realms of childish or academical shoreside theology. The God John Mackinnon had discovered from the life he had led at sea. It had never been a matter of doubt, though the precise nature of God's substance raised itself occasionally as a matter for mild private debate in the Captain's mind. Nor did Mackinnon nurse the ridiculous and rooted prejudice that

162

God in any way, by placation or prayer, by supplication or sacrifice, took any real interest in him personally. Sparrows might fall and God might notice, but God did not prevent their death.

But God did exist; of that the Captain entertained not the slightest doubt whatsoever.

Now, as the typhoon worked itself steadily up the Beaufort scale he wondered why he had never before noticed God's presence in the wind. This howling madness had a primeval quality about it as it clawed at them and forced the mighty ocean to do its bidding. It was a delusion to think that it obeyed studied and recognised patterns of behaviour, for it did no more than conform to a predictable average. In truth it reserved to itself the right to do as it pleased and to manifest itself as chaos, a random storming of atoms, a noise that drove into his brain, numbing him, assaulting his innermost self and demanding entry into his very soul.

Such a thing *had* to be God!

Mackinnon passed from the world of men. From the planes of puny power; from the world of directors and chairmen, of politicians and playboys. He stood upon his tiny bridge amid a world of elemental force and numinous presence.

He, too, felt his isolation now, not merely the loneliness of command, but that of judgement before Almighty God. And, oddly, he felt no fear, only a great wonder.

Macgregor had never known God. God came in the same category as art, justice and love. God was bullshit. Macgregor knew fear and hunger, loneliness and hate. Just now he was full of fear. When Pritchard had got him out of his bunk and he had pulled himself together he had emerged on deck to claw his way to the bridge.

Out on the open boat-deck he had seen for the first time the size of the seas rushing at them from the hellish darkness

163

astern. God was not in the wind for Macgregor, only the devil of a fate that had forever had a down on the Macgregors of this world. Macgregor was not awestruck, for his imagination was incapable of encompassing anything bigger than his own enormous grudge.

For Magregor the boat-deck was a lonely place inhabited by malignant demons intent on impeding his progress to the bridge. Eighty feet of bucking teak planking ran wet with spray, inches deep across its surface, so that it plucked at his feet. Lit harshly by the minimal lighting the *Matthew Flinders* burned at sea, it was a place of steel corners and jutting dangers, of winches, boat davits and ventilators. Magregor was sodden and bruised by the time he had been buffeted forward to the bridge ladder.

Pain was the spur that goaded Macgregor. Pain had always unleashed a venomous resentment in him which generated its own hatreds, feeding his enmity for all things. Deprivation, poverty and neglect had been Macgregor's world since birth and even the tolerant, pragmatic regime of the Merchant Navy was something to be fought and resisted in a hopeless, endless fight with a world of circumstances always implacably hostile.

He had sworn viciously as he had been bruised but, taking the wheel, fear and the enduring instinct to survive kept him company again, compelling him to do his duty and keep the ship on the course Mackinnon desired. But Macgregor was no true seaman and lacked the instinctive response that makes a good helmsman. He was unable to anticipate the movement of the ship and was, at best, merely a reactive operator. For a while he kept a tolerable hold on the ship, but then, from time to time, he lost her and she threatened to skid round towards the dreaded position of broaching.

On each occasion Mackinnon stirred from his post to stand like Nemesis at Macgregor's elbow, silent, forbidding and all-powerful. Unperceiving of much existing outside his immediate self, Macgregor feared Captain Mackinnon more than the typhoon and fought, in self-justification, for control of the ship again.

Taylor was there too, threatening Macgregor in a more physical way, and by his very presence as the Captain's satrap triggered off Macgregor's smouldering resentment against all whom providence had elevated above and thus against him. Macgregor had not forgotten the threats made by the Third Mate. The insensate hatred that ran bilious in his personality poured itself into his ego.

In the radio-room Sparks finished writing to the dictates of the dots and dashes crackling through on the airwaves. Bracing himself he tapped out his acknowledgement of the signals then made his way to the bridge. Halfway along the boat-deck, fifteen minutes after Macgregor had traversed it, he paused and took stock of their situation.

'Christ,' he muttered, unaware the wind had actually dropped a little, even though the effort of moving forward made him gasp, 'if the wife could see me now . . .'

He found the Captain and stirred him from his trance. On Mackinnon's instruction, he read out the contents of the messages by torchlight.

'Both from Hong Kong Radio, sir, for the Master, *Matthew Flinders*. The first one's an acknowledgement of our typhoon information and then a request for clarification of our flag state, sir.'

'What the hell do they want that for? They can find it out by ringing the agent.' Mackinnon's voice was genuinely puzzled.

'I, er, think it may have something to do with the refugees, sir. It's my guess they want you to admit you're not British.'

'What d'you mean I'm not British?' Fatigue made Mackinnon testy.

'Well, the ship's no longer British, sir.' Sparks's voice bore traces of the patience of the experienced. He had never

165

aspired to command, settling early in his career for a specialisation that made him forever subordinate. It was, he was fond of saying in his cups, why he made such an excellent husband.

'You think we may have a problem with the immigration people?'

'It's very likely, sir. I read something in the *Straits Times* about the camps in Hong Kong being overcrowded.'

'Were we supposed to leave those people to drown?'

Sparks was wisely silent at Mackinnon's outraged rhetorical question.

'It's just a guess, sir.'

'Yes, yes, I know. And you're probably correct. What's the other message?'

'It's from Dentco, sir and personal. D'you want—'

'No, no, read it out.'

'It's confirming your wife's time of arrival, sir, tomorrow evening.'

Tomorrow evening. Mackinnon turned once more to the wheelhouse window. Tomorrow evening. Where would he and his ship be tomorrow evening? It seemed an eternity distant.

CHAPTER ELEVEN

Oil and Water

On the bridge Mackinnon considered what to do next. With the wind on the starboard quarter the *Matthew Flinders* would slowly move out of the path of the advancing typhoon on a curving course. This was a result of the indraught of the air as it circulated and was drawn towards the eye of the storm. The wind-generated waves did not alter their angle with the same speed, they lagged slightly, so the nearer the eye an observer was, the more the angle increased until at the centre all was confusion as waves rushed in from every point of the compass.

As the actual wind constantly created new waves, the 'old' waves, the cumulative residue of air that had now moved on, were left behind as swell waves. Dispensing with the landsman's notion of 'waves', the seaman refers to the inequities in the sea's surface as 'seas' and 'swells', a precise rather than a pedantic differentiation. A swell, though it might be monstrous in size, is a decreasing force; losing its angular shape it becomes rounded, like an ancient mountain. It possesses no breaking crest, but if unimpeded it will travel thousands of miles across an ocean as it gradually decays, long-distance evidence of a gale or storm, an observable early warning. In this decaying state it will do no more than cause a ship to roll if she is beam on to it or pitch if she heads into it, with a consequent corkscrew motion at

167

other angles. With sea and swell astern the motion is called scending, for it contains a precipitate forward motion not unlike a sleigh-ride.

The swells then assaulting the *Matthew Flinders* were still relatively young. They possessed enormous kinetic energy and it would be a long time before they became mere benign ground swells, low and slow. Their rolling and pitching motion was a danger because they were still steep and the period between the passing of their crests remained short. More important, their angle was not yet significantly different from the wind-made waves that were constantly being produced by the screaming air as it rushed towards the vortex. The combined effect was to produce a very steep, comparatively short sea that flung the ship wildly about and in which the danger of being pooped remained.

Captain Mackinnon was well aware of this and it presented him with a dilemma. In theory there was a classic remedy: oil. The less easily answerable part of his problem was how to deliver the oil and who was to do it. There were notable examples quoted in the seamanship books of, as it was quaintly put, 'the efficacy of oil in quelling the sea'.

Oil, and only a little of it, was necessary, spread in a thin film which damped down the breaking seas, robbed them of their crests and therefore rendered them much less dangerous.

Captain Mackinnon had seen plenty of oil slicks during the war and could vouch for their practical value; moreover, Mackinnon knew that God helped those who helped themselves.

There were drums of lubricating oil stored in the steering gear. They could be reached by going aft from the engine-room through the shaft tunnel and up the escape, the route by which he had earlier ordered the greasers, accommodated aft under the poop, to use. From the after end of the shaft tunnel, access to the poop was achieved by ascending the vertical ladder of the tunnel escape shaft. The

168

steering flat was conveniently close to the greasers' lavatory. Half a bale of waste dropped into one of the pans there and kept sodden with viscous lube oil would, with an occasional flushing, spread astern of them, damping down the seas and rendering them, at least on a comparative scale as things now stood, relatively harmless. Resolved on this course of action, Mackinnon turned from the window.

In the wheelhouse Taylor stood keeping a watchful eye on the useless runt Macgregor. Taylor would organise the matter, Mackinnon concluded. Judging by his recent performance he was at his best with a task to attend to. After amputating legs this would be simple.

Holding on to the engine telegraph, then edging round Macgregor, Mackinnon began to shout an explanation of what he wanted done.

Taylor bent to hear what the Captain was saying, taking his attention from the helmsman. For some time Macgregor's steering had been steady; he seemed to be getting the hang of the thing and, in any case, had only about another fifteen minutes before he was relieved. Standing over Magregor, glad of something to do, Taylor's mood had swung back again to one of groundless optimism. He was actually amused by the grunting effort Macgregor put into his exertions, writing off fifty per cent as being for his benefit. Had he been less introverted, Taylor might have smelt the musk of the man, the exudations of fear and anxiety. For a man unused to any form of real responsibility, this supervised torture was a hell to Macgregor from which there was no escape.

By now he understood the danger to which his neglect might expose the ship, and it overawed him, chiefly because his own life, rather than the lives of others, was at stake. Experience had early marked out the priorities for Macgregor; the fact that he came low on the list of others made him aware that to survive he must look after himself. In his own way he too understood that God helped those who helped themselves. He had observed its truth since his boyhood.

However, his character lacked staying power and the whisky he had drunk nurtured his grievances. Supervening his fear at losing control of the ship again, resentment grew at having such a responsibility thrust upon him. Paradoxically he equally resented the supervision. He knew his job. He did not need Third Officers and Masters to stand over him as though he was a child. He had an AB's ticket just like Braddock and Williams and Pritchard. Fear, incompetence and pride spawned this complex, deadly peevishness, and it welled up within him, submerging the fear and breeding carelessness.

But Taylor and Mackinnon were impervious to his spite. Instead he had begun to hate the wheel. It had knocked his knuckles twice as he released it to spin back admiships under the equilibrifying forces of the hydraulic fluid in the telemotor. It had humiliated him, just as the corner of the winch on the boat-deck had caught his ribs fifty minutes earlier. He had begun to resent steering the ship and the typhoon had become a thing to be hated, defied and spat upon.

Then, out of the night, came a periodic series of those coincident crests which Mackinnon had studied before turning. Distracted, Macgregor did not notice the ship's head begin to pay off and the swing had accelerated beyond redemption when he did. He lost control of the ship on the advancing face of the first of the cumulative waves.

As the stern lifted it was thrust to starboard, almost cartwheeling in an attempt to overtake the accelerating bow. Driven deep, the ship's head slewed rapidly to port, increasing the swinging moment as the angle of the supporting ocean abruptly inclined towards the vertical. The *Matthew Flinders* rolled to starboard as her head flew to port. And she failed to swing back as the rudder bit, for Macgregor had quite forgotten the ship was inanimate and

170

needed sympathetic human intelligence to nurse her through her ordeal.

Perhaps Macgregor should never have taken the wheel as custom ordained and Mackinnon ordered; perhaps Macgregor should never have been isued with a certificate of competency as an able seaman which allowed him the privilege. Whatever misjudgements had been made where Macgregor was concerned, and they had doubtless been made (whatever *he* thought of them) by giving him the benefit of the doubt, they were now proved wrong. His application of counter-helm was too late for, lifted high, nine tenths of the *Matthew Flinders's* rudder turned uselessly in the spray-sodden air.

The *Matthew Flinders* broached at the first of the oncoming quartet of heavy seas. It burst against her port quarter with an impact that could be felt throughout her fabric, further pushing the ship's stern to starboard and lifting her as she continued slewing to port. The flung spray arched over her in a pale, wind-riven cloud and the wave passed under her. The *Matthew Flinders* rolled back to port as the second huge sea heaped up alongside her, rearing over her entire length as the decks, even the exhaust tubes poking up through her buff funnel, pointed invitingly towards it. The crest came roaring down upon her as she lay like a drunk in the gutter.

As hundreds of tonnes of water cascaded from the summit of the wave, the inherent stability of the *Matthew Flinders* asserted itself. A reaction between the downward thrust of her weight and the upward thrust of her buoyant self reacted with a levering effect. Whilst each might be considered to act at a single point, the first at her centre of gravity, the second at her centre of buoyancy, the first remained constant whatever the ship's attitude in the water. The other moved according to the body of the hull actually *in* the water. As the centre of gravity acted downwards through the ship's centre, a roll to port moved the upward thrust of her centre

171

of buoyancy dramatically to the left. This was increased by the rising of the port waterline for the ship now felt the upward buoyancy of the next wave. These two forces, gravity and buoyancy, acted in opposition, and since they were not in the same vertical line they formed a moment known as a righting lever, throwing the *Matthew Flinders* back to starboard away from the breaking torrent that swept down upon her.

Although it was not the decks upon which this vast volume of water struck, it hammered with tremendous force upon the whole exposed length of the port side, inducing a fast roll the other way. At the same time it swept the ship, like a woodchip in a mill race, bodily sideways.

Mackinnon turned in those few fateful seconds to correct Macgregor's steering. He knew instantly he was too late. He was level with the open wheelhouse door as the ship went over to starboard, with Taylor somewhere above him on the canting deck and Macgregor scrabbling at the telemotor for support. Mackinnon was flung into a half-run, half-stumble out on to the bridge-wing. The outboard rail dipped down, down to the seething blackness that was the sea on their lee side. For an instant he thought he was to be flung from his own bridge, then he made gasping, winded contact with the starboard gyro-bearing repeater pedestal and collapsed, clinging to it as the water came over him, roaring in his ears, deceptively warm.

In the wheelhouse Macgregor was flung from his handhold on the wheel, hitting the engine-room telegraph with a yelp of pain and falling to the deck as one of the port wheelhouse windows was stove in. The armoured glass shattered into long slivers and one slashed across Taylor's forearm as he reached out to seize the abandoned wheel, bracing himself against the steep angle of the deck. Anxiously he scanned the starboard bridge-wing for a sign of the Captain.

Yet none of the water that poured aboard the old cargo-liner at that moment was solid, or constituted what sailors call a 'green' sea, for the bulk of the wave had gone *under* the ship; it was merely the mass of water flung *upwards* from the impact of the colliding breaker which was then shredded to leeward, smashing the wheelhouse window, deluging Captain Mackinnon and pressing him to the deck at the foot of the repeater pedestal.

A deck below the bridge Rawlings found himself lying on his cabin bulkhead. Once relieved by Taylor he had crawled to his bunk in search of an hour or two's rest and had actually fallen asleep. When the *Matthew Flinders* rolled to leeward he was jerked from his fitful slumber. As the ship lolled on her side, Rawlings was pierced by anxiety for her stability. It was his particular responsibility and he was aware of the potential variables that such a roll might cast loose in the ship's cargo spaces. He lay still, his whole, frightened being concentrating on listening for distant rumblings from the holds.

Stevenson had been unable to sleep. He was keyed up, excited as much by the presence of the Vietnamese girl as the typhoon. Who was she? *What* was she?

She seemed to be alone and he nurtured ridiculous ideas about her vulnerability. A ship was a libidinous hothouse. He thought of Macgregor and Rawlings as threats to her. Then, being a sensible man, he dismissed the whole thing as stupid fantasy and tried to sleep, only to find he could not drop off. He got up and realised he felt hungry. He recollected he had eaten no dinner that night; his hunger gave him the excuse he subconsciously sought to make his way back down below.

He went first to the galley. Fred Thorpe was still about. The Chief Steward never turned in early but normally led a small school of the ship's hardened drinkers who, off watch or on day work, congregated nightly in his cabin. He was a sociable host and, being Chief Steward, had the keys that

173

circumvented Captain Mackinnon's bar-opening hours. Tonight, however, Thorpe was occupied on more humane matters. Being a pragmatist he felt no humiliation from passing out over the amputations. Mackinnon had himself quailed, handing the job over to Taylor. Taylor always was a superior, heartless sort of bastard, and if his detachment only confirmed this in Thorpe's eyes, he had been too long subservient to worry about social pecking orders. Basically, as exemplified by his discreet drinking school, at the end of the day, Freddie Thorpe did just what he wanted.

He was not a voluptuary, however. No seaman can ever be that entirely. Bred to the service of others, it was Thorpe who, with one of his Chinese assistant stewards, cleared up the swilling muck in the officers's duty mess. After that he had made it his business to supervise the feeding and bedding down of the refugees. The women and children had settled first in the smoke-room, then the men had been attended to in the saloon.

He was in the galley discussing the arrangements for feeding the increased numbers the following day when Stevenson found him. The galley was at main-deck level in the approximate centre of the ship, directly above the forward end of the engine-room, the nearest habitable space to the ship's centre of gravity. More than anywhere else, the motion of the ship was least here.

Thorpe and Wang Lee, the cook, stood, braced easily, their hands clutching the guard-rail that ran round the Carron electric range.

'Hullo, Freddie, any chow left?'

'You no come dinner, Mr Steven-song. Your favourite – *Nasi Goreng*.'

'Got any left, Wang Lee?' Stevenson grinned.

Wang Lee shook his head. 'Mos' go boat people.'

'Oh.' Stevenson's regret was tempered by the thought of Tam. 'Never mind.'

Thorpe was looking amused. 'We've got a drop of soup,

Alex, and some bread rolls.'

'They'll do.'

'You'd better have the soup in a mug,' Thorpe said, taking a ladle from the jingling row that swung from a hook above the range. He lifted the lid from a huge pot held on the warm hotplates by horizontal bars. Wang Lee handed the Chief Steward a mug from the half-dozen hung from hooks in the deckhead above, then turned and produced a basket of crisp brown rolls. Stevenson could smell the freshness of them and his mouth watered.

'Thanks.' He took a roll and then the mug just as the ship dipped her bow and began to broach and roll.

'Steady there . . .'

Bracing themselves, the three men waited for the ship to right herself. She shook at the impact of the first quartering sea. Stevenson, the mug in one hand, stuffed the roll in his mouth and seized the range grab-rail as the rolling increased. A moment later they each knew something had gone seriously wrong.

'Holy shit!' swore Thorpe as the *Matthew Flinders* rolled to port and they felt her rise as the approaching sea heaped itself under the hull. They felt her thrown over to starboard as the breaker slammed against her with an immense, terrifying jar.

Like Mackinnon three decks above him, Stevenson was caught partially off balance with only one hand free. Wang Lee and Thorpe cannoned into and clung to each other, skidding down the galley's tiled deck and crashing into the stainless-steel lockers to starboard. The ladles and straining spoons dangling above the range were flung from their hooks, the port-side lockers burst their turn-buckles and pots and pans, knives and utensils tumbled down upon them with a clatter.

Stevenson was precipitated towards the hooked-open entry door. He had dropped the mug, but he had the fleeting impression that gravity drew it chest height, parallel to his

175

own direction of descent, the soup slopping from it in a dollop. He spat out the roll as his hands went out to save himself; the entrance loomed, he caught at the side of it and, with a sickening blow, his shoulder fetched up against the door jamb. A wave of nausea tore through him as the intervention of the door jamb spun him round and shot him backwards into the alleyway beyond.

Simultaneously water burst in upon the accommodation. Stevenson fell full length and it washed over him as it rushed like a miniature bore the length of the alleyway, diminishing only where it spewed into adjacent cabins and down, over the low sea step, into the storeroom alleyway and master-gyro room below. The air was filled with the screams and howls of the boat people. The security of their exhausted sleep was abruptly terminated by this terrifying change in their apparently secure circumstances. The motion of the ship was suddenly a suffocating extension of the exposed horrors of the junk. The edge of their tiredness removed by two or three hours' oblivion, they woke to be revolted by the smell of diesel oil, of European cooking, of the Europeans themselves in this battened-down, enclosed, staggering, drunken steel box.

In the Chief Engineer's cabin the telephone rang about thirty seconds before Macgregor lost control of the ship.

After Mackinnon had visited Mr York prior to amputating the feet of the Vietnamese woman, the Chief had gone below and told the Second Engineer, who was then on watch, that he wanted the engines put on to diesel oil. Normally, when on passage between ports, the *Matthew Flinders*'s Burmeister and Wain diesel engine ran on fuel oil, a cruder, cheaper means of power than the more expensive pure diesel oil. This was only fed to the engine on 'stand-by', when the ship manoeuvred in and out of port. Reliability being essential at such times, the more volatile diesel oil was used as the engine was stopped and started.

176

Mackinnon, mindful of the worsening weather, had ordered the ship back on to diesel oil, anticipating the need to adjust the engine revolutions in the coming hours. Mr York had already hurriedly changed over from fuel oil to diesel once that afternoon, as Mackintosh had manoeuvred close to the drifting junk. Having recovered the boat people and increased speed, Mackinnon had telegraphed 'full speed away' and they had reverted to ordinary fuel oil.

But Mr York had a problem. Since the ship was to be paid off for scrap when she arrived in Hong Kong, Mr York had been instructed by the company superintendent before leaving the United Kingdom not to take more bunkers than was absolutely necessary. Calculating fuel consumption being both part of the Chief Engineer's domain and something in which Mr York took a particular pride, he had left Singapore congratulating himself that he had done so to a nicety. He was in complete agreement with the company's policy and had always abhorred waste.

During the course of their chat, Mackinnon had revealed that the old ship was to be sold to the Chinese for further trading. Not that the fact altered the matter of bunkers, York thought; it was too late for that! Nor did it bother him if the Chinks took the old lady over with empty double-bottoms. Let them buy their own bloody fuel; he intended remaining true to his principles. His standards had already saved the ship, though he did not, nor would he ever, appreciate the fact. As in the matter of the steering-flat door, the amount of bunkers generally, and diesel oil in particular, now became a matter of importance.

Mr York was a little older in years than Captain Mackinnon, and a lurking heart ailment he refused to admit to made him tire easily. He had no trouble falling asleep and was prostrate on his bunk when the insistent ringing of the telephone recalled him to consciousness. It was situated on the bulkhead above him and he reached up for it and heard the voice of the Second Engineer.

177

'Chief? There's something wrong. Can you come down?'

'What's the matter?' The obvious note of concern in the voice of George Reed worried York. His normally competent and imperturbable Geordie Second sounded extremely anxious. Still holding the telephone York began to heave his legs over the leeboard of his bunk, bracing himself against the sudden roll of the ship.

'I think there's been a bit of a cock-up, Chief. Best if you come down.'

'Right.' York stood, leaned over the rumpled bunk and hung up the phone. He turned to reach for his boiler suit, worrying over Reed's words, and had one leg in the garment when the *Matthew Flinders* flew over to starboard. Hopping and cursing, York cannoned into the edge of the partition separating his night cabin from his dayroom. Losing his balance he fell and struck his head on the corner of the steel filing cabinet beside the end of his desk. He was unconscious before his body subsided on the deck.

The ringing of the telephone impinged upon Taylor's consciousness above the terrible boom of the typhoon and his anxiety to locate Mackinnon. He was the first of the trio on the bridge to recover his senses, aware the wheel was untended. Despite the deep gash on his arm from the flying shards of armoured glass, Taylor realised the perilous position of the ship. He clawed at the wheel, dragging it over to port in a desperate attempt to heave-to. Beside him in the darkness Macgregor whimpered.

'Here, Macgregor! Take the wheel again! Hurry, man!'

The pale shape of Macgregor's face shook itself as the telephone continued its insistent noise.

'Taking the fucking wheel!' Taylor shouted.

Macgregor lay inert, his face eclipsed as he hid it in the crook of his arm. Like an animal, Macgregor had lain down to die.

'You gutless, fucking bastard!' Taylor screamed, ignoring

the telephone and looking frantically about. Something else was clamouring for his attention, something more urgent than the telephone. Something was wrong. Very wrong. For a moment he was unable to identify the source of his fear, for the deafening, booming roar of the wind dulled his wits and numbed his reflexes. All he could do was cling on to the wheel spokes and drag the rudder over to port. Then he knew it was useless.

The main engine had stopped.

CHAPTER TWELVE

Typhoon David

In that awesome moment Taylor felt a surge of adrenalin. Macgregor's folly followed by his abject surrender made him intensely angry. His unnaturally elated mood sustained him, for he alone knew what was happening. Until Captain Mackinnon was located, he, the officer of the watch, was in command.

Drawing himself upright he looked at the dimly lit overhead magnetic compass. The ship's head was unchanged. The *Matthew Flinders* lay a-hull, his efforts to heave her to were futile without the main engine. He let go of the wheel and it spun back to amidships.

He struggled uphill kicking aside large slivers of glass and answered the jangling telephone.

'Hullo? Bridge?'

'I was beginning to think you'd all died up there.' Geordie Reed's frustrated sarcasm was apt, but he rushed on, preoccupied. 'I can't get hold of the Chief. I spoke to him before we rolled. Anyway, we've got an airlock in the fuel line, bloody engine's stopped.'

'I know.' A chilling and distant rumble sent tremors through the ship. The *Matthew Flinders* continued to roll, but the roll no longer oscillated either side of the vertical, for she already lay at a mean angle of ten degrees to starboard. Taylor asked the question all hurrying, hastening navigators ask: 'How long will it take?'

'How the fucking hell would I know? Twenty minutes if you bastards'd stop rolling the sodding ship. In this lot, Christ knows!' The phone slammed angrily down.

Taylor turned. The lights still glowed, so the auxiliary generators were unaffected, but the rumblings in the hold were ominous in the extreme. For a moment he stood still in the darkness, trying to listen for more noises despite the thrumming boom of the typhoon's terrifyingly powerful note.

Someone loomed in the starboard doorway, a hunched, unfamiliar figure.

'Who . . .? Sir? Are you all right?'

'I'm alive, Mr Taylor,' Mackinnon gasped.

'The main engine's stopped,' Taylor reported, 'some sort of fuel problem. The Second's below and doesn't know how long it will take to get going again. He's sent for the Chief.'

'Then we shall have to be patient, Mr Taylor,' said the Captain, stumbling over Macgregor. 'Is this you, Macgregor?'

The pale oval of Macgregor's face rose from its supine funk and grunted.

'Anybody ever tell you,' Mackinnon said, his voice shouting above the wind roar yet sounding menacingly low in the wheelhouse, 'that you'll never make a helmsman as long as your arse points downwards?'

Incredulous in that primordial blackness in which the wind reached a crescendo of mind-numbing noise and with its gusting beat about the ship making his head ache, Taylor cleared the glass away and watched Captain John Mackinnon step over Macgregor with a disdain visible in the gloom. With a sigh the Captain resumed his post in the forward corner of the wheelhouse.

'Patience,' he said, half to himself, 'patience and daylight.'

Then, as the motion of the ship eased slightly, her lolling

roll settling to a more regular pattern, Stevenson and Rawlings reported to the bridge having come up the internal companionway.

The stilled rumble of the engine had summoned them.

Rawlings announced his presence with lugubrious news. 'I think the cargo's on the move, sir.'

'You can hear it down below,' said Stevenson. He was nursing his shoulder.

'I'm not surprised,' Mackinnon said. 'How are our passengers?'

'Pretty frightened, sir. When that green one hit us, I was in the saloon area,' Stevenson volunteered.

'Clean swept us, sir,' added Rawlings.

'That,' said Mackinnon in a tired voice, 'was little more than heavy spray, gentlemen.' He paused to let his words sink in. 'I fear we can expect more of the same – if not worse. We'll have to lie a-hull now while the engineers do what they can. Any oil we can get to windward of us will help. How much leeway we are making I leave to your imagination.'

'We could get some out of the galley sink. The scuppers are amidships and there's cooking oil down there . . .'

'See to it, Mr Stevenson, then reassure our passengers. We mustn't forget the news you brought aboard.'

'Aye, aye, sir.' Stevenson turned to go below again. He made way for Sparks, hauling himself up the companionway by the handrails with an air of exhaustion.

'Mr Rawlings,' Mackinnon went on, addressing the Mate, 'I want you to try and assess what's happened below. Better assume the worst. We can expect to have heard something from forrard and not from Number Five 'tween deck. See what you can do.'

'Very well, sir.'

'And Mr Rawlings . . .'

'Sir?'

'No risks.'

'No risks, aye, aye, sir.'

182

Mackinnon could guarantee Rawlings would take no risks, but the public instruction not to might stiffen his resolution. He caught sight of another figure in the wheelhouse.

'That you, Sparks?'

'Yes, Captain, d'you want . . .?' Sparks's voice tailed off as if unwilling to form the words. Mackinnon caught his meaning.

'No, no, not yet. We're down, but not out. You can make yourself useful by sending another typhoon report. Say: wind north, force twelve.'

'Position?'

Mackinnon grunted. 'Same as the last, near enough. What we made to the north we lost to leeward long ago. I'll work out something more accurate later.'

Give them all something to do, Mackinnon thought; keep them busy, thinking about their own tasks. Only way to save the ship. No one would get to them in this weather, if they did send a distress signal. Maybe, if they survived until daylight, he would change his mind. Not now. 'Got that, Sparks?'

'On my way, sir.'

'Be careful on the boat-deck.'

'Don't worry, sir.'

But Mackinnon did. As the *Matthew Flinders* leaned away from the wind her decks were in the lee of the weather rail. So strong was the wind now that in such areas it created a partial vacuum, sucking a loose object to leeward. Sparks, exposed on the boat deck, was one such loose object.

In the days of wooden hatch-boards and canvas tarpaulins such a suction could tear a vessel's holds open. Fortunately the *Matthew Flinders*'s steel Macgregor hatches were proof against that, though the irony of both their plight and their survival being synonymous did not escape the Captain's divagating mind. The unreliable owner of the proud clan name sat hunched in a corner.

'Mr Taylor?'

'Sir?'

183

'Get another seaman up here and then have that arm of yours dressed. You're leaking rather badly.'

Taylor looked down. His bare forearm was black with blood and, now that Mackinnon drew his attention to it, it throbbed painfully. He began to laugh.

'What's the matter?' Mackinnon asked sharply and Taylor muffled his hysteria with an effort. If he bled to death the loathsome gonococci would leach from his body! The image of his pale, putrified corpse sinking in the ocean was irresistibly funny.

Going below again Stevenson thought of the ammunition clip. The Captain's remark had reminded him. Funny how one forgot things, how events overlay each other eclipsing one concern with another. He tried to remember the boat trips in detail. There had been so many of them and only the last stood out, but by then he was alert to the possibility of one of the boat people having a gun.

Yes, some bundles had gone aboard, slung over the shoulders of at least two women and, he was certain, one of the men. They might have concealed a gun, but so what? The poor devils had been running for their lives. If one of them had a gun it did not, in itself, mean he nursed any sinister intent now. Was old Gorilla not being a bit over the top with his apprehension?

As he reached the main-deck level Stevenson heard the babel of the boat people. The cries of the children, the keening of frightened women and the helpless anger of the men had subsided now the ship had steadied somewhat. Animated shouts came from the saloon. They *could* get ugly, Stevenson thought, but would gain nothing by it. Their chances of survival were entirely dependent upon the crew of the *Matthew Flinders*. Such a consideration revived the feeling of protection towards the girl, then he tossed the silliness aside. He had a more urgent task.

In the galley he found a disgusting mess of flour, cooking

oil, spices, salt and rice mixed with seawater swilling across the deck. The ready-use lockers had disgorged their contents, their doors banging back and forth with a metallic clatter. Not all the sunflower oil had been lost, however, and, dragging his feet through the muck, Stevenson reached the large, stainless-steel sink on the port side of the galley. Grabbing a passing tea-towel he stuffed it down the plug hole to stop the oil running out in a dollop. With infinite caution, his wrenched shoulder paining him, he got hold of a five-litre can of oil and laid it in the sink. Then, looking round, he saw a large cooking knife, picked it up and hauled himself back uphill. Clinging to the rim of the sink with his left hand, his shoulder racking him, he stabbed furiously down with the knife, perforating the thin tin-plated can. The golden oil glooped viscously into the sink. He realised it would take one entire can to bring the slopping level up to the elevation of the plug hole. Patiently he worked round the galley and discovered two more cans in a leeward corner. Feet slithering and his now oily hands slipping on the handrails, he painfully dragged each to the high side of the galley.

When he had finished he stood panting. The simple task had taken twenty minutes and he felt exhausted and ill-tempered by it.

'Like the poor bloody Viets,' he muttered. Nothing was more truly exhausting than enduring. When he had caught his breath he turned and slid across the heaving deck. Back out in the alleyway, where he had fallen earlier, the chatter of the boat people surged like the filth borne by the water up and down its length. Drawing himself forward as much by the handrails as by walking, he approached the saloon. From the noise one imagined some sort of seething mass of wildly protesting humanity. Instead the men huddled against the bulkheads, their knees drawn up under their chins, emaciated elves clustered beneath the overhanging, toadstool-shapes of the dining tables. About their haunches the watery muck sluiced back and forth, while above their heads hung a thick blue haze from the glowing cigarettes they smoked.

Catching sight of Stevenson their voices rose in an arsis of misery and uncertainty. Bracing himself spread-legged, he held up his hands, palms towards them, fingers splayed, then pressed downwards, as though against resistance. Seeing the gesture they grew quiet.

'Everything o-kay,' he said with a calm deliberation. He glanced round the circle of hollow faces with their dark, tenebrous eyes. And smiled.

They watched, silently impassive. He waited, wanting a response, unable to leave them on so unsuccessful a note.

'Everything o-kay,' he repeated, but still they stared back. He had begun his retreat when a man called out, the syllables short and sharp and loaded with conviction like pistol shot.

'Everything no good!'

The noise welled up again and the speaker rose to his feet, two or three others following suit. Stevenson found Thorpe was beside him.

'Noisy lot of slant-eyed bastards, aren't they?' said the Chief Steward flatly, wading into the saloon. 'Sit down, sit down, too much makee noise, call Captain bottom-side very angry.'

Inexplicably as far as Stevenson was concerned, the refugees subsided, those standing sat down again and the glow of their cigarettes seemed, to Stevenson's heightened perception, to glow with renewed brightness.

Number One Greaser sent in search of the Chief Engineer bent and shook Mr York.

'Ay-ah . . .' The man let out a double syllable that might have meant anything. He stood and retreated from the cabin. Having regained the engine-room he located the Second Engineer.

'Chief dead man, Second.'

For a moment the young Tynesider stared uncomprehending at the elderly Chinaman.

'Dead? Are you sure?'

'I sure. I see plenty dead man.'

'Okay,' Reed said at last. 'First we start engine, then go topside look at Chief.' Reed had never seen a dead man; nor did he feel particularly curious.

Stevenson reached the smoke-room and found the easier motion of the ship had almost immediately pacified the women. The old woman was still awake and showed him her inane gold grin. He experienced a pang of extreme irritation, for Braddock was there, squatting close to Tam with something in his arms. Stevenson stepped over the inert bodies and crossed to the girl.

'Braddock,' he began, 'what are you—?'

'Hullo, Sec.' The seaman looked up. In his arms he held the baby. 'Got to turn to now, and thought I'd bring the little bloke up for a cuddle.' He offered the child to Tam. 'Can you look after 'im for a bit, love?'

Stevenson watched her. She stared uncertainly at the tiny bundle. Its swaddling clothes were none too clean, but Stevenson recognized a bath towel with Eastern Steam's compass rose trademark.

Tam took the child and cradled it to her breast, rocking the tiny form as it whimpered and puckered its lips.

'Is it hungry?' Stevenson asked.

Braddock barked a short, dismissive laugh. 'I doubt it, Sec, it's eaten more than I've seen any kid stow away. I reckon it's full of wind and shite.'

Stevenson grinned. 'You okay?' he enquired of the girl.

She nodded and smiled, then regarded the baby again. 'Sure.'

'You going forrard with the Mate, Brad?' The seaman shrugged. 'Mind how you go,' Stevenson said.

187

Captain Mackinnon stood on the bridge and waited for the dawn. Patience and daylight, his twin watchwords. Silently he mourned his dead, for George Reed had telephoned the bridge with the news of the Chief's fatal accident.

'One leg in his boiler suit,' Stevenson had reported after Mackinnon had sent him below to investigate, 'and one out. Must have lost his balance and struck his head on the corner of his desk or the filing cabinet.'

Mackinnon knew the filing cabinet well enough. He used to stand the occasional beer on it when he and old Yorkie had a pow-wow. Poor Ernie. Mackinnon sighed; they had been shipmates a long time. He wondered how Brenda would take it, a sharp, dark little woman whom he had met upon the odd occasion. Now she would never have her man home again and all the long voyages, investments against a better day when the plans for a life together after retirement would be fulfilled, were wasted.

'You all right down there, George?' Mackinnon had asked Reed after digesting the news.

'Oh, aye. Ah'll manage reet enough.' His voice sounded strained with shock and sudden responsibility. Old Ernie York had led a pretty sedentary life lately, but his presence had been reassuring to the younger man. Now Reed was on his own.

'Do your best, George,' said Mackinnon, 'that's all we ask, lad.'

'Ah can fix her, Cap'n. I just need time. Aye an' . . .' Reed broke off.

Mackinnon smiled in the gloom. 'I know. You want the bloody deck ornaments to stop rocking the boat.'

He was rewarded by the grin in Reed's voice. 'Ah'll be getting on then.'

Mackinnon left him to 'get on'. Reed would receive no reward for the effort he must put in. It was part of the job, the

188

job which ended when the ship reached Hong Kong.

Captain Mackinnon did not permit himself to consider the ship failing to arrive at Hong Kong. There were some things best ignored at times.

Rawlings's sortie had been an abject failure. A sea had come aboard in the darkness washing Able Seaman Braddock into the lee scuppers from which he had only been recovering with difficulty. Clearly frightened and very wet, Rawlings had returned to report nothing more than a confirmation that something, several things, were loose in Number Five 'tween decks as well as Number Two. The proximity of the Chief Officer to the thumps only increased his nervousness. Mackinnon regretted sending him; he should have relied upon Stevenson, or even Taylor, but you could not pass over the ship's Chief Officer. He was all right with routine or simple tasks; he was a good organiser but . . .

And it was a bloody big *but*.

He thought of the boat people. He could let his mind drift a little. There was nothing to do until either Reed got the main engine going again or daylight came. Besides, the loose bulldozers would beat their way out of the ship's side if they were going to and his fretting about them would do no good. So he thought of the boat people. They were part of his responsibility anyway.

Funny how he had had the premonition about them. And on his last voyage. Fate again . . .

But what about them?

What had made them leave their homes? The Vietnam War had ended years earlier, though what its aftermath meant to the South Vietnamese he could only guess. Were they just ordinary people, driven out by intimidation of one sort or another, victims of bullying, by whom did not matter much, beyond the fact of its hostile intent?

And what, the Captain's imagination asked his soul, would he have done? Could he imagine it, from his

189

comfortable, predictable western career-orientated point of view?

Well, yes; perhaps imperfectly, grasping a fraction of its effect. He did know what desperation was like, for he had felt it in the lifeboat and a hint of it was present aboard the *Matthew Flinders* on his last voyage, particularly among the young men. And he knew a little of surrounding hostility, for this, too, he had experienced, on Shelagh's father's Ulster farm when they had visited as young newlyweds. He had never understood it, or taken sides, a fact which had not endeared him to his father-in-law, but the sectarian hatred was palpable enough, and, for him, intolerable. He was always glad to leave, always glad to return to the crowds and squalor of Liverpool, for all the beauty of the Antrim coast.

But what would he have done at the final extremity of his wits and resources when escaping or driven from his home? Men liked to think they would fight, but they seldom did, or could, alone. They had first to think of wives and children. Single men and irresponsible men could run away and join bands of like-minded fools. And there were always cunning men to sell them arms. Men like that found it very easy to fight; it was courageous, a manifestation of the magnificence of the human spirit; a thing of primitive tribal satisfactions upon which whole civilisations were based. It possessed the grandeur of a selfless principle. Except that it was a lie, as the wastelands and refugee camps of Africa could testify. A vast lie, a lie so bloody huge the contemplation of its truth could so easily be covered up. Governments did it all the time and half their populations acquiesced, desiring the status quo and a quiet life.

It seemed sometimes to Mackinnon that the world (the 'postwar world') was composed of only two kinds of people: of young men in khaki drab, machine carbines clasped languidly at the extremity of their powerful forearms, muscled and well-fed; and the old, very young, infirm or female of the species, hurrying, hurrying away towards the

190

illusory horizon. Even, Mackinnon thought, where prosperity reigned, both types existed in an uneasy truce, hidden under the veneer of civilisation, waiting to reveal their allegiance. It occurred to Mackinnon, in a flash of enlightenment, that mankind was nowhere civilised, merely sophisticated.

The temptation to lie down and wait for the end must be overwhelming after a while. When the belly had shrunk from hunger and after the first strike of death, a child perhaps, while you begged your retreating way. Every door would be closed against you because you spread the contagion of fear, and assistance rendered meant sympathy given. Sympathy invited reprisal and reprisal was too dreadful to contemplate.

Besides, where was there to go? What was it he and Sparks had said about it that morning in Singapore? Once you could relocate deprivation and dissent, now it goes to sea?

Perhaps. But it was so much easier to lie down and die, of hunger or disease or the bullet which was bound to find you eventually if you had the effrontery to go on being alive.

To cast oneself and one's family adrift seemed both the height of folly and, at the same time, an act of magnificent faith and courage. Most ducked their heads and paid lip service and who could blame them?

But these people had taken to the sea! They were quite obviously not fisherfolk, therefore their act was a last resort. Or was it? You did not think of the awfulness of being adrift. You thought a boat and the sea led you to the rest of the world; to other places where things were different. Better.

Mackinnon remembered the message they had received from Hong Kong Radio and Sparks's suspicions as to its underlying meaning.

The poor bastards were about to find out just how 'different' the rest of the world was. There were no more places to go. They would end up like those poor, utterly

191

hopeless people they had seen towed into Singapore. At the utter extremity . . .

He caught himself on the wings of this fantasy. They were not. They had simply swapped the coffin of the junk for the catafalque of the ship. Perhaps, and here Mackinnon slid off into another flight of fancy, they had been picked up by the *Matthew Flinders* to draw the British and Chinese crew into a sharing of *their* fate; perhaps it was not a rescue after all, but the reverse. And Mackinnon could think of no English noun that served.

'We are so used to success,' he murmured. He could think of a cliché, though, and it assuaged his guilt to be able to do so. 'We're all in the same boat . . .'

And, despite his circumstances, he smiled.

Captain Mackinnon did not entertain the slightest doubt the encounter with the refugees was no coincidence. It was a conceit of his, albeit a small and private conceit, that his apprehension in Singapore had been premonition. Of what use was a man once his sexual appetites had dulled if he could not bring a little wisdom into the world? Premonition was no magic thing; it was generated by experience, circumstances, an awareness of what was happening around one – and a spicing of primordial fear. It was just that the process was obscure, misunderstood, automatic. Instinctive.

What the preoccupied, self-absorbed world of what it was pleased to call 'everyday affairs' knew as coincidence was rarely so, Mackinnon mused. Some reflection, or an examination into the whole, would reveal the linking threads. It was not only murders which were chained together by motive, cause and effect. They were merely solved by applying the rules governing most things.

He could enumerate several stories as proof of providence. Well, perhaps not quite proof, but suggesting *something*. They were marvellous, but not mystical. More conclusive evidence had come to Mackinnon after the war.

192

Having lost over half its ships to the enemy, as a temporary stop-gap until new tonnage had replaced these the Eastern Steam Navigation Company took over vessels surplus to the Ministry of War Transport's requirements. Along with most major British liner operators their fleet spawned numerous 'standard-ships': United-States-built 'Sams' and 'Victories', British and Canadian 'Forts' and 'Parks'.

Eastern Steam renamed the *Fort Mackinac* the *George Bass* and as such, in the spring of 1951, she had passed through the Kiel canal on passage to Målmo and Turku-Abo. It was a gloomy voyage and no one was looking forward to the Baltic. It was not only the ice, for to the south of them most of the former Reich and the countries of eastern Europe lay under the heel of Stalin's Russia, while the unknown vastness of their quondam ally, the Union of Soviet Socialist Republics itself, lay beyond the sunrise.

The mood had been set during the canal transit between Brunsbüttel and Kiel. The enforced contemplation of Germany had awoken old emotions and their departure from the former *Kriegsmarine* base with its mixture of ruination and rebuilding had been complicated by the presence of an ice-pilot.

The man's appearance was so much that of the expected stereotype that it was almost impossible to take him seriously. Tall and thin, of an indeterminate age with prematurely greying blond hair under his white-covered cap, he wore a black leather coat and calf gloves. Only a red scarf wound round his neck stopped him looking like the archetypical Nazi bully then currently causing the laughter of relief in British cinemas. Tolerated for his expertise on the *George Bass*'s bridge, he became a figure of fun, for neither Second Officer Mackinnon nor Captain McGrath wanted to enquire into his past; it would have made any kind of professional relationship impossible. Only the *George*

Bass's Chief Engineer, Mr King, was unable to conceal his true feelings.

'The arrogant bastard,' Mr King would say with compelling intensity, 'he'd never *dare* wear a white-covered cap if he hadn't been in command, and the only thing a Kraut of *that* age could have commanded is a U-boat.'

He said this with such conviction nobody considered the possibility of the ice-pilot having commanded a mine-sweeper. For the apprentices, boys who had not been at sea during the war, their figure of fun turned into an object of sinister curiosity (though still to be aped).

Although Mr King was not alone aboard the *George Bass* in having been torpedoed, nor in taking to an open boat several hundred miles north of the Arctic circle, he was unique in having been witness to an atrocity.

Alone, after being separated from any consorts of a convoy bound for Murmansk by a northerly gale, his ship, the *Henry Hudson*, was torpedoed and sunk with her load of tanks and chemicals bound for the Red Army.

In the half-light of the Arctic winter day, the blown-out gale was succeeded by a freezing mist out of which ghosted the sinister shape of the U-boat which had sunk them. Figures could be seen on her conning tower and she had stopped between the two lifeboats. Several of her hands had run down on to her casing and fished about in the water. They recovered a lifebuoy bearing the legend: *Henry Hudson – Liverpool*. An officer had called down asking which boat contained the ship's Master. The Captain had held his silence and no one had betrayed him, for the masters of some British ships had been taken prisoners alone, as living trophies. The German officer had repeated the question, with the same result. The U-boat's commander, distinguishable in the gloom by his privileged white cap cover, had given an order. Off the casing by now, the hands gathered swiftly about the conning tower machine gun. A few rounds stuttered and flashed, ripping into the boat on the far side of the U-boat. A moment later the barrel lengthened, then foreshortened as it swung towards King's boat. A frantic scrabbling at the oars was swiftly terminated. Mr King was knocked to the bottom boards as an oarsmen cannoned into him from the impact of the bullets.

When King struggled up again, the grey shape had vanished in the mist. He could hear the noise of its surface diesel engine for a long time. By true nightfall he was the only man left alive, for the last of the wounded had succumbed to loss of blood, or the cold.

Mr King was picked up by the corvette *Nemesia* sixteen hours later. That much his shipmates knew; it was in incontrovertible print, part of the company's history, though Mr King himself never spoke of it. They did not know they were to witness the delayed finale.

The ice in the Baltic was thick that spring, a northerly gale packing it southwards and impeding the progress of the *George Bass* through the Fehmarn Belt.

'It is better we wait, *Kapitan*,' the pilot advised McGrath, 'these wartime ships, zey are not so strong, no?'

For two days they drifted slowly off the Lolland coast, engines stopped, waiting for the wind to change.

This enforced inactivity compelled the *George Bass*'s Master to offer a little hospitality to his guest. The ice-pilot said he preferred *schnapps*, but under the circumstances Scotch would do. This condescending attitude was characteristic of the man, and prevailed as several pegs of whisky were downed in McGrath's cabin below the bridge. After a while Mr King loomed in the doorway seeking enlightenment as to how long the weather was likely to delay them. The barbed remark was addressed more to the ice-pilot, as the Captain well knew, being himself an easygoing and tolerant man well-used to his Chief Engineer's embitterment. Chiefy King, as everyone in Eastern Steam knew, had had a bad war.

The ice-pilot shrugged with massive condescension. 'Ach,

195

the Chief Engineer comes mit de questions, *ja*? Always the engineers ask questions impossible to answer. You are too long working mit the logical things in life, my friend.'

King turned a glance of withering contempt at this insolence, but accepted a glass of Scotch from the Captain.

'How you English say? Cheers, *ja*?'

King remained stonily silent, raising his glass to McGrath in appreciation. The Captain, slightly amused, watched the two of them.

'You remember too much the war, eh? When we seamens all do our job. Dat is right, *ja, kapitan*?'

'Sure.'

'Now we have all to be together, soon we fight the Russians, eh? Then you will need our help.' The ice-pilot smiled confidently. 'The Russians, they build many submarines, eh? You British will need good help of Willi—' and here he tapped his leather breast, and roared with laughter.

'You were in submarines?' the Chief asked in a choked voice, speaking directly to the German for the first time.

The ice-pilot's face was whisky-flushed. 'Sure, Chief. I do my job, like you, *ja*? You were in dis company's ships?'

King nodded, his eyes noticing the ice-pilot's left hand, unconsciously lying a-top the white-covered cap on the settee beside him. Picking up the whisky bottle King filled the German's glass. 'Yes.'

'I have sinked one of dis company's ships, you know,' the ice-pilot said solemnly. 'Very sad, very good ship, maybe 'bout ten t'ousand tons, *ja*. Good ship . . . good people, but—' he shrugged again – '*c'est la guerre, n'est-ce pas*?'

Captain McGrath shifted uneasily in his chair as King leant forward, his face a mask of anticipation.

'And you were Captain of a U-boat, weren't you?'

The German patted the white-covered cap. '*Ja*.'

'Do you know the name of this ship you sunk?'

The ice-pilot's ruddy face cracked in a wide, boyish grin.

196

'*Ja, ja*, I know, sure. *Henry Hudson* 'bout ten t'ousand ton . . .'

But King was no longer listening, he had slammed down his glass and walked from the cabin. McGrath refilled the ice-pilot's glass.

'He had a bad time in the war, Pilot.'

'Sure, sure. We all have a bad time.'

They lay stopped all day. After his dinner the half-drunk German fell asleep in the small cabin set aside for his use. As the sun set, the bridge was left to Mackinnon, an apprentice and a lookout. They would not move until the wind shifted and a south-westerly was forecast for the morning. In the approaches to Målmo an ice-breaker was busy and Captain McGrath was confident in making port the following midnight.

But during the evening Mr King entered the ice-pilot's cabin with a heavy fire axe. He struck the German's head repeatedly until the man's skull was unrecognisable and the screams had gurgled into silence. Second Officer Mackinnon was the first on the scene.

The *Matthew Flinders* lay a-hull for the remainder of the night. Below, in the engine-room, George Reed and his men carefully bled the main fuel lines of air, closed off the empty diesel tank and then, with infinite patience and considerable difficulty, man-handled six forty-gallon steel drums out of the shaft tunnel. Rigging up a plastic pipe, they hand-pumped this small, reserve quantity of gas oil (actually kept for the emergency fuel pump, the lifeboat engine and two portable salvage pumps) into a header tank ready to restart the main engine. It was dawn before they had pressed up the main service tanks with ordinary fuel oil and an exhausted Reed climbed wearily to the bridge to report.

He found Stevenson up there with the Captain. Able Seaman Pritchard had made a pot of tea and Reed clung to the engine-room telegraph and gratefully accepted a mug.

'You've got half a dozen starts left if ah put her over to fuel oil reet after she fires this time, Captain.'

'Let's hope that's enough, Mr Reed,' Mackinnon said, heaving his bulk out of the corner.

They stared from the windows as the light grew, luxuriating in the warm sweetness of the tea like voluptuaries. Despite the angle of loll they had not rolled excessively during the last few hours and Reed remarked on this unexpected phenomenon, though he had to shout to do so.

'It's ironic, George,' Mackinnon bellowed back, 'but the sea has actually reduced in height as the wind has increased in strength. It no longer peaks and breaks, d'you see, lad? The wind won't let it, slices it off, smashes each wave to smithereens as it rises.

'Out there' – Mackinnon waved his hand forward where the outline of the heeling masts and sampson posts of the *Matthew Flinders* were dark diagonals in a grey blue – 'the air is no longer breathable. It's filled with salt spray. You could not stand it on your skin. It would burn you . . .'

And Reed gazed through the armoured glass as the light grew and looked upon a world that was full of the great roaring rush of air and sea co-mingled, a confusion in nature itself, back eddies of which flurried in through the smashed side window and the open doors of the exposed bridge wings.

He turned to Mackinnon, his face a boyish mixture of wonder and relief, for the ship seemed perfectly safe; battered, but safe. He had known in his heart of hearts she would be! This was the twentieth century and she was built for the trade. Yet the faces in the wheelhouse looked strangely sober, and it was odd that Captain Mackinnon had taken this trouble to explain to him.

'We're not out of the wood yet, George. Oh, she's comfortable enough at the moment, but we've been making leeway like a train for hours, beam on and dead before the wind . . .'

'I don't understand.'

198

'We're in the dangerous zone. We're going to need that engine of yours. We're being blown directly into the vortex.'

Mackinnon shouted the short, staccato sentences. Reed caught the look in Alex Stevenson's eyes and felt the flutter of real fear in his gut. He turned away and stared out at the impenetrable, spume-laden air, the very essence of the *taifun*, the 'great wind' of the China Seas.

Then he turned and went below.

CHAPTER THIRTEEN

Juggernaut

With the growing light Captain Mackinnon felt an increasing strength. So strong is the body's metabolism that even after a sleepless night in which the only rest had been momentary catnaps, in which tired muscles had adjusted constantly to support its weight on the heaving deck, and its ravaged organs had resisted the onslaught of the whisky, it reacted to the dawn of the new day.

For Mackinnon's conscious self this revival came with copious yawnings and a gritty irritation behind hot eyeballs which sizzled in the sockets of his skull. But, just as he had dutifully encouraged George Reed, his body clock now roused his own combative spirit.

Not that he actually felt better, far from it. Despite the tea he was still thirsty, he realised, and stiff as a board, but his mind sloughed off the metaphysical preoccupations of the night. The contact with Reed and the real world of immobilised engines had merely engendered a helplessness; the depressing knowledge that without the beating of her diesel heart, the ship was a hulk, a derelict, like the junk. And from somewhere down below the ominous thump of loose cargo sent a periodic tremor through the ship.

Suppose they could not get the engine going again? Reed would return to the bridge and report his failure, looking to Mackinnon to tell them what, in the last resort, they should do.

What *could* they do?

Mackinnon knew that, in the days of sail, even a dismasted ship was capable of being restored to basic movement by a jury rig. Even when her holds were awash she might be pumped, because her company could use the basic resources they found to hand.

Nor had the situation become entirely irredeemable in a steam or motor ship until recently. Mackinnon had heard of a case where an enterprising master had rigged wires from sampson post to sampson post, down both sides of the ship, each with running blocks controlled by ropes. Between pairs of these blocks he had stretched hatch tarpaulins as rough, trimmable sails, and the ship had made port, or at least within hail of a tug or two.

But the *Matthew Flinders* had Macgregor hatches, steel covers not canvas tarpaulins, and though she did not rely upon technology to the extent of her most modern competitors, she was beyond the redemption of her crew's ingenuity if Reed and his men failed.

Helplessness in the face of failure was the price mankind paid for the easement of their lives conferred by the wonders of science. Technology not only robbed men of their ancient skills, simple though they might have been, it laid them open to appalling hazard when it failed.

Mackinnon's newly roused spirit nearly foundered with the reflection. But the desire to do something triumphed. If they could not make the ship mobile, they must at least secure her in her immobility, giving her the chance to lie supine and watertight. Without engines it was their only chance and delay might cause the loose cargo, whatever it was, to burst through the ship's side. *That* would be disaster; the bottom line. They must avert the possibility at all costs. At that moment, Mackinnon set his hopes no higher.

'Another cup of tea, sir? And we've made some toast.'

Mackinnon turned. The three deck officers were on the bridge now, their faces grey in the dawn light, their white tropical shirts and shorts stained and torn. Stevenson was holding out a mug of tea. The smell of hot buttered toast brought a smile to Mackinnon's face.

'By heaven, that's most welcome.'

He sipped at the hot, sweet brew and took a slice of the toast Taylor offered.

'You look like bloody scarecrows,' Mackinnon said as he chewed.

'I feel like the bottom of a parrot's cage,' said Rawlings, the flippancy betraying his nervousness.

Mackinnon grunted, 'Your arm all right, Mr Taylor?' He nodded at the dirty bandage.

'It's okay, sir.' Taylor's reply was flat, toneless. Preoccupied and in the half-light, Mackintosh failed to notice the high-strung tension in the man's voice and bearing.

'Have you done something to your shoulder, Two-O?'

'Nothing much, sir. Gave it a wrench,' Stevenson answered sheepishly.

'Right. Well, we don't know how long Geordie Reed is going to be before he gets the main engines going—'

'*If* he gets them going,' interrupted Taylor, oblivious of having spoken aloud. Rawlings and Stevenson cast sidelong glances at the junior mate.

Mackinnon ignored the impertinence. 'So, here's what we've got to do . . .'

He had barely outlined his intentions when with a loud and startling jangle the telegraph pointers jerked round to *Stand by main engines*.

Jubilantly Mackinnon repeated the signal. Down below Mr Reed was ready.

'Right, one of you grab the wheel.' Taylor stepped forward while Rawlings went to the telephone and rang the mess-room for a seaman. 'Any one but Macgregor,' he bellowed into the mouthpiece.

Mackinnon stared out of the forward wheelhouse

windows. Rain and spray filled the air. Another ship, an island, a whole confounded continent might be a hundred yards ahead of them, but they would not know it. Even the radar was almost useless, the surrounding sea returning the echoes from wave tops in dense ranks.

'Here we go then. Hard a-port!'

Taylor repeated the order and spun the wheel. Sweating profusely, his fist slippery on the brass telegraph handle, his heart thumping in his breast and a worm of apprehension writhing in his lower gut, Mackinnon swung the handle backwards and then forwards, hard down against the stop: *Full ahead.*

'Shit or bust,' muttered Rawlings, still holding the mess-room telephone lest his shaking hand betray his fear.

From below the answering pointer jangled its reply.

In normal conditions they would have heard the hiss of compressed air, the faint, then growing rumble as the engine fired until the tremble of it permeated the steel hull. But they could hear nothing above the hideous boom of the wind, nor feel anything except the painful fluttering of their hearts. The tachometer needle lifted off its stop.

'She's answering!' Taylor's shout was triumphant. They watched the steady swing of the compass card, sensing the increased heel as the *Matthew Flinders* turned slowly into the wind, then fell if ease as she baulked and steadied, the wind on her port bow, her helm hard down.

'That's it, sir,' said Taylor, 'she won't come up any further.'

'Very well,' said Mackinnon, 'let's count our blessings. She's comfortable enough.'

And she was. Relief was clear on all their faces, the thrust of rudder and propeller balanced the mass of air built up to windward of the ship's bulk, holding her with the wind broad on her port bow. She was pitching again, and rolling less, though from below the thud, thud of loose cargo still demanded their attention.

Beside Rawlings the engine-room telephone rang. Rawlings nodded assent, said, 'Well done,' and relayed to Mackinnon:

'George reports all's well. We're back on fuel oil, sir.'

'Very well. Then let's get organised and secure this cargo without further delay. I've no desire to get caught in the eye. You know what to do . . .'

Able Seaman Pritchard loomed in the wheelhouse doorway. 'Come to take the wheel, Cap'n.'

Taylor handed over and the officers muttered their 'aye, ayes' before departing.

'What's it like below, Pritchard?'

'Bit of a pigsty, sir.'

'Much water got in?'

'Yeah, quite a lot. They're squee-geeing it down the alleyways and bucketing it out.'

'What about the woman?' Mackinnon asked, suddenly aware that he had forgotten about her.

'The Chief Steward sat up with her, I t'ink, Cap'n. She fell out of the bunk once, but he and the Bosun got her back in okay.'

'Christ!' Mackinnon muttered under his breath, making a mental note to ring down in a moment and order her given more morphine. Good old Freddie Thorpe, he thought; self-centred, not above a bit of graft and an expert practitioner of the trading of *cumshaw* for favours, he had nevertheless sat up with the patient.

'The kid's okay, too. Had the best kip of the lot of us.'

'The kid? Oh, the baby . . . who looked after it?'

'Braddock got broody, Cap'n. Filled the little bugger up wi' connie-onnie. He's back wid his own lot now, like.'

Mackinnon grinned, imagining the ugly, bronzed features of Able Seaman Braddock forcing condensed milk into a rose-bud mouth. Then, with a pang of intense pain at the reference to the baby, he turned away.

The group of men were roped together like mountaineers as

they made their slow way up the foredeck. The ship's attitude at a broad angle to the wind gave them some shelter up the starboard side, in the lee of the contactor houses. Fortunately they did not have far to go to reach the small access hatch beside the huge, heavy trackways for the Macgregor slabs which they dare not now open. The access hatches, one to each hold, were small, raised trap doors, protected from slopping water by a high steel coaming and secured by heavy dogs, like the door to the steering gear.

The *Matthew Flinders* was still shipping water, but it was not the green mass they had endured earlier, for the immense power of the wind flattened the sea, and though they waded through a foot or two of swirling seawater slopping about the deck, it was the wind that tore at them, a stinging, plucking force that was saturated with millions of tiny droplets and against the strength of which they were roped.

Taylor led, his bandaged arm not appearing to trouble him as he thrust himself forward. Rawlings, back in the shelter of the accommodation, had said, 'Right now, who's first?', making it clear the Mate's role was going to be supervisory. While Stevenson dragged a coil of flag halliard forward, Taylor had organised the first group.

'I'll take Braddock and Williams with the Bosun as anchor man. Okay?' he had bellowed. They had jostled for position, uncoiling the rope and flaking it out in the alleyway. 'You see it runs clear, sir,' Taylor ordered brusquely, surveying the streaming foredeck with the eye of a reconnoitring grenadier.

They had heard the bump-bump of the loose cargo and Rawlings had offered the opinion it was the heavy industrial cement mixers in Number Two 'tween deck.

When he was ready Taylor had checked the small VHF handset on its strap about his shoulders and turned to the Second Mate.

'Okay, Alex?'

'Okay.' Almost inaudible above the wind, Stevenson gave the thumbs up.

'I'll let you know the score and expect you up in support,' Taylor mouthed, agreeing the plan they had contrived in the wheelhouse.

Out on deck Taylor's party moved forward slowly, clawing their way along like ham film actors faking a cliff climb on a horizontal surface. Rawlings fed the long length of halliard dutifully through his hands while Stevenson, radio pressed to his ear, took occasional peeps round the corner of the accommodation, where the droplets of rain and spray stung his face. After a while he rolled back into shelter, his thumb jerking again.

'Reached the access hatch.'

It seemed they had to wait for hours, buffeted by the wind as it whipped in fits and starts, seeking them out to pluck them from their imperfect shelter. Then the handset crackled in Stevenson's ear:

'Mate's right. Bulldozers are okay, but the fucking cement mixers are going walkabout . . .'

The transmission suddenly ceased, then came to life again.

'Alex, d'you hear? Over.'

'Roger. Copy the cement mixers are problem. D'you want ropes or chain snotters?'

'Ropes – at least to start with.'

'Right. I'm on my way.'

The short lengths of mooring rope, six fathoms to a man, were wound round the shoulders of Stevenson's party and they hitched themselves up. Stevenson's shoulder ached, but he tried to ignore the pain, able to cope with all but the heaviest demands upon it.

'Off you go!' shouted Rawlings and Stevenson led the Carpenter and Macgregor forward.

Clear of the accommodation Stevenson stopped and then crawled, aware that the wind, passing over his curved back actually sought to *lift* him from the deck. They progressed through water which also threatened to sweep them into the scuppers as the ship lurched and rolled so that they were sodden as they inched forward dragging the weight of the ropes coiled about them. From time to time they stopped, gasping and clinging on to a ringbolt here or a hatch support there with no clear idea of how long it was taking them. Stevenson realised he was favouring his weak arm and as a consequence of this distraction the handset dangling round his neck outside the rope was dragging in the water.

After what seemed an eternity of struggle, they reached the access hatch in the lee of which crouched the Bosun, the halliard an umbilical to Taylor, Braddock and Williams below. Stevenson beckoned his men with their heavy coils of rope and indicated with his index finger they should follow him. The Carpenter nodded and gave the thumbs up; Macgregor contented himself by looking sour.

The hold spaces of the *Matthew Flinders* consisted of six hatches numbered from forward, beneath each of which extended a three-metre-high 'tween deck and then a deep lower hold. The bottom of the latter was formed by a double skin used as a fuel oil tank. In Singapore much of the cargo had been discharged from the 'tween deck. Exposed 'faces' of cargo for Hong Kong had been 'tommed off', shored up with heavy timbers and planks, a surprisingly effective, if time-consuming and expensive, method of preserving cargo stows. But where the bulldozers' own inertia combined with the heavy chain lashings had held against the worst ravages of the typhoon, the lighter rope lashings about the cement mixers had parted. It would have started with a small movement, a tiny, imperceptible sawing of the ropes, tensioned by twisted toggles of timber to form a 'Spanish windlass'. The lighter cement mixers were less stable than the massive, track-mounted 'dozers. The rolling had exaggerated their movement, increasing the sawing and slackening of the lashings, gradually casting them loose. As

Stevenson dropped from the dull grey light of the overcast morning into the stale, dusty air of the 'tween deck, lit by the orange pools of the intermittent cargo lights set behind grilles in the deckhead, he was overwhelmed by a sense of claustrophobia.

When Braddock plucked at his arm he almost jumped, then steadied himself.

'Third's over there.' Braddock pointed and Stevenson could see Taylor's grubbily white form dodging about a monstrous shape as it lurched and slid with a squealing of steel on steel and a shower of sparks that in themselves sent shivers of apprehension down Stevenson's spine.

'He wants to get a rope on each mixer, Sec. That's what he told me to tell yer. Once we've restrained 'em we can get some chains down 'ere.'

'Got it!'

Stevenson scrambled forward over a stow of cases of beer. In the airless 'tween deck, in marked contrast to the atmosphere on deck, a faint but insistent queasiness seized him. A melange of stinks, chiefly that of stale alcohol filled the available space. Uncoiling his length of rope he advanced towards Taylor who, he could now see, was, with Williams, circling the nearest of the three mixers.

'Look out!'

Taylor, wary as a hunter, had been watching his quarry and already sensed the coming movement of the ship as the *Matthew Flinders* began to climb a long swell and roll lugubriously to starboard. All at once the relative peace of the 'tween deck was shattered. The three loose cement mixers moved towards Stevenson, approaching from the after starboard corner of the 'tween deck. To his left a tumbled and crushed heap of cardboard cartons, their contents spewed across the deck and burst by successive impacts of the rogue mixers, had formed a cushion and clearly saved the vulnerable shell plating of the ship from the worst damage the mixers might have done.

208

'Here, Alex, quick!'

Dragging his rope clear of two of the lumbering juggernauts, Stevenson edged round them as they crashed together. Instantly Stevenson perceived the Third Mate's intention. One of the mixers had not quite broken free. A single strand of its original lashing had caught and it swung, not yet an agent of indiscriminate destruction. As he reached Williams and Taylor, they grabbed his rope and cast a double turn round the heavy vertical pillar that supported the deck above. After a few minutes exertion, interrupted by only a single threatening lurch of the other cement mixers, they had one of them secured.

'Okay,' Taylor yelled in triumph, 'now for number two!'

Freddie Thorpe propped the woman up and, with an arm about her shoulders, held the cup of hot, sweet and milky tea to her trembling mouth. He was sweating with the effort of the task, bracing his fat, overfed body against the bunk in an attempt to ease the buffeting of the ship's motion as the *Matthew Flinders* climbed laboriously over a succession of low, wind-shorn waves. As she finished the woman spoke, searching his rheumy eyes for some knowledge. Instinctively Thorpe nodded, setting the cup down and lowering the woman back on to her pillow. She too was sodden with perspiration.

'Your baby okay.' He cradled his arms and swung them back and forth. 'Okay.'

'Okay,' he thought the woman replied. As she closed her eyes he picked up the ampoule of morphine.

Behind him the empty cup fell to the deck and smashed.

When the officers had gone Mackinnon ventured cautiously from the wheelhouse to stare at the panorama daylight revealed. It was awesome. A world circumscribed in its visibility by the white mist, for salt spray transfigured the dark surface of the heaving sea, evidence of the titanic brutality of the wind as it scourged the sea's surface. It was as though air and sea were fused together into a new element by the catalytic effect of the wind. In this new element he, John Mackinnon, master mariner, commander of the motor vessel *Matthew Flinders*, found it difficult to breath. A feeling of panic gripped him as he gasped for breath, until sense drove him back within the wheelhouse where the pressure on his eardrums was bearable and the curtains of spray constantly hitting the windows obscured his view from the dreadful desolation of the scene beyond.

'Never seen anyt'ing like it before,' Pritchard remarked and Mackinnon, unnerved by the experience, was about to squash the Able Seaman's presumption when he realised Pritchard too was scared.

'Quite a blow,' he said, jamming himself into his observation post in the forward starboard corner of the wheelhouse.

He had to face the fact that, until the men below secured the loose cargo, he must remain hove-to. Assuming they eventually succeeded in achieving what was, he knew, a damnably dangerous task, a task for which all legislation respecting safety might be thrown aside, displaced by the invocation of 'the safety of the ship' clause in the Articles of Agreement between him as Master and them as crew at the long-ago signing on, he had to turn round again. And that, in the present wind strength, was demonstrably impossible. Their bow would not turn further into the wind and to pay off the other way, to 'wear ship', as the old sailing men would have said, meant exposing her to more violent rolling with no guarantee that they could hold her stern to the wind or, failing all else, return the ship to her present position of relative safety. Another engine failure could not be contemplated and so it became paramount in Mackinnon's mind to maintain the status quo.

But that now meant, he was certain, risking the ship in the typhoon's eye. The wind circulating the first upward rush of

210

damp tropical air, the polewards spin of coriolis and the initiation of the whirling storm system were simple enough to grasp. As the warm air rose, it cooled, releasing moisture in the form of the rain they had experienced and this cooling liberated energy, shooting the mass of tropical air higher and drawing in beneath it the cooler, damp air around the storm's path, fuelling its own violence and causing the great winds they now endured.

But a thing spinning tends to fly outwards, so that the indraught of the vacuous centre and the centrifugal force balance. The winds about the vortex of so violent a storm as Typhoon David, had undoubtedly created this tempestuous equilibrium, forming a vast, invisible column, impenetrable to the inrushing air, but into which the ship could be drawn and in which the waves, once released from the immeasurable suppression of the winds, would clash from every direction of the compass.

Then, only fate and her builders could save her . . .

'Now!'

Taylor, Stevenson, Braddock, Williams and the Carpenter circled the second cement mixer. As the men moved forward with the ropes looped between them, the ship lurched again. Instantly the disciplined cordon broke down and each man ran for the bolthole he had selected. Hanging back beneath the access hatch just outside the square of pale daylight and the view of the Bosun, Macgregor sniggered. No one appeared to miss him, so he told himself he had relieved Braddock as the link man between the 'tween deck and the Bosun above. He kept his head down.

The two loose cement mixers skidded together with a crash and rumbled jerkily downhill, bringing up separately, one embedded in the crushed beer stow, the other against a pillar with a jar that transmitted itself to Mackinnon again leaning his feverish forehead against the cool of the wheelhouse windows.

211

'Funny how the bastard things hit together but don't jam,' Taylor called to Stevenson as they emerged from cover again, ready for another attempt. It was their seventh, though they were not counting.

'Sod's law,' shouted Chippy as they jumped first one way and then the other in a hiatus of the ship's motion.

'Get away, get clear!'

'No! No! We've got it! We've got it!'

The confusion of shouts, their alarms and their triumphs sounded like battle cries in the sickeningly foetid air in which the dust rose beneath the imperfect lighting. The *Matthew Flinders* was pitching again, and rolling to leeward in a motion they had all by now become accustomed to, recognising the fact that her roll to windward was just sufficient to move the mixers back a little before the harsher, more violent roll to starboard sent them 'downhill'. Here they were beginning to cause real damage, for the pulverised cartons were already broken through to the ship's side.

No one was very clear quite what happened. All Stevenson knew was that he and Braddock, attacking the mixer nearest them, caught a turn around its drum which this time did not slip off and had it instantly belayed in a manner that suggested they should have achieved the thing with ease long before.

'Got the bugger!' They howled with elation.

'Now Chas . . .' In the half-light they closed on the second mixer.

Their triumph was short-lived. Taylor was infuriated by his failure to secure the cement mixers. He had almost done it three or four times, but a failure on the part of his team-mates to belay in time, or the twisting free of the bight he had caught about a section of the machine, or a simple missing of his throw, had maddened him to recklessness. It became paramount to his highly strung spirit to tame the things. They were as bestial as the germs he had debrided from the woman's flesh, as horrible as the filthy gonococci

212

that swarmed in his own blood, things to be fought to the uttermost point of defeat. He howled in his angry frustration as he assaulted the remaining cement-mixer yet again. It rumbled malevolently towards him as he stood his ground undaunted, a *matador* waiting to execute a flawless *veronica*.

This time . . .

Now!

He skidded in the mess of beer and filth swilling about the deck and went down heavily on one knee. Williams saw what was happening and shouted a warning. Taylor struggled to rise, caught one foot in a coil of the rope that stretched across to the Able Seaman and the Carpenter who already had a turn round the adjacent pillar. The cement mixer struck him on the breast. Badly winded, Taylor grasped it instinctively to prevent himself falling under it, seeking to fling himself clear as soon as he had drawn breath. Instead he was borne on its front as the ship leaned to leeward in a heavy roll.

Taylor's voice pierced the gloom in a scream of agony.

'Look to your steering,' Mackinnon grumbled, turning from his window.

'Haven't moved the wheel, sir,' Pritchard remonstrated. 'Had her hard over all the time. That bugger knocked her down a bit.'

Mackinnon grunted assent and Pritchard grinned, pleased with his own ability to match old Gorilla's *sang froid*.

'She's coming back now, sir,' he said as the ship recovered from her heavy roll.

The roll that pinned Taylor between the heavy industrial cement mixer and the ship's side prevented them from extricating him. If ever they had wanted the mixer to slide back across the deck it was now, but the thing stayed immobile, though a torrent of invective accompanied the slithering and puny attempts they made to drag it off the Third Mate.

213

Above the shouts, Stevenson became aware of Taylor's voice and he bent to see the Third Mate's face. It was a pale oval, held rigid by a rigor of neck muscles, distorted by pain and something else which he could not, at the time, put a name to.

'Alex . . .' Taylor's mouth gaped in a rictus of agony, the syllables attenuated into a gurgle.

'Chas, for God's sake!' Stevenson felt his own body shake, and then blood burst from Taylor's mouth and it went slack as his head fell to one side. Into Stevenson's mind slipped unbidden the phrase 'gave up the ghost', and the mystery brushed him in its passing. Then the heartless pragmatism of the seaman, fighting for the safety of his ship, asserted itself.

'Get the lashings passed! Now!'

'But . . .'

'Now, damn it! He's dead! There's nothing else we can do.'

The difficulty of holding the ship hove-to persuaded Mackinnon his assumptions were correct. They now had no alternative but to submit, nursing the ship through the coming hours as best they could. He hoped the working party could succeed before they entered the confusion of the vortex, and he peered down to where he could just make out a pair of figures moving aft, their oilskins beating their backsides as they crouched and half-crawled along. They had been toiling for over an hour and he was impatient for news.

'Sir?'

'Mmm?' Mackinnon turned to find Sparks behind him, holding a pink message form and with an ominous look upon his face.

'What is it?'

'Message, sir, from Hong Kong.' Sparks threw a significant look at Pritchard and Mackinnon dragged himself reluctantly from the comparative comfort of his corner. In

214

the chart-room Mackinnon cast about for his reading glasses.

'I seem to have lost . . . what does it say?'

'Basically, sir, they don't want our passengers in Hong Kong.'

'The authorities refuse us entry because we've picked up a load of boat people?' Mackinnon exploded incredulously. He took the pink chit but the letters were illegible to his tired and long-sighted eyes and he handed it back.

'Well, not quite, sir, not in so many words. The message is from Dentco but we're ordered to Shanghai direct. Apparently most of the cargo was originally for transhipment and now our resale—'

'God damn and blast the bastards! What do they actually say about the Vietnamese?'

'Er . . .' Sparks consulted the form. '*In view your unauthorised acquisitions divert direct Shanghai whence bulk of cargo destined*. They'll save themselves transhipment.'

'And dump those poor devils back where they started, more or less. It's a bloody outrage. How the hell are we going to tell them?'

'Hey, Cap'n . . .'

Both men looked round. Dripping wet and with a strange look upon his face, Able Seaman Macgregor stood in the wheelhouse door. He was gasping with the effort of reaching the bridge first, maintaining the illusion of having been at the forefront of affairs both for his own and others' benefit, and now he had his reward.

'What the hell do you want?' Mackinnon asked angrily.

'It's the Third Mate . . .' Macgregor paused, suppressing his excitement with difficulty.

'Well, man,' Mackinnon snapped impatiently, 'what about him?'

'He's dead.'

Time for Stevenson had slowed to a stupefied rate. The dissolution of the watch system and general disruption of the ship's routine had been caused by the unusual events of picking up the boat people and running into the typhoon. These circumstances had in some measure contributed to this sense of detachment, but it was the physical intrusion of the typhoon itself, the altering of atmospheric pressure, the power of the great wind, the violent motion it caused the ship, which created an alien environment in which time, as a measure of relative solar progress, was dissolved.

Everything took so long and was so exhausting: the struggle in the galley to get oil to drain from the sink; ordinary progress about the ship in which the very air was altered. The stale atmosphere of the accommodation with its taint of vomit and urine, of faecal matter and the noxious perspiration of fear, was at least breathable. And then the 'tween deck, like an anteroom of hell, had been full of mephitic gas in which they had performed prodigious exertions. The dim lights and the dust disturbed by the cement mixers and crushed beer cans sending out the sickly sweet effluvia of stale ale had torn at their lungs as they had finally secured the cement mixers with chains, working about Taylor's bloodily mangled corpse. Then, back on deck an age later, with the shock of loss and the brush with death to clog the rational mind, the salt-and-water-laden medium in which they gasped was not air but the ocean itself, lifted and less dense than in its familiar state, but undoubtedly the ocean. Stevenson had seen for himself the great breaking waves and their decapitation by the *taifun* and he was under no illusion as to the whereabouts of that white mass of foaming and tumbling water. He, like Mackinnon above him, experienced the alien sensation.

But, despite his exhaustion, it was chiefly reluctance that slowed his final climb to the bridge. He had found Rawlings reeling in the lifelines and met the Mate's eyes. Rawlings already knew; had sent the odious Macgregor to the bridge with the news. Stevenson was the last man back into the

216

shelter of the starboard alleyway. Words were unnecessary, for both officers felt a measure of guilt, their professional training making them receptive to such a reaction. Failure always carried its burden of responsibility and lodged easily in the souls of men bred to assume it. Macgregor felt no such constraint, hence his excitement in the presence of death. It had brushed him but chosen one of *them*.

Stevenson nodded his head upwards, towards the bridge, and Rawlings had nodded too, dragging the lifelines into the shelter of the accommodation. On his upward trek Stevenson had stopped at the smoke-room door.

The girl was sitting bolt upright, her back to the bulkhead, a look of abstraction upon her face. She did not see him, looking at her, and he was oddly bothered by what was in her mind's eye.

CHAPTER FOURTEEN

Vortex

At all costs, Mackinnon had told himself earlier, at all costs he must secure his ship. Now, with Ernie York already gone and another death to pay the old currency for the poet's 'admiralty', he wondered if it was enough. He had tempted providence, too, when he had spoken to Shelagh: 'We'll be in Hong Kong the day after tomorrow.'

But they had cheated the sea of one hundred and forty-six lives. Would he really have rather lost them and preserved Taylor and Ernie York? God alone knew the true secrets of a man's heart, for they were often obscure to the bearer, but he was relieved the engine had restarted, relieved to the point of a muck sweat!

And now Stevenson stood before him with the burden of his detailed report.

'I'm sorry, sir, we couldn't get him out.'

'I understand,' Mackinnon said, though his eyes asked the unspoken question.

An awful sensation of uncertainty swept Stevenson, then he remembered the enigmatic expression on Taylor's face. 'He was quite dead, sir.'

'Safety of the ship, mister,' Mackinnon rasped harshly, giving absolution and extreme unction before turning back to his window. 'We'll be passing through the vortex soon,' he went on, his back to the Second Mate. 'You'd better go and warn the refugees then let the crowd know. Don't forget the engine-room, or the greasers aft. I want a personal appearance, Mr Stevenson d'you understand?'

'Aye, aye, sir.'

Did the Second Mate understand? Mackinnon wondered. He had not needed to see Rawlings hanging back, coiling the lifelines, to know the Mate had already risen as far as he could to the occasion. Taylor had done bloody well, better than Mackinnon would have thought, and been sacrificed. Now there was only Stevenson. . . .

No,that was not true: there was Freddie Thorpe and George Reed, and Able Seaman Pritchard and Braddock and the stalwart Bosun, and Chippy, and Reed's Chinese greasers who they called by numbers at boat drill.

He could feel the soft, warm bundle, see the wrinkled face that looked like no one else, yet was indubitably Shelagh with a touch of his own mother.

The drinking had started the day he had received the news of the child's death. They had been in port; perhaps if they had been at sea it would have been different. He had asked Eastern Steam to relieve him, even telegraphed an offer to pay his own fare home to be with Shelagh; but the company had refused and he had been devastated. The binge had lasted four days before he came to himself and had exhausted the patience of others. They had covered for him, of course, out of pity and sympathy and friendship. A bloke could go on a bender if the cause was great enough and they were mostly absentee fathers, sentimentalists who understood the solace of the bottle.

But it happened again at the next port, and then the next, until they knew the worst was looming and the Master, a tolerant man, carpeted Mackinnon and warned him about alcoholism and dismissal, telling him he was the best Chief Officer in the line and now his reputation hung by a thread.

It straightened him for a bit, but then, with letters from

home that revived his bitterness, he relapsed ashore. They found him in a gutter, half-naked, his face bruised and cut, his wallet missing. He could not remember what had happened. The Master locked him in his cabin and stood his watch. He thought he had lost his job, but the Master proved a true friend and gave him a final chance. Mackinnon pulled back from the abyss. Despite the company's heartlessness, he had subsequently proved unswervingly loyal.

Long afterwards he had asked his commander why he had been so forgiving. 'Because if we had been in an office or a factory,' the Master had said, 'you'd have gone sick. Here you can never leave the job.'

Even now the memory made him shudder.

Stevenson went directly to the smoke-room. His shoulder hurt badly, for he had further strained it in the fight with the cement mixers. He was absurdly glad to be going to find Tam, glad of the excuse Mackinnon had given him, 'to find the interpreter and get her to tell them they would be all right soon, that although it was going to be very uncomfortable for a few more hours, the ship was very, very strong. Be confident and reassuring.' Mackinnon had concluded.

She was not in the smoke-room. The old woman said something, her gold teeth flashing in the electric light, and pointed. He went aft and found her in the alleyway, talking to two Vietnamese men. As he approached they caught sight of him and the three fell silent. It was obvious he was intruding.

'You okay?' he asked her, feeling far from confident and reassuring, remembering the loose ammunition clip.

She tossed her lank hair back. 'Sure.'

'I come from the Captain,' he began portentously, looking from one to the other, not liking the blank, uncommunicative expression in Tam's face or the outright hostility of the two men. One had his hand in the pocket of

220

his slacks and the angular outline of a bulky object made Stevenson's mouth run dry. 'We will have very bad time for about four or five hours' – he held up his fingers – 'but soon typhoon pass and everything will be okay.' He smiled, a thin, insincere grimace. 'Then we go Hong Kong.'

'Hong Kong?' one of the men asked, then fired a question at Tam. She asked: 'We go to Hong Kong?'

'Of course,' Stevenson said, then the second man snapped something and spat on the deck. As Stevenson stood uncomprehending the three of them pushed past him and left him staring after them.

'You were on the fucking bridge when we broached,' Pritchard, who had been relieved on the wheel, accused Macgregor, his finger stabbing at the Scotsman. Braddock stood beside him and the other men in the mess-room, halfway through an extempore breakfast of cornflakes and tea, grew silent.

'Aye, and we've got to stand your bloody trick for you,' one of them added.

'You're no bleedin' seaman, Rob Roy. You're shit!'

Macgregor smirked. 'You smell like what you're treated like,' he said obscurely, 'an it wasna my fault we broached. That daft bastard Mackinnon—'

'What would you know about it?' Pritchard said contemptuously. 'You couldn't piss in a swimming pool.' He exchanged glances with Braddock. Macgregor had hazarded the ship and with it all their lives.

'I'm going to see how that nipper is,' Braddock said.

'I'm coming wid yer.'

But Macgregor refused to rise to the insults. He had bigger things on his mind.

'What d'you mean "conspiratorial"?'

'I don't know, sir, it was just a feeling. Up to now the girl was quite friendly.' He paused, then went on, 'But in the

221

presence of those two men, she seemed suddenly the opposite.'

'And one of them had a gun?'

Stevenson shrugged. 'Again, it's only a hunch, sir, but I'm pretty sure. I can't ignore it. We know it's a possibility.'

'We do indeed.' Mackinnon's voice trailed off, then he thought of something. 'You say they asked about us going to Hong Kong?'

'Yes.'

'I wonder why they asked that. You'd already told 'em we were bound there, hadn't you?'

'Yes, I think so, sir.'

A nasty suspicion was forming in Mackinnon's mind. He nodded. 'Right then, mister, search 'em, search every one of them and disarm them.'

'Me, sir? Or Mr Rawlings?'

'I haven't seen the Mate, Mr Stevenson, so I want you to do it. Get the Bosun and Carpenter to help you, otherwise keep it as low key as you can. Get the girl to interpret. I don't want any misunderstandings.'

'Aye, aye, sir.'

'By the way, Mr Stevenson.' Mackinnon beckoned him into the chart-room and lowered his voice. 'For your ears only, but we've received orders to proceed to Shanghai.'

'Shanghai? But that means. . . .'

'Exactly.'

'Jesus!'

'Go on, get on with it and if you see the Mate, tell him I'd like a word.'

He almost tripped over Tam. She was with Braddock and Pritchard, cradling the baby in her arms. The wrinkled face peered from a swathing of blanket. Her two boyfriends seemed to have disappeared. The contrast with the last time he had seen her not ten minutes earlier was marked. The quartet were sitting on the steps of the main stairway, like a

222

small social group waiting for a photographer. A thin film of water still trickled about their feet. They were laughing together, though Stevenson noted a shadow pass over Tam's face as she saw who it was stepping down past them.

'Can I speak with you a moment please,' he said. 'I have a message from the Captain for your people.'

'I already tell them about everything all right.'

'No, this is more important.'

Tam stood unsteadily as the ship rolled. 'I'll take the baby,' Braddock volunteered.

'No, it okay. Baby sleep.'

Stevenson put his hand out to steady her, forgetting it was his injured arm. The pain of her sudden weight made him wince, but she drew sharply away from him.

'Ask Chippy and the Bose to come here, please,' he said to Braddock.

'Okay.' The two seamen shuffled reluctantly away and Stevenson turned to the girl. She looked very uneasy, as if frightened to be alone with him.

'Listen Tam, you must interpret for me. I am going to take you into the saloon and speak to the men. I think – the Captain thinks – someone . . . one of you people, has a gun; perhaps more than one. D'you understand?'

Her pale face had drained of colour and he saw her long throat undulate as she swallowed.

'D'you understand?' he repeated.

For a moment she stood, eyes downcast, then she looked up at him. 'Alex, you tell me ship go Hong Kong, yes?'

He nodded, fearing what was coming. 'Yes, I told you.'

'Is true?' she asked directly, setting aside any recognition of the subtleties of tense as a preliminary to explanation. Slowly he shook his head. 'No. Ship now go Shanghai.'

She jerked as though he had struck her. Her large eyes widened as she backed away, and then she turned and was running aft bouncing off the bulkhead as the *Matthew Flinders* rolled, and the alleyway was full of the baby's wailing.

'Shit!' muttered Stevenson vehemently.

'Did you make her an offer, Sec?' Macgregor grinned from the far end of the alleyway, but vanished when the Bosun and Carpenter appeared. Stevenson was caught up in the necessity of instructing the petty officers.

They started with the saloon. The Bosun and Carpenter closed off each of the two doors and stood impassively while Stevenson strode forward and motioned for all the men to stand. Anger lent a grim purposefulness to his task. After turning over their pathetically few bundles he frisked each man in turn, as he had seen done on the movies. Their limbs were thin as sticks under their cotton trousers, their ribbed chests bare of holsters, their armpits sticky with nothing more sinister than sweat. Once he drew back sharply from a young man woken from sleep, his erection rigid. The ensuing laughter defused what might, in its aftermath, have been unpleasant. He found no guns and, smiling as courteously as he was able, he thanked them. Only as he left did he realise neither of the men he had seen earlier with Tam had been among those searched. Then, as the three white men were leaving, the two missing Vietnamese burst into the saloon.

'What for you do this?' one of them demanded in passable pidgin. Struck in the back by the imploding door handle the Bosun had the man spun round and spread-eagled against the bulkhead in a trice. Frisking him he straightened and shook his head. The other man, his hands voluntarily lifted above his head, was equally devoid of arms.

Stevenson went up to the first. 'You savvy English, eh? Okay, we check. Make everything okay.' Then he led the trio from the saloon and left a babel of voices noisily debating the intrusion.

'Do we get to do that with the women?' queried Chippy facetiously.

Stevenson sighed. 'I suppose we'd better.'

224

But it was a half-hearted affair, despite the explanation rendered by Tam to ease the embarrassment of both parties. As he left the smoke-room, Stevenson caught the girl's eyes and held his hands up in an eloquent and hopeless shrug. But as an appeal it was a useless gesture; Tam merely looked away.

Stevenson escaped to the wilderness of the upper deck.

Immediately he noticed the change. Emerging on deck it was lighter, the mastheads no longer seemed to scrape the heavy overcast. He caught sight of a glimpse of the sun, a pale disc, but visible again as the fractus edged away. Against it a shape, ragged, batlike, then another, and another, a hideous nightmare of exhausted birds flopping like filthy rags tossed out of the sky; the grey and white of sea birds, and the brilliant greens, iridescent blue and scarlets of land birds. Unnerved, Stevenson stood for a moment, aware too that the wind had dropped and the ship's motion had become irregular.

Climbing towards the boat-deck, only half-comprehending what had happened and sensing again that elemental shift in the relationship of air and water, he realised the spray had fallen back, that a vague and misty horizon was visible. The surface of the sea no longer wore the scourged, abraded appearance it had done; instead its battered waves seemed to gather themselves, not wind-driven and tumbling crests, but highly charged repositories of kinetic energy released from the thrall of the *taifun*.

On the bridge ladder he paused and turned, scanning the surface of the ocean. This was the very eye of the storm, and as if to confirm his diagnosis the sun finally broke through. Looking upwards he could see the sky, a mighty dome of cobalt blue edged by a great mass of towering cloud, a huge curtain of cumulonimbus on a gigantic scale.

All about the ship the sea was suddenly blue and white and the comparative silence was unnerving after the hours of wind-rushing noise.

'Is this the vortex, sir?' he asked Mackinnon as he slid back the wheelhouse door and met the Captain's drawn face.

'Only the edge, laddie, only the edge. The worst is yet to come.'

Stevenson looked at the helmsman. He was steering a course again, and though the *Matthew Flinders* rolled and wallowed and threw her bow in the air and continued to shoot curtains of spray and ship the occasional sea, her motion, bad enough in normal circumstances, was nothing to what it had been earlier. It was clear to Stevenson that Mackinnon had his ship under command again and was making north and east as fast as possible to cut his way out of the typhoon as it moved west-north-west.

'Did you find anything?' Mackinnon asked.

'Nothing, sir.'

'You checked everyone?'

'Yes.' Stevenson paused, remembering. 'Oh, except the woman you operated on.'

Mackinnon shook his head. 'I've just had word from Freddie. He's been with her all night.' The Chief Steward had also let him know the woman had had another dose of morphine sulphate. 'What about the baby?'

'The baby, sir?' Comprehension dawned in Stevenson's eyes. Without a word, he turned and ran below, banging from bulkhead to bulkhead, bruising his shoulder again, his heart in his mouth. Of course! The baby . . .'

He was convinced he had been deceived, convinced Tam had been holding the gun in the child's blanket even as she had talked to him. Why else had she looked so guilty? Why else had she refused Braddock the bundle? And why else had she reacted the way she had when he told her they were bound for Shanghai, not Hong Kong.

Now he would have to confess to Mackinnon the refugees knew of the re-routing, knew it from himself, to whom Mackinnon had imparted the news in confidence.

It became imperative that he discover the gun.

226

She was in the smoke-room, sitting where he had seen her earlier, back straight against the bulkhead, staring in front of her. What *was* she seeing? Her village under the nipa palms, the dusty road on its low dyke, the rice paddies spread out on either side and the range of blue mountains in the distance? Or a noisy, teeming street in Saigon; a street of endless comings and goings, of jostling and haggling.

To his relief the swaddled baby was still in her arms, though it whimpered quietly.

'Tam.'

She looked up at him, but no warmth kindled in her eyes. She merely gazed at him as he squatted down next to her. The old woman in the corner sucked in her cheeks and muttered to herself.

'Tam,' he repeated, his hands going out for the baby, 'you hide gun, eh?'

She thrust the baby at him and it stirred, crying as Stevenson took it. The blanket concealed nothing more than a damp patch. Sheepishly he handed the baby back to her and stood up.

'You tell me lie,' she snapped.

'No . . .'

'You tell me ship go Hong Kong.' Her voice was sharp with accusation, betrayal.

'Yes.' He nodded vigorously. 'Ship go Hong Kong, then – he held up his hand to stop her protest – 'then we have radio message, just now, savvy? I didn't know when I spoke to you before. We have a change of our orders,' he went on, seeing her expression alter and abandoning the attempt to tell her in pidgin. 'I came and told you when I knew.' He switched to the offensive, dropping down on his haunches beside her and lowering his voice. 'Tam, those two men. They had the gun, yes? They told you to hide it, didn't they?'

For a moment she stared at him impassively and his heart sank. 'I not want to go Shanghai,' she said. 'Everybody all finish.' She was silent, her eyes imploring him to understand

227

what would happen to them. 'Okay Hong Kong bad; maybe prison camp but not – not finish.' She whispered the last word. Stevenson thought of Taylor's dead face.

'Those men,' he began, but Tam interrupted.

'Not good men, Alex, no, but they maybe fight for us.' She paused, then added, 'Maybe you fight for us too, maybe you not let me and' – she indicated the whimpering bundle – 'baby go back to Communists in Shanghai.'

Stevenson could not bear the look in her eyes. What could he do? Whatever happened his loyalties lay with Mackinnon.

'The gun,' he persisted, 'where is the gun?'

She lowered her eyes, aware she had lost. 'Ask Phan Van Nui.'

Deeply troubled, Stevenson climbed once more to the bridge. The ship was moving with an increasingly erratic motion. He was too late, too involved, to carry out his encouraging mission to the engine-room.

'No luck?'

'Not yet, sir, but,' he temporised, thinking of the two Vietnamese men running into the saloon in mock outrage, 'I think they've hidden it somewhere.' He hesitated, knowing he would have to confess he had inadvertently let the refugees know their destination was Shanghai.

'That's bad,' Mackinnon mused. 'I think they know by now that we are not going to Hong Kong.'

'Sir?' Stevenson frowned.

'When Sparks brought the message about our diversion, Macgregor overheard us discussing it.'

Relief flooded Stevenson. 'Yes, they know, sir,' he said flatly, confirming the Captain's deduction.

'There's always one rotten apple in the barrel,' Mackinnon said, and Stevenson's self-esteem shrivelled under this vicarious disapproval. 'Anyway, we've got to get through this lot yet. Did you find the Mate?'

'No, sir, I haven't seen him.'

'Checked his cabin?'

'No.'

'You'd better have a look.'

Rawlings was fast asleep, spread-eagled on his bunk, his face slack, almost boyish in its innocent detachment from responsibility. Stevenson gazed at him for a moment, recalling his escapade with his niece, Dawn Dent; 'Double-D' the crew had nick-named her for her nubility. It took all sorts, Stevenson thought.

'Leave him be for a bit,' Mackinnon said, staring again at the depressed needle of the aneroid barometer. 'He'll wake up soon enough.'

And they were not long left in their situation of relative comfort, for as they moved across the vortex and it, in its turn, moved over them, the residue of the wind in which they had been hove-to sent the waves in towards the centre. For some twenty minutes, as they passed out of the wind through the invisible 'wall' bordering the typhoon's eye, this continued. Then, imperceptibly at first, cross swells ran in, the sea began to heap, to fling itself in the air as unseen waves collided with an increasing turbulence. After the pressing violence of the great wind, all now seemed a random of chaos.

The *Matthew Flinders* was flung about, her hull protesting as a violent roll terminated abruptly in a premature counter-roll, only to turn with a monstrous jerk which bodily twisted her into a sky-climbing pitch from which her suddenly unsupported bow fell with an immense, jarring crash.

There were no harmonics in this anarchy of water, nothing recognisable as a pattern of waveform, nothing in the least predictable beyond the knowledge that the vast energy the storm had unleashed on the surface of the sea, an energy which unimpeded could send an ocean swell from one side of the Atlantic to the other, had concentrated its power to propel a gyration of swell waves to a small centre perhaps twenty or thirty miles across.

Mackinnon clung to the handles of the wheelhouse windows. It was no wonder that the combination of low pressure and the inward heaping of the sea could raise the very sea level by estimated heights of sixty to seventy feet! Indeed, he knew of a ship that had been carried over a shoal which would normally have ripped the bottom out of her. He thought of the words of the psalmist: *They that go down to the sea in ships and occupy their business in great waters; these men shall see the works of the Lord . . .*

Mackinnon watched the foremast whip back and forth across the blue of the sky with its table, making of it an elongated cross. 'Let's hope the builders made a good job of her,' he said to no one in particular.

The extreme erratic violence of the ship's motion increased the misery of all on board. Only those with strong stomachs and good sea legs could move about. Without exception the boat people lay down, many choking up their recently eaten food so that the reek of fresh vomit was added to the stench of human neglect filling the accommodation. Rawlings woke, as Mackinnon had predicted, but he dragged his mattress on to the deck and fell upon it, dead to all thought of duty, aware someone would call him out if he were wanted. Freddie Thorpe was driven from his patient's side by sheer exhaustion. He also crashed on his deck-laid mattress, as did the remainder of the crew who were not on duty.

At their posts there now remained only a handful of men. On the bridge were Captain Mackinnon and the duty seaman at the helm; Sparks in the radio-room patiently waited for a further incoming signal he knew was due from the inclusion of the *Matthew Flinders*'s call sign on the last traffic list transmitted by Hong Kong Radio. Far below, in the shaft tunnel, Greaser Number Twenty-three, Wang Ho Lee, tirelessly worked his way along the shaft bearings while his colleague, Chan Xao Ping, clung like a limpet above the generators and main engine and checked dashpots and tundishes with an impressive devotion to his duty. Below him, on 'the platform' beside the engine controls and the terminus of the telegraph, George 'Geordie' Reed stood listening to the beat of his engine. Somewhere above him Assistant Engineer Curtis again checked the level of the service tanks.

'Wi' her tossing herself aboot like this, ah doon't want no more fooking air locks,' Reed had told him, 'or ah'll hae yoor fooking bollocks for a necktie.'

Without seeking permission, Stevenson had left the bridge. Phan Van Nui, he guessed, was one of Tam's boyfriends. He wanted to call him an 'intimidator', but he was no longer sure. He had been a fool to think a slight rapport could signify anything.

East was east, and west was fucking west, he thought savagely.

He went first to the radio-room. He had no real idea why, beyond acknowledging he should perhaps have been here earlier. Sparks removed one of his headphones.

'Hullo, Alex,' he said. 'Bad news about Chas.'

'Yes.'

'You were . . .?'

'Yes, I saw it. Poor bastard.'

'He wasn't a very happy bloke.'

'No. I wonder if any of us are.'

Sparks pulled a rueful face. 'Soldier philosophers are to be admired as historical heroes; sailor philosophers are a pain in the arse.' He smiled, taking the sting out of the rebuke. 'He's at peace now, anyway, out of this bloody mess.'

Stevenson was about to remonstrate and then he recalled the expression on Taylor's face, the expression he could not quite define, that had mystified him. 'Yes,' he found himself saying, 'he is.'

'You've heard the news?' Sparks went on, ignoring the warning as to the confidentiality of radio telegrams that was framed under glass on the adjacent bulkhead.

231

Stevenson nodded. 'Shanghai? Yes. The boat people have got wind of it, too.'

'It's fucking Dent's,' Sparks said, 'probably James Dent himself. I was told he'd be out in Hong Kong when we arrived. He'd happily do the government's dirty work for them. Probably sucked his way to dinner with the Governor. There's nothing that bastard likes better than kicking arse. He must get a great big stiffie out of it.'

'I think there may be trouble with the boat people,' Stevenson interrupted, 'once we're out of this lot. They've got a gun of some sort. It's my guess they might try and take over the ship.'

Sparks's mouth dropped open. 'You're kidding.'

'No, I'm not. I wish I was.'

'Does the Old Man know?'

'Yes. I think he's guessed what might happen.'

'What's he going to do?'

Stevenson shrugged. 'I've no idea; but I thought I'd better put you in the picture.'

'Thanks,' replied Sparks ironically. 'What about Randy?'

'Rawlings is crashed out,' the Second Mate said, 'and frankly I don't think he's going to be a lot of good.'

'No,' said Sparks, 'he's a bit of a broken reed at the best of times.' He smiled again. 'You won't forget old Sparky, Alex, will you, if things start to hum? Perched down here at the after end of the boat-deck I'm a bit isolated and they may take it into their heads to fuck up this lot.' He gestured at the radio sets before him.

Stevenson grinned. 'Okay, I savvy.'

'I mean I'd hate to end up like poor Chas. My wife still loves me – at least so she says in her letters.'

Outside, on the boat-deck, Stevenson almost trod on the fluttering of an exhausted bird. It was a parakeet of some kind, a tangled bundle of brilliant colours, one wing broken and its long tail feathers bent. He stood for a moment staring at the unfortunate thing, then looked out over the wild

232

confusion of the sea. He had never seen anything like it, for it beggared all description, a leaping, heaving mass, the tall columns of imploding waves sparkling in the benign sunshine.

Suddenly he made up his mind. Turning forward, he began to run.

CHAPTER FIFTEEN

A Roosting of Pigeons

A man running on a wildly bucking deck experiences two sensations: that of weightlessness as the deck drops from under him; and that of weighing far more than mere avoirdupois as it changes and rises rapidly beneath him. The first makes him run on tiptoes, the second causes his knees to buckle; in neither case has he control of himself, for a lateral movement of the ship may set an unanticipated sideways component into the equation of balance, and a deck has too many excrescences to allow unimpeded movement. Thus Stevenson fetched up sickeningly against a boat-hoisting winch, just as Macgregor had done hours earlier.

When he reached Captain Mackinnon's cabin, he sank to his knees on the damp carpet before the ship's safe. Catching his breath he tried to recall the combination number. Miraculously the safe opened at his first attempt. Lifting out the revolver he carefully inserted the handful of bullets and snapped the magazine into the handle. Finally he put the weapon inside the waistband of his uniform shorts and buttoned his shirt over his belly.

Outside in the alleyway he paused by Rawlings's door. Then he knocked and, opening it, put his head into the Mate's stuffy cabin.

'Mr Rawlings,' he called. Stretched out on his mattress the

Mate stirred.

'Eh? What is it? What's the time?'

'I think the Old Man could do with a relief on the bridge,' Stevenson said, 'or some moral support. We're in the vortex. I think you should be up top.'

'What about the Third Mate?' Rawlings asked, still fuddled with sleep.

'He's dead,' snapped Stevenson, bringing Rawlings to his senses, before backing out and slamming the door. He peered for a moment up the stairwell to the chart-room. He could hear the low buzz of conversation, presumably Mackinnon and the helmsman. He slipped below.

He thought of all the places the Vietnamese might have gained access to: the gyro-room, the stores alleyway. He quizzed the assistant stewards, but no one had released a key or opened a locker for hours. The galley, a worse shambles than on his earlier visit, yielded nothing, and he probed yard after yard of cable tray with a mounting hopelessness. His task daunted him, for there were so many hiding places on a ship.

He clambered gingerly through the heavy engine-room door, its weight swinging dangerously against his injured shoulder. A wave of hot air and a thunderous noise met his entry. It was to Stevenson, despite his long years of sea service, an alien place. The strict lines of demarcation drawn up by the twin, inter-related disciplines of the British Merchant Navy existed to its bitter end. Class, tradition, personal inclination and sheer English snobbery ensured it.

Thus, even in the extremity of near-desperation, Stevenson entered the huge space, as big and awe-inspiring as an English mediaeval parish church, with a sense of being a stranger. For him to search the vast labyrinth was impossible, but to communicate his apprehensions to Reed was no more than common sense demanded.

As Mackinnon stood on his bridge, Reed still occupied his own command post: the platform. Stevenson shouted the

235

nub of his intelligence and Reed shook his head and pointed upwards.

'Ah can see the engine-room door from here. Every time it opens ah can tell – the draught alters a bit. You become used tae these things. Nobody's been below, Alex.'

Somewhat reassured, Stevenson made his way aft along the shaft tunnel. Number Twenty-three Greaser nodded and smiled.

'Okay?'

'Okay.'

He climbed upwards through the escape into the sodden squalor of the poop. Here Chinese faces greeted him.

'No good,' said Number One Greaser, 'plenty water come in. No good. Come Hong Kong-side, go home. Ship finished. No good. Big wind no good. Company no good. Bastards Ay-ah . . .' and he swore a complex Cantonese oath, continuing all the while to bale out his cabin.

'You okay, Number One?'

'Oh, sure, Secon' Office' all okay.'

'You see boat people come aftside?'

'Boat people?' the old man queried incredulously. 'Fucking boat people plenty no good,' an they too were united genealogically with the oath. Admiring the greaser's incredible fortitude, Stevenson made his slow way back to the accommodation via the shaft tunnel and the engine-room while the *Matthew Flinders* crashed and banged her wracked way across the airless void of the vortex.

Guilt, Mackinnon knew, wore a man down more surely than anything. It acted upon the soul with a persistent corrosive power.

If he was susceptible to the workings of conscience.

The qualifying afterthought made him smile wryly to himself. Mackinnon could see little guilt about Rawlings.

'Thought I'd come up and see if you wanted a relief, sir,' he drawled.

'Very kind of you,' Mackinnon replied dryly, undeceived.

'We should be out of the eye soon, the cloud's beginning to build up ahead,' Rawlings went on.

'Aye, it is. It'll be a head wind and we'll keep her away to the north-east until the wind moderates to an eight or nine before we haul round to the north.'

Rawlings moved forward and jammed himself in the port forward corner of the wheelhouse in imitation of his commander. 'Wind's stripped miles of paint off the derricks,' he remarked.

'So it has,' said Mackinnon unmoved from his own vantage point. For a moment they were silent, both thinking it no longer mattered, then Rawlings asked:

'Are you going below, sir?'

Mackinnon shook his head. 'Not yet.'

'Well, there's no point in both of us—'

'I quite agree,' broke in the Captain. 'I'd like you to go below and have a look at the woman.'

In the absence of the Mate, Captain Mackinnon resumed his train of thought. Characteristically, he rejected the theory his over-active brain was erecting as a carapace to cover its own inner secrets. Guilt was not universally destructive; it was not even universally acknowledged, for no one of the Captain's generation was able to grant a grain of goodness to *all* mankind. He was dissembling: guilt lay heavy on the Captain's ageing soul. Guilt had once driven him to the verge of alcoholism. Guilt had sprung the metaphysical locks of his fate-laden philosophy, guided his thinking as he jostled his lonely conscience through the current crisis wherein he pitted his skill against the typhoon. He recalled the ideas he had had earlier, seeking to drive them further, closer to the truth.

In order to make judgements a man needed more than experience, experience merely gave him options. What he had drawn on in the past hours was more than cunning, in its original sense, the sense that linked it with knowledge. What

237

had guided him was his intuition, his own luck, a sense bounded by its own restraint: his guilt.

Again and again, in these moments of enduring, of waiting until the ship battled her way out of the typhoon, his mind went over and over these abstract obsessions: how things turned full circle, of cause and effect; luck and guilt, opportunity and misfortune; and overall – fate. Somewhere – Conrad, wasn't it? – he had read that life was a 'droll thing', a 'mysterious arrangement of merciless logic for a futile purpose'.

The concept chilled him.

No landsman could ever truly know the loneliness of the sea life; how omnipresent was the job, how few the distractions. If a man's conscience was troubled, guilt grew like a wart upon his nose, conspicuously, unavoidably. And from an early time Captain Mackinnon had acquired his measure of guilt to hump about the world's oceans; no very great thing, perhaps to a landsman. No very great thing to many seamen either; a peccadillo, one might say, except the indiscretion was passionate and, in its own intense way, sincere. Its power to trouble him lay in this sincerity; its power to destroy, in the fact that it was inimical to his sworn love for Shelagh.

He had for many years enjoyed his share of inconclusive skirmishes with the whores of Hong Kong and Japan; the willowy, long-haired Chinese in their brocaded silk *cheongsam*, the dainty, erotically tantalising Japanese in either traditional *kimono* or cheap copies of Yankee fashion. On a cold night in Yokohama, the tiny, brightly lit bars, each with its glowing brazier, hot towels and the solicitous attentions of willing and concupiscent women, were a welcome distraction. Jubilant *mama-san* welcomed the foreign seafarers like Trojan heroes and their blandishments were well-nigh irresistible. Mackinnon recalled, too, the lost world of Blood Alley in Shanghai, closed down by the crusading Communists not long after he had been bombed in the Whang-Po on the old *James Cook*. There a man, no matter how perverse his tastes, or how far gone in debauchery, could find satisfaction for the most bizarre appetite.

For the young Mackinnon most of this had been no more than a colourful backcloth, something to be enjoyed as an accompaniment to a run ashore, but never indulged in seriously, for at his shoulder stood the constant shadow of Shelagh. Nothing, he had consoled himself when the temptation became unbearable, was worth losing her, for she had come into his life after he had faced death in an open boat and only a fool would hazard so obvious an intervention of fate.

But, in the end, Mackinnon had been a fool.

It was his first voyage as Chief Officer. As almost her last influential act before her death, the elderly Mrs Dent had sanctioned his appointment to the *Sir Robert Fitzroy*, Eastern Steam's newest cargo-liner. They had completed their discharge of the outward cargo at Kobe and been ordered into dry dock, since the ship was suffering problems with her tail shaft and stern gland. There they had suffered delay, first from a typhoon, then from the prolonged attempts of the original builders to evade responsibility for a scored shaft. The wranglings of solicitors in the distant United Kingdom drew a curtain of idleness on the ship; her crew awaited the outcome uncomplaining, for the bright lights, the girls and the cheap shops of post-war Japan beckoned. Eventually even Mackinnon's pretence to being busy could be sustained no longer. A night in a bar loosened his appetites. Warily he refused a second. Instead he took a train to Kyoto, intent on enjoying the sights. The young woman sitting opposite him was dressed in the western fashion with a cotton print dress and high-heeled shoes. Her black hair fell to her shoulders with the seductive curve of a permanent wave copied, Mackinnon thought, from Jean Harlow. She was reading a copy of the *Mainichi Daily*

Times, betraying a knowledge of English, and his restiveness must have communicated itself to her, for despite the demure attention she paid to her newspaper their eyes met several times. Though both shied nervously away, this mutual avoidance in so confined a space inevitably caused Mackinnon's nervously crossed legs to brush her precious nylons.

'I'm sorry,' he stammered as she lowered her paper, sensing antipathy from the other occupants of the carriage, sober, serious middle-class Japanese in dark *kimono* and business suits.

'Okay,' she said, her accent American. 'You are English, *né*?'

'Yes,' he replied.

'But not a tourist, you have not any camera,' she said, 'and not army.'

'No.' He smiled. Her accent and her deductions, together with her aping of western fashion, reminded him that her contact with westerners was a result of American occupation. He tried to place her age. Ten years his junior? 'Well, perhaps today I am a tourist,' he admitted. 'I am going to see Kyoto.'

'*Ah-so*. Kyoto is very beautiful.' She smiled wistfully. 'So, I think you come here on ship.'

'Yes.'

'And you are the Captain, *né*?'

'Not quite.'

She frowned. 'You are Lieutenant-Number-One?'

He nodded. 'More or less.' She shook her head at the idiom. He leaned forward in his seat, aware of the increase in hostility the conversation was generating in the compartment. 'In a British ship, a cargo ship,' he added, eager to dissociate himself from all engines of war. Then, inspired, he reached for her paper. 'May I show you?'

He found the shipping pages and pointed to the announcement that the MV *Sir Robert Fitzroy* was dry-docked but it was anticipated she would be open for loading in a week's time and that prospective shippers should contact her agents.

'*Ah-so.*' She pronounced the unfamiliar syllables of the ship's name. Gently he corrected her.

'Fitz-roy,' she said carefully. 'This is English name, yes?'

'Yes. Your English is very good. Do you read the *Mainichi Times* for your work, or to improve your English?'

'For both,' she replied, 'but it is always best I talk to somebody.'

'Better,' he said, grinning at her, 'always better. . .' He tried to explain the difference between the comparative and superlative.

When he had finished she said, 'I show you Kyoto.' Her eyes sparkling, she added, 'And you talk English to me. That will be *good.*'

'What is your name?'

'Akiko.'

'Okay, Akiko-san, I agree. My name is John.'

He sat back content, looking at her as she stared from the window. The train raced on. The factories and smoking chimneys surrounded by the tiny, fragile houses of the inhabitants passed in a blur. Already the burgeoning of Japan's industrial might was rising from the ashes of defeat.

He was never quite certain where Akiko was going that day. He learned later, when they sat in a small tea-house and he asked her about her family, that her only relatives were an aunt and uncle.

'You have no mother or father, no brothers or sisters?'

'My father was a soldier,' she said expressionlessly. 'He was killed in the war. My mother . . .' She turned her head and caught the eyes of an elderly couple in drab *kimono* of brown, her voice faltering. Mackinnon regretted his question.

' . . . was in Nagasaki, with my brother . . .'

She blinked at him, her dark, almond eyes brimming.

241

Without thinking, without considering the impulse would break the normal barriers of convention, he put out his hand and touched her arm.

What else could one human do for another in the circumstances?

'*Pikadon**,' he said quietly, and the elderly couple stirred as though a wind had passed through the room.

Looking back over the intervening years Mackinnon could recall much of the day. It had not been cherry-blossom time, though a few petals had burst from the bud to brave the chill March wind. They had exchanged a first kiss as they left the tea-house, a clumsy and precipitate act on his part while he had pulled her coat about her shoulders. He remembered the bright sunlight on the gilded walls of the Kinkakuji pavilion, and her laughter at the squeaking floor that surrounded the Shogun's palace and upon which it was impossible to move without making a noise.

He explained to her the meaning of the word 'intruder', against whom the floor was designed to guard and give warning. And he remembered with painful vividness, how, when he had first entered her, she had squeaked lasciviously in his ear and whispered the learnt word back to him.

They lay that night, and all the subsequent nights until the *Sir Robert Fitzroy* left dry dock, loaded her cargo and sailed, in a small, discreet hotel off the Motomachi. To his astonishment, she met the ship as it berthed at Nagoya, Shimizu and Yokohama.

When at last the vessel left the Japanese coast for Hong Kong, he knew the anguish of a broken heart. Akiko returned to her job as an industrial interpreter and never had the holiday she intended at her aunt's and uncle's house in the hills.

A wise man would have let the affair die; but Mackinnon

* 'Flash-bang' – the name the Japanese gave the atomic bomb

was not wise. He had also been eight months from home when he next called at Yokohama. The anguish of conscience accompanying his reunion with Shelagh was short-lived, as he thought, for he loved his wife and had left her pregnant, though neither knew it at the time. Nor did he get her letters, for the disrupted schedule of the ship was due to the Suez crisis and Eastern Steam, not slow to capitalise on world instability, had picked up a rival's conference schedule from Australia to maintain the service and keep the butcher's shops of Britain stocked with frozen lamb.

It could only have been fate that decreed another docking at Kobe. He had spent two nights with Akiko when the news of his parenthood reached him. Now his remorse overwhelmed him and he knew he had only shelved it, buried it in the sensuous delights of his marriage bed.

He told Akiko. They spent a weeping night which he dismissed afterwards in a pathetic attempt at bravura. Ashamed, he returned to Shelagh and the wonderful joy of their child. Months later he learned of the child's death. Its mysterious cause troubled him. Fate had demanded a price for his affair with Akiko.

Perhaps he had directly contributed to it. The descent into drunkenness followed.

Mackinnon stirred at the bridge window, his belly rumbling uncomfortably. He looked at his watch; it was almost noon and he had only the haziest notion of where they were. Ahead of the ship the wall of cloud grew, darkening the horizon. Already her motion had eased, the swell coming down from the north-east was predominating, superimposing itself in a regular wave formation.

'Nearly out of the typhoon's eye,' he remarked, turning and speaking to the man at the wheel.

Beside Able Seaman Braddock stood Macgregor.

Mackinnon grunted. 'What are *you* doing up here?'

'Come to take the wheel.'

'I said you were relieved of that duty,' Mackinnon said curtly.

'They're all kickin' up fuck down below, Cap'n, because ah'm no pullin' me weight. Ah've come to take the wheel.'

Mackinnon shook his head. 'No, you're not. She'll be all right on automatic pilot now. In another hour or two this'll be no more than a Force Eight gale.' He bent to the Arkas, ordered Braddock to put the helm amidships, and switched over.

'Carry on, Braddock,' he said, and the seaman turned to go below. His glance of contempt at Macgregor was not lost on Mackinnon.

'D'youse want me tae keep lookout then?' Macgregor asked truculently.

'Bugger off,' Mackinnon growled. He wanted to be alone, whatever the regulations said. His train of thought and the memories of Akiko had stirred too much in his mind to want even the silent company of a lookout to distract him.

For Captain Mackinnon wanted somehow to make amends.

The smell in the accommodation was asphyxial and Stevenson choked on the nauseating stench. The ship's gyrations had reduced the refugees to a supine state. They stretched out inert, moving only involuntarily in response to the ship. He looked in on Tam. She lay with her eyes closed but was not asleep, for she pulled a strand of hair from her mouth, then replaced her hand protectively over the sleeping baby.

As he went forward towards the main stairway he met Rawlings.

'Just going to see the patient,' Rawlings said breezily, as if he had occupied the entire forenoon in such busy errands. 'Motion's getting easier,' he went on, one hand on the spare cabin door handle. 'We'll be out of it soon and be able to ventilate this pigsty.' He smiled and threw open the door as the *Matthew Flinders* rolled away from him. The smile vanished from his face.

'Jesus Christ!'

She had been flung from the bunk and her stumps had struck the deck, rupturing the ligatures. The haemorrhage had been enormous, the square of carpet adorning the spartan room squelched darkly under their feet. Both men bent over the woman, gasping as the stench of gangrene rose from her imperfectly debrided wounds.

'God . . .' Rawlings backed off, puked, and put a hand to his mouth. A stream of vomit spewed through his fingers splashing Stevenson as the two of them bumped in the doorway. The Second Mate gagged as they both retreated into the alleyway. Rawlings grabbed the handrail that ran along the bulkhead as the ship began a long upward pitch. Stevenson closed the door.

At that precise moment the *Matthew Flinders* dropped from the crest of a wave and rolled to port. The forward port teak door, its hinges already weakened, tore from the frame. Water burst into the end of the alleyway, funnelling down it in a torrent and swept them to the deck.

Stevenson got to his feet and assisted Rawlings to recover. Macgregor was splashing towards them, grinning at the spectacle of the two wallowing officers.

'We're out of the bloody vortex then,' Stevenson remarked grimly.

'But not out of the shit, eh, Sec?' And Macgregor shoved past them still amused.

'Insolent bastard,' said Rawlings, wiping his mouth and trying to recover his dignity. 'I say, Alex, is that the Old Man's pistol you've got there?'

Looking down at his flapping shirt tail, Stevenson realised his belly was exposed and the gun butt stuck from his soiled waistband.

'I understand,' said Rawlings with a hint of reproach that he had not been informed earlier by the Captain himself, 'we are now bound for Shanghai, sir.'

Tired, Mackinnon shifted at his window. 'Yes.'

'I do think, sir,' Rawlings ploughed on, 'I might have been told.'

'You were asleep at the time,' Mackinnon said irritably, 'besides, Stevenson was quite capable of handling things.'

'So I believe, sir,' said Rawlings. 'I notice he enjoys your full confidence to the point of toting your automatic.'

Mackinnon swung round. 'What the hell d'you mean?'

Rawlings elaborated and Mackinnon realised Stevenson had helped himself to the pistol before searching for the weapon he believed the Vietnamese to have brought aboard. He found he did not mind, that he applauded Stevenson's lèse majesté, regarded it favourably as initiative and preferable to Rawlings's petty-mindedness.

'Oh that,' he said dismissively, 'he was only doing his job. *That* isn't a threat to your manhood is it, Mr Rawlings?' He threw the barb and enjoyed seeing it strike.

'There is something you don't appear to have considered, sir,' Rawlings countered.

'Oh? What's that?'

'Apart from the dead woman, we've Ernie York and Taylor. We can't shove them over the side without the consent of their families,' Rawlings said roughly, enjoying the look of real anguish which passed over Mackinnon's ravaged features. 'As for landing them in China, well . . .' Rawlings ended the sentence with a shrug.

Mackinnon heaved himself out of his corner, Rawlings was right. Dead British bodies in Shanghai would embroil him in a bureaucratic nightmare, whereas burial at sea . . .

Outside the wind was no more than force nine or ten. Their ears no longer popped in the gusts and although the air was full of spray and the sea white with spume, they were making nine or ten knots to the north-north-east. He could not commit poor Ernie or the unfortunate Taylor to the deep in such conditions, for the ship continued to roll and pitch, sluicing green seas across her decks. His relief at knowing the ship had survived the worst was tempered by Rawlings's reminder of the officers' fate.

'You've got a point,' he said. 'I'll send a signal.'

'I suppose if Dent insists on Shanghai we can always bury them when this lot moderates,' Rawlings temporised, waving his hand at the view beyond the wheelhouse.

Mackinnon paused, remembering Rawlings's loyalty to his clan. 'I'm going below for a spell,' he said. 'You can take her. I'm relying on you obtaining a fix at twilight. Course o-two-five.'

It was time the bugger pulled his weight, Mackinnon reflected as he first made his way cautiously aft to find Sparks. Besides, it was only in fiction the Captain stood on the bridge for a week without a bloody break . . .

He did not go directly to his cabin after sending the message. Instead he made his way down through the accommodation, putting his head into the saloon, unregarded by the inmates. They did not know who he was. Passing on towards the smoke-room he discovered for himself the corpse of the woman. Holding his breath he knelt beside her for a moment, touching her lifeless thigh in a small gesture of regret at his failure.

In the smoke-room only the baby seemed awake, its dark eyes focussed on him. He felt a compulsion to pick it up, but drew back as its forehead wrinkled and it began to sob. Hurriedly he backed out.

'Ah, sir, there you are,' Stevenson came towards him. 'I've just come from the radio-room, sir. There's a message coming in.'

'Very well. You'd better get the woman's body into the fridge.'

Stevenson swallowed. 'Yes, sir.'

'And, Mr Stevenson,' Mackinnon said, stepping closer and

247

lowering his voice, 'have you still got my gun?'

'No, sir. I put it back.'

'Good. I presume you found nothing.'

'I'm afraid not, sir.'

Mackinnon left the Second Mate to his gruesome task and clambered up to the radio-room via the open ladders at the after end of the superstructure. The air was still thick with spray, but breathable now, no more than a strong gale on their starboard bow and diminished in speed by the retreat of the typhoon.

Mackinnon opened the radio-room door. 'Can I come in?'

'Ah, perfect timing, sir.' Sparks peeled off his headset and stood up, handing the Captain a message form. Mackinnon shut the door and took the fluttering pink chit. 'Dent hasn't wasted any time getting back to us,' Sparks said.

'What a bloody nerve!' Mackinnon muttered and read the signal through again aloud.

'*Pilot ordered for 0800 local time Wednesday Yangtze Bar stop all necessary clearances made stop Immigration procedures a formality stop Native crew to pay off locally stop Hong Kong Chinese to travel by train stop Non native crew ditto to pay off Hong Kong stop Arrangements to effect fifty-fifty Hong Kong stroke US dollars stop UK flights arranged local stopover likewise stop Reference your last please commit to deep am contacting nok stop Kind regards James Dent ends.*'

'This is insufferable.' Mackinnon was flushed with anger. He read it through a third time, punctuating the stuffy air with his outrage:

'Eight o'clock Wednesday – doesn't the bastard know we've been caught in a typhoon? Necessary clearances . . . immigration a formality – good God, has he bought off the incorruptible Maoists? No choice for the poor bloody Shanghai Chinese and as for non-native crew – does the cunt mean British officers?' He looked up at Sparks, angry Dent's patronising signal had made him sound like an anachronistic imperialist. 'As for this fifty-fifty pay-off deal, I'd like to know how much that saves Dentco on the exchange market.'

'Good of him to book us a flight home, I suppose,' remarked Sparks drily.

'And he made sure we knew it was the Chairman and Managing Director himself who made these sumptuous arrangements for us. Christ, Frank,' said the Captain, using the Radio Officer's Christian name in a rare moment of fraternity. 'I've never in all my life seen so cynically manipulative a piece of, of . . . Jesus, I don't even know what to call it! As for disposing of poor Ernie York and young Taylor *before* contacting the next-of-kin.'

Mackinnon had exhausted himself with protest. The postscript appalled him.

'Sign of the times, I'm afraid, sir,' consoled Sparks.

'Yes,' Mackinnon agreed, staring out of the single window giving on to the outside world. The grey, streaked escarpments of the sea seemed suddenly familiar, preferable, for all its miseries and endless challenge, to the shore. 'Yes, sign of the times.' He was about to add, *sotto voce*, that perhaps two could play at the game, but Sparks had not yet finished with him.

'He did send his kind regards, sir, and there's another one. Personal.'

Mackinnon took the sealed brown envelope, smiling at Sparks's diehard professionalism and thinking what fools they were to continue these charade-like touches when their world was falling about around them. He tore open the envelope. When he had read it he handed it back to the Radio Officer.

'That's the real pay-off, isn't it? The thing that buys me out, eh?'

Sparks gave him a rueful grin. 'I rather think that's what's intended, yes.'

Both men stared down at the pink slip: *Mrs Mackinnon will await her husband's arrival at the Mandarin Hotel at company expense stop Dentco stop*

By a supreme effort on the part of most of the *Matthew Flinders*'s crew an air of normality had returned to the ship by six o'clock that evening. No one was summoned to duty, they came voluntarily: prostrated seamen to the mess-room; Chinese stewards and cooks to the galley; Chinese greasers to the engine-room. Men began to clean up, to shovel the mess of water, food and filth out of the main deck alleyways, to brew tea and think about a meal.

In the galley, Freddie Thorpe and the Chinese cooks tossed omelettes through into the mess-room and men rinsed their hands in sequence, devoured the omelettes, and turned to again without thought of a full meal break. Unable still to reach his workshop, the Carpenter 'borrowed' a sheet of plywood from the engine-room and fitted it in the empty door-frame, sealing the accommodation off again from the ingress of the sea.

In the after fridge locker, Stevenson, Braddock and Pritchard, the latter in breathing apparatus, lashed the bodies of the Vietnamese woman and the Chief Engineer. When they had finished, Braddock stood for a moment beside them and crossed himself.

With a rough but not unkind solicitude, the Bosun swabbed out the saloon and the male refugees were persuaded to shower themselves. In the smoke-room Thorpe shook Tam into full consciousness and explained the women could use the shower reserved normally for himself.

'You get all bodies clean like number one special,' he said with tactless condescension, 'and I fix chow-chow very soon. Okay? Savvy?'

Recalled to the present beyond which stretched a dreadful future, Tam, her eyes swollen and lacklustre, looking worse than when she had climbed from the lifeboat, acknowledged him.

'Sure. I savvy.'

By midnight the ship's routine had been re-established. The only difference was that instead of Third Officer Taylor, Captain Mackinnon would stand the morning eight-to-twelve watch. By then he would have had a night in his bunk.

Shortly after four the following morning, when Able Seaman Macgregor judged the relieved men of the middle watch had turned in and Scum-bag Rawlings was scratching his arse over his third cup of tea in the chart-room, he put his two fingers in his mouth and gave a low whistle.

CHAPTER SIXTEEN

Mutiny

They had promised Macgregor the girl. There were three of them, led by Phan Van Nui, unscrupulous gangsters, men who had each run their 'girls' in down-town Saigon and cleared out when their attempts to live under Communist rule proved impossible. They were either related to the other refugees, owed them favours or had sold them places on the junk at extortionate prices. Tam was a distant cousin of Phan's, but he nevertheless bartered her with the same facility as he had traded his sister with the American military, back during the 'good times'.

Macgregor was a type he was familiar with, an unconscionable man, a survivor, cunning and street-wise, but unintelligent enough to be ultimately outwitted. They had had dollars as well as the girl, and Macgregor took the bait with enthusiasm. It was his big chance. He could quietly bank the dollars in Hong Kong and screwing the girl to cheat Stevenson would be pleasure enough, while screwing her for himself would be seventh heaven!

His own part in the affair would, he had been promised, be covered up. They wanted some hiding places, routes of access and inside information as to certain procedures on board ship that would enable them to seize control with the minimum of disturbance.

Macgregor held out his hand to shake theirs as though

some chivalric purpose existed between them. 'It'll be a piece o'piss,' he had promised. And so it proved.

The key to the enterprise was the taking of hostages. Chief Officer Rawlings was secured, gagged with rigging tape and with his hands tied behind his back forced to sit in a damp locker-cum-urinal abaft the chart-room.

As he divined the purpose of the sudden appearance of the three Vietnamese men, he shouted for Macgregor, his duty lookout man, on the bridge-wing. But his cry was cut short, sounding no more than a cough to anyone below curious enough to be listening at that dead hour of the night.

With Rawlings immobilised Macgregor satisfied his aching and inchoate lust for revenge. The conspirators' next targets were the Radio Officer and the radio-room. Five minutes with a handy fire axe was sufficient for Macgregor to render the tall, stacked medium-frequency sets a wreck. The auxiliary VHF sets soon followed. Macgregor lowered the axe and wiped the sweat from his forehead, a lupine grin illuminating his face. As he went out he swung the axe at the light bulb. The glass shattered and the arcing axe split the top of Sparks's neat desk.

Meanwhile, with Phan Van Nui on the bridge, shortly rejoined by Macgregor, the two other Vietnamese first gagged and then dragged from his bunk a struggling Sparks. Forcing him chest down on his cabin carpet, they wrenched his hands behind his back and tied them with flag halliard provided by Macgregor. Then they forced him to sit beside Rawlings in the locked bridge urinal. Both men had seen the muzzle of Phan Van Nui's machine pistol.

The seizure of the ship had taken less than twenty minutes.

In the chart-room, out of sight of the two bound officers, Macgregor stared at the chart. Rawlings had been unable to secure a stellar observation at evening twilight, but the dead-reckoning positions were neatly marked for 2000, midnight and 0400. To Macgregor's untutored eye they were

253

absolutes; he had no idea of the misgivings privately assailing the officers who had marked them. He found Hong Kong on the chart, laid the long parallel rulers between the 0400 position and the magenta flash denoting Wang Lan lighthouse, and inscribed a pencil line. Then, as he had seen the officers do, he 'walked' the rules to the nearest compass rose and read off the course.

Captain Mackinnon had decided to maintain a course that took them out of the baleful influence of Typhoon David with the greatest possible speed until the overcast broke sufficiently for a star sight. This, he hoped, would occur about 0630. The fact, therefore, that Macgregor found the *Matthew Flinders* on a course of north-north-east gave him the impression of their heading for the Taiwan Strait and Shanghai.

Cocksure, Macgregor marched into the wheelhouse. The dull gleam of the binnacle and telegraph light reflected off Phan's weapon as the man stood in the unfamiliar darkness.

'You fix?' he asked.

'I fix real good,' said Macgregor, bending to the Arkas auto-pilot and altering the course as he had seen done. 'A piece o' piss,' he affirmed.

'How long before we get Hong Kong?'

'Don't you worry, mate. We'll be there tomorrow night. We'll get Mackinnon or Stevenson tae take her in an' then you can vanish. By the time a pilot gets off tae the ship an' the arguin' starts, you'll be awa', ah'll be twa blocks up that bit o' stuff wi' ma pillow stuffed fu' o' dollars.'

The fantastical prospect made Macgregor relapse into his native vernacular, mystifying Phan Van Nui who shrugged impassively in the darkness. He knew disappearing into the teeming streets of Hong Kong would not be as easy as Macgregor naively insisted, but he knew, too, of the lubricating power of money. Besides, while he held the machine pistol, he could eliminate *any* opposition; even that of his friends.

'Tomorrow night, eh?' he asked in confirmation.

254

'Yes,' grinned Macgregor, who had been at sea long enough to know how many days it took to steam from Singapore to Hong Kong. 'Tomorrow night.'

'Okay, you go now.' Phan looked at his watch. They had agreed it was unnecessary to disturb too many people prematurely. Besides, Phan Van Nui wanted to secure the allegiance of his ally. 'Come back one hour.'

And suppressing a wild and triumphant yelp, Macgregor withdrew like a shadow.

Before midnight, Stevenson had slept like a log. He had relieved Rawlings (who, by himself relieving Mackinnon, was compelled to stand the evening eight-to-twelve before being called for the morning four-to-eight) and kept his watch in a strange, disembodied sense of achievement. It was not elation, for the horrible death of Charles Taylor whose mangled corpse still lay in Number Two 'tween deck, had affected him deeply. But he could not deny a feeling of having stood his ground undaunted in the face of death, of having come through a test satisfactorily. His short, deep sleep had left him full of energy and this feeling of having been tested and proved worthy made the forthcoming arrival at Hong Kong less a termination of his career than the start of something new.

In the wild darkness of the night he attempted no rationalisation of these feelings. In his imagination he wrote mental drafts of letters to Caroline Taylor, letters that praised her husband and slighted her own trivial existence and spoke of her unworthiness; accusatory letters which made of her faithlessness a cause of Taylor's heroic death. Finally, he chose one of tragic content and mixed metaphor: of her neglect and Taylor's misery, drowned in the arms of a beautiful whore, of his conscience and immolation in losing his life to save his ship,

It was all nonsense, a product of Stevenson's hyped-up state. In the cold light of day when, he knew, he would have

255

to retrieve Taylor's body from the 'tween deck, the whole train of thought would be anathema to him, but in the graveyard hours he indulged in a savage, misogynistic reaction.

Finally relieved by a grumbling Rawlings, he had gone below in no mood for sleep. Instead he had found his way to the lower alleyway and met the Third Engineer coming out of the engine-room.

'Getting better,' the Third remarked as they enjoyed a companionable chat, referring to the easing of the ship's motion. 'I'm for my pit,' he said after they had gossiped. 'Got to get my strength back for Hong Kong.'

As he bade the Third good night, Stevenson realised Mackinnon had not yet broadcast the change of destination to the ship's company.

A moment later he was quietly opening the door of the smoke-room. It lay in darkness, apart from the splash of light from the open door and a faint gleam filtering through the jalousies pulled up against the windows. Tam lay among the sleeping women. Her face was toward him, no more than an indistinct oval. He could not understand what drew him back to look at her like a middle-aged *voyeur*. Even a plain woman, they said, grew beautiful in proportion to the number of days you were at sea, but that was insufficient explanation.

She possessed none of the allure of Cathy, yet Cathy had not had the power to hold him. Had he truly loved Cathy, would he have been able to make the grand, reasonable gesture, bowed to the pragmatic and let her go? If he had truly loved her, would he not have fought for her? Remonstrated, pleaded, cajoled, even accepted the infidelity he knew was a concomitant risk of his prolonged absence?

Yet here he was, like a thief in the night, without the excuse of the typhoon to explain his prowling among these sleeping women. It was, he realised with a start, a situation that would be hard to justify if discovered. Yet, unwilling to end it, wanting only somehow mitigate the ordeal he knew she must face in Shanghai, to explain to her he had nothing to do with the change of orders, that none of them did, being almost as powerless as the refugees themselves when it came to challenging the authorities, he stepped inside and stood in bizarre communion with her in the darkness.

Then as if to echo his fear of discovery he heard the outer door of the alleyway open and felt the rush of cold air die as someone closed it behind them. He drew back, shrinking against the bulkhead, his heart thundering in his chest. The steps did not go on down the alleyway: they had stopped outside the door and the very stopping alarmed Stevenson. A man with an innocent purpose would scarcely pause like that.

Slowly, as the door cracked to admit a sliver of light from the solitary bulb in the alleyway, Stevenson slid his back down the bulkhead until he squatted against it, almost indistinguishable from the other exhausted, breathing shapes about him.

A torch beam zig-zagged across the deck, stopped on a face, moved on, stopped again and then went out as a muttering stirred the recumbent forms. The door closed as the figure entered the room and Stevenson had trouble distinguishing what was happening. His first guilty fear of discovery kept him from jumping up immediately. Part-guessing that the target of the intrusion was Tam, the most desirable of the female refugees, part-fearful of the intruder being one of her boyfriends and this whole thing being nothing to do with him, he kept still. At first he thought this course of action justified, for though overwhelmed by disappointment at her apparent acquiescence, she appeared to rise in conspiratorial silence, embracing the stranger, to step over her neighbours and leave with him.

It was only when the door was pulled open that he saw he

had misinterpreted the intimate configuration of the entwined bodies. The dark slash of the sticky rigging tape gagged her and the arm twisted up between her shoulder blades kept her close to her abductor. Then he saw the light fall briefly upon Macgregor's triumphant features as he forced the writhing girl swiftly through the door.

Stevenson rose in pursuit. Macgregor was struggling forward with the girl ten yards away when Stevenson slipped into the alleyway. Behind him in the smoke-room the women slept undisturbed. Occupied with the girl, Macgregor was unaware of Stevenson's presence, muttering obscenities into her ear, shaking her so that her feet left the deck. The two of them slammed into the bulkhead as she resisted. Drawing back, Macgregor hefted her a second time into the steel wall, driving the wind from her. A moment later Stevenson caught his shoulder and pulled him round.

Macgregor's astonishment faded quickly, and was replaced with an expression of feral savagery. He thrust the girl aside so hard that she fell and, unable to draw sufficient air into her gasping lungs, fainted.

Stevenson drove his right fist into Macgregor's face, but the seaman parried it with his left forearm. Stevenson's fist struck the bulkhead and the next instant he was reeling back. Macgregor hit him first on the jaw, then in his gut and Stevenson doubled up. The Glaswegian's upthrust knee caught his bruised shoulder and he sagged uselessly to his knees.

Macgregor had not finished yet. He caught Stevenson's hair and cracked his head into the steel bulkhead so hard Stevenson saw stars and fell full length.

For a moment he thought he would pass out, but Macgregor had let him go and he was dimly aware of the seaman leaving him and bending over the girl. As the breath rasped in Stevenson's throat, Macgregor hove the unconscious girl on his shoulder and turned aft. Instinctively Stevenson drew his knees up to his belly, spoiling the kick

Macgregor aimed at him in passing. A moment later a cool draft of air and then the bang of the alleyway door marked Macgregor's exit.

For a moment Stevenson lay where he was, overcome by nausea, the pain in his shoulder and his split head which bled copiously. Something beyond his pain stirred in him and very slowly, using the alleyway handrail, he groped his way to his feet and staggered aft.

He had been so sure, so Goddamned sure . . . the test . . .

And now this . . . humiliation . . .

On the after deck the sting of salt-laden air partly revived him. Despite the hiss of the sea, the rumble of the engine and the keen of the wind, a noise above him galvanised him to further action.

'Come *on* you fuckin' whore!' A door banged and Stevenson began to climb towards the radio-room as quickly as his shaking limbs would allow.

Tam was naked by the time he tore open the door. Under the dim twenty-watt bulb of the emergency lighting her slender body was the ivory colour of the dead woman's corpse except for the red weals where Macgregor had ripped her rotten clothing from her and lashed her shoulders to the chromed handles on the wrecked radio stacks with lengths of flex from the head and hand sets. With eager lust he had already parted her legs and his own jeans were round his ankles.

'Come on,' he insisted through gritted teeth, thrusting forward, 'you'd better get used tae it!'

'No!'

As Macgregor swung round his rigid member bounced obscenely from his loins. Stevenson's right hand flicked out, finger extended, and it was Macgregor's turn to double up. Snarling with fury, Stevenson was on him. Seizing the handset from which Macgregor had torn the flex, Stevenson repeatedly swiped it back and forth across the seaman's face

259

in a frenzy of rage, reducing Macgregor to a sobbing supplicant kneeling, half-naked, at his feet.

Breathless and unable to lift his extempore weapon any
more, Stevenson leant back and fell through the opening
door, the sea step catching him behind the knees. For a
moment no one moved, then Stevenson got slowly to his feet
and stepped towards Tam. She had come round as Macgregor
stripped her and remained rigid with shock, the ugly rectangle
of the metallic rigging tape disfiguring her stricken face, her
eyes like dark holes in her skull. Stevenson peeled back a
corner of the tape and roughly pulled it from her skin. She
gasped with pain and relief as she dragged air into her lungs.
He tore at the wires securing her arms, whimpering in his own
pain and inability to release her fast enough.

There was an old stained duffle coat on a hook beside the
door. Grabbing it from him she pulled it round her and
appeared to shrink away from him.

'It's okay,' he gasped, trying to soothe her, 'it's okay . . .'

He realised she was staring in horror at Macgregor and he
slowly drew her past him and out on deck. He put his arm
tentatively round her. He could feel her shaking as they edged
forward towards his cabin. Halfway along the deck she
stopped. Like a frightened mule, she would go neither one
way nor the other.

'What's the matter?' he asked. 'Is it me? I won't hurt you!
God, I couldn't hurt you . . .'

She muttered something, the syllables chattering inco-
herently through her uncontrollable sobbing.

'Not Shanghai, not Shanghai,' he thought she said.

'You don't want to go to Shanghai? I know.'

With an effort she shook her head. '*Not* Shanghai,' she
repeated, gradually mastering herself. 'They stop you, make
you go Hong Kong . . . Phan . . . the gun. They catch
ship . . .'

'*Catch* ship? You mean *seize* the ship? When, for God's
sake? *When?*'

'Now!' she almost shouted at him, 'Now! *He* help them!'

Comprehension dawned on Stevenson. He looked forward at the extension of the bridge-wing, pale against the already lightening sky. What the hell was going on up there?

'Come,' he said with a sudden, harsh urgency, 'I take you my cabin. You have wash, take my clothes, lock door. You'll be quite safe.'

The habits of half a lifetime spent as a watch-keeping officer die hard. Despite his years as Master, Mackinnon could never sleep longer than seven hours without waking. Moreover, a man with a problem which has pierced him to his soul will wake the moment his tired body lifts from its deepest slumber, not stopping at that dreaming plane of shallow sleep from which most of us emerge every morning. In Captain Mackinnon's case, with several problems claiming his attention, he rose like a breaching whale to lie anxious and wide awake in the first grey glimmer of dawn.

His initial anxiety for the ship was thrust aside the instant he knew from her motion that the typhoon had passed and they ran through nothing more than a near-gale. It was swiftly replaced by a deep anger. He felt demeaned and insulted by James Dent's message, not merely because it would cause ructions amongst the majority of the crew, but because it was manipulative, dragging Shelagh into the matter of the disposal of the *Matthew Flinders*. He began to suspect some skulduggery attendant upon the sale of the ship, in which the unplanned arrival of the refugees had somehow served James Dent to his profit.

It was the sort of luck fate doled out in abundance to his ilk: Mackinnon did not like James Dent. Putting aside an old man's prejudice against a younger man set above him, he disapproved of Dent's cynical attitude to his company's ships. Bent on preserving Dentco as a viable commercial house, James Dent had diversified into other fields, bought into other interests, none of which had anything to do with

261

shipping. His ships had receded from the forefront of his business; they had been flagged out, their crews subjected to an erosion of their conditions of service and their quality of life. In competition with the cheap labour of the Third World, his employees, many having given long years of service with the proud tradition of being part of Britain's Merchant Navy, were unashamedly reduced to Third World status.

For Mackinnon such a thing was unforgivable, an arrogant disregard of a great trading house's responsibilities; a squandering of a national asset in the squalid name of profit and, worst of all, a betrayal of the thousands who had died in war.

Musing in the twilight, Mackinnon could hear Able Seaman Bird's tirade against shipowners as the lifeboat tossed on the heaving bosom of the grey Atlantic. It had not proved the rantings of a crank Bolshevik, after all . . .

Whilst Mackinnon did not trouble himself to fathom the scam Dent was working, beyond the obvious reason that the *Matthew Flinders* would have fetched a better price sold for further trading than for scrap, it disturbed him to realise how they had unwittingly played into Dent's hands by their humanitarian rescue. Of course, Mackinnon reasoned to himself, humanitarian acts were inimical to the cold logic of profit. By complicating the arrival of the ship in Hong Kong with the presence of the Vietnamese, Mackinnon was in no doubt Dent had enlisted the weight of the authorities by way of counter-measure. He would have played the game of influential contacts so that the Hong Kong government would refuse entry to the ship. There was no evidence for Sparks's hunch, but Mackinnon's instinct endorsed it and now he feared the worst.

But what of the refugees themselves? How could he, complaining of Dent's capitalist logic, deliver them to Shanghai? On the grounds that it was his duty? Duty to whom? To Dent? Was Dent so powerful that the fate of those wretched people depended upon John Mackinnon's sense of obligation to James Dent?

What exactly *was* his duty? He had built his life upon duty and obedience; to duty and his obligations to his owners just as he had expected obedience from those who served under him. But the pure responsibility of a Master for his ship and its people were ineluctable. This very obligation had sustained him and his men in the past hours and, with God's help, brought the ship and all but three of the souls confided to her, through the typhoon. Any dereliction of such a duty was a spiritual matter for his conscience, and a temporal matter for the Department of Transport . . .

No, it was not! He realised that the formal apparatus of government to whom he was responsible was no longer that of Britain; Sparks had pointed *that* out. Furthermore, Dent himself had flagged the ship out and he, Mackinnon, was answerable to a government in Central America!

Surely then the duty he was now laid under by Dent's signal was a different matter. The company as Mackinnon knew it was finished, the *Matthew Flinders* their last ship. When the voyage ended James Dent would wash his hands of all her people; they would, in that term of disposal hallowed by usage, be 'discharged'.

And among those luckless people, among whom even the detestable Macgregor was a prince, were one hundred and forty-six Vietnamese refugees.

How could he deliver them to the cousins of their Communist persecutors?

He found sleep had increased his desire to do *something* for the refugees. It would doubtless be confounded, the unfortunate boat people would end up in a wire cage on Stonecutter's Island in Hong Kong harbour, but he had to make some gesture, no matter how quixotic. Nor could he remain detached for much longer; his influence over their lives would last only until the ship reached port, and if he chose to flout Dent's order and go to Hong Kong, that time diminished rapidly.

263

It struck him with poignant urgency, so much a part of him had it become, that he would cease to command the *Matthew Flinders* when they arrived – and Hong Kong was less than twenty-four hours away . . .

Mackinnon threw off his bedclothes and drew back his window curtains. A grey daylight revealed a grey sea, the streaks of spume no more than old scars and no threat as the ship ploughed doggedly along, throwing out her bow wave as she plunged and drove northwards. Overhead the cloud was breaking up; the cold fire of fading stars showed against the sky.

Where *exactly* were they? Had Rawlings got his star sights?

Mackinnon was seized with a sensation of sudden panic. He shoved his feet into his slippers and reached for his red silk dressing gown. It occurred to him with a sense of gut-wrenching haste, this was his last morning in a sea-going command, perhaps his last at sea. He wanted to be on the bridge, to draw the stars down to the horizon and swing the arcs of their altitudes against the rim of the world and find that most exciting thing a navigator can: exactly where in all the wide oceans of the globe they were.

He struggled into his dressing gown, cursing the fact that he had drawn one sleeve inside out when last he had taken it off. The crepuscular moment when star and horizon were visible did not last long. Stumbling out of his day room he squelched on the wet mess of his cabin carpet. The book about the Uffizi lay face down, its glossy paper ruinously welded by the water. Stupefied by fatigue, he had not noticed it last night. He felt a momentary pang of conscience for Shelagh, picked up the sodden book and put it on his settee. He must hurry!

His last dawn . . .

In his haste he fumbled with the girdle of the red silk dressing gown. How many dawns had he spent taking star sights as Chief Officer? And afterwards, before the news of

264

the child's death, how many hours had he paced the bridge, cock of the walk, amid the smell of bacon and eggs floating up from the galley, waiting for the Third Mate to relieve him at eight o'clock, recalling Akiko's quickly responding body arching with pleasure as he made those last thrusting movements before the torrent of release . . .?

He stepped into the alleyway and collided with Stevenson.

'Thank God they haven't caught you, sir!'

CHAPTER SEVENTEEN

Signs of the Times

'What the hell . . .?'

Mackinnon staggered back white-faced as Stevenson thrust the Captain into his cabin.

'Not much time to explain,' hissed Stevenson urgently, 'but please listen, sir.' The Second Mate flung himself to his knees before the ship's safe, as if suddenly mastered by an impulse to pray. For a moment Mackinnon thought he had taken leave of his senses, seeing the bruise and broken skin on his forehead, then the younger man looked up at him, anxiety etched in every muscle of his face.

'Best get some clothes on, sir.' He turned back to the safe, explaining in a torrent of words as he twisted the combination lock. 'A small group of Vietnamese have seized the bridge. Tam, the girl, told me. I stuck my head over the after end; they've got a gun up there, it must be the automatic we were looking for. Two of them are somewhere around; I thought they were after you. Macgregor's in with them . . .'

Stevenson yanked open the safe door, pulled out the pistol and closed it again. Mackinnon was struggling into shorts in the doorway of his night cabin, trying to digest what Stevenson was telling him after a moment's total incredulity.

'You don't have any more slugs, sir?' Stevenson asked, looking down at the handful of dull brass cartridges.

'No.' Mackinnon pulled on socks and shoes. 'Where's Macgregor now?'

'I left him laid out in the radio-room. He'd wrecked the place.'

'The bastard,' Mackinnon swore. 'They've got Rawlings, then?'

'Yes, Macgregor was his first lookout . . .'

'Christ . . . what do they want, the Vietnamese? Did the girl know?'

'I know what they *don't* want. They don't want to go to Shanghai, sir.'

Something in Stevenson's voice caught Mackinnon's attention. Buttoning his shirt heavy with the stiff epaulettes of Master, Mackinnon asked, 'And where exactly do *your* sympathies lie, Alex?'

Stevenson paused. He had been relieved to find Mackinnon unmolested. He was now anxious not to be delayed, to rush back to the bridge ladder and storm it as quickly as possible. Mackinnon's cool appraisal steadied him; besides, the Captain had never addressed him by his Christian name before.

'Me, sir? Why, I . . .' He dropped his eyes.

'If you're fond of the girl you can't want her given back to the Communists.'

Stevenson looked Mackinnon squarely in the eyes. 'No, I don't. How did you know?'

A faint smile curled Mackinnon's weathered features. 'I guessed that at six in the morning with you not in your bunk.'

'Ah,' broke in Stevenson ruefully, 'it wasn't quite like that.'

'The thing is, Alex, I have no intention of taking this ship to Shanghai. Ironically, I had already decided that a wire compound on Stonecutter's Island was probably preferable to turning them over to the Chinese.'

Stevenson's face brightened. 'That's fantastic, sir.'

'Up to a point, perhaps,' Mackinnon said drily. He ran his thumbs round his waistband, pulling the front of his shirt tight across his paunch, 'but Hong Kong or Shanghai, it's *my* decision, and *my* responsibility; not some bloody Glaswegian cowboy and his unlikely allies.' Mackinnon paused, then added, 'So are you with me?'

'Of course, sir.' Stevenson grinned, then held out the gun.

Mackinnon shook his head. 'No, you hang on to that, just tuck it out of sight.' With a kind of fascination Mackinnon watched Stevenson's brown forearm bend as he stuck the dully gleaming pistol into his waistband. He remembered his earlier vision of a world full of gun-toting young men. It was tragic that now among them his own Second Mate had to be numbered.

God, he was becoming an old fool! Had he not long ago decided the lot of the world was turmoil and tragedy? How could he stand dithering philosophically when a few feet overhead his ship was in alien hands?

Perhaps he was already unfit for his job.

'Come,' he snapped with sudden harshness, 'let's go and see how to get out of this mess.'

Macgregor came to his senses through a red blur. The whole of his face throbbed and his exploring hand pulled back reflexively from the sensitive bruising. He stared at it, his eyes focussing on blood. Stevenson's battering had broken the skin over his cheekbones and his nose felt huge on a face he sensed was grotesque.

'The *bastard*,' Macgregor groaned, but the venom had gone out of him: he had been beaten yet again. He lay back, one of life's perpetual underdogs, only then becoming aware of what he had been cheated of. His bare loins, the jeans twisted round his ankles, the sheer discomfort of his position, gradually spurred him to movement more than any motive for vengeance.

Standing, hands on the desk he had smashed earlier, he

268

remembered the fire axe. Very slowly it seeped into Macgregor's brain that with such a weapon he could bring an overwhelming superiority to bear upon Mister Fucking Stevenson.

For, in Macgregor's battered brain, Stevenson had had only one purpose in intervening: *he* wanted the girl. The lassie would never grass on what was going on on the ship, for she had no more desire to go to Shanghai than the others, so she would either let Stevenson screw her or fight him off – and Macgregor flattered himself that she had little fight left in her. But the thought brought him no comfort: Stevenson was a winner and the bitch would let him have her . . .

With ponderous intent Macgregor went in search of the fire axe he had discarded earlier.

On the bridge Phan Van Nui awaited the return of his two confederates. He had told them that before they dealt with any of the sleeping crew, the engine-room door had to be secured. It was at the after end of the main-deck alleyway, abaft the galley and not far from the saloon. It was from there they had heard and seen it open and close, felt the blast of warm, oily air as the boiler-suited engineers went in and out. They needed no assistance from Macgregor to devise a way of lashing the outer dogs so that no one could get out. In fact it was the simplicity with which they had discovered this fact that had led them to conceive the plan, once the rumour of their destination became fact. In the circumstance it was of no great importance. Phan did not know of the other means of access to the engine-room. The small door in the funnel was not commonly used, and although the shaft tunnel had provided entry and exit during the typhoon, Phan Van Nui did not appreciate it.

As soon as his men returned and reported the task completed it would be time to take the Captain hostage. Then they could dispense with Macgregor's help altogether.

Phan Van Nui did not trust Macgregor. Giving him the girl got him out of the way and would occupy him for long enough to complete their stratagem. Afterwards . . .

Phan Van Nui lit a cigarette and smiled. Far away in the east, unseen behind rolls of thick cloud, the sun rose.

Mackinnon left his cabin with no plan as to how he intended to recapture his ship. He was motivated by outrage and anger that anyone should have the effrontery to take it from him to the extent of leaving the pistol in Stevenson's possession. It was an irrational act in itself, but to Mackinnon the very thought of dispossession was so inimical that he wanted no fuss, no risk, no misunderstanding to attend the simple fact of his reassuming what was rightfully his.

He was not in any doubt at all that morally and legally he was in the right. He had no intention of delivering the boat people to Shanghai, but he was damned if the flouting of James Dent's 'order' was going to be perceived by anyone as anything other than his own decision. He strode towards the foot of the ladder to the chart-room, reaching it at the same moment Phan's confederates ran up from securing the engine-room door.

The confrontation was brief. The panting Vietnamese saw before them the bulky figure of Captain Mackinnon. The alleyway light gleamed on his epaulettes and the gold-braided peak of the cap that he had seized instinctively as he left his cabin. They paused briefly at this formidable apparition and lost any initiative their sudden appearance might have gained them. The affronted Mackinnon let out a bull roar and drove at them. His huge fists reached out and each grabbed a handful of singlet, thrusting the wearers back against the bulkhead with a jarring impact. The two Vietnamese howled as their heads cracked against the steel and then, down the stairwell from the dark shadows of the bridge above, came the ear-splitting rattle and the zip and clang, the sparks and wild ricochet of automatic gunfire.

Maddened by this further outrage, his hands still on his two would-be captors, Mackinnon twisted to one side and hurled them both down the stairs to the promenade deck. They were small men, light from under-nourishment, out of breath from their exertions and fearful of the furious strength of the starched white figure assaulting them. They fell in an ungainly bundle, bruised but not seriously hurt in their ignominious tumble.

As he disposed of them, Mackinnon turned back and roared at the man on the bridge. 'Stop firing at once!'

Stevenson had been a yard or two behind the Captain and had never made the turn round the bottom of the bridge ladder. At the terrifying burst of machine-gun fire, he had drawn back towards the Captain's cabin. The noisy effect of the ricochets in the confined space paralysed him as flying wooden splinters were flung from the door frame of a cabin in the athwartships alleyway. Already aware of the situation and fearful of the outcome, he was not encouraged by Mackinnon's fury. In the wake of the Captain, the stream of automatic fire seemed specifically directed at himself. He found himself sitting, his legs kicking back up the alleyway until he felt the coarse coir of the doormat outside Mackinnon's cabin rasp his bare thighs. At that moment Mackinnon roared out his command to cease fire.

Miraculously Phan Van Nui obeyed. His thin, reedy voice floated down into the officers' flat.

'Who speak?'

'This is Captain Mackinnon. I want you to know ship not go Shanghai. Ship go Hong Kong. You savvy?'

Another voice, Tam's, quickly translated and Stevenson saw the door of his cabin opened a crack. A torrent of Vietnamese poured down from the bridge above and when it was over Tam's disembodied voice, speaking in English, filled the air.

'He says how can we trust you? You can tell us anything.'

'He's going to have to trust me,' snapped Mackinnon

271

truculently, stepping forward, but an explosion of sparks and splinters burst like a small bomb at his feet where Phan's slugs cut up the composition of the decking.

Mackinnon danced backwards. Stevenson had got to his feet and crept aft. He could see Mackinnon round the stairs pressed back clear of Phan's line of fire. Phan remained out of sight to Stevenson. The movement caught Mackinnon's eye as he recovered from the gunfire.

'Look here,' he had begun and Stevenson mouthed and gestured for him to keep talking. 'Look here,' Mackinnon went on, 'stop this shooting at once. You have the gun and I must negotiate with you.' Mackinnon turned to the girl whose face he could just see peeping through the slit in Stevenson's cabin door. 'Can you explain that to him?'

She nodded and began to translate. To Mackinnon's relief the translation grew into a dialogue. His heart was hammering uncomfortably in his breast as the full import of exactly what was going on overcame his initial outrage. He was aware that the two Vietnamese he had thought he had disposed of were now behind him. They joined in the row and Mackinnon said in stentorian tones, 'Will you tell these men, miss, that I, I,' he repeated the word, tapping his chest for emphasis and aware that their argument was subsiding and they were listening to him, '*I* am taking this ship to Hong Kong. Never mind what you have been told. It is true we were ordered to Shanghai, but now it is all changed.' He thought fast: 'Because of the typhoon we cannot go to Shanghai.' He paused, sensing a lowering of tension. 'You tell them.' Perhaps Stevenson's ploy, whatever it was, would not be needed. Mackinnon wanted to avoid the young man being tempted into foolish heroics, knowing his ancient pistol was no match for the automatic weapon held by the man above.

Stevenson had retreated into the Captain's cabin. In addition to the door into the officers' flat and the internal ladder to the chart-room, there was a door leading directly on to the boat-deck. It led out under the ladder to the starboard bridge-wing and Stevenson reached the top of this and lifted his head cautiously above the level of the deck to locate Phan's exact whereabouts.

To Stevenson's relief the Vietnamese was half-hidden; standing at the head of the chart-room stairwell, only his back and one elbow could be seen through the open wheelhouse door. Cautiously Stevenson moved upwards. Once on the bridge-wing he could pad swiftly to the door and prod the stub-barrelled revolver into Phan's ribs. The man would have to relinquish the machine gun and all would be well. He strained his ears to catch Phan's voice above the noise of the wind. He was still negotiating, saying something in Vietnamese. Stevenson hesitated, thinking he heard Tam's voice and drawing strength from it.

He gathered himself for the final move, his right leg bent under him, the other ready to launch himself forward.

'Gotcha!'

Macgregor's hand closed round his left ankle, but Stevenson was already moving off the top of the ladder. With one leg trapped he fell full length and the pistol flew from his hand. He barked his shin on the lip of the bridge-deck and then suddenly Macgregor let go of his ankle and leapt up behind him. To his horror, Stevenson found the Able Seaman standing over him brandishing a fire axe.

'Now you bastard . . .'

Fighting for his life, convinced Macgregor was out of his mind, Stevenson twisted violently to one side. Macgregor had seen the gun slide across the deck and hesitated, unsure whether to commit himself to an attack on the Second Mate with the fire axe, an attack that to succeed could only have one outcome, or whether to try for the abandoned revolver.

Action without much fear of the consequences had been a watchword of Macgregor's uncontrolled and wild childhood, but survival, he had soon learned, often depended upon an escape route. In his many confrontations with authority the early acquired skill of pushing things just so far had stood him in good stead. At times it had deceived his victims into thinking he was resolute. If so it was part of their perception of their own intimidation. Resolution, however, took no notice of consequences; it pursued its ends regardless, taking no note of escape routes, even of self-preservation. It was one of the building blocks of courage, but not part of Able Seaman Macgregor's make-up.

Stevenson was at his mercy; an unalterable fact which Macgregor paused just long enough to savour. The fire axe, which had seemed so attractive a means of revenge a few minutes earlier, might now be replaced by the revolver, a weapon of greater potential, lethal, but also intimidating. He *could* kill Stevenson. The axe would make short work of the prone body at his feet, but Macgregor knew the chances of pulling off the complete and irreversible seizure of the ship was unlikely. He was not used to considering himself on the winning side. Oh, he had won skirmish after skirmish, certainly; but never a real battle, never mind a campaign; the winning of a war was beyond his imagination. For this reason, a reason of great cunning, the arrangement he had come to with Phan Van Nui had allowed his part in the seizure of the ship to be kept from his shipmates. He wanted to fuck the girl and get ashore in Hong Kong with a fistful of greenback dollars.

But his thirst for revenge on Stevenson had compromised him. A seed of doubt was germinating in his mind. The axe was too dangerous, the pistol offered a way out. As Stevenson sought to roll out from under the imminent descent of the axe, Macgregor jumped forward towards the gun.

The shout and sounds of a scuffle on the bridge-wing had alarmed Phan Van Nui. He stepped back into the wheelhouse, casting a quick look to his left, out over the starboard bridge-wing. A man was lying on the deck,

274

another had got past him, had an axe in his left hand and was picking up a pistol, pointing it at the wheelhouse . . .

Phan spun round, whipping up the machine gun which had been depressed to cover Mackinnon below him at the foot of the chart-room stairs.

'No! It's me . . .'

An orange burst of fire stuttered from its ugly muzzle. Macgregor, his moment of triumph turned in the split second of Phan's alarm and incomprehension into bloody tragedy, jerked obscenely with the impact of the slugs. Blood seemed to spray out of him as his rent muscles were torn apart, convulsing his body in a last fling.

Stevenson, flat on the deck in a long, attenuated moment of absolute terror, felt the warm splatter of the stuff strike him. Through the teak planks and his own taut and apprehensive nerves, he heard and felt the heavy axe clatter to the deck, and then the unforgettable slump of Macgregor's body and the long, long rattling exhalation of his last breath.

For a moment Stevenson stared into the wide, staring and sightless eyes. Then with a violent retch, he was sick.

Looking up and watching the effect Tam's explanation was having on the Vietnamese gunman, Mackinnon was alarmed when the man swung to his left and the air was again split apart by the evil death chatter of the machine gun. Certain that it was Stevenson at whom Phan fired and with no thought for himself, Mackinnon charged up the internal stairs. He was oblivious to the fact that his precipitate movement released the other two Vietnamese bandits from their torpor. His sole consideration was for Stevenson and the horror he might find on the bridge, a horror he was already blaming himself for.

As Phan's five-second burst ceased with the realisation he had shot Macgregor, he turned back to the others. He was too late. Mackinnon was at the top of the stairs and although

Phan rounded on him with a cry and brought the snout of his weapon toward the Captain's ample belly, Mackinnon crashed into him. Phan fell back, lost his balance and the tall brass column of the engine-room telegraph struck him in the small of the back, winding him badly. As his slight frame bounced forward, Mackinnon drove one fist into Phan's stomach while the other tore the machine gun from his loosening grip.

Staring out of the wheelhouse door Mackinnon saw Stevenson getting to his feet, wiping a dribble from his mouth, his eyes on the inert body sprawled at his feet.

'Are you all right?' Mackinnon called in a voice harsh with anxiety, and then, as he took in the whole ghastly scene, asked, 'Is that Macgregor?'

Stevenson looked up and nodded.

'Are you all right?' Mackinnon repeated with more emphasis.

Stevenson pulled himself together. 'Shaken but not deterred,' he joked.

Mackinnon smiled. Behind him there was a movement he thought came from Phan Van Nui, the would-be hijacker. He turned, realising his mistake. Phan had not recovered, but his accomplices had the girl between them, her arms pinned back behind her shoulder blades so that the pain made her walk on tiptoes, her mouth stopped by the hand of one of her countrymen. The trio were edging forward into the wheelhouse, working their way round to Phan whose laboured breathing rasped loudly.

Mackinnon raised the machine gun. He had no idea how to use it, but he waved it and snarled, 'Let her go!'

Above the hand across her mouth, Tam's eyes were wide with fear. She tried to shake her head, knowing men with machine guns usually used them.

Behind Mackinnon, Stevenson saw what was happening. For a moment his mind was a blank. He thought of the revolver and how he had dropped it, remembered

276

Macgregor had been going to get it when Phan mistakenly shot him, and then saw the dull gleam of the thing almost at his feet with congealing gobbets of Macgregor's blood across it in a trail that led from his corpse to the eau-de-nil paintwork of the bridge bulwark.

Bending he picked it up. It seemed to jump in his hand, the kick of its recoil shocking his arm. The whine of the ricochetting bullet whanged off forward somewhere. The shot made them all jump. Mackinnon half turned again, Tam was jerked by her nervous captors and Phan, drawing his knees into his agonised stomach in an attempt to stand, slumped down again.

It had all happened very quickly and the situation was resolved by Mackinnon who recovered and reacted first. Realising what had happened, he turned on the hijackers holding Tam. With a quick stride he had closed the gap between them, shoving the muzzle of the machine gun into the ribs of the nearer Vietnamese, and was bodily forcing the trio backwards. The two men lost their nerve. With a strong, cuffing sweep of his powerful left arm, his right still pressing the firearm into the ribs of the right-hand bandit, Mackinnon detached Tam, flinging off her other captor as he roughly slammed the two of them against the flag locker across the rear of the wheelhouse.

Cushioned by the man, Tam was only shaken. Observing Mackinnon's purpose in separating Tam, Stevenson called, 'Here! Come here!'

'Where Chief Officer? Where *Dafoo*?' Mackinnon asked harshly of the quailing bandits. The two men shrank back as Mackinnon continued to menace them with the gun. 'Give me another shot, Alex.'

Gingerly Stevenson pointed the gun upwards and pulled the trigger. A shower of splinters leapt from the teak rail round the monkey island. Involuntarily, he squeezed the trigger again and a second shot rang out. The next moment, pushed out of the wheelhouse on to the port wing, the two

Vietnamese suddenly broke and fled, scrambling down the port ladder.

'Shall I follow them?' Stevenson called, but Mackinnon shook his head.

'Leave 'em. Let 'em stew awhile in their own juice. If they'd had a gun they'd have used it. I think we hold all the cards now.' Mackinnon nodded at Phan. 'You can tie this bugger's hands behind his back and secure him to the telegraph.'

'Where belong Chief Officer?' Mackinnon turned to Tam and Stevenson. 'Ask him, will you?' Mackinnon said as Stevenson found a length of flag halliard and crouched beside Phan. 'Tell him if anything has happened to them it'll be the worst for him.'

Tam spoke to Phan and he replied slowly and with some difficulty. Watching, Mackinnon regretted hitting him and felt sorry for the man. His anger waned rapidly now he had control of the ship again. A few moments later Stevenson had released Rawlings and Sparks from their imprisonment.

They appeared somewhat sheepishly in the wheelhouse doorway.

'Trust you two old ladies to be locked in the lavatory,' Mackinnon remarked.

'Have you seen that ship, sir?' Rawlings riposted, and Mackinnon looked round. Not three miles away, south-bound for Singapore, a large container ship thrashed past at speed. It recalled Mackinnon to the present.

'I suppose we didn't get stars?' he asked.

'No, sir; I'm sorry,' Rawlings said, pleased old Gorilla had used the first person plural and did not blame him for their lack of a position fix.

Mackinnon grunted. 'I wonder where the hell we are.'

'I'll go and try for a D/F bearing, sir, from Wang Lan,' volunteered Sparks, equally anxious to wipe out the humiliation of time spent in close proximity to a urinal pan and the nervously perspiring Rawlings.

'Good idea, Sparks,' Mackinnon said.

'I don't think you'll find your radio-room in the state you left it,' Stevenson advised the Radio Officer as he made to go below.

'Oh, Christ.' Sparks pulled a face and went down the ladder.

Mackinnon stepped out on to the bridge wing and called Rawlings over.

'Let's have this cleared away,' he ordered, pointing at Macgregor's bloody body, 'and this mess hosed down.'

He watched the huge grey 'box boat' sweep past. She flew the Panamanian flag, like themselves, but Mackinnon knew she was owned by a *taipan*'s house in Hong Kong.

'Looks like the Chinese finally won the opium war,' he muttered. The sea had gone down and the wind, veering steadily in the wake of the storm, was blowing across the run of the waves so the long hull of the passing vessel lifted and rolled with graceful ease.

Mackinnon caught Tam's eye. She was standing in the wheelhouse door watching with preoccupied fascination as Braddock and Pritchard lifted Macgregor's corpse. He realised he had forgotten the forlorn duffle-coated figure isolated at the back of the wheelhouse. He indicated the container ship.

'Sign of the times,' he said kindly, aware she had no idea to what he alluded. 'Alex will look after you,' he said slowly.

Why had he said that? True, Stevenson had not demurred when Mackinnon had referred to his interest in the girl earlier, but it was not the real reason he had pushed them together. Mackinnon was aware he saw something of himself in Stevenson, and something of Akiko in Tam. He chid himself for his silliness; it was nothing other than an old man's fancy. Far more likely the girl would get her claws into Stevenson to keep her out of the cages in Hong Kong. He hoped Stevenson was wise enough to see through such a ploy. Anyway, Mackinnon had more important things to think about; *he* could not marry them, despite what Hollywood

279

thought! He raised his binoculars and swept the horizon ahead of the *Matthew Flinders*. 'D'you think there's the remotest chance of some breakfast?'

It was the old woman who put the idea into Tam's head. 'He wants you,' she had said, 'take him, he will make a good husband.'

Tam had considered the matter. She dreaded the future and knew what the old woman said made sense, but she had no affection for white men. Her earliest recollections of them were all of horror. They had destroyed the village where she had been born in an inferno of searing heat. The remnant of her family had migrated to the city where the insecurity of survival had broken it up. Since the day she had first known the stench of napalm she had been on the move, a nomad. The tranquillity of those long-ago, childhood memories of village life had goaded her on until, in her search for the unattainable, she had been caught up in the escape in the rotting junk.

'He's not an American,' the old woman had explained, exasperated with Tam's finer feelings, 'he's a strong man, a young man.' She had sucked her gold teeth and swayed back and forwards. 'Ah, if I was young again . . .'

Obeying Mackinnon's order, Stevenson led her below, aware of her nakedness under the heavy duffle coat which she clasped tightly about her. He must find something for her to wear, he thought, and it was difficult for him to throw off the image of her slender body exposed to Macgregor in the wrecked radio-room.

He opened his cabin door and stood aside for her to enter. Their eyes met and the prickling spur of lust at their sudden concupiscence gave way to an overwhelming pity.

He began to pull open drawers and his hanging cupboard. He found her a coloured shirt, some flip-flops, a sweater and a spare sarong he wore at night.

'That's a bit of luck,' he said, holding it out to her. She

took the thin cotton garment, let it fall from its folds and draped it from her waist. As she looked down at herself, her hair fell across her face. Impulsively he put out his hand and stroked the lock away. She raised her head and he caught her chin in his cupped hand. Very slowly he bent to kiss her, but she drew sharply back.

For a moment they confronted each other, Stevenson momentarily affronted by her rejection until his good sense reminded him of the ordeal through which she had just been.

She felt confused, repulsed by his touch, yet moved by his obvious concern. She recalled the old woman's advice and realised she did not want to take advantage of the man before her. She shook her head.

'I'm sorry,' he said, exuding a deliberate, if forced cheerfulness and returning to practical matters. 'We will get you some proper clothes when we get to Hong Kong.'

'Hong Kong?' she queried, still suspicious. 'Captain say Hong Kong but . . .'

'Yes, Hong Kong, Tam, I promise. It was not a trick,' he said insistently, delighted at the effect his words had upon her. 'You put those on.'

'Alex . . .' her hand was on his arm, restraining him. 'You not tell me lie now?'

'No!' he said vehemently. 'No, of course not. Why should I lie now?' He saw the cloud lift from her face. 'Make yourself at home.' He waved expansively at the appointments of the spartan cabin and left her to herself.

CHAPTER EIGHTEEN

Bloody But Unbowed

A long time ago, it seemed now, before the *Matthew Flinders* reached Singapore and he had swum daily in the pool, wallowing in the balm of the ship's routine, Mackinnon had imagined these last hours. They would be heavy with nostalgia, poignant with sadness but full of a sense of achievement, of effort sustained, of a job well done. His life, he would console himself, had been well spent, a good one and if it wound down on the back of the great institution of the British Merchant Navy, there was a certain, selfish satisfaction in the thought; a graveyard consolation that an old man might hump with him, a sense of being part of a last stand.

If life had taught him that expectations were rarely fulfilled, the sense of that ludicrous propriety was shattered now. The vision of his last days afloat, in command of a British merchantman, had been clouded by that fear of meeting the boat people. Ironically that *was* an expectation which came true and from it, and the typhoon, and the deaths of four people arose his present, far-from-nostalgic last approach to a port.

He raised his glasses. Ahead of the ship as it cleaved a sea of innocent and sparkling blue, the purple hills of China and the Crown Colony of Hong Kong were hardening in their outline, gathering mass and form as they changed to dun and dark green. On the port bow, stared at by Alex Stevenson over the prism of the azimuth mirror on the bearing compass, the white tower of Wang Lan Lighthouse reflected the sun. All about them the bag-wing sails of fishing junks dotted the calm sea and half a dozen ships, container vessels, two tankers and two ro-ro ships, converged or departed from the focal point of Hong Kong's landlocked harbour. It was a scene of tranquil normality; perhaps, Mackinnon thought, the only thing about this day likely to conform to his imagination.

Stevenson straightened from the compass and smiled at Mackinnon as he went into the chart-room to plot the ship's position. How did the young Second Mate feel? Mackinnon's was not the only career due to terminate in the coming hours. He supposed Stevenson's grin was one of those tiny miracles which passed unnoticed in daily life.

'Starboard easy; steer o-one-five,' he said automatically, altering the *Matthew Flinders*'s course to avoid a junk just then hauling her nets two miles ahead of them.

'Starboard, o-one-five.' The helmsman's abbreviated reply came in Pritchard's inimitable accent. Pritchard, Stevenson, Sparks, Thorpe, all good men, *true* characters, the bearers of men of indifferent qualities, men of Rawlings's and Macgregor's stamp. Mackinnon felt nothing towards Macgregor. Like Rawlings, he was simply part of the warp and weft of the sea life.

Mackinnon remembered some lines which had once won a poetry competition run by the old Seafarer's Education Service. In Mackinnon's opinion they were not poetry, for they neither rhymed nor scanned, but they had stuck in his mind:

In passing, I have seen deep sea-scapes,
Been ashore, adrift and drunk
with this world's soiled glories.
Ships and men and places all within
my compassed horizon . . .

In passing, some few sweet kisses,
Given, taken; at hazard and wind
Swept dreams away; alone.
Gale and calm and chilling dawn
and watches stood . . .

How true; of all of them, good, bad and indifferent.

He raised his glasses again and stared at the junk as they swept past. The high, square stern, the peaked, bamboo-battened sail had not changed in a thousand years; its elderly helmsman leaned on the tiller indifferent to their passing. Mackinnon acknowledged a *brüderbond* with so ancient a mariner. Perhaps, he mused, that man's great-grandfather had stared incredulously as the steam dragons of the *fan kwei* moved against wind and current and forced the passage of the Bocca Tigris in the first Opium War!

'Well, old fellow,' Mackinnon muttered, 'you've the last laugh. No more red barbarians.'

And then the extent of his self-deception hit him with an almost physical impact. Below, on the foredeck, walking forward to the foremast, Able Seaman Braddock carried a fluttering red bundle. Mackinnon watched him hitch the Inglefield clips to those on the flag halliard and then, with a smooth, hand-over-hand motion, began to haul the red ensign up until it flew, brilliant in the sunshine, against the cerulean blue of the sky.

'God damn!' Mackinnon swore. The flag of the British Merchant Navy, once the senior squadron flag of the *Royal* Navy was not going to fly as a bloody courtesy ensign on his last morning in command, by God!

The insignificant consequence of their *not* being a British ship (as he had earlier stupidly deluded himself), and therefore having to fly the merchant ensign of the port they were approaching, stung Mackinnon to the quick. Suddenly the day turned upside down, a position from which it was never to recover.

'Braddock!' Mackinnon roared. Just short of the yardarm the red duster halted its ascent and flew as if at half-mast, in mourning, reminding Mackinnon of something else, of an old flag etiquette that in this world of commercial pre-eminence he had almost forgotten. Braddock spun round, looking up at the bridge. 'Take that down,' bellowed the Captain. 'Go and hoist it aft, at half-mast!'

'Sir . . .'

The tone of reasonable protest came from Rawlings, standing in the wheelhouse doorway in his smartly ironed white shirt and shorts. He must have sent Braddock forward with the courtesy ensign.

'Well, what is it?'

'I've already ordered the ensign to be half-masted, sir.'

Mackinnon looked aft. The red and blue squares and stars of the Republic of Panama flew its own depth below the truck of the staff.

'That's not the red ensign, mister,' snapped Mackinnon. 'Ernie York and Charles Taylor arrive in Hong Kong under the red ensign. Even that bastard Macgregor was one of us.'

'But . . .' Rawlings began, then shrugged his shoulders. It was none of his damned business.

Sparks had contemplated his wrecked radio-room with dismay. Not that the ship was out of communication with the rest of the world, for there was a VHF radio telephone on the bridge. It was intended for inter-ship and port operational use, but Sparks had harboured an inner resentment against surrendering the ship's prime communications function to the deck ornaments up there. He made a gallant effort to restore his office and succeeded to the extent of repairing the medium frequency receiver and tuning it to Hong Kong Radio.

To his alarm not only was the *Matthew Flinders* on the traffic list, but was being repeatedly called by the duty operator. He quickly found it impossible to repair the transmitter; Macgregor had destroyed it with the sure hand of instinctive vandalism. Swearing comprehensively, cheated of his final operational function as a ship's Radio Officer, Sparks made his way forward along the boat-deck to the bridge.

He found it crowded. Although Mackinnon stood alone on the port wing, Stevenson ran in and out of the chart-room plotting the ship's approach to Hong Kong every ten minutes, Rawlings fussed about in the wheelhouse, and Able Seaman Pritchard stood at the wheel steering. Over the bow a cleft in the coastline revealed the position of the Lye Mun Pass.

Sparks found the volume control of the wheelhouse VHF set turned down. With a savage satisfaction he twisted the knob and the wheelhouse boomed with the weary voice of the operator:

'*Matthew Flinders, Matthew Flinders, Matthew Flinders*, this is Hong Kong Radio calling the Panamanian ship *Matthew Flinders*, come in. Over.'

Sparks was suddenly surrounded by staring faces. 'You had the volume turned down,' he said with collective accusation, 'they've been calling for ages.'

'Well answer them, then,' snapped Rawlings, irritable at Mackinnon's behaviour and secretly pleased at the operator's correct use of their formal nationality.

Sparks shot the Chief Officer a resentful glance; what did it matter now when the voyage was all but over?

'Hong Kong Radio, this is the *Matthew Flinders*, come in. Over.'

'Chop channel twelve,' came the curt reply. Sparks changed frequency.

'Hong Kong Radio, this is the *Matthew Flinders*. Over.'

'Ah, *Matthew Flinders*, been trying to contact you for two hours. What are your intentions?'

'Tell him,' said Mackinnon, looming in the wheelhouse doorway, his face dark with anger. '*I* intend entering Hong Kong Harbour.'

Sparks swallowed and a sense of foreboding, of having

touched something he could not quite comprehend swept over him. He felt a hammering of his heart at that emphasised monosyllable of mastery.

'Hong Kong Radio, this is *Matthew Flinders*, intend entering Hong Kong Harbour . . .'

'Bound for the quarantine anchorage. Pilot required in half an hour,' prompted Mackinnon.

'Bound for the quarantine anchorage. Pilot required in half an hour. Over,' Sparks dutifully repeated.

There was a short silence, then the operator's voice came back: 'We have no knowledge of your ETA, *Matthew Flinders*, minimum notice for pilotage is—

'Pettifogging bugger,' snapped Mackinnon, 'give me that bloody thing.' Mackinnon's voice drowned the operator's as he shoved Rawlings aside and took the handset from Sparks.

' . . . Your entry not permitted at this time. Over,' the Operator's voice concluded.

'Hong Kong Radio, this is the *Matthew Flinders*. Master speaking. My radio sets have been damaged, my ship is short of fuel after weathering Typhoon David. I intend entering Hong Kong as port of refuge. I have four dead on board. I require a doctor and can manage the pilotage if necessary. Over.'

Mackinnon lowered the handset and Sparks noticed he was biting his lower lip. Behind him Rawlings expelled his breath with an audible incredulity.

'*Matthew Flinders* this is Hong Kong. Wait one.'

In the wheelhouse the atmosphere was tense as they waited for the reply. Mackinnon broke the silence.

'Starboard easy.'

The pale blue hull and white upperworks of another container ship appeared through the cleft in the hills and its profile foreshortened as it altered course towards them, coming on to the reciprocal of their own headings.

'Midships. Steady on o-one-five.'

Pritchard repeated the order and the waiting officers

watched, apparently mesmerised by the simple evolution. With every passing moment the *Matthew Flinders* drew closer to the port. Details stood out on the shoreline. The sparse scrub on the hillsides, the houses and the gleam of sunlight in metallic reflection from a moving car.

Like marionnettes they jerked to the sudden squawk of the VHF radio.

'*Matthew Flinders*, please confirm you received orders for Shanghai. Over.'

'Hong Kong, this is *Flinders*. Confirm affirmative.'

'Roger. Please also confirm you have refugees on board.'

'Confirm affirmative,' Mackinnon repeated, adding, 'one hundred and forty-five souls.'

'Wait one.'

Again the deadly silence of shoreside consultation and the expectant hiatus on the bridge. At a mile every four minutes the *Matthew Flinders* ate up the distance to the gap in the hills beyond which lay the harbour of Hong Kong. Already, ten knots faster than themelves, the huge, blue container liner bore down upon them. The officers continued to watch her, thinking the same thing: that she was their supersessor. The hull colour and the logoed funnel were familiar to them. As she swept past, the flag of Liberia was a mere handkerchief above the one-hundred-feet-wide transom. On her bridge they could see two tiny figures staring at them through binoculars as once steamship men had looked at the last, rusty windjammers.

'*Matthew Flinders*, this is Hong Kong Radio, do you receive? Over.'

'Loud and clear, Hong Kong. Go ahead. Over.'

'Entry forbidden, Captain. Do you understand?'

Mackinnon opened his mouth, then shut it, his teeth bearing down on his lower lip. Slowly he looked at each of his officers.

'I don't think I do understand, gentlemen,' he said grimly.

'But sir . . .' protested Rawlings.

288

'What have we got to lose?' he asked, aware of the irony in Rawlings's case. 'And how can you object in the name of common humanity? I'd like to know who exactly made that decision. One of your relatives, I expect, Rawlings.' And Mackinnon turned forward, ordering Pritchard to swing to port, to begin the final approach to the Lye Mun Passage and the entrance to Hong Kong.

The disembodied voice of the VHF persisted to query them.

'*Matthew Flinders* this is Hong Kong Radio. Do you read me? Please confirm you received my last. Over.'

'Be a good fellow, Sparks,' Mackinnon said, 'and turn the volume down.'

The Captain was smiling as he walked nonchalantly back on to the port bridge-wing. Behind him in the wheelhouse Sparks and Rawlings exchanged glances.

Mackinnon was aware that he had thrown down the gauntlet. Leaning again on the rail he was aware, too, that below him, crowding the main-deck rail, the Vietnamese were mingling with the idlers among the crew, seamen waiting to go to stations, stewards and off-duty greasers, chattering together and excitedly pointing to where the first pale tower blocks appeared beyond the shoulder of the headland. Mackinnon shook his head in wonder; it was unusual for the ship's company to fraternise even on the approach to so popular a port as Hong Kong; it seemed the Vietnamese had acted as a social catalyst. It was just as well they did not know what was awaiting them on Stonecutter's Island.

'Sir . . .'

The note of alarm in Stevenson's voice alerted Mackinnon. The Second Mate, his glasses in one hand, pointed ahead with the other.

'I was expecting some such visitation,' muttered Mackinnon.

The Bird-class patrol vessel, pale grey with a feather of

289

white at her forefoot, came clear of the land and headed out towards them. Immediately the twinkle of a signalling projector flashed imperiously from her bridge.

'Shall I answer, sir?' asked Stevenson.

'No,' replied Mackinnon languidly, 'ring down and ask the Bosun to put the pilot ladder over on the port side.' Mackinnon glanced up, amused at the outrage and confusion on Rawlings' face.

'Put the engines on stand-by, mister.' he ordered.

The patrol craft swept across the bow and circled under the stern of the *Matthew Flinders*. On her tiny bridge they could see the white-capped naval officers studying them. A white ensign fluttered above the stern and they could read her name in small red letters on her quarter: *Starling*. Mackinnon was reducing speed progressively as he slowed his ship for the Lye Mun. As he did so, with a dull roar, HMS *Starling* gunned her engines and began to overtake them. Members of *Starling*'s crew in the berets and blue cotton of Number Eight rig were taking the canvas cover off the 40mm Bofors gun on her foredeck. As they clustered round the exposed gun they pointed at the gaggle of refugees and crew that stared back at the *Starling*'s unnecessarily aggressive appearance.

'Bloody hell, James Dent's aboard.' Rawlings was clearly more apprehensive at the appearance of the chairman of Eastern Steam than the hostile intent of Her Majesty's Navy.

As the little warship ran up alongside and slowed to match her speed with that of the elderly cargo-liner, Mackinnon stared down on the blond, swept-back hair of the ship owner, saw him point, presumably recognising the figure above them, and watched the naval officer beside him put the portable loud-hailer to his mouth.

'Captain Mackinnon!'

The naval Lieutenant's voice echoed eerily off the old

liner's wall side, as though they were in some vast cave rather than the open air.

'You must stop your ship. You are forbidden entry into Hong Kong Harbour. I am empowered to arrest your vessel if you attempt to enter.'

Mackinnon watched the patrol boat's First Lieutenant lean over the bridge front and the Bofors was trained sharply to starboard. Bristling at the indignity of being brought under the cover of a gun his taxes paid for, he disdained a hailer and bellowed back at the young officer:

'I demand a port of refuge. I am almost out of fuel and I have four dead on board in addition to the boat people you can see. Furthermore I am committed to the Lye Mun Pass now and unable to turn around. I suggest you take that ridiculous gun off us and send someone on board . . .'

A clatter of wooden rungs striking steel told where the Bosun and Braddock had thrown the pilot ladder over the side.

Aboard *Starling* there was a brief moment of consultation.

'So, James Dent represents the government of Hong Kong, does he?' Mackinnon muttered to himself. 'He must have been pulling some high strings.' He called over his shoulder. 'Go down and welcome our guests, Alex . . . You stay here, mister,' he added, as Rawlings made a move towards the ladder. Mackinnon watched while the *Starling* edged closer and bumped gently alongside the rope ladder.

Below him, the patrol boat's skipper handed over to his Number One and led James Dent down on to her deck, then forward to where the *Matthew Flinders*'s pilot ladder dangled. The two men scrambled aboard and, with a grumble of her Paxman diesels, HMS *Starling* pulled off and ranged herself off the *Matthew Flinders*'s side.

Mackinnon heard the step on the ladder and swivelled to meet the intruders. Stevenson appeared first and, proper to the last, introduced the naval officer.

'Lieutenant Drinkwater, sir,' he said, adding after a slight pause, 'And Mr Dent.'

291

'So, the Navy's here, Lieutenant Drinkwater,' Mackinnon said, holding out his hand and marvelling at the youth of the naval officer. 'I recall another *Starling*, d'you know? *She* was the toast of the Western Approaches.'

The apparent cordiality disarmed the boy as Mackinnon detached his hand, turned to the civilian bringing up the rear and with deliberate impudence greeted his employer.

'Well, well, what seduces a shipowner from his VDU, James?'

Dent with equally offensive purpose ignored Mackinnon's outstretched fist.

'I thought so,' he said quickly. 'This is done on purpose, isn't it, Mackinnon?'

'That might be a perceptive remark, James,' Mackinnon replied smoothly, 'it might even do your conscience credit in respect of my shortly to be out of work crew, but it is a foolish one.' Mackinnon addressed the naval officer. 'Lieutenant Drinkwater, my ship has just suffered an ordeal in passing through Typhoon David – you may inspect the logbook and the damage if you are not inclined to believe me – and we are desperately short of oil fuel. The Chief Engineer, who was, incidentally, killed in the typhoon, was under orders from this gentleman here not to over-bunker, to have only enough fuel to reach Hong Kong . . .'

'Just a minute,' broke in Dent, but Mackinnon discarded his mask of exaggerated bonhomie in a flash.

'Hold your tongue, young man. I still command this ship. My demand for refuge is paramount. Moreover,' he went on, addressing Drinkwater again, 'I have had to put down a misguided attempt to take over the ship.'

'By the Vietnamese?' the naval Lieutenant asked.

'Yes. They have an understandable aversion to going to Shanghai.'

'You say you are in command now, Captain, so you are clearly not in need of our traditional support in quelling insurrection,' Drinkwater said, revealing either a quick intelligence or a good briefing, 'nor are you a British ship.'

Mackinnon knew Rawlings was behind him, heard his noisy exhalation of satisfaction as the perceptive Drinkwater cornered him. He wished his Chief Officer was neither so abominably crude, nor so insufferably stupid. It pained him, after so long an acquaintance, not to have earned a better opinion in Rawlings's estimation. The Chief Officer seemed to derive even greater satisfaction from Lieutenant Drinkwater's next remark; or perhaps his noises of concurrence were for Dent's consumption, non-verbal communications of being in dispute with his Captain, caught on the fence of loyalty and conscience but thereby revealing he was really on the side of the twin shibboleths of law and order.

'You are flying the red ensign of Great Britain quite illegally, Captain.' Lieutenant Drinkwater gestured aft.

'Alter course position coming up, sir,' prompted Stevenson. Ahead of them green hills rose on either bow and between them could now be clearly seen the harbour with its throng of anchored and moored ships, its criss-crossing traffic of ferries, junks and *wallah-wallahs*. On the port bow a shanty town appeared to tumble down the side of the headland. Beyond, office buildings rose from the city's traffic haze and houses climbed the slopes of the Peak almost to the summit, where, shrouded by a light swirl of cloud, the villas of the *taipan* squatted amid rich foliage. Above the urban sprawl of Kowloon opposite, a Jumbo jet lifted from Kai Tak, angling above the harbour as it swung and headed south towards Singapore.

This was, Mackinnon thought, a crazy moment, a moment of true farce, the end of everything for him, for there could be no going on beyond it. Here, at the doorstep of Britain's last colony, the 'fragrant harbour' nicked from the old moribund Celestial Empire, a British master-mariner on a ship whose nationality was a commercial expedient, was about to be threatened, bullied, or perhaps arrested by an

293

officer in the armed services of the state to whom he paid his taxes, for the crime of claiming the ancient right of refuge. The young officer, brought up on a diet of 'my country right or wrong', was angry at Mackinnon's truculence as much as by the embarrassing presence of the unwanted refugees below them.

Beside the naval officer the ship's owner, himself brought up on the self-justifying and apparenly irrefutable dictates of profit, sought immediate disencumbrance of the human flotsam his ship had picked up. Moreover, he had enlisted, through God knew what network of artifice and connivance, the help of the Royal Navy.

'Take her in Alex, if you please.'

'Aye, aye, sir.'

Mackinnon turned his attention back to Dent and Drinkwater. 'It may be a technicality that this ship is not British, Lieutenant, and I'd personally be quite glad to stand up in court and tell you and the rest of the world why I have a nostalgic and hopelessly out-of-date affection for that bit of bunting hanging over the arse end of my ship, but that's all airy-fairy nonsense. The fact is, I've no fuel, my ship's company have taken some knocks, I've a dead woman and I have had a British national killed on board, in front of witnesses, by a Vietnamese gunman. I have had a second British national die accidentally, and another in the line of doing his duty. I therefore insist you allow me to anchor in the quarantine anchorage until we solve this little impasse.'

'Mackinnon . . .' Dent began, but Mackinnon rounded on him.

'*Captain* Mackinnon to you, and before you say anything, there is nothing further you can do to me. I shall walk down the gangway the instant the anchor brings up. British or Panamanian, it doesn't matter, I command until the ship is brought safely to port. You are both powerless to prevent my doing anything else. Whatever the circumstances, gentlemen, illegal flags and frustrated owners notwithstanding, I alone am responsible for the ship.'

Leaving them staring open-mouthed after him, he addressed the eavesdropping Rawlings.

'Have the Carpenter stand by the starboard anchor, Mr Rawlings,' he said, and he was consoled by the astonished obedience of the Mate. 'Perhaps, Lieutenant,' Mackinnon threw over his shoulder, 'you'd like to make the necessary arrangements with the authorities. Help yourself to our VHF radio. Turn it up, will you, Sparks?'

Lieutenant Drinkwater was about to remonstrate, thought better of it and took the handset from the Radio Officer. Mackinnon crossed the wheelhouse and confronted Rawlings.

'Get that man out of the urinal, mister,' he ordered curtly, ignoring Dent, who was recovering from his discomfiture.

'Captain Mackinnon, you'll regret this, you know . . .'

Mackinnon paid no attention to the dialogue Drinkwater was having with the shore authorities. Instead he watched approvingly as Stevenson conned the ship through the narrow passage. The Second Mate had a natural aptitude; what a pity it was going to go to waste.

Drinkwater put down the VHF. 'I've cleared the matter for the time being, Captain. You may use the immigration anchorage.' A certain relief was obvious in the naval officer's tone.

'I'm obliged to you, Lieutenant.'

Dent spun on his heel and went out on to the bridge-wing. Drinkwater looked sheepishly around the wheelhouse.

'I think you'd better take charge of this,' Mackinnon said, picking up Phan's machine gun from the flag locker and handing it to the Lieutenant. 'You're the gunnery expert . . . ah Mr Rawlings.'

Rawlings appeared in the wheelhouse doorway with the trussed and downcast Phan. Mackinnon grinned at Drinkwater. 'And you have custody of this fellow, Lieutenant. *He* tried to take the ship from me too.'

CHAPTER NINETEEN
The Blessings of the Land

Mackinnon did not quite carry out his threat of walking down the gangway directly the ship was brought to her anchor. In fact the *Matthew Flinders* was forbidden to lower her gangway and Lieutenant Drinkwater's departure heralded the arrival of a squad of police while a police patrol launch circled the ship ceaselessly.

Disarmed by Mackinnon's obduracy and reduced to impotence when Drinkwater found no grounds to enforce the prohibition of the *Matthew Flinders*'s entry, Dent had departed in a fury. Imprecations had been muttered about old fools and ingratitude and something about what Mrs Mackinnon would think about it all. Even the young naval officer, confused and embarrassed by the obvious innate honesty of Mackinnon's claim, had been drawn into these half-hearted threats.

'A sound and fury signifying nothing,' Mackinnon had said to the wheelhouse as HMS *Starling* bore away their visitors.

'I shouldn't be too sure,' the cavilling Rawlings had mouthed in a low voice behind Mackinnon's back. He could still not quite believe the audacity of Mackinnon's act, for Dent had repeated the order to take the ship to Shanghai and the Captain had refused it.

'Let Rawlings do it,' Mackinnon had said, 'he'll be able to retire to the shires and stick 'Captain' in front of his name. No one will ever know it was only for four days.

At almost that very moment a deputation from the crew, led by the Bosun, had arrived to announce their refusal to take the ship beyond Hong Kong.

'I'll get a local crew to do it,' raged the thwarted Dent.

'Then there's no problem, is there?' Mackinnon had temporised mildly, escorting Dent to the bridge ladder. If the appearance of the Bosun had not been evidence enough of the undercurrents racing through the vessel, of others settling their own individual fates while the political aspects of the ship's entry into Hong Kong were being disputed on the bridge, the crowd assembled at the foot of the ladder proved it beyond doubt.

They had stood mute, a triangle of upturned faces with Tam, clutching the baby, at their apex. For a moment Drinkwater and Dent had paused, their vulnerability as individual men overriding the pomp of their respective offices. Then the expectant seven score of supplicant souls drew back and allowed them to pass with a noise like wind through dry grass.

Now, lying in his bath contemplating the mound of his hairy belly, Mackinnon could find himself wishing they had not consented to so smooth a passage for the twin emissaries of authority. But perhaps, he chastened himself, a show of hostility would have destroyed what little hope of official compassion existed. Pragmatically he knew he had provided the hard-pressed Hong Kong government with but one more burden. But politicians and diplomats, he consoled himself, should have to earn their money and privileges in the same harsh world as common dogs like seamen.

The thought amused him and he fumbled for the soap, thinking of Shelagh and that the day was not yet over.

There was a general air of resentment at the refusal of the Immigration Officers to clear the ship and allow the crew shore leave.

'More days more dollars,' advised the Bosun, grinning at the padre from the Mission to Seamen who had been allowed on board, alone among the queuing tailors, vendors, barbers and sew-sew women bobbing alongside in *sampans* and *wallah-wallahs*. Even Dent could not deny the rights of the dead to decent burial.

'It's odd, you know, Padre,' said Stevenson, deputed to liaise, 'the man Macgregor was a holy terror – if you'll pardon the expression – when he was alive, but dead he was the trump card the Old Man played to get us in here.'

'The ways of God are passing our understanding . . .' In the alleyway the words had a hollow, insubstantial ring, like a primitive, meaningless incantation, yet something in the manner of their utterance struck Stevenson, whose mind revolved round certain preoccupations.

'You really believe that, don't you?'

'D'you think I'd do a thankless job like this if I didn't?' replied the priest, a twinkle in his blue eyes. 'I'm not aware of having made a single conversion in over twenty years of this work. Nowadays I don't even minister to nominal Christians, like yourself. Most of my pastoral care is with Asiatic seamen, Filipinos and the like, but . . .' The man shrugged as if mere words could not encompass the spiritual enormity of his situation. Then he caught Stevenson's eyes. 'Anyway, what is reality, eh?'

'A bit like Voltaire's definition of history, I guess,' said Stevenson, 'a fable upon which we are all agreed, more or less.'

'Yes, and our indifference to its unpleasantness is but a conspiracy of concurrence. So, my friend, we go on.'

'What will happen to them, Padre?'

'The boat people? Oh, they'll join the thousands already held in the camps around the colony. This is Asia, after all.'

'Not a very happy ending to our joint ordeal, is it?'

'The only ending of this temporal life any of us can look forward to is the common one of death.'

298

'Yes, but . . .'

'Are you still under the illusory influence of things like justice and the freedom to seek happiness? Surely you've been at sea long enough to know the nonsense of that?'

'I suppose I have.' Stevenson grinned ruefully. 'It's not a comfortable feeling though, is it? Why were we equipped to dream of it?'

'Ah, there you hit the eternal mysteries bang on the head. But don't let an old cynic like me influence you. The world needs romantics like you. Come to communion in the mission chapel and hear what comfortable words our saviour Christ said . . .'

' "Come unto me all that travail and are heavy laden and I will refresh you".'

'You are not such a nominal Christian after all.'

'I'll come to communion, Padre, and afterwards I would like a word with you. I'm sure the fable of reality can be manipulated a touch.'

The peculiarity of the day pursued Mackinnon to its very end. Allowed to leave the ship to make a deposition concerning his need of refuge and to note protest in case of claims of damage to cargo during Typhoon David while the authorities debated the fate of the boat people, he boarded a *wallah-wallah*. The little launch swung round and crossed under the stern of the *Matthew Flinders*. Mackinnon stood looking at his last command. Men who serve aboard ship only infrequently see them from the outside and to Mackinnon the sight brought satisfaction. The topsides were rust-streaked, and fresh corrosion showed on her white upperworks, evidence of her ordeal in the typhoon. Above him Stevenson was lowering the 'illegal' red ensign.

'Sunset,' he called down by way of explanation and Mackinnon nodded, raising a hand in a half-wave that was also a kind of instinctive, valedictory salute. As the *wallah-wallah* drew away, the ship's side seemed to blaze like molten metal, high-lit by the near-horizontal rays of the sun as it set behind banks of inky cumulus hanging above the distant hills of China proper. The light flared, too, on the jagged and rusty wreck of a huge ship lying on the bottom of the harbour, a burnt-out hulk which was one more symbol in this eventful day.

The great wreck had once been one of the wonders of the maritime world, the Royal Mail Ship *Queen Elizabeth*, pride of the Cunard-White Star Line, whose first task had been the swift transportation of Canadian and American soldiers across the North Atlantic Ocean before she settled to her true, post-war business of carrying passengers between Britain and the United States.

Now she lay discarded, a gravestone of a merchant fleet of which she had once been cast, quite spuriously, as the flagship. It hardly seemed to matter now; she was nothing more than a consumed relic, a metaphor for all the thousands of ships that had once been part of something greater than the sum of its separate parts.

The great transatlantic liner's corroding superstructure rose from the grubby waters of the harbour like a gigantic tombstone. Mackinnon turned away profoundly moved. Then, unable to restrain himself, he looked back. Not a gravestone: she was the burnt, awry totem of a disinherited tribe.

Darkness crept over the water. The sun had set and the gentle breeze was suddenly chilly.

Shelagh was waiting for him in her hotel room. Their meeting was undemonstrative. They hugged each other and kissed, as though only a day or so had separated them.

She seemed older, he thought, the smart formality of new clothes setting off her still comely figure, but emphasising the lines of her face.

'You look tired,' she said, and he knew she was thinking the same thing.

'It's been a long day.'

'I expected you earlier. I saw the ship come in.' The lilt of her voice was ageless, the voice of the young Irish farm girl he had first met as a shipwrecked apprentice forty-odd years earlier.

'We had some problems,' he said shortly. 'Picked up a load of boat people which the locals didn't want and I had to note protest and then go to the police mortuary.'

'Mortuary?'

'One of the crew.' He did not enlarge. It was better not to try and tell her everything all at once. Besides, he wanted to tell her *all* about it, most especially how she had inspired him to turn surgeon, and he knew this was not the moment. He was emotionally drained from informing York's widow of her husband's death and the frustration of being unable to contact Taylor's widow.

'I've some gin and some tonic.'

'Bless you.'

'Did you read the book about the Uffizi?'

Mackinnon laughed and shook his head. 'Somehow I never quite got round to it.'

'Mr Dent rang me this afternoon.' She tinkled ice into two glasses. 'He said something about the company being unable to pay my hotel bill after tomorrow. You've fallen out, haven't you?'

'Not before time. The presence of the boat people embarrassed him. He had sold the ship to the Chinese in Shanghai. I'm supposed to take her up there but,' he shrugged, 'I've told him it's not on. Rawlings can do that.'

'I'm pleased, darling,' she said, handing him the drink and sitting down opposite him. 'Dent mentioned the boat people . . .'

At the prompting Mackinnon began to tell her. He spoke of their arrival at Singapore and his sense of foreboding, of the approach of the typhoon and Taylor's mistake; of the rescue and its awful sequel, the operation; of the long

301

struggle through the worst weather he had ever experienced, the deaths of Ernie York, of Taylor, the Vietnamese woman and then Macgregor.

Finally he explained his feelings at the end, as the *Matthew Flinders* arrived at Hong Kong.

'James Dent and this young naval chap came on the bridge as though they owned the whole bloody world. It was quite odd, you know. I had this overwhelming sense of solidarity with those unfortunate refugees; suddenly I had nothing in common with the two representatives of my own nation. It struck me that nationality meant nothing in the circumstances. What *does* it mean, beyond acknowledging the fact that one is born on the same chunk of earth as others? Like institutionalised religion I felt it was a superimposed doctrine, an idea become fact and a fact become chains. In the war, running cargoes to Russia and across the Atlantic, we were taught to feel part of something greater, part of the *Allied* war effort. This morning I thought I was part of something greater even than that. After all, I am a seaman; whatever else we may be, we're an international confraternity, sharing the common perils of the sea, beyond the boundaries of men like Dent. Moreover, with my career ending, I had become something else, something the very end actually conferred upon me: I am a free spirit. I could do what I liked, do what I thought was right. What was Dent but a trafficker? So, for lots of reasons,' he ended on a note of abrupt self-deprecation, 'I defied the bugger, and brought the ship into Hong Kong. Not that she had the fuel to go much further.'

'I never liked James Dent.'

'It's strange, you know, but you've seen the wreck of the old *Queen Elizabeth*?' She nodded. 'I'm a bloody old fool, but I thought it looked symbolic, lying there. Made me think of my feelings about nationality and whether I might not be a traitor, or something. Then I realised my repudiation of nationality was as rational as the shipowners'. Don't you think that's odd?'

302

'Not as odd as what happened to me on the flight out.'

'What? I don't understand.'

'You remember how she died . . . how we never knew . . .'

Shelagh never mentioned their child by name. It was her way of coping, of coming to terms with the indifference of death. 'I sat next to a woman, an Army wife coming back out to rejoin her husband. You know the way people chat on long flights. She'd just lost her son, a four-year-old. It sounded just like *her* . . . the symptoms, the lethargy, the weakness . . .' She fell silent.

'Go on,' Mackinnon prompted, his voice low, thinking how attractive she looked to him. The single bedside light threw her face into sharp focus, revealing the beauty of it.

'It's rare, but it's got a name, an auto-immune disease, dermatomyositis.'

The name meant nothing to him beyond the realisation that it pleased Shelagh to have discovered the cause of their child's death.

'In a sense,' she went on, her explanation ruthless in its long-deferred pursuit of the truth, 'the body starts to consume itself.'

'It's odd,' he said quietly, 'how life goes round in circles.'

Neither Stevenson nor Rawlings expected Mackinnon to return aboard before the morning. This irritated Rawlings, partly because of the confusion and irregularity inherent in their arrival, and partly because, with Taylor dead, he had perforce to split the night duty with the Second Mate. By contrast, Stevenson could not have cared less.

He had had no sleep before climbing to the bridge, for to him, in his capacity as liaison officer, had fallen the sad duty of seeing ashore the bodies of Chief Engineer York, Third Officer Taylor, Able Seaman Macgregor and the Vietnamese woman.

The padre had made the necessary arrangements and

Stevenson had seen the bodies into police custody. Tomorrow, almost as his last act as Master, Mackinnon would have to register the deaths. He had already formally identified the bodies.

The inactivity of a midnight-to-six anchor watch brought home the fact that it was all over, and with a finality outside the normal emphasised by the presence on the bridge of the smartly uniformed Chinese policeman. Whatever happened to the ship, her true voyaging finished here, tonight, along with that of Mackinnon and himself and the rest of them. In a prescient moment Stevenson knew Rawlings would find, as time passed, his three – or four-day tenure of command a mild mockery. Stevenson wished him well, indifferent to the Chief Officer's inner self, knowing he was adequately provided for.

A figure loomed at the head of the starboard ladder and Stevenson turned at the intrusion. 'Can't you sleep?'

'No.' Sparks settled himself beside Stevenson, elbows on the dew-damp teak rail, and they stared in companionable silence over the waters of Hong Kong harbour.

The night was overcast, the glow of the colony's millions of lights were reflected in an orange glow from the cloud base. Crowded at the waterfront level, lessening in density higher up the Peak, they sparkled or flashed in the myriad colours of the advertising logos. The Chinese and Roman characters spelled the familiar names of companies known the world over, the American conglomerate, the Japanese *daibatsu*, the German corporations; airlines, electronics companies, beer and soft drinks manufacturers silently screamed the message of their commercial insistence like precocious children demanding attention. Both men felt the incongruous contrast of their situation compared with the peril through which they had so recently passed; yet neither could express the dichotomy, for in its brazen embrace they felt the comfort of normality.

On and off the lights flashed, the brilliance of the neon

colours thrown back by the black, soulless waters of the harbour.

Opposite, from the lower levels of Kowloon, answering broadsides flickered from the environs of Nathan Road, fading into the dark hills of the New Territories beyond which brooded China.

Criss-crossing the harbour, ferries and *wallah-wallahs* made their ceaseless way while clusters of brilliance marked the merchant ships. Here and there the matrix of shore light was obscured by the batwing sail of an ancient junk ghosting silently through the crowded waters, its oil lamps ineffective in the prevailing glare.

'Bit of an anticlimax, isn't it?' Stevenson said at last, as though the phrase was the final precipitation of his thoughts.

'Yes; but the end of a voyage always was.' Reasonably, Sparks temporised, the eternal optimist, though the use of the past tense was evidence of the importance of the moment in their shared lives.

'You're not going on to Shanghai?'

'I've got no choice,' Sparks replied. 'Unless Dent kicks us all ashore. I can't afford to jeopardise my pay off. Not now, not after all these years. What about you?'

'I've been doing some thinking. I don't know for sure yet.'

'Other fish to fry, ch?' Sparks looked at the younger man, half-envying him his foot-loose youth.

'I don't know that either, yet.'

'Well good luck. I suppose we must chalk it up to experience.'

'Yes.'

'You had a rough time from what I hear. I only got locked in the shit-house!' They chuckled together, reviewing their respective luck.

'I'm sorry we didn't save the woman,' Stevenson said, thinking of the baby.

'Pity, after what the Old Man, Chas Taylor and Freddie did.'

'Yes, poor Chas . . . I keep thinking of him and poor old

305

Ernie York; even Macgregor. He was going to fill me in here, if he got the chance.'

Sparks grunted. 'Man proposes and God fucks him up,' he philosophised.

'Old Gorilla did pretty well, though, didn't he? Took us all by surprise.'

'Especially Rawlings,' said Sparks, and they chuckled at the Mate's discomfiture. '*He*'s not so bad really. Did a good job with the boat people.'

'Yes. He's okay.'

'I wonder what'll happen to the Viets.'

They relapsed into silence and then Sparks straightened up, slapping the teak rail. 'Well, Alex, I've a busy day tomorrow, up to my bollocks in bumph. Better get some shut-eye. Good night.'

'Good night.'

'Come on, Pritch, drink up.'

Braddock stood with the mess-room rosy in one hand and the other held out for Pritchard's beer can.

'Tidy bugger. You're wors'n my old woman.'

Leaning back in his steel chair, Pritchard tipped the last drops of lager into his upturned mouth with exaggerated finality. Then he lobbed the empty can neatly into the rosy, simultaneously letting his chair slam back on to the deck. The crash of the chair and clatter of can was accompanied by a loud belch.

'You are a coarse sod,' said Braddock inoffensively, returning the rosy to its corner.

'Dat's what my old woman used to say.'

'She'll be able to tell you regular now, remind you what we've had to put up with.'

'Yeah.'

'Funny about Macgregor.'

Pritchard hoisted himself unsteadily to his feet. 'What's funny?'

306

'Don't know, really. Didn't like 'im, but . . .' Braddock shrugged. 'Well, I didn't wish 'im dead.'

Pritchard stretched, his extended fingers reaching the deckhead. 'What's it fucking matter, Brad?'

On the deck above, the refugees were almost all asleep. Armed Chinese constables guarded the doors of both the saloon and the smoke-room. For long into the night the men had smoked and talked in undertones, their voices hissing like waves breaking on a beach. At about one o'clock Freddie Thorpe had made his last rounds before turning in. Peering into the dimly lit saloon he watched the last debate end, the last cigarettes glow in the darkness.

'What happen Vietnamese people?' he asked the policeman, who shrugged. The Chinese officer had seen too much during his service among the Alsatias of Hong Kong's overcrowded purlieus to produce a compassionate response.

'Maybe go to camp, maybe be repatriated.'

'There's cholera in the camps.'

'Maybe. They' – the Chinese constable jerked his head at the settling forms beyond the double doors – 'are a problem; Hong Kong is too small. Hong Kong has plenty of problems.'

'Too many problems in the world,' Thorpe said, turning away.

'Too many people,' said the Chinese policeman to his retreating back.

At two in the morning Stevenson shared a pot of tea with the Chinese constable on the bridge. Their conversation was monosyllabic and neither sought to prolong it. With his cup the policeman retired to the bridge-wing. Stevenson remained in the chart-room writing up the log when Tam, having evaded the guard on the smoke-room door, whispered his name:

'Alex!'

He spun round, pleased to see her. 'Hullo,' he whispered, and quickly drew her out of the policeman's line of sight. 'No can sleep?'

She shook her head and tried to peer out on to the dark bridge-wing in search of the police guard.

'He's okay,' Stevenson reassured her. 'You're all right with me. I'll make you some tea.'

While he bent to the task she asked, 'What happen tomorrow?'

He shook his head, handing her the hot mug. 'I don't know, Tam. Now you are here, in Hong Kong, the padre says the authorities will let you stay. You'll know tomorrow.'

'We'll go to a camp, yes?'

'Yes, I'm afraid so.'

The girl nodded. Illuminated by the dim chart lamp her face was like ivory, a beautiful mask, Stevenson thought, hiding the turmoil and uncertainty within. His heart was thundering in his breast as he braced himself, knowing that her evasion of the police guard and her appearance on the bridge may have been motivated by fear, but hoping something more personal had triggered her action. He felt a prickling shame that despite his bold resolutions all he had done for her was make her a cup of tea.

'There may be cholera in camp,' she said and he felt the force of implication in her dark eyes. He guessed the opportunist desire which might lie beneath the bald statement, yet she had made no effort to entrap him. He suddenly found he did not care, and with the carelessness came the conviction that life was an act of faith. He had cast Cathy aside, but he did not want to lose this girl.

'Tam,' he began huskily, the ridiculous fluttering in his belly inexplicably making his voice quaver so that it faltered. Instead he held out his hands to her.

The morning was a suffocating sequence of bureaucratic obligations for Captain Mackinnon. The crew had to be paid off, statements made in the presence of the Panamanian vice-consul; the deaths had to be registered and depositions made at the Coroner's office. From the agent's he made a telephone call to York's son seeking instructions about the body, followed by a fruitless attempt to do the same for Macgregor. The wretched man had no next of kin, he discovered, and Mackinnon wasted an hour tracking a sister who had long ago deserted the only address they had for her.

Nothing seemed real. His interference with those distant lives as he blundered into their night hours gave him a sense of remote detachment.

A further hour was devoted to locating Caroline Taylor. A man's voice sleepily answered the number he had been given. He refused to let Mackinnon speak to Taylor's widow.

'D'you know what time it is?' the voice protested.

'It's about her husband. She should have been informed . . .'

'Yes, yes, she heard yesterday.' There was an edge of complicit guilt in the man's tone. 'Look, I'm afraid she's not very well at the moment.'

Mackinnon felt a rising anger. Taylor's preoccupied misery came back to him. He held on to his temper and explained he wanted instructions regarding the body.

'I don't think she knows,' the man said after a pause in which, Mackinnon hoped, he had at least consulted the young woman. 'You'd better contact his family. Wait, I'll give you a number.' A strong sense of the lovers divesting themselves of any responsibility came to him, and he imagined it bouncing up to the satellite and back to the other side of the earth while he hung on. In her deceit, Caroline Taylor was, he guessed, far beyond the point of remorse. Perhaps Taylor had known.

When the man finally provided the information Mackinnon dialled again and waited. In his mind's eye the telephone rang in the empty darkness of a large house.

Taylor's mother was icy in her self-control, only her silences betrayed the effort it cost her.

'How did it happen?' she asked and Mackinnon explained at length. From what she subsequenly said Mackinnon concluded she was a widow or lived alone.

'Bury him in Hong Kong, Captain,' she said at last. 'Let me know when it is to be and I will . . .' Her voice caught.

'Are you sure?' Mackinnon asked.

'Yes,' she said, her voice stronger, 'It is what he would have wanted.'

'Yes, I rather think it is,' Mackinnon agreed.

He put the phone down. He was stiff with sitting and rose slowly to his feet. The reactive fatigue after his ordeal was beginning to catch up with him. Wearily he shook his head to clear it, bracing himself for the encounter with Dent.

James Dent received him in an opulent office high above the streets. It commanded a magnificent view of the harbour and Mackinnon knew he was supposed to feel awed, to be trepanned from his familiar environment of a ship's bridge and caught at a disadvantage upon the acre of blood-red carpet. Dent sat behind a large desk, staring out of the window. Over his shoulder the *Matthew Flinders* looked no bigger than a child's shoe.

'I have effected the change of Master,' Mackinnon reported formally. 'Apart from your agent's attendance with the money to pay off the crew, that concludes our business together.'

Dent turned with a studied and intimidating arrogance. 'I looked at your file before I left London, Captain. You've been with us a long time.'

'I knew your grandmother.'

'There's no room for sentiment in business, Captain.'

'Quite so. But you've had your pound of flesh.'

Dent's expression became hard, the handsome, proud young face flushed beneath its cow-lick of blond hair. 'You've

310

caused me a lot of trouble.'

'It doesn't matter much now, does it? Pay off the crew—

'I'm going to,' Dent said with a sudden petulance, and Mackinnon saw, beneath the bland assurance of the businessman, the thwarted youth. 'The whole bloody lot are going. You've made things very awkward for me by bringing the ship here instead of taking it to Shanghai.'

Mackinnon mastered his rising anger. He was too old and tired to change the world. A sudden, terrible and perverse yearning came over him, a poignant desire to be once again on the bridge of the *Matthew Flinders*, to be pitting his wits and his ship against the insensate fury of the typhoon. Odd so awful a situation should seem preferable to giving this spoiled, overpowerful brat a piece of his mind. But it did not matter, could not matter, for he was without influence.

'Call it an act of God, Mr Dent,' he said calmly. 'That's the official designation of the typhoon through which we passed. It made things very awkward for us too.'

'I'm afraid the company will be unable to foot the bill for your wife's accommodation after all,' Dent went on, 'and her air fare is being deducted from our final settlement of salary to you.'

The meanness of Dent's decision failed to outweigh the irony of his action. Despicable as it was, Mackinnon's contempt overcame his affront.

'As you say, Mr Dent, there is absolutely no room for sentiment in business.'

He went out into the wide atrium. A huge and abstract oil painting thick with impasto hung above the beautiful Eurasian receptionist. She smiled mechanically at him. Mackinnon glared ferociously back. In his mind's eye a hundred and forty-six pallid faces stared up at him from the deck of a derelict junk.

'You know nothing,' he said to the astonished young woman, 'nothing at all.'

311

CHAPTER TWENTY
Endangered Species

The room at the Orient Star Hotel was much cheaper and closer to the true heartbeat of Hong Kong. 'More like the *pensiones* of Florence,' Shelagh said, smiling and reminding Mackinnon of the prospect of a leisure limited only by death.

He grunted, sitting on the edge of the bed. Death had obsessed him lately. First the funerals, then the days in court reliving those few, climactic moments of Macgregor's end . . .

'What's the matter?' Shelagh asked.

'Eh? Oh, nothing. Just missing some air conditioning.'

'And I thought you such a tough guy,' Shelagh said, still smiling as she stepped out of her dress. 'I'm going to take a shower.'

He lay back exhausted after their day of sight-seeing, wanting his own turn in the shower, followed by a drink. For Shelagh's sake he would endure these dog-days of tourism, but already he missed the ship's routine and had begun to consider the galleries of the distant Uffizi preferable to this haunting of a waterfront upon which he now wished only to turn his back.

He had discharged his final duties two days earlier. There had been the court appearance necessary to try Phan Van Nui for the murder of Macgregor. The witnesses were called, unfamiliar figures out of their uniform. Stevenson boyish and almost a different person from the young officer with whom Mackinnon had spent the last two months of his life. It was always like that, Mackinnon mused, at the end of a voyage.

Under the circumstances, justice had been swifly done. Alone among the boat people, Phan's life imprisonment was a decision easier to reach than the fate of his fellow Vietnamese. The irony of the life-long detention at Her Majesty's pleasure struck Mackinnon forcibly. Was it an old man's indulgence to question so solemn an institution as the law? Somehow he found it impossible not to, to contrast the limbo into which the innocent boat people were cast with the solicitous incarceration meted out to Phan Van Nui. In a sense Phan had won.

Even now Mackinnon found the situation's flaws outweighed the law's remorseless majesty, so much so that the memory of the defence's claim that in the person of Captain John Mackinnon Phan Van Nui had met 'great and insupportable provocation' only made him chuckle. Something had happened to him during the typhoon, something he was only just beginning to understand, to recognise as a profound change within himself. He was not yet certain what it was, but he seemed to see things with a bewildering clarity, as though for the first time. There had been a craziness about the courtroom proceedings to match his own madness in defying Dent and his gunboat cronies, a fact obliquely referred to at one point in an unwise attempt to demonstrate his, Mackinnon's, despotism.

Fortunately the judge had directed the snide remark inadmissible and Phan had been sentenced to life imprisonment, but Mackinnon was uneasily aware that this collision of variant stupidities begged the question of which was *reality*.

In his exhaustion he shelved the matter. Since he had relinquished the bridge of the *Matthew Flinders* his power was diminished. Such lofty considerations were set aside in place of more lugubrious duties.

Chief Engineer York's body had been flown home at the request of his widow, but they had buried Taylor and Macgregor side by side in the Anglican cemetery on Hong Kong island. The twin graves awaited the simple tombstones Mackinnon had paid for. Both would bear the ship's name.

'There's a kind of satisfaction in that,' Mackinnon had growled. The mission padre had agreed, assuring him matters would be concluded as he wished.

'I *wish*,' Mackinnon had responded fervently, 'that James Dent had bothered to put in an appearance. After all Taylor died saving the last of his ships.'

'I expect he's a busy man, Captain,' the padre had soothed.

'That's the excuse we always concede the likes of him,' Mackinnon had said. 'Whatever happened to *noblesse oblige*?'

He had almost drifted into sleep when Shelagh came out of the shower, her hair wrapped in a towel, the robe wet from contact with her body. She filled the room with her scent. He felt cheered by her pink presence and obvious contentment.

'Oh, that does feel better; your turn now, darling.'

Inert, he watched her move to the window and shake her hair free.

'You've not been asleep, have you? I don't know, you seamen can sleep anywhere.'

'I'm not a seaman any more. I'm a bloody tourist.'

'Well you look like a beached whale.'

Mackinnon chuckled and threw his legs over the side of the bed. Shelagh vigorously rubbed her hair, staring out over the harbour.

'Isn't that the old ship?' she asked suddenly. Mackinnon hove himself to his feet with dizzying speed, fumbling for the binoculars he had kept handy.

314

The *Matthew Flinders* was standing out past Wanchai, heading for the Lye Mun Pass and the eastward passage to the Taiwan Strait. Mackinnon focussed the glasses on her, an uncomfortable lump forming in his throat. Under her rusty flare, a patch of bright new paint reflected her bow wave as she increased speed. Her old name had been blacked out, a new one added in Chinese characters. Mackinnon wondered what her new owners had called her.

'Well I'm damned!'

Over her stern the red flag of China lifted languidly in the following breeze. Mackinnon shifted his scrutiny. From the starboard yardarm on her foremast the red duster flew as a courtesy ensign. Even as he watched a *sampan* went alongside and the tiny figure of the pilot clambered down the ship's side. Then a roil of water appeared under her stern as she increased speed, obedient to another's hand. Forward, the red ensign fluttered downwards.

Mackinnon felt the tiny hairs on the back of his neck crawl.

'God Almighty,' he murmured, then coughed to clear his husky throat. 'It looks as if Randy Rawlings was cheated of his command after all. He didn't deserve that!'

Side by side, Mackinnon and his wife watched until the ship disappeared.

'I remember . . .' He stopped. What did it matter now what he remembered? Shelagh turned aside and picked up a paper bag.

'Here, John, I found this today. I think it's time we arranged our flight.'

He drew the large format book from the wrapping: it was about the Uffizi.

Mackinnon drew the strap on the last case and wondered how Shelagh had managed to collect in a fortnight more than he had garnered in a lifetime of ocean wandering.

'Is there anything else?' he called to his wife, but her reply

315

was interrupted by a knock at the door. 'Come on, Shelagh,' he added, 'the taxi's below.'

But it was not the taxi. Alex Stevenson stood on the threshold, and behind him was a figure Mackinnon did not realise at first was Tam.

'Hullo, sir. I hope you don't mind . . .' Stevenson's smile vanished as he caught sight of the cases beside the door.

'Come in, come in,' said Mackinnon. 'We've only a few moments, we're catching a flight.'

'Oh I didn't know . . . well, perhaps we'd better go.'

Stevenson's confusion and embarrassment held a note of desperation. He stepped back, but Mackinnon put his hand out and restrained him.

'Hang on, you've obviously got a problem.'

'It's all right, sir . . .'

'No it's not!'

Neither man realised the incongruity of their continuing, unconscious adherence to the formalities of their dead shipboard existence.

'But if you're leaving . . .'

'Mr Stevenson,' Mackinnon was almost bawling, 'come in and sit down!'

'What on earth's the matter?'

Mackinnon turned to his wife. 'Shelagh, tell this young man to come in, we've got five minutes.'

'We've got more than that, Mr Stevenson. My husband has a horror of being late for anything.'

Reluctantly Stevenson stood aside and motioned Tam into the room. Mackinnon hardly recognised the young woman in the pale blue cotton dress. Gone was the greasy, lacklustre hair, the thin, pinched face, the awkward, gauche stance.

An unsettling, guilt-laden image of Akiko intruded.

'We were married this morning,' Stevenson said. 'The padre arranged things.'

'Why on earth didn't you tell us?' Shelagh broke in, 'we would have loved to—

'We wanted to keep it quiet.'

'My dear fellow, we must send down for a drink.'

'No, Captain Mackinnon.' Tam spoke, for the first time. The long, dark lashes lay upon her cheeks and then she looked up at him, her eyes dark, like Akiko's. 'We just come to tell you and say goodbye. I want to thank you for stopping your ship.'

'We were the third ship, sir,' Stevenson said, 'two others went past them. Bit like the good Samaritan.'

'We didn't do very much for them,' Mackinnon said deprecatingly. 'Took them out of the frying pan and threw them into the fire.'

He had watched the boat people taken in police launches to the caged encampment on Stonecutter's Island, a prison by another name.

'You did something, Captain,' Tam said.

'Perhaps,' Mackinnon said, unconvinced. His bold stand against authority seemed inconsequential now; an illusory victory, revealing no truth greater than his own self-conceit.

'Well,' he said, addressing Stevenson, aware his miserable tone was inappropriate to the occasion, 'I'm glad you managed to rescue one.'

'Two, Captain,' said Stevenson, a hint of mischief in his eyes. 'I got Sparks to alter the list. We decided Tam should be a mother a little prematurely.'

Comprehension dawned on Mackinnon. 'The baby?'

'Yes. We wanted to let you know, sir, in case there were any questions asked.'

Mackinnon smiled and then began to chuckle. 'Bugger the bureaucrats, Mr Stevenson. Shelagh, let's get a drink organised.' He looked at his watch. 'We've ten minutes.'

'No, Captain, we leave the baby at the mission, we must get back. The padre is a kind man, but he is not good with babies.'

'Wait a minute' put in Shelagh with a flash of perception, 'you only married this morning, you say?' Stevenson nodded.

Shelagh turned to her husband. 'John, get those bags

unpacked at once. Ring and cancel the flight. They came to see us to ask us to baby-sit. The poor padre . . . You came to ask us to baby-sit, didn't you?'

'But Shelagh . . .'

'Cancel the flight, John, don't fuss. Even *we* managed to have a honeymoon.'

'What are you going to do?' asked Mackinnon as the two men enjoyed a gin and tonic in the absence of the women who had taken the expected taxi to the Mission to Seamen to collect the baby.

'Well, it's rather an odd thing, really,' Stevenson said, rolling the glass between the palms of his hands. 'You recall the naval officer, Lieutenant Drinkwater? I met him again and he seemed quite friendly, as if he had been embarrassed to have been caught up in the boarding operation. He insisted on buying me a drink and in the course of our chat he mentioned his tour was nearly over. I asked him how he'd enjoyed it, and, well, to cut a long story short, he and his officers had formed a syndicate and bought a boat. There were three of them and they were looking for a buyer.'

'You bought the boat?'

'Yes; she's a forty-two-foot ketch, a bit old and wanting a lick of paint, but,' Stevenson shrugged, 'we thought we'd go south to Borneo and Aussie.'

Mackinnon stared in open admiration at the young man. 'You're not bothered . . . I mean suppose you were caught out in weather like . . .?' The thought appalled him. He got up, walked to the window and stood looking out. 'A few days ago I stood here and watched the *Matthew Flinders* on her way to China. She's renamed now; God knows what the Chinks have called her. It was like the end of the world, you know. *My* world . . . *your* world. There aren't many of us left, Alex.'

Stevenson rose and stood beside Mackinnon. He smiled. 'I saw Sparks off on the plane from Kai Tak, sir. He and

Rawlings were travelling home together. They were both a bit pissed. They wanted to take the ship to Shanghai, but Dent knocked it on the head. Poor Sparks was pretty emotional.'

'He was a good man.'

'Yes,' Stevenson agreed. For a moment they stood side by side, staring out over the darkening waters of the 'fragrant harbour' as twilight fell, the shadows stretched out and the lights of the moored ships twinkled with increasing brilliance.

Suddenly, round the shoulder of the intervening land, a monstrous, glittering structure appeared. Like a fantasy spaceship in a film, it seemed to float, suspended above the sea, line after horizontal line of lights, some of which coruscated in variegated colours, others pulsed on and off in time with a faint, rhythmic beat that came up to them.

'Christ,' muttered Mackinnon, real shock making his voice tremulous, 'is that a *ship*?'

'It's the *Lotus Princess*,' Stevenson said, a tone almost of apology in his voice, as if embarrassed to be compelled to explain to Mackinnon, 'they call it discotheque-shipping.'

'We are diminished by such . . . such . . .' Mackinnon fought for the right word. Contempt and anguish filled his voice, and something worse, much worse, some sense of ultimate worthlessness opening like a void.

'They are very profitable,' Stevenson went on. 'The income generated from the cruise passengers' fares is compounded by spin-offs in the duty free shopping malls, the bars . . .'

'God save us.' Mackinnon abruptly swung away from the window. Such rank commercialism on the littoral of China smacked of an obscene insensitivity. James Dent would approve, God damn him.

'Tell me about Sparks.'

'Nothing much to tell, sir. As I said, he was a bit emotional. As a matter of fact, he was pretty near to tears.

He said we were extinct, dinosaurs . . . he gave a pretty good impression of a diplodocus,' Stevenson laughed at the recollection. 'Though it looked more like an elephant to me. Rawlings tried to shut him up, but you know Sparky he was having none of it and went roaring round the airport bar waving his arm in front of his nose and lumbering into people.'

'Jolly jack ashore,' Mackinnon said, smiling, 'but he's right. We're finished, the last, and we thought it would never end, that there'd always be a red duster in every port in the world.' He sighed, then added, 'So good old Sparky danced the jig at our wake, eh? Well, what the hell?'

Mackinnon held out the bottle and Stevenson reciprocated with his glass.

'It may sound an odd thing to say,' Stevenson said, 'but I am glad I had the experience of the typhoon, sir.'

'That's not odd, Alex . . . cheers.'

'Cheers.' Stevenson lowered his glass. 'I don't feel like a dinosaur.'

'Well,' said Mackinnon, suddenly brightening, 'you're not, are you? You're off to Aussie with your lassie. We're not dead yet, not quite.'

'More an endangered species then.'

Mackinnon met the younger man's eyes. 'Endangered species?' he said, as if repeating the words somehow validated them. 'Yes, it's not quite an epitaph, is it, though I doubt anyone will notice our rarity value before it's too late.'

'I'll do my best to survive,' Stevenson said, grinning, and Mackinnon smiled back, again envying him his youth.

'I'm sure you will,' he said as, from outside, there came the sound of the returning women.

Later, when he had persuaded the hotel to let them have the room another night and the airline to cancel their booking; after Shelagh had crooned and fussed to her heart's content over the wrinkled yet alien bundle and gone at last to her bed, he sat in the darkness and stared out over the harbour. He could not look at the sleeping child without thinking of the shambles of the mother's wrecked legs, or of how Taylor had rescued him and finished the operation only to be killed for his trouble; nor could he forget the utter pointlessness of it all, since the woman had not survived their clumsy ministrations. It seemed to him a parable of the futility of all human existence, of inevitable failure.

As he stared at the harbour he saw again in his mind's eye the brilliant intrusion; the fantastic ship that was not a ship but seemed to float miraculously above the sea's surface like a star ship, impervious to typhoons and acts of a mere omnipotent god. Events had overtaken him: he was an old man, thinking an old man's thoughts, and the bitterest pill to swallow was the pill of obsolescence.

He tried to console himself with thoughts of Stevenson and Tam, and the bright promise of their youthful optimism. Yet even here he was disappointed. They would sail south, to Borneo, Stevenson had said, the land beneath the wind it was called by the sea-Dyaks, the land whose latitude lay below that at which the great wind, the *taifun*, was generated. What would they find? A land already being denuded of its hardwood jungle in response to humanity's insatiable desire for the ramin and scraya timber of the rainforest.

It was all too depressing to think about and he was moved by the terrible thought of his own death. He stirred, chilled by the cool wind which at last blew into the stifling room.

How did the boat people feel, mewed in their cage across the bay on Stonecutter's Island? Did they feel beleaguered, an endangered species like himself? Did he, Captain John Mackinnon, sometime a ship-master in the British merchant marine, share the sense of being an outcast with the refugees?

He shivered; not in the material sense, certainly, for he had his uncaring country to return to, a modest house and the soporific comforts of modernity to pamper his old age. But something of their plight had touched him, marked him with the common bond all humans share.

'John,' Shelagh stood in the doorway, 'are you all right?'

'Yes.' he said, 'I couldn't settle. I thought you were asleep. Didn't want to disturb you with tossing and turning.'

'I don't mind.' She was beside him and he felt her hand reach for his and smelt the warmth of her and the familiar fragrance of her hair.

'Is the baby all right?'

'Of course.'

'I was thinking of those two. Alex and Tam.'

'They seem very happy.'

'Yes,' he said abstractedly.

'Romantic even,' Shelagh added.

He grunted agreement. Yes, they were romantic all right; but what was romance other than someone else's life, at a distance, uncomplicated by the minor irritations of daily trivialities?

'But that wasn't what you were thinking, was it?' Shelagh asked.

'No . . .' He paused, uncertain how he could explain it, knowing the task was impossible, quite beyond him, the fruit of his own unique experience. Perhaps she too had arrived at similar conclusions by other paths; perhaps there had been another, Akiko-like, in her own life.

'What *were* you thinking, John?' Shelagh persisted, and her voice was huskily intense, a measure of her desire for intimacy.

It struck him then that he must explain, that he had time to explain if only he could marshal the words. Moreover he was obliged to explain, for no longer had he to discard a train of thought because she was not within a thousand miles of him; no longer had he to try and spell it out in his awkward way in a letter or, worse, abandon it as still-born, forgotten, a small piece of the deprivation suffered by every sea-estranged couple.

'I was thinking about hope,' he began at last, willing her with every fibre of his being to comprehend what this simple sentence had cost him, 'Without hope, we're finished.'

And he took her in his arms, seeing again the girl in the farmhouse and forgetting the daily burden of infirmities he increasingly bore.